Rum Luck

Rum Luck

Ryan Aldred

FIVE STAR
A part of Gale, Cengage Learning

PASADENA LIBRARY, FAIRMONT
4330 Fairmont Pkwy
Pasadena, TX 77504-3306

GALE
CENGAGE Learning®

Farmington Hills, Mich • San Francisco • New York • Waterville, Maine
Meriden, Conn • Mason, Ohio • Chicago

GALE
CENGAGE Learning®

Copyright © 2016 by Ryan Aldred
Five Star™ Publishing, a part of Cengage Learning, Inc.

ALL RIGHTS RESERVED.
This novel is a work of fiction. Names, characters, places, and incidents are either the product of the author's imagination, or, if real, used fictitiously.

No part of this work covered by the copyright herein may be reproduced, transmitted, stored, or used in any form or by any means graphic, electronic, or mechanical, including but not limited to photocopying, recording, scanning, digitizing, taping, Web distribution, information networks, or information storage and retrieval systems, except as permitted under Section 107 or 108 of the 1976 United States Copyright Act, without the prior written permission of the publisher.

The publisher bears no responsibility for the quality of information provided through author or third-party Web sites and does not have any control over, nor assume any responsibility for, information contained in these sites. Providing these sites should not be construed as an endorsement or approval by the publisher of these organizations or of the positions they may take on various issues.

LIBRARY OF CONGRESS CATALOGING-IN-PUBLICATION DATA

Names: Aldred, Ryan, author.
Title: Rum luck / Ryan Aldred.
Description: First edition. | Waterville, Maine : Five Star Publishing, 2016. | Series: A bar on a beach mystery ; 1
Identifiers: LCCN 2016001556 (print) | LCCN 2016013045 (ebook) | ISBN 9781432831899 (hardback) | ISBN 1432831895 (hardcover) | ISBN 9781432831875 (ebook) | ISBN 1432831879 (ebook)
Subjects: LCSH: Mystery fiction. | BISAC: FICTION / Mystery & Detective / General. | FICTION / Humorous.
Classification: LCC PR9199.4.A397 R86 2016 (print) | LCC PR9199.4.A397 (ebook) | DDC 813/.6—dc23
LC record available at http://lccn.loc.gov/2016001556

First Edition. First Printing: June 2016
Find us on Facebook– https://www.facebook.com/FiveStarCengage
Visit our website– http://www.gale.cengage.com/fivestar/
Contact Five Star™ Publishing at FiveStar@cengage.com

Printed in the United States of America
1 2 3 4 5 6 7 20 19 18 17 16

For Andrea. Now and always.

ACKNOWLEDGMENTS

The people of Tamarindo, for creating the kind of place that gets inside of you and refuses to let go. Any errors and inaccuracies are entirely mine.

My beta readers—Seb, Sheri, Omar, Janet, Graham, and Robyn—for your honest feedback and your words of encouragement. And the balance between the two.

My mentors—Garry Ryan, Vicki Delany, Dinah Forbes, and Morty Mint—for your introductions, endorsements, and the benefit of your hard-earned experience.

Deni Dietz and the team at Five Star Mysteries, for helping this novel reach its full potential.

My family—Andrea and Eric, and my mother and father—for your unending patience and unconditional support.

And, of course, the readers. I hope you'll drop in—www.ryanaldred.com—and tell me what you thought of the book. May this be our first adventure of many.

CHAPTER ONE

The hot, humid air wrapped around Victoria Holmes the moment the driver opened her door. She stretched her legs, rose from the chauffeured car, and absently plucked one of her long auburn hairs from her skirt. She wished, not for the first time, that she'd had time to unearth a summer-weight suit before catching the flight late last night. Her driver returned to his seat and cut the engine, spilling silence onto the sleepy side street.

She glanced down the road toward the center of Tamarindo, where the rolling verdant hillside gave way to beach houses and brightly colored hotels, their yards punctuated by massive trees. Across the street, rusted corrugated roofs gave way to towering resorts and half-finished condominiums, framed by the glittering Pacific. Dense foliage hummed, chirped, and chittered. Life atop of life, atop of life.

Victoria allowed herself a small smile. This was the Costa Rica she'd hoped to find, if only . . . She took a deep breath of air scented by salt, earth, and diesel exhaust, covered her dark eyes with a pair of designer sunglasses, and headed up the drab concrete walkway.

A holiday in Costa Rica had been on Victoria's list for years, but had never quite reached the top. Her friends had always dragged her someplace more exotic or luxurious. But she could already feel there was something here that went beyond infinity pools and corporate cruises.

Not that this trip would be much of a vacation. Even a lawyer of her caliber was unlikely to find time for piña coladas between bail hearings.

Victoria kept a bag packed for such calls, but never thought she would haul it out of the closet on account of dear, sweet, predictable Ben. There may have been a time when his antics seemed certain to land him in prison—or a morgue—but ever since he'd left university, his idea of going off the rails was watching two movies in a single night.

Had it really been more than a decade since them? Ahem . . . since *then*?

Tamarindo's police station was a small, squat building, with walls of white painted concrete and the ubiquitous metal roof. The police crest was hand-painted over the door—a shield that featured a hulking police officer with one arm around a pair of expressionless children, set before a lush mountain at sunrise. The station itself looked clean and in good repair, as did the handful of parked white pickup trucks and squad cars with *Policía* emblazoned on their sides. All good signs.

She swung open the door. The inside looked like any other police station, with a handful of tired-looking officers pecking away at reports on antiquated computers beneath the fizzing glow of fluorescent lights, sipping coffee from Styrofoam cups. But there was a hum to the atmosphere, a speed at which papers were shuffled, a gleam in the eyes of the constables. This was not just another day at the office.

Victoria stepped up to the desk sergeant and handed him a formal request to see her client.

Miguel Valares made his way down the stone path to the beachside café. The raucous shouts from the hotel pool washed over him unnoticed as his eyes flicked from one face to the next. Searching. His hands hung by his sides, palms open. Ready. Years of experience kept that readiness from showing on his face. Better if he didn't scare away the other diners.

He seated himself away from his fellow patrons, in a chair that gave him a decent view of the beach without forcing him to turn his back to the restaurant. Waiting was the worst part. Particularly for matters that were out of his control. Even the crashing waves and the endless parade of Tamarindo's most eccentric visitors failed to provide distraction.

He eyed a pack of Camels a few tables over, next to a discarded plate of scrambled eggs. Empty, but for one lone cigarette poking out from the crumpled aluminum wrapper. He hadn't had one since . . . Well, not for a long time. Not long enough, apparently. Miguel pulled his phone from his pocket and set it on the table, willing it to buzz with an update. No such luck.

He thought back to last night. The beachside bar bathed in revolving blue lights. The crackle of police radios. Ben, slumped in the back of a squad car. And the choice Miguel had made. It had gone against every instinct to leave Ben there and call Victoria instead, but he'd had few options. Even unarmed, Miguel had no doubts about his ability to break open the squad car and disable the handful of *Policia Turística* on-site. But what then? And at what price?

The waiter cleared the table, scooping up the pack of cigarettes in the process. Miguel breathed a small sigh. He glanced down at his phone once more. Nothing. What was taking so long? The pounding of his heart overtook the rhythmic drumming of the hotel's samba music. He could feel the darkness creeping up the back of his neck, whispering in his ear. Searching. Ready.

Waiting was the worst part.

Ben Cooper had had his share of hangovers over the years, but this one deserved to be immortalized in poetry. Where lesser ones faded with time, this one was still returning on a winged tequila worm to take him to Hangover Valhalla. Unfortunately, his other senses were now coming into focus, including his sense of smell. His cell reeked of hot sweat, stale beer, and bitter disappointment.

He tried to remember what happened the previous night. His hands were bruised and scraped, and his shirt was speckled with blood. He ran his fingers through his hair and found it caked with sand. The flesh around his right eye was sore to the touch and his nose felt broken. If he was lucky, that meant the blood on his shirt was his own.

So, not wrongfully arrested. He didn't know whether public intoxication was a crime in Costa Rica, but he must have disturbed the peace. Running his hands through his hair and down his face was disturbing enough.

Miguel would know. Assuming his friend wasn't lying in the cell next to his.

"Miguel?" Ben asked through the bars.

The dull hum of the fluorescent lights overhead was the only reply.

Ben slumped back on the concrete floor, struggling to remember more of last night. They'd been at the bar, having drinks with . . . what was that guy's name, Alberto? Antonio? And then . . . and then . . .

Ben remembered the flash of police lights and the overwhelming smell of salt and copper. Oh God, what had he done?

The clack of the lock echoed in his head like a cannon shot. A guard pushed open the door and ushered in a young woman wearing a business suit. If Ben didn't know better, he would say she looked like—

"Victoria?"

"Hi, Ben." She gave him a wan smile. "You look like hell." Victoria, as ever, was class personified . . . a fashionista's dream.

An errant fleck of seaweed tickled Ben's nostril.

"Please, make yourself at . . . home." He gestured to the thin mattress that he had abandoned at some point during the night for the blessed coolness of the concrete floor.

Victoria glanced at the mattress, but remained standing. "Thanks, I'll pass."

"What are you doing here?" Was she some sort of withdrawal-induced hallucination?

"Miguel called me," she explained with a shrug.

Her arrival cleared the fog from a dozen missed engagements. When they graduated—him to IT consulting and her to her father's law firm—Ben had known his best friend from university would be busy trotting the globe and building her career. It took a few years to realize that meant she'd only be available to meet up between 3:08 and 3:11 p.m. when the moon was waxing gibbous.

Yet here she was. Ben would have to get Miguel a trophy that read "World's Best Best Man" to thank his Colombian friend for his quick thinking. Except there was no best man, not after what had happened between Ben and Tara Whitmore, his former fiancée. "World's Best Ex-Best Man" didn't have quite the same ring to it, somehow.

"He said you needed me to take your case," Victoria finished.

Case? It couldn't be as bad as that, could it? "It's great to see you. It's been ages. But I'm sure they'll let me out of here once I sober up and pay the fine." He fought back against the fear creeping into his voice. "I don't think Miguel meant for you to fly down from Toronto in the middle of the night . . ."

Victoria took a deep breath. "Ben, you've been arrested for murder."

Ben moved his mouth to speak, but it seemed to have malfunctioned.

"Listen carefully," she said. "I don't know if you remember

what happened last night and, right now, I don't care. For now, you don't say a word. When we leave—and we will leave today— let me do the talking. Do you understand?"

He stared through Victoria into a lifetime of sweltering inside a concrete box. *I can't go to prison here,* he thought. *I don't know nearly enough Spanish.*

Victoria nodded at the guard standing by the open cell door. He readied his keys as she strode past him into the hallway, her high heels snapping on the concrete floor. By the time he slammed the lock back into position, Victoria had already passed the desk sergeant and swung left toward the captain's office.

"Señora!" the desk sergeant called, while the guard fumbled with his heavy key ring.

Victoria rapped twice on the captain's office door, then pushed inside to reveal an older, overweight officer sitting at a heavy wooden desk with a coffee in hand, reviewing the morning paperwork. He glanced up at the intruder, his eyes narrowing. The lines on his face spoke of too many late nights and early mornings spent reading print that grew smaller by the year.

With a flick of his hand, the captain dismissed the desk sergeant and the guard, who had finally caught up with Victoria. He shot them a glare that made it clear they should not make any plans for their next days off.

"Buenos dias, Captain Reyes. I am here to arrange the release of Mr. Benjamin Cooper," Victoria said in flawless Spanish. She took a seat in one of the chairs before the heavy wooden desk and extracted a thick manila envelope from her leather attaché case.

Captain Reyes slowly set aside his barely touched coffee. "I am afraid you have the advantage of me, Miss . . . ?"

"Victoria Holmes of Holmes, Holmes and Wright. I am Mr. Cooper's attorney."

"Are you aware that Mr. Cooper has been detained in connection with the violent murder of Mr. Antonio Guiterrez?"

"I am."

Captain Reyes paused.

Like many veteran officers, he believed he could gain the advantage by trading time for silence. Victoria had studied at the same school of thought. They stared at each other for several moments, the office silent but for the slow thrum of the ceiling fan as it struggled to move the leaden air.

The captain finally asked, "Do you intend to present your request?"

"In a moment." She gave the wall clock the slightest of glances. "I believe you are expecting a phone call."

"Is that so?"

Again, silence. Then the phone rang. Captain Reyes's eyes flashed as he brought the heavy black receiver to his ear.

"Reyes."

Victoria couldn't decipher the other side of the conversation, but she had a good idea of what was being said.

"I see, Minister." He paused. "You understand of course, Minister, that I will require a written order to that effect." His grip on the receiver tightened. "Oh, she does? That *is* most convenient. Good day, Minister." He slammed the receiver down.

Victoria slid the manila envelope across the captain's desk. "You will find everything in order."

Reyes opened the envelope and wordlessly flipped through the documents until he reached the release authorization at the bottom. Seeing the rage flare in his pale green eyes, Victoria wondered if she had perhaps been *too* prepared.

"Oh, look. There is even a little sticker to tell me where to sign. How thoughtful of you and your . . . *friends.*" Reyes spat out the last word, but reached for a pen and signed the document.

"We realize you are a very busy man, Captain." Victoria smiled, taking back the release form. "This is all I require. The remainder is for you to retain, for the time being."

Reyes grunted. He picked up the envelope and seemed mollified by the weight of Ben's passport, though he'd know well enough how little a passport mattered in a town like Tamarindo.

Victoria rose from her chair triumphant. "Thank you for your cooperation, Captain. I will not take any more of your valuable time."

"Good day, Miss Holmes." To her surprise, he rose with her and inclined his head in farewell.

A gallant police captain—how quaint. She closed her attaché with a click and reached for the door. There might be time for that piña colada after all . . .

"Oh, and Miss Holmes?" Captain Reyes sat back down and took a sip of coffee. To her surprise, he switched to fluent English. "So you are aware, I am releasing Mr. Cooper into your care solely due to evidence that he left the scene prior to the murder. Despite what you may have heard about the police in Costa Rica, I would not simply turn a homicide suspect loose in Tamarindo, not even into the custody of the Minister of the Interior himself."

His tone sharpened. "Should our opinion of Mr. Cooper's involvement change, he will be arrested. Should Mr. Cooper attempt to leave Tamarindo, he will be arrested. Should Mr. Cooper fail to deposit a chewing gum wrapper in the proper receptacle, he will be arrested. And should either of you interfere with the investigation, you will both be arrested. And *that* release will not come with a convenient signature sticker." He took another sip. "Please close the door behind you."

Victoria met his gaze and returned his nod, inclining her

head a moment longer than etiquette demanded. The heavy wooden door swung closed behind her.

The guard yanked open the door to Ben's cell, shouted something at him in Spanish, and motioned for him to get out. He assumed they were moving him to another prison. Perhaps, if he asked nicely, the guard would teach him how to say, "I wish to join your gang in exchange for protection" in Spanish.

He was surprised to find Victoria waiting for him at the sergeant's desk, next to an evidence bag containing his personal effects. He gave her a bruised but grateful grin, and she flashed him a quick smile. She seemed on the verge of setting the world record for securing the release of a suspected murderer from a Central American prison, assuming he still had the dexterity needed to put his belt back on.

Apart from the belt, there wasn't much: a broken watch, a cashless wallet, and the key to his hotel room.

"No phone?" he asked the sergeant as Victoria peered over the desk, looking for his other belongings. "The case has a Canadian flag—a red maple leaf—on the back."

The desk sergeant shook his head and hunched over the desk as he filled out the receipt for Ben to sign.

"Ben," Victoria whispered, inclining her head to direct his gaze. "What's that piece of paper, the one in that evidence bag?"

He spotted the evidence bag. Inside was a document typed in Spanish with his name and signature at the bottom. It looked as though someone had spilled . . . Was that blood?

"That's my signature, but I don't remember signing anything."

Victoria held a single finger to her lips as a warning, then spoke to the desk sergeant politely in Spanish.

Ben could barely order beer or fajitas, but the sergeant's tone made it clear he wasn't handing over the bag. He and Victoria argued back and forth. The sergeant shook his head.

Victoria raised her voice and slapped her palms on the desk. Then she slid her phone out of her jacket and looked as though she was threatening to . . . call someone? Who would she call? Ben wondered what strings had been pulled to get him out.

Thunderclouds passed before the sergeant's eyes, and the guard strode toward the desk, his hand on his baton. Ben tensed. All he wanted was to go back to his hotel and have a nap. Was that so much to ask?

But before the guard reached them, the storm passed. Victoria threw up her arms in resignation and slid the phone back into her pocket. The sergeant gave Ben a look that was equal parts pity and disgust as he thrust a clipboard into Ben's hands.

"Sign. *Now,*" Victoria hissed.

Ben needed no further prompting. He signed.

He and Victoria walked out the front door of the station toward the waiting car, leaving the stained document in the custody of the Tamarindo police.

Miguel's phone buzzed twice. He snatched it off the table and read Victoria's text message. He smiled, the weight of last night's decision lifting from his shoulders. Now, how had she—?

He felt . . . something.

Miguel grabbed the hand sliding into his pocket and twisted. The would-be thief sank to his knees. He tried to pull away but found no escape, only agony.

"You'll break your wrist that way," Miguel said mildly.

The man grimaced. "I thought you were someone else."

"I'd hope so." Miguel plucked the wallet from the thief's twisted fingers and whacked him on the forehead with it, just hard enough to make a point. "What did you learn?"

"Huh?"

Miguel twisted further. The man yelped. Miguel smiled, hopefully reassuring his fellow diners. "I said, what did you learn?"

"I'm a lousy pickpocket?"

Miguel twisted just a bit further.

"And I should find another job."

"Sounds about right to me," Miguel said, releasing his grip. "Now get the hell out of here before I change my mind."

Between his crushing exhaustion and pounding headache, Ben barely had room to feel relieved. He sank into the car's plush back seat and let the chill of the air conditioning gently waft over him. A strong whiff of barnyard and moonshine reminded him how long it had been since he last showered.

He looked in the rearview mirror and saw his familiar slate blue eyes, set in a face so swollen and bruised it was almost unrecognizable. He turned to Victoria and drew his swollen lips into a humorless grin. "It's a modern-day fairy tale—*Beauty and the Beast.*"

Victoria wrinkled her nose and rolled down a window. "More like *Lady and the Tramp.*"

He glanced back in the mirror and locked eyes with the driver, who stared at him as though examining the bottom of his shoe. Ben scowled back as he wriggled deeper into the seat. The driver made a noise of pure disgust, then eased the car through the still-quiet side streets of Tamarindo.

Victoria stared out the window at faded wooden shacks and the latest Costa Rican fashions drying on clotheslines. Ben wondered how he could repay her for what she'd done for him.

"Thank you," he said simply.

She gave him a small smile. "Don't thank me yet."

The car lurched to a halt beside the stone walls of his hotel, the Tamarindo Diria. Ben got out and savored the victory of returning here once more. Inside, bellboys bustled with bags while guests lounged on dark wicker furniture, flipping through brochures for marlin fishing and sunset tours. Past the open-air lobby, a trio of stone tribesmen spat streams of water into a glittering swimming pool.

Yet it was the beach that held his eye. Beyond the pool and its leafy, gnarled trees, a stretch of fine golden sand paved the path to the turquoise and navy bands of the Pacific, sparkling in the late morning sun. The surf whispered rhythmically against the shore.

He took a deep breath of sea air and salivated at the aroma of cayenne and searing meat. "I'm famished."

"I think you mean 'filthy.' " The disdain in Victoria's eyes shone through her oversized sunglasses. "Go clean up. Miguel and I will be waiting out on the patio, once you no longer look as though you've washed ashore from a desert island."

He realized then that his fellow guests had stopped studying their brochures, and were instead studying the strange man who had apparently escaped Davy Jones' Locker to pillage their passport pouches.

He sighed with resignation. "Order me a burger, will you?"

She nodded in reply, then waved for a bellhop to gather up a surprisingly large number of Louis Vuitton suitcases.

The cheerful beep the door made when Ben slid his room card inside the slot was perhaps the loveliest beep he had ever heard, in a life full of beeps. Much the same could be said for the shower that followed.

He returned to the lobby a new man. Or a bruised man in a new shirt, at least.

"Brother!" Miguel cried, wrapping his lengthy arms around his friend, slapping his back heartily, and re-bruising most of Ben's injuries. Miguel had greeted him this way since they became friends midway through university; Ben had never got used to it for the simple reason that Miguel easily outdid him in height, fitness, and strength.

No wonder Miguel rarely talked about his mandatory stint with the Colombian Army, part and parcel with growing up there. With a build like that, his term as a conscript must have been little more than a glorified camping trip. His current job as a bartender at one of Toronto's premier clubs seemed a much better fit for his gentle, friendly nature. Even so, some of their acquaintances had indelicately suggested that pouring shots and wiping up spilled pints wasn't exactly a dream job for a university graduate. Miguel would shrug and say he'd put his sociology degree to better use in a barroom than a boardroom.

He dragged Ben through the lobby to a small, shaded table in the far corner of the restaurant's patio. Victoria was waiting for them with a cappuccino in hand, her dark wool suit replaced by a simple linen skirt and a colorful, flowing blouse. Soaring palms waved in the wind behind her, dappling the patio with shade.

"So," she said after the waiter had taken another round of drink orders, "what the hell happened last night?"

"I don't exactly . . . remember everything, precisely." Ben gulped his water, wondering how something with no taste could taste so good.

"What *do* you remember?"

"We drove down to Tamarindo from San José . . . and then . . . Miguel?"

"Ben got *really* drunk last night." Miguel's eyes were ringed with exhaustion. Ben wondered whether his friend had also overindulged last night. More likely, he was up late talking with Victoria, plotting Ben's jailbreak.

The waiter returned with their coffees, then vanished once more.

"I gathered as much." Victoria stirred sugar into her fresh cappuccino and looked back at Miguel. "I assume you don't remember much about last night, either?"

"We stopped in at one of the beach bars. Ben looked fine when I left, sometime around ten. He and the bartender were getting along like long-lost cousins," Miguel said. "He was drunk. Sure. But he's on holiday, you know? I got back to the Diria before one. I thought I'd find him sleeping it off, but he wasn't in his room, so I went back to the bar."

"You left him there on his own?" Victoria asked, eyebrow slightly raised.

"I met someone," he stammered.

If Ben didn't know better, he would swear his Colombian friend was blushing.

Miguel looked at him. "I'm sorry, man. I never should have left you on your own after . . . you know . . ."

"Not your fault," Ben said. "I shouldn't have tried to drink Costa Rica out of rum."

"Jesus, Ben. Not rum again," Victoria said. "I thought you gave that up."

"Yes. Rum. Again." There had been a time, early on in their friendship, when Ben occasionally overindulged. But that was ages ago. He hadn't tried to tie a shopping cart to the top of a tree in well over a decade. "Like Miguel said, I'm on holiday."

Miguel finished, "By the time I got back to the bar, the whole place was wrapped up in police tape and you were asleep in the back of a squad car. Once I knew where you were headed, I ran back to the hotel and called Victoria."

"Sounds like that's the only smart decision either of you made since you got here." She frowned at Ben. "Thanks for the wedding invitation, by the way. Aren't you supposed to be on your honeymoon?"

Ben had been hoping to avoid that subject until he'd had a chance to eat. Or, ideally, forever.

"It's a long story, but the wedding's off. The airfare and the hotel for the honeymoon were nonrefundable, so Miguel and I decided to get out of town for couple of weeks." He would have liked to invite Victoria to the wedding, but he'd sooner have convinced Tara to add laser tag to the day-of itinerary.

"You should call her. She'll be worried," Victoria said.

"If the next time I talk to Tara is from my deathbed, it'll be too soon," Ben replied evenly.

Victoria's eyes flickered with surprise. She started to ask another question, but Miguel spoke up before she got a word out. "How did you get him out of prison so quickly, anyway? I thought we'd be here for weeks."

Ben shuddered. "If we were lucky."

She waved a hand dismissively. "Mansion has a friend who went to St. Andrew's with the Minister of the Interior. Our firm vouchsafed that Ben will remain in Tamarindo until the investigation is concluded."

Victoria always referred to her father, Jonathan Holmes, as Mansion—a backhanded tribute to both his greatness and his size. Ben had met him. Once. They might have exchanged two or even three words; the man had an unnerving knack for ignoring anything he found distasteful.

The waiter emerged from the kitchen with their meals. Ben's stomach rumbled at the sight of the thick, juicy hamburger and the piping hot mound of fries. It took all his self-control to wait until after his friends were served before tucking in.

They were lucky to have come when they did. The patio was starting to fill up with last night's bar crowd medicating their hangovers with greasy fare and chiseled surfers fueling up. They chattered happily to one another, laughing and smiling. Ben tore himself away from people-watching so he could eat. "That's all it took? One call from your dad to his grade-school chum?" he asked between mouthfuls.

"The Ministry of the Interior has the utmost regard for the

solemn word of our law office. Particularly after it hands over two hundred thousand dollars in bail bonds."

Miguel whistled.

"Try not to skip town, Ben. We'd like our money back." Victoria dabbed her lips with a napkin. "To be honest, I'm not sure it was necessary. From what the captain said, you're not an active suspect, though I did have to surrender your passport."

Ben shook his head. "I wish I could remember something about that damned piece of paper I apparently signed last night."

"Oh, thanks for reminding me." Victoria slid out her phone and pulled up a picture. "It's not a great shot. The paper is pretty filthy, but I can make out a few words. Miguel, can you have a look?" She handed the phone over to him.

"What is that?" Ben asked a second before he clued in. "Did you take a *photo* of the document in the evidence bag?"

"So?"

"So, you stole evidence from the police! Good God, what if you were caught?"

"Relax, Ben. 'Stole' is a very harsh word. It's only a picture. Think of it as a souvenir."

Miguel looked at the photo. His eyes went wide.

"Oh, no . . . no . . . You couldn't have . . ."

Ben and Victoria looked on in horror as Miguel clutched his chest and doubled over in agony.

CHAPTER TWO

"Miguel!"

"My phone!" Victoria cried at the same time.

Ben rose to his feet to help, but Miguel held out a trembling hand to ward him off. Miguel's breathing turned ragged and devolved into a coughing fit while Victoria deftly scooped her phone from the ground, looked it over, and buffed it on the hem of her skirt. By then, Miguel had stopped gasping, though sweat still beaded his face.

People nearby looked over at the commotion for a moment, then turned back to their meals. It was poor street theatre by Tamarindo standards. Ben waved off a concerned-looking manager and turned his attention back to his friend. Miguel appeared to have come around. Victoria, apparently unconvinced, flicked ice water in his face.

"Hey!" Miguel recoiled. "You're getting lemon in my eye!"

"He's fine." Victoria rolled her eyes. "Looks as though Ben wasn't the only one who overdid it last night."

Ben wasn't so sure. If he didn't know better, he would have sworn Miguel had suffered some kind of panic attack. Despite the heat, the hair on Ben's arms stood on end. "Are you okay?"

"I'm fine. I just . . . choked on a fry, that's all." Miguel refused to meet Ben's gaze. "I never thought you would actually do it. I mean, you talked about it. We've all thought about it. But, doing it . . . If I'd known . . ."

"Miguel?"

"The photo. It's the deed to the bar. It's in your name."

"Bar? Which bar?"

"*The* bar. *Your* bar."

"*My* bar?" The thought slapped Ben. "The *murder bar?*"

"Don't call it the murder bar. It's bad for business," Victoria said. "Miguel, what are you talking about?"

"I own a murder bar," Ben muttered to himself, horrified. Shards of last night returned to him—the flimsy plastic pen he'd clutched as he scrawled his signature across the bar's wrinkled deed, the gleam in Antonio's eyes, and the rush of raw elation that followed. But he hadn't really meant to buy a bar. *Had he?*

"Around the time I left, Ben was telling the owner how much he'd always wanted to own a bar on a beach," Miguel said. "The owner offered to sell the place cheap. Only sixty thousand dollars."

Ben's mouth dropped open. "And you left me there to *haggle?*"

Miguel threw his hands in the air. "You were drunk. And crazy. You called it Bar on the Beach Enterprises. You kept saying everyone wants to run their own beach bar some day and they'd pay good money to call the shots for a week." He glared at Ben. "Besides, it's not like you were sitting next to a suitcase full of newly minted fifties. Where were you supposed to get sixty grand?"

The blood drained from Ben's face.

"Back up a minute," Victoria said. "What's this about hiring out the bar?"

"Ben had the idiotic idea of offering tourists a taste of owning a real beach bar. One week it's a jazz club, the next a Scotch lounge. He was going to put together a list of experiences—handing out drinks, kicking someone out of the bar, firing a clumsy busboy—that clients could pick off some damned menu, like they were ordering chicken fingers."

Victoria tapped her chin with a manicured finger. "It's actually not a bad idea."

He snorted. "Ridiculous."

"I've seen businesses built on less." Victoria gazed out over the stretch of pristine sand. "It might sound like paying to do work, but it could be a true vacation—the chance to step outside of your life and have a bit of fun without worrying about the consequences."

"Are you joking? Ben was totally smashed. After he scrawled out his business plan on a cocktail napkin, he tried to steal a sombrero off the wall."

Ben suddenly remembered trying to steal the sombrero. Sort of. Mostly, he remembered looking up at the sombrero from where he lay on the floor.

"What does it matter, anyway?" Miguel said. "It's not like Ben found sixty grand hidden under his bar stool. I'm sure he didn't actually pay for the bar."

Ben dropped his burger on the plate. "I *had* that kind of money—before I bought a murder bar."

"Stop calling it that," Victoria said.

"Tara and I are—were—planning to buy a house. The down payment was sitting in our joint account, ready to be transferred out."

"You couldn't have sent that much money out in one night, could you?" Miguel asked.

Ben wasn't so sure. Memories of last night flickered in the dark. He took a deep breath. "Victoria, I need your phone."

"Why?" she asked, clutching it to her chest.

"I have to check my bank account."

She reluctantly handed it over. Ben loaded the website for Greater Canadian Financial and tried to access his account. And tried. And tried.

27

"Any luck?" Victoria asked.

"I'm locked out of my account," Ben said.

"Any chance you could have entered the wrong password?" Miguel asked.

Ben shook his head. "Tara is going to kill me. Most of that money belongs to her parents."

Victoria smiled. "It never hurts to have a few extra investors."

"I need a drink."

"It's a good thing you own a bar, isn't it?" she said.

"Don't you mean a family-friendly tropical beverage establishment?"

"Shut it, Miguel."

Ben found the short walk to the bar surprisingly pleasant. His aches and pains faded as he stretched his muscles, and the ocean air cleared his head, though he did find himself lagging behind Miguel and Victoria. At one point, he found that he'd unknowingly come to a halt in front of a glass-fronted bookstore bustling with tourists and locals. The idea of lying on the beach with a good murder mystery seemed enticing until he remembered there had been a real murder, here, last night, in a bar he'd bought on impulse, the one he now had to run. He'd have little time to read.

He knew deep down that buying the bar was insane, and he started walking once more, determined to do everything in his power to get out of the deal and out of Costa Rica. His pace was brisk until he pictured himself slinking back to Toronto, which made him think about why he'd left in the first place and all the events that had led to his signing the deed to the bar. Had they all happened for a reason? That seemed silly, and yet . . . Perhaps something good could be salvaged from this mess. Something better than the nothing that waited for him in Toronto, at least.

Was there such a thing as a fresh start?

He quickened his pace and caught up with the others. He spotted the bar's massive dome of palm fronds rising up from the fine, pale sand, and as they got closer, he realized that, right now, he wanted nothing more than to enjoy an ice-cold beer in his very own bar. Instead he found a powerfully built man in a suit yelling at a terrified police officer in Spanish.

The uniformed officer appeared to be trying to appease the man—was he a detective?—while taking down caution tape as fast as possible. The man spun around and kicked over one of the bar chairs. It landed with a crash.

"Hey, that's my chair!" Ben yelled. He immediately wished he hadn't.

The man strode over to him, "You watch your mouth, or I will—"

A growl emanated from the back of Miguel's throat. His posture stiffened, and his eyes turned blank and cold. Perhaps Miguel's military training lay closer to the surface than Ben had realized. Even so, the other man's stare remained fixed on Ben.

"Threatening my client, Detective? Do you have a name to go with that badge number?" Victoria asked casually, her eyes on the golden insignia hanging from a chain around his neck.

His eyes flicked over to Victoria. "Detective Vasquez." He turned back to Ben. "I am investigating the brutal death of Mr. Antonio Guiterrez. A death that you seem to have profited from rather handsomely." The veins in his forehead bulged.

"Ms. Victoria Holmes, Mr. Cooper's attorney." She reached out her hand. Vasquez made no move to take it. "I never met Mr. Guiterrez, but I can tell you that we have a great deal invested in helping the authorities find whoever committed this horrible crime." She lowered her hand, the offered handshake unrequited. "Did you know him well?"

"Well enough, Ms. Holmes," Vasquez said, his eyes still locked on Ben. "Establishments like this often require the assistance of the police. Not that my friendship did Mr. Guiterrez much good, in the end." He turned as though to leave, then looked squarely at Victoria. "In Tamarindo, connections only get you so far, and then they get you dead." He stormed out of the bar, climbed into an unmarked police car, and sped away.

"What the hell was that about?" Miguel unclenched his fists.

"I've met cops like him before," Victoria said. "First they pick the perpetrator, then they find the evidence. One way or another."

They stepped inside Ben's new purchase. Thick, knotted beams from an ancient rainforest rose out of the ground and branched outward like the ribs of an umbrella, holding a vast, soaring dome of palm fronds aloft over the entire cantina. The tables and chairs looked as if they'd been hewn from the same ancient wood, the chairs strung with old hemp rope. The vast bar counter was a single slab of timber worn smooth by thousands of glasses, its rich, swirling grain deep enough to drown in.

Terracotta tiles stretched through the spacious dance floor to the pristine, soft sand beach, where a scattering of lounge chairs lay nestled beneath towering, emerald palms. Surfers skidded over the crashing waves and dozens of yachts and fishing trawlers bobbed at anchor in the shelter of the bay. To the north, jungle-capped hills rose from the sparkling ocean.

"Nice bar," Victoria said. "I feel quite motivated."

"Thanks." Ben smiled.

"Motivated to clear your name and get you out of this deal as quickly as I can."

He looked around the bar again, noticing for the first time the chair legs held together by duct tape and hope, the torn posters of scantily clad women astride motorcycles, and the layers of grime on every surface. Sunbeams were streaming through holes in the rotting roof. A pale, pudgy tourist in a bright yellow Speedo frolicked in the distant surf. Ben's shoulders bowed.

A young woman in a tidy black apron walked out of a hallway beyond the bar.

"I think you have enough legal problems already," she said with the musical inflection of a faint Spanish accent.

Victoria tilted her head. "You must be one of those famous lawyer-waitresses I've heard so much about. Otherwise, you're sadly mistaken if you think I can't get the sale overturned faster than a table in a bar fight."

The server ignored the slight, looking instead at Ben. Where had he seen her before? And why was Miguel trying to hide behind a bar chair?

"Hello, Miguel," she said with a wry smile. "It's nice to see you again so soon. You left without saying goodbye, you know."

"You work here?" Miguel blurted. "I mean . . . hello, Ana. It's good to see you, too. Uh, last night was great. Sorry I ran, er, left." By the time he finished mumbling, he was staring at his shoes.

A half smile lifted the corner of Ana's mouth. "Yesterday was my day off. Today, I am here as the bartender. As for tomorrow, that is up to the new boss."

"I think we can work something out," Ben said. "Ben Cooper. Nice to meet you." He extended his hand over the bar and she took it gently.

"It is good to see you too, Ben. You probably do not remember meeting me last night. I am Ana Guiterrez Rojas."

Ben's hand froze mid-shake.

"Guiterrez?" Miguel asked, eyes widening.

"Yes. Antonio Guiterrez was my uncle." Ana delicately extracted her hand from Ben's grasp.

"Ana," Ben said, "I don't know quite how to say this, but the

31

police consider me a suspect in your uncle's death." He steeled himself for her reaction.

She laughed. "You could not even take a sombrero from the wall last night. Do they really believe you could kill Uncle Antonio?"

Ben felt relieved. Insulted, but relieved.

"You convinced the police to let Ben go, didn't you?" Victoria said.

"After I tell them what I saw last night, one of the officers said they would let Ben go in the morning, when he was sobered up."

Being back in the bar was making Ben's head swim with vague memories, each fading as he tried to bring it into focus. He was left with only a sense that something important had happened here last night, something he should be able to recall, beyond signing the deed. The harder he tried, the more his brain itched.

"What happened last night?" Ben asked.

Ana gestured to a circle of semi-clean chairs. "Have a seat, please. It is a long story." She disappeared into the kitchen, emerging moments later with a pitcher of ice-cold sangria and a handful of wine glasses. She moved quickly and gracefully across the bar, her slender arm easily bearing the weight of the heavy jug.

She sat down in a chair, poured them each a glass, and downed hers. She poured herself another, then began, "I spent last night here, as I usually do on my days off. Miguel and I started talking and then we go to my place—around ten? Yes, ten."

Miguel turned crimson.

Ana continued, "I came back to the bar after Miguel left. Even on my nights off, Antonio had me come back to help him close. It was around midnight. Antonio was here by himself. He tell me he had sold the bar to some drunk from Canada and that Uncle Jorge would call about the money early today." She smiled at Ben. "Congratulations, you own the bar now."

"Uncle Jorge?" Had Ben sent his life savings to the Costa Rican mafia?

"Antonio's brother. He lives in Canada, where he has a travel agency. Antonio has a sailboat that he used for fishing charters, sometimes. The tourists can make a—what is it?—an online bill payment to Jorge's company, and he send the money to Antonio's account."

"That's convenient," Victoria muttered.

"Much harder to stop than a credit card payment, if he change his mind." Ana's smile belied the hard glint in her eyes.

"So, what? I punched Jorge's account into my phone, pushed a few buttons, and sent him sixty thousand?" Ben asked.

Ana shrugged. "More or less."

How was that even possible? Then he remembered the pink silk ribbons, artisanal quinoa salad, and ice sculptures of amorous doves—but a few of the reasons why he and Tara had removed the spending limits from their joint account in the weeks leading up to the wedding. He groaned.

"And Antonio would sign over the deed, just like that?" Ben asked.

"He would if he see you make the transfer on your phone. Besides, Antonio did not make it easy on the people who owe him money." Ana's face wrinkled in disgust for a moment, then she perked up. "This one time there was a fisherman from Vancouver, who decide he wanted to go fishing at two at night and then changed his mind when we got out to sea. He . . ."

As Ana poured herself another glass of sangria, Ben caught Victoria's eye and furtively mimed talking into a telephone with his thumb and pinkie. She rolled her eyes almost imperceptibly, but slid her phone from her purse and left it perched on the arm of her chair.

Ben rose to his feet, somewhat unsteadily. "Where's the bathroom?"

Ana pointed over her shoulder. As she did, Ben snapped Victoria's phone off the chair and stuffed it into his pocket. "Be careful, it is a bit of a mess," Ana said, then continued her story.

He shouldered his way through the bathroom door. Ana wasn't kidding. The lid to the toilet was chipped and cracked, the shattered mirror over the basin was held together by clear tape, and the paper-towel dispenser looked more like a modern art project. The walls had gaping holes where the drywall was caved in. This wasn't where Antonio was murdered, was it?

Or was this Ben's handiwork? He'd done the same to the bathroom in a Burger Duke years ago, although he thought he'd learned his lesson after that one. Apparently not, given his latest purchase; punching up a bathroom seemed downright responsible compared to blowing sixty large on a ramshackle beach bar.

He shook his head and remembered his mission. He slid a plastic card from his near-empty wallet and dialed the number on the back. After a few painful moments spent navigating menus and punching in his client number, he finally tracked down a living, breathing person.

"Greater Canadian Financial, how may I help you?"

"I'd like to check my bank balance," Ben murmured, hunched over the handset.

"Eight dollars and seventeen cents," the agent said.

He closed his eyes as the shattered bathroom swam around him. A bead of sweat trickled down his cheek as the tinny chords of Latin dance music wafted in through a cracked window. "I'd like to issue a stop payment." The words tumbled out before he could stop them.

"I'll need to ask you a few more security questions," the

agent said. Ben took a deep breath, then rattled off his birth-date, address, and other personal trivia. If nothing else, he needed to reset his online banking password. At least, that's what he kept telling himself.

"One last question, sir," she finally said. "What do you want to be when you grow up?"

"Pardon?" Ben asked.

"That's your personal verification question. It's required for major transactions."

That was not Ben's personal verification question. It was . . . The color of his childhood cat, Baron Von Whiskers. Something like that. He might not remember the exact question, but he *would* remember the answer. He said as much.

A keyboard clacked. "Sir, we called you last night to verify a large payment leaving your account. You answered all of our security questions, and then you changed your online banking password and your personal verification question."

Through the fog, Ben could almost hear the distant, muffled ringing of his phone. He had confirmed the transfer, and then . . . "What if I can't remember the new answer?"

"No problem, sir. Just visit any of our twelve hundred branches across Canada with two pieces of photo identification, and you can change your verification question."

That wasn't going to work.

This was like one of those horrible classroom discussion ques-tions. Did Drunk Ben want Sober Ben to have a way out of this mess? Or would Drunk Ben try to force Sober Ben to spend the rest of his life running a bar in Costa Rica, next to a ready sup-ply of alcohol? Would it be the Lady, or the Tiger? The Bottle of Rum, or the Prison Cell?

He tried his luck with the usual suspects. Astronaut. Firefighter. Race car driver.

"I'm sorry, sir. You are now locked out of your account for

the next twenty-four hours."

Ben hung up, splashed some water on his face, and returned to the seating area as Ana finished her tale.

". . . Deserted island and a rowboat. That was the only time Antonio did not get paid."

Victoria glanced over at Ben. He shook his head slightly.

"What happened later that night, after Antonio told you Ben had bought the bar?" she asked.

"We chatted for a bit and then I went home. I was sleeping when the police called."

"Was there anything about that night that struck you as unusual?" Victoria asked.

"Only he seemed a bit jumpy. He did not tell me about selling the bar until I ask him if anything is wrong." Ana shook her head. "I am surprised he sold the bar so cheaply. He had wanted to sell for years, but always said that he would die behind the bar before he got less than a hundred thousand. He dreamed of spending his last few years on his sailboat. Maybe he thought he could get by with less money, now that he was older."

"Was Ben around when you were closing up?" Victoria asked.

"Antonio said Ben had stumbled down the beach, singing. Well, kind of. I could hear him, far away from us."

Ben had a sudden, vivid memory of belting out "Yo-ho, yo-ho, a pirate's life for me!" while staggering down the deserted beach, a half-empty bottle of rum in hand. Worse still, he only knew that one verse. He'd sung it over and over.

He searched his mind again for other fragments knocked loose by Ana's account. Nothing. "Do you know where I got all these cuts and scrapes?"

Ana paused for a moment before pointing at Ben's face. "You got the bruise on your cheek from trying to take the sombrero and the cut on your lip from drinking a beer without taking off

36

the bottle cap first. Other than that, you looked all right when I left."

Ben's face deepened in color.

"Is there anyone who would have wanted to harm your uncle?" Victoria asked as she casually slid her notebook from her briefcase.

"Only about half of Tamarindo. Tourists come and go, but there are a lot of expats who stay here for years. Some of them come here for reasons other than surfing and tanning." She took another long pull of sangria. "Drugs are everywhere. Colombia is close by. Antonio tried to keep the dealers from doing their business in the bar. When he caught them selling, he threw them out, but they always come back a few days later. *Diay?*"

Miguel had taught Ben some Costa Rican slang on the flight down. *Diay* was a term of equal parts surprise and annoyance that effectively meant, "Well, what can you expect?" Efficient, that.

"Did it ever get violent?" Victoria asked.

"Sometimes. Antonio kept a bat behind the bar that he used to settle arguments."

"Is it still here?"

"The police took it." Ana poured herself yet another drink.

Victoria looked thoughtful.

"Do you think a drug dealer could have done this?" Miguel asked.

"Bad for business. This . . . this felt personal." Tears welled in her dark brown eyes. She took a deep breath.

Miguel's hand inched toward Ana's before awkwardly pulling back.

"Did Antonio ever get the police involved?" Ben asked.

"They do what they can, but a lot of money is tossed around. A police officer sees a crooked judge throw out his arrest a few times and he wonders why he misses out."

Miguel's eyes darkened. "You make it sound like they have no choice."

"Oh, they have a choice—*plato o plomo.*"

"Silver or lead," Victoria muttered.

"Get paid, or get killed. *Diay,* most of the police are honest even so, but it only takes a few."

"What about Detective Vasquez?" Victoria asked.

"Uncle Antonio liked Vasquez. He's one of the few who is not afraid to go after the drug dealers. Antonio would call him if there was a problem he could not solve with his bat," Ana said. "Vasquez can be a real son of a bitch, though. He once break a rookie's nose, teaching him to use the baton. He works alone, now."

Victoria jotted a few notes down in her agenda. "Any current or former bar staff with grudges?"

"I cannot think of any. There are only the three of us now. I tend the bar, Luis is the busboy, and Oscar does some cooking and looks after the place."

Ben glanced around the bar once more. A small bright blue bird flew in through one hole in the roof and out another. He was going to have a little chat with Oscar.

"We grumble now and then, but who does not?" Ana said.

Miguel nodded. He sometimes said you don't have to worry when soldiers complain. You worry when they stop complaining.

"Did the police mention anything else?" Victoria asked.

"Most of them seem to think it is a robbery. The register was cleaned out, and Antonio's watch is missing." The corner of Ana's mouth twisted.

"You disagree?"

"Antonio knew how to handle robbers. He would be sweet as roses and hand over the money. Then, when the robber's hands were full and his back was turned, he would knock him senseless with the baseball bat." Ana mimed her uncle knocking a robber over the head, splashing her sangria in the process.

Ben smiled. He wished he could have got to know Antonio. All he remembered was the gleam in the man's eyes.

Ana leaned back in her chair. "It feels wrong. The bathroom is a mess, but the back room with the safe was untouched. They take his watch and his wallet, but not his rings or credit cards. They do not even take the good Scotch. Maybe I just do not want to believe that my uncle was killed by some lowlife looking for quick cash." She rose on unsteady feet. "Please excuse me. I need to take care of the cleaning up. Those cleaners the police send, they barely do anything."

Ben and Victoria paled.

"Ana?" Miguel took a deep breath. "Do you want any help?"

Ben froze. He had to force himself to wash the dishes; he couldn't imagine cleaning up after the murder of someone he loved. He thought of Tara, then remembered that he wasn't supposed to be in love with her anymore. He blinked twice. He had enough to worry about without feeling sorry for himself.

"Thank you, but I would like some time by myself," Ana said. "Ben, please talk with Luis when he arrives. He has not answered any of my calls." A shadow crossed Ana's pretty face as she disappeared behind the bar.

"Victoria," Ben said once Ana was out of earshot, "did the police say anything about how Antonio died?"

"He was beaten to death with his own baseball bat."

CHAPTER THREE

It took a full hour for Ana to finish her grisly task. By then, Ben had taught himself how to work the draft tap and had poured himself and Miguel a pair of frothy pints.

"So," Ana asked, "what is the plan for tonight?"

"Plan?" Ben didn't have a plan, other than sitting in a lounge chair, drinking beer, watching the sun set, and trying not to think about Tara. Victoria had already left for the hotel to change her clothes, and wouldn't return until sometime after dinner.

"Are you going to open?" Ana asked, hands on her hips.

"Doesn't that seem a bit soon?" *Soon* was one word for it. *Callous* and *ghoulish* were two more. Besides, all he really wanted to do was have a pint or three and go to bed.

"It is better than sitting in my apartment, worrying if anyone will show up for Uncle Antonio's funeral." She sighed. "Also, it is Friday night. We do half of our business on the weekend. Unless you have enough money for us to fix the place up before we open again, maybe?"

Ben looked at Miguel, who nodded his approval. "Okay. Let's open."

Ana walked behind the bar and flicked a switch, lighting up the large neon sign that read "Antonio's." She stabbed her finger at another button, and the speakers by the dance floor crackled to life with Latin dance music. She checked her watch. "It is almost five. Customers should be here any minute."

"Here's one now," Miguel said.

40

A young man with impeccably spiked hair sauntered into the bar, clad head to toe in designer duds.

Ana scoffed. "That is Luis, the busboy."

Luis flinched when he saw Ana glaring at him.

"Luis, where the hell were you? I leave five messages on your phone."

"Sorry, Ana," he said, hands thrust into the pockets of his tailored jeans. "My battery died."

"Those missed hours come out of your pay." She looked at Ben, who nodded. "Meet Ben Cooper, the new owner."

Luis brightened. "Pleased to meet you, Mr. Cooper. Can I stay on as a busboy?"

"Sure, Luis," Ben said, puzzled. His silk sport shirt alone must have cost more than Ben's first car. "We're glad to have you."

"Wait until you get to know him." Ana turned back to Luis. "Get changed. Customers will be here any minute."

Luis hustled into the kitchen without saying another word.

"He's our busboy?" Ben asked.

"If you ask him, he's God's gift to fashion design," Ana said, rinsing their sangria glasses and hanging them to dry on the metal rack above the bar. "He's always telling us how he's going to bring Costa Rican style to the international stage." She snorted. "*Diay.* It would help if the sleeves stayed on."

Ben exchanged puzzled looks with Miguel, then shrugged. "So, is there anything in particular I should be doing tonight?"

"If you knew how to mix drinks, I would ask for your help behind the bar." She moved on to cutting up limes. "No offense, but until you learn how to bartend, you are more trouble than you are worth on a busy Friday night." She looked Miguel up and down. "I can use your help, though."

He hopped across the bar and started rummaging through the fridge. It sounded like the two lovebirds had gotten to know each other rather well last night. Miguel had tended bar at one of the top clubs in Toronto for close to three years, despite once dropping a two-thousand-dollar magnum of champagne. Ben eyed the row of dusty liquor bottles along the back wall of the bar, then appraised the way the thin vintage polo shirt clung to his friend's muscular form. Whatever damage Miguel might cause in breakage would be more than made up by the boost in sales.

Ana turned to Ben. "Talk to the customers. Keep them happy and buying drinks."

"And if they don't speak English, I can smile and wave like a finalist in some damned beauty pageant," Ben groused.

"Now you are getting the hang of it." Ana gave him a re-assuring smile. "The rest will have to wait until tomorrow. Otherwise—trust me, you will know when you need to help."

Ben grabbed his pint and sat down on a bar stool. Customers started to trickle in, alone and in pairs at first, then in small groups. There didn't seem to be a single age group that called Antonio's home: a couple of local surf instructors preceded boisterous women of a certain age, followed by graying men clad in Hawaiian shirts boasting of their marlin catch.

Ben wondered if they were among the expatriates Ana had mentioned. What secrets lurked beneath those bronzed, smiling faces? He tensed at the thought of Antonio's killer returning to the bar this evening. He gazed down at his bloody knuckles. Perhaps the killer was already here.

He grabbed a tray full of colorful drinks to deliver to a bachelorette party that had taken over the beach lounge. He managed two steps from the bar before the heavy daiquiri glasses slid off the tray and exploded on the terracotta tiles. The crowd was silent for a moment, then someone started a round of lively applause.

He closed his eyes and wished he could sink through the

floor. Ana coughed twice, and he looked up to see Luis standing next to him, with a mop, broom, and dustpan.

Next he tried mingling, with mixed success. Half the customers spoke no English, at least not while Ben was around, and the other half avoided eye contact altogether. He handed out a free drink to a middle-aged woman sitting alone, but she turned out to be almost as drunk as Ben had been last night and tried to drag him onto the dance floor. And into a table. He politely disengaged from her grasp.

He reached for his phone and its dizzying array of distractions before remembering it was lost. After drumming his fingers on the bar for several minutes, he headed to the men's to splash some water on his face, gather his thoughts, and escape the growing din.

The bathroom was still a wreck. Oscar had done what he could to put it back together in time to open, but it looked like a war zone. The cracked toilet lid had been filled in with globs of putty, while the shattered mirror had been replaced with a burnished metal tray. A roll of paper towel now hung from a coat hanger on a nail, and circles of fresh plaster marked where the drywall had been crushed.

Sloshing water on his face didn't revive Ben as he had expected. The haphazard repairs couldn't mask the lingering sense of boundless rage. He again wondered if the fight had started there, though Ana hadn't mentioned blood anywhere other than behind the bar.

By the time Ben got back to the bar, the trickle of customers had become a flood. Surprised, he turned to Ana and asked, "Hey, is this usual for a Friday ni—?"

A tipsy, sunburned tourist bumped him from behind. "Hey man, get a picture of me at the scene of the crime," he shouted, mugging for his friend's camera. "Sucks that they got rid of the chalk outline so soon, but what can you do? Hey, look at me,

I'm a dead bartender." He lay down on the ground with his tongue sticking out, twitching around for comedic effect. His friends—flabby college kids in pink polo shirts two sizes too small—laughed until they doubled over.

Ben turned to the crowd of drunks. He wanted to bellow at them—all of them—that they were miserable human beings. He wanted to force them to apologize to Ana. Then, he wanted to toss them to the curb with the rest of the garbage. If only that baseball bat were still behind the bar.

The moment balanced on a knife's edge. Then the pounding stopped.

Ben turned back to the bar. "Miguel. Ana. For the rest of the night, I want those punks to pay twice as much for half the booze."

"Sure thing, boss." She unclenched her jaw and smiled. "If Antonio was here, he would be proud."

Luis looked up from sorting dishes and muttered, "If Antonio was here, he would sell T-shirts that said, 'I got wasted at Antonio's.' "

Ana opened her mouth to yell at Luis, then stopped herself. Ben couldn't tell if she was furious or fighting the urge to laugh. He wasn't sure if she knew, either.

Ben said, "Keep up the good work."

Ana gave him a small smile and lifted a glass to pour another pint. He turned around and ran straight into Victoria, now wearing a vibrant blue sundress.

"What the hell is going on here?" Her eyes darted around the room, trying to count the people who'd come for the thrill of partying at a real crime scene.

"We opened."

"I'll say you did," she said. "Good idea. Looks like you're doing well."

Ben glanced at the pack of college kids, emptying their wallets in exchange for a tray of watered-down rum-and-Cokes. "Business is booming."

"Do you have a minute?" she asked.

"Let's step into my office."

Victoria seemed impressed. "Certainly, Mr. Cooper. Lead the way."

They walked past the bar into the back hallway and opened the first door on the right. Ben noticed closed doors farther down the darkened corridor. He'd ask Ana to give them the grand tour sometime soon.

The office hadn't been touched during the struggle, but it still looked as though it had been struck by a miniature tornado. Papers covered every surface, including a large safe and a row of filing cabinets. The stained walls were plastered with photo after photo of Antonio Guiterrez, smiling down at them from cliffside restaurants, sisters' weddings, children's birthday parties, and the ever-present sailboat. The effect was unpleasant.

Ben waved Victoria toward one of two wicker chairs and shut the door behind them. Rather than trying to wedge himself behind the battered wooden desk, he sat in the second wicker chair.

"What's on your mind?" he asked.

Victoria squinted at him. "Are you feeling okay?"

"Never better." For the first time in a while, he actually meant it.

"Bad news. Mansion's landed a big client and he wants me to take the lead on the file. I'll need to head home the day after tomorrow," Victoria said. "Sorry, Ben. I wanted to stick this one out. If I can't clear your name before I leave, I should be back within a week."

"I understand. We'll miss having you here, but we'll figure out a way to make it work." Two days wasn't much but, with luck, it would be enough. As for later—well, he was due to fly back in a week, but it was anyone's guess whether he'd be on that plane.

"I've found a local law firm that should be able to ensure you get fair treatment until I return. I'll meet with them tomorrow to sort out the details."

Ben grinned lopsidedly. "By 'details,' do you mean how best to keep Vasquez and friends from tossing me back in jail on a trumped-up charge?"

"That's exactly what I mean."

"Just making sure," Ben said. "Was that everything?"

"No, actually. I wanted to talk to you about Ana." Victoria weighed her words carefully. "Have you considered that she might have the most to gain from Antonio's death?"

"How so?"

"First, it seems she was Antonio's closest relative, which means she will likely inherit the sixty thousand dollars you paid for the bar plus the remainder of Antonio's assets. That's more than ten years' wages in Costa Rica. Second, she has no alibi for the time of his murder and is the last known person to have seen him alive.

"Third, she knew everything there was to know about the bar, including where Antonio kept his bat and how he'd react during a robbery. And finally, we have no idea whether her version of events is true. For all we know, she sold you on a discount fishing charter to get you to access your online banking, drugged you, stole your money, and forged your signature on the deed."

Ben opened his mouth to explain that he remembered signing the deed, but he couldn't recall *exactly* what had happened, apart from holding a pen, seeing the gleam in Antonio's eyes, and feeling really good about it afterwards. That was hardly conclusive evidence in Ana's favor, but Victoria's litany of charges still seemed extreme.

"What about the bathroom? Why would she trash it?" he said.

Victoria deflated slightly. "That's the part I can't figure out. Perhaps she did it so the police would suspect a male robber. Maybe she wanted to muddy the waters." She leaned forward, lowering her voice. "I'm worried about Miguel getting too close to her before we have all the facts."

"I'll keep an eye on him," Ben promised, although inserting himself into Miguel's love life was the last thing that he wanted to do. He briefly wondered if this was more about Miguel than Ana, but, no, he couldn't imagine Victoria and Miguel romantically involved with each other. Could he?

Victoria looked around the office. "This all feels too convenient to me."

Ben leaned back. "Let's look at what we know. Fact: Antonio is dead. Fact: Antonio was killed the same night I bought the bar."

"That's a rather large coincidence," Victoria said.

"I agree. Especially considering what Ana said about my paying less than Antonio thought he could get. That's worth looking into."

"I'll make a call to the office. They should be able to check what a place like this usually fetches," Victoria said. "What if Antonio knew someone was coming for him, and that's why he dropped the price?"

"But who? And why?"

There was a knock and Ana eased the door open. Her face was a grim mask. "There is something you need to see."

Ben rose from his chair, wondering how long Ana had waited before knocking.

The sky flushed red and gold, backlighting the beachside bargoers as they watched the Pacific swallow the last sliver of sun.

Ben let out a heavy breath and wished he was out there with them, watching the sun set on his first day as the bar's owner, worrying only whether his ice cubes were getting lonely.

Ana grabbed an envelope from the counter and handed it to Ben. "I turn my back for a second to get some clean pitchers. When I turn around, I find this on the bar." She reached under the sink and drew out a pair of cheap yellow cleaning gloves. "Put these on when you open it."

Feeling nervous—and a little ridiculous—Ben pulled on the sour-smelling gloves and extricated a single sheet from the envelope. Letters cut from newspapers and magazines spelled out two short sentences:

Antonio died well. Will you?

Ben shivered.

"Seriously? Letters cut from a magazine?" Victoria asked, peering over his shoulder. "Do criminals even still do that?"

Ana shot her a glare. "Not everyone in Tamarindo has a fancy office with a printing laser."

"Laser printer," Victoria corrected.

"Have you ever seen anything like this before, Victoria?" Ben interrupted.

She shook her head. "I haven't. Then again, I wasn't practicing law in 1972. We also don't get a lot of anonymous death threats at a corporate law office."

"Really? That is a surprise," Ana snapped. "What do we do with this, Ben?"

"Victoria, take a photo of it. Then Ana will put the letter in the safe. We'll give it to the police tomorrow."

"That's not necessary, Ben," Ana said as Victoria took a picture of the letter with her phone.

"You have another idea?"

"No, no. Captain Reyes is here. You can give it to him now."

Ben shut his eyes. *What's next, a plague of locusts?*

He looked down the length of the bar and spotted the captain standing alone. He was in street clothes—a dark green golf shirt tucked into pleated khakis—presumably to avoid drawing attention to himself. He wore the civilian attire awkwardly, like a man who lived and slept in uniform. There was a distinct tan line across his forehead where his forge cap usually sat.

"I can handle this," Victoria said, using a folded glove to hold the letter by a corner.

"I'll go with you," Ben said. "This isn't a social call."

Victoria glided over to the policeman, a death threat in one hand and a bottle of rum in the other. "What can I get you, Captain?" she asked smoothly.

"Nothing more for me, thank you." He raised a glass of soda water. "I simply wanted to see how you were getting on."

"Just glad to be part of Tamarindo's thriving economy, Captain."

"I have no doubt." He laughed. It almost sounded genuine. "Business does seem to be thriving. Perhaps a bit too well? You are aware that the fire code limits you to two hundred customers at a time, yes? You seem to have rather more than that."

Victoria clucked her tongue. "Captain, what sort of establishment do you think we are running here? We only have 187 customers at the moment. You are more than welcome to count them yourself, if you'd like." She gestured at the mob of patrons.

He smiled. "As you say, Ms. Holmes."

"May I ask how your investigation is proceeding?"

"You may not," he replied. "I'm sure you appreciate that any information we release would be limited to Mr. Guiterrez's family until after the investigation is concluded."

"Of course." She looked pointedly at the other side of the bar, where Ana was smiling at something Miguel had said. "Speaking of your investigation, I believe this might be of interest." She held up the letter so Reyes could get a good look.

He slid a pair of reading glasses from his pocket and quickly scanned it. "This could be important. Or it could be a rather cruel practical joke."

Ben scoffed.

"I do not mean to seem insensitive, Mr. Cooper. If there is a credible threat against you, we will of course offer you the same protection that we would offer any other resident of Tamarindo," Reyes said. "I'm sure you understand that this kind of unfortunate incident always draws curiosity-seekers. Some are more curious than others."

He produced an evidence bag from a pants pocket and slid the threatening letter inside. "That said, I will certainly enter this into evidence and send an officer to take your statements. We will let you know if we learn anything more."

"Thank you, Captain," Victoria said.

"For future reference, gloves do not always prevent fingerprints from transferring to the paper. At least you had the foresight to hold it by the corner." He turned to Ben. "Mr. Cooper, how are you this evening?"

"I'm all right, Captain. Thank you for arranging for the crime scene to be released so quickly."

Captain Reyes's face twisted in annoyance. "Do not consider that a personal favor, Mr. Cooper. There are a great many people in Tamarindo who rely on tourism for their livelihood and who think that police tape anywhere in town is bad for business." Reyes looked down at his barely touched soda water. "I believe I am no longer thirsty. Good evening to you both." He slid from his stool and slowly made his way out through the crowd.

"Well played, Ben," Victoria said.

"Do we really have 187 customers?"

"How on earth would I know?"

The crowd swelled until it seemed to swallow the bar whole. Ana and Miguel battled back, filling glasses as fast as the patrons could drain them. At one point, Ben saw Miguel spinning a bottle of rum with his right hand while igniting a cloud of cinnamon with his left. He looked like he was having the time of his life. Even Ben and Victoria had the chance to get behind the counter and sling a few drinks. Victoria took to it as if it were second nature and Ben enjoyed it, once he'd picked up a few tricks. Then, after what seemed like both an instant and an eternity, the crowd receded and the four of them were left to close up.

Ben staggered to the beach and flopped down on a lounge chair beneath the stars. He had no problem leaving the inventory and the accounting to Ana and Miguel; last he'd checked, neither of them had woken up that morning on a concrete prison floor. He would learn how to close up another night. Whenever it was they closed. He was used to the set hours required of Canadian bars. Clearly Costa Rica played by its own rules.

He lay still, enjoying the murmur of the surf and the cool breeze that tugged gently at his sweat-stained clothes. To his surprise, Miguel sat down on the chair next to him and handed him an ice-cold Imperial, a local beer Ben had favored when their holiday was still a holiday. "Victoria insisted on taking over the accounts," he explained. "She said she wasn't willing to entrust vast sums of money to a man who almost set himself on fire with a household spice."

"Sage advice," Ben said.

Miguel groaned.

"What sort of vast sums are we talking about here?" Ben asked.

"I'm not sure, but Ana said it was a solid take. Victoria

promised to give us a rundown on the finances tomorrow."

"How was your night? It looked like you were having a good time out there."

Miguel looked up at the sky. Even with light spilling from the bar onto the sand, countless stars gleamed above their heads.

"I want to be your partner," he said.

"That's very flattering, Miguel. But I only think of you as a friend."

Miguel punched his arm. "In the bar, you idiot."

Ben laughed. "I'd like that." He turned serious. "Why the sudden change of mind? You said buying this shack was a crazy idea."

"It is crazy. All of this is crazy. But how can you say no to something like this? The chance to own a bar in the tropics."

Ben silently added the other perks that came to mind. Staying up late. No more winters. Swimming in the ocean every morning. No more winters. All the bar nuts he could eat. No more winters. The list went on.

"I talked to a lot of people at the bar," Miguel said. "Most are tourists down for a week or two, but some have been here for ages. A few came down for a holiday and stayed for ten years or more. I don't know. It's like Tamarindo chooses you."

Ben had felt it, too—for an instant, somewhere between Miguel snatching a spinning rum bottle from midair and Victoria dashing Tabasco in the eyes of a customer with more hands than brains. Then reality had sunk back. Tara. The money. Tara and the money. Oh, and the looming criminal charges. He'd almost forgotten about those.

"Did Ana show you our fan mail?" he asked.

"I don't like it. Not one bit. I don't care what the captain says, that's no practical joke."

"And you still want in on this?"

"Definitely."

"Then welcome aboard, partner," Ben said, extending his hand. Miguel shook it firmly.

The sun had already peaked by the time Ben returned to the bar the next day. Clearly, he'd needed the sleep. His face and body were still covered in bruises, but the ache had faded from his muscles and he'd finally sweated out the drink.

Once the last of the lunch crowd left the bar, Ana switched the sign to "Closed" and brought over the large platter that Oscar had left in the pass-through—skewers of blackened shrimp, spicy chicken wings, battered calamari, and bowls overflowing with nachos, cheese, and sour cream. They tucked in.

"Do we know when the police are coming by?" Ben asked after polishing off the last of the wings.

"They were here this morning," Ana said.

"Do they have any leads on who made the threat?"

"The officer said he would look into it." Ana frowned.

"That's good, isn't it?" Ben said.

"They sent Constable Andino."

"Oh?"

"I would not trust him to find sand at a beach."

"Oh."

Ben turned to Victoria and said, "How are the accounts?"

She wiped her hands, then flipped open a leather notebook. "Do you want the good news or the bad news?"

"Let's start with the bad news." He looked longingly at the draft tap.

"You have about three weeks to raise roughly twenty thousand dollars, or you'll be forced to sell the bar."

"Twenty thousand!"

"Give or take."

He rubbed his forehead. "I thought we had a good haul last night."

"You did. That's why you have three weeks instead of two," she said, flipping pages. "You're facing a death of a thousand cuts. The bathroom needs to be properly repaired, the roof is going to shred in the next high wind, and Antonio had yet to pay for a new keg fridge due to arrive in a few days." She flipped another page. "We're still six weeks from peak season. Based on last year's figures, the bar will bleed more than a hundred dollars a day until then."

Miguel moaned, his massive hands covering his face. "Can't we put *some* of this off until later?"

"You could try, but chances are the weather will get wetter and windier before you can make more cash. That could double or even triple the cost of fixing the roof. Even if, by some miracle, the roof isn't turned into palm confetti, there aren't many customers who'll want to sip margaritas to a power tool serenade, especially during the prime season." She closed the notebook. "Cut your losses in three weeks and you'll only take a twenty thousand dollar bath."

Twenty thousand dollars. That was more than Ben's entire life savings; far more than his share of the down payment on the house. He'd have nothing. Worse, he'd owe Tara money she hadn't agreed to lend him.

"Otherwise, you risk losing it all," Victoria finished. "Look on the bright side, at least that ancient walk-in freezer is still going strong. If that was shot, you'd be done before you even started. At least you have a fighting chance."

"More like a beating, if you ask me," Ben said.

"No one will give you a loan right now," Victoria said. "Not without your kneecaps as collateral. But if we handle these problems, you should be able to get a line of credit from one of the banks."

There was silence around the table.

Finally, Miguel spoke up. "I'm staying on as a partner. I've got five thousand in the bank. It's yours if it will help."

"Thanks, man." Ben was relieved, though a small voice in his head said, *Five down, fifteen to go.*

He straightened his back. "Ana, could you give us a tour of the bar? I'd like to see what we're up against."

They gathered up the greasy wicker platters and placed them on the pass-through to the kitchen. Ana walked back into the bar and gestured to the cantina under the leaky roof. "There are four different areas here. The dining area is there." She pointed to the raised section, where they'd eaten lunch. It held ten round tables, each large enough for four people. "The lounge area is here." She indicated the stools in front of the bar itself, the pool table to the side, and the collection of low-slung wicker chairs and couches clustered around wooden coffee tables in the middle of the bar. They'd sat there yesterday while Ana recounted the details of her uncle's murder. The doors to the washrooms were beyond the lounge chairs, on the far wall.

"The third area is the dance floor." She waved at the open expanse of tiled floor, one step below the lounge area, which ended at a low stage dominated by massive speakers. The dance floor itself was ringed by high tables and bar stools.

"And the beach lounge is the fourth." To the right of the dance floor, an archway built from large wooden logs led to a small section of beach, fenced off and furnished with a collection of faded beanbag chairs and a dozen metal and nylon loungers. Ben assumed the lounge chairs weren't wooden because they were exposed to the elements. More exposed, he corrected himself, as he peered through one of the holes in the thirty-foot-high dome of palm fronds.

Ana continued, "Behind the bar, we have a sink and two fridges, one for the beer and wine bottles and the other for the kegs of beer." Ana pointed at each in turn.

"Do we really need a new keg fridge?" Miguel asked.

Ana shrugged. "It is too late now to cancel the order. Even if we could, this fridge is about to die. The beer gets warmer each day, and one tap pours only foam."

Ben looked down at the fridge to judge for himself. Until now he hadn't even noticed the fake wood grain on the fridge door, let alone the compressor that sounded as though it housed a robot wrestling league.

He looked up at Ana. "I think that's the right call."

"Thanks, Ben." She pointed at the pass-through to the kitchen. "When a meal is ready, Oscar will leave it there for one of us to pick up and carry out to the table."

As if on cue, Oscar's face appeared in the pass-through. It was caked with fine white powder, and when he smiled, a gold incisor glinted in a stray sunbeam. His long dark hair was tucked in a net. Before Ben could ask whether he was covered in drywall dust or flour, he had disappeared back into the kitchen.

"Now the back area." Ana ushered them into the back hallway as Oscar stepped out of the first door to the left. He hung his apron on a peg as he pushed through the heavy swinging door, revealing a tool belt underneath. He and Ana chatted in Spanish for a moment, and he went off to fix something. She had told Ben last night what his chef-cum-handyman would be working on for the next few days, but the list was so long that Ben had forgotten the first half by the time they'd reached the end.

Ana led them through the swinging door into the kitchen and stepped them through the array of fixtures, appliances, and cooking utensils spanning more than four decades. The room was small, but the stainless steel counters, black-and-white tile floor, and the well-worn appliances were all spotless. Particularly the stove, which looked as though it hadn't been used in months. The deep fryer, on the other hand, seemed to have many miles on it. The massive walk-in freezer was an equally ancient Kelvinator. Some of the chrome letters had fallen off, rechristening the freezer *Ke vin*.

Ben opened *Ke vin* and peered inside. Cold air washed over him as he squinted into the darkness. The freezer smelled clean, if stale, but it was hard to tell its state in the dim light from the kitchen. "I'm guessing this walk-in was invented before the age of automatic lighting?"

"There should be a candle in there," Ana said.

Ben chuckled. "Good one, Ana."

"No, really." Ana reached through the door and took a half-melted candle from a shelf. "The rest of the freezer works fine, but the light is broken." She pulled a lighter from her pocket and offered both items to Ben.

"No, thanks. I'll take your word on it."

"Suit yourself." Ana put the candle back, then pointed at a small metal latch on the inside of the door. "I never lock the freezer, but Oscar and Luis sometimes do. If you are ever inside when that happens, this will unlock the door."

So Ben would leave Canadian winters behind to end up inside *Ke vin*, chiseling out fish sticks by candlelight? He considered that a moment, then made a mental note to delegate anything freezer-related.

"Good to know," he said aloud.

Ana closed the freezer and pushed her way back out through the kitchen door, leading the group farther down the hallway.

"That's the office." Ana pointed at the door opposite the kitchen.

"Mind if I have a look?" Miguel reached for the doorknob, but stopped when someone inside started pounding a hammer. Oscar was fixing a loose floorboard, if Ben's memory served. Or building a catapult.

"Maybe tonight," Ben said.

Ana finished the tour by showing them the four storerooms at the end of the hallway. They seemed to store cobwebs and boxes filled with other boxes more than anything else.

The four of them returned to the bar lounge to plan their next move, where they sat in silence for a while. Eventually, Ben remembered something.

"Didn't you say you had some good news?" he asked Victoria.

"Right. Almost forgot," she said. "The problem now is that the bar loses money in the off season, and there's little to lose. Morbid curiosity helped us last night, but that won't last." She pulled out her notebook once more. "I did some calculations, and I think your scheme of renting the bar to wanna-be owners could save you from certain financial doom."

"I remember that plan," Ana said. "You should stick to stealing sombreros."

He fixed her with a glare, then turned back to Victoria. "What do you mean?"

"If you can get enough pretend-owners to sign up, you can use their deposits to cover the costs. You'll still be cutting it close, but it's either that or try to hold the world's largest bake sale."

Ben rubbed his stubbled cheek. "Where do you even start with something like this?"

Miguel sat bolt upright. "Bongos!"

"What?" Ana asked.

"My uncle," Miguel said. "He's a world-champion bongo drummer."

Victoria laughed. "You're making that up . . ."

"Seriously," Miguel said. "Bongos are big business in Costa Rica. Uncle Enrico always said he wanted to own a bar one day, but he's always been too busy with his bongos."

Too busy with his bongos. Ben mouthed the phrase silently. So this was what his life had become.

Ana's mouth dropped open. "Enrico Morales is your uncle?"

Miguel smiled broadly. "He sure is."

"What do you think he'd be willing to pay?" Ben asked. He'd tried looking for the business plan he'd scribbled on the cocktail napkin, but he must have used it to staunch his bleeding nose while in prison.

"Enrico Morales? *The* Enrico Morales? You want *him* to pay *us*?" Ana asked.

"If we ask nicely, he might perform for us in trade," Miguel said. "He's a huge draw. Fans will line up around the block."

"It could bring in some extra revenue," Victoria admitted.

"Uncle Enrico could get the story out about how much fun it is to pretend-own a bar. We'll get some reporters out to cover it. For all we know, some tourist could come for the bongo show and sign on as our next client."

"It beats waiting for the roof to fall in," Ana said.

"Bongos it is," Ben said. "Call Uncle Enrico."

CHAPTER FOUR

"A bar owner?"

"That's incorrect, sir."

"Innocent?"

"No."

"Sober?"

"I'm sorry, sir. You are again locked out of your bank account for the next twenty-four hours."

So much for his plan to stop payment on the bar. Ben hung up and dialed another number. The line clicked and went to voicemail. Again.

He still had no idea where he'd lost his phone. That was the third time he had tried calling his own number, always with the same result. He'd hoped that he left it in his hotel room, but he'd searched every nook and cranny without success.

Not for the first time, he debated reporting his phone stolen. He'd used the hotel's business center to check his phone bill online, but no new calls had been made. Either the phone was powered off somewhere or had been wiped clean and sold on the black market. He drummed his fingers on the hotel desk for a few moments, finally electing to hold off another day or two.

TravelerAdvice rated the Diria as one of the finest beachside resorts in Tamarindo; it was certainly among the more expensive. Tara had chosen it, as she had decided most of their wedding details. At least Ben had got more use of the hotel room than she had of the chocolate-bourbon wedding cake or the three-piece jazz band. Presumably.

God. How many times had he and Tara practiced that ludicrously elaborate swing-dance to the aptly titled "Love Me or Leave Me"? How many walls had he spun into before he finally learned how to segue an under-arm turn into an exchange in triple time? And how many years would go by before he forgot those utterly useless dance steps?

But he did own a bar now. So there was that.

It took real effort to be melancholy in a place like Tamarindo, particularly when staying at the Diria. His room's walls and bedding were cheerful hues of red and yellow and yet, as bright as they were, they paled against the view from the window. Swaying palms reached toward the terracotta balcony, patterning the rippling blue of the hotel's vast pool, and the golden beach and its long row of white lounge chairs with bright blue umbrellas. An enterprising local paused between chairs to drop a straw into an ice-cold coconut for one of the many sun seekers. Ben and Miguel might be facing imminent financial ruin, but at least they'd live the high life for one more week.

Ben looked over his wrinkled list once more. They needed to pick up a lot of supplies before Enrico arrived. It'd taken Miguel all of five minutes to persuade his uncle to sign on. He was wrapping up a road tour that evening in nearby Brasilito and would be ready to begin his week of pretend-ownership tomorrow afternoon. That didn't leave them long to prepare, but at least they'd know soon whether this scheme had even a faint hope of success. Or if they'd need to put up flyers saying, "Bar for Sale. Cheap. Warm Beer. Only One Murder."

He glanced at the bedside clock. Almost two in the afternoon. Time to meet Miguel. Ben headed to the hallway, his leather sandals flapping against the clay tiles. He knocked, and Miguel opened his door a few inches, enough for Ben to spot the puddle of clothes poised to ooze into the hallway and envelop the ice machine.

"Two minutes," Miguel said through the crack before closing the door.

For all his confidence, Miguel was clearly ashamed of his messiness. Ben had offered to lower the cost of the trip by exchanging his honeymoon suite for a basic room with two queen beds, but Miguel had insisted on booking a room of his own. He wouldn't even let Ben pay half the extra cost. Before, when Ben had spent a week on Miguel's couch after breaking up with Tara, Miguel had kept the door to his room locked. Who cared that much about a mound of wrinkled shirts, anyway?

At precisely two o'clock, Miguel strode out of his room, impeccably dressed in linen slacks and a brown V-neck T-shirt from some up-and-coming Toronto fashion designer. It occurred to Ben that, if Miguel actually allowed anyone to disturb his messy room, he might transform into a pudgy, polyester-wearing slob.

The two walked down the stairs, through the lobby, and out the large wrought-iron gate at the front of the hotel. The midday heat had descended upon Tamarindo, and Ben could feel it radiating from the asphalt as they crossed the road to the parking lot where they had left the rental car.

At least, where Ben thought they'd left the rental car.

They searched for a minute or two before realizing that the car was at the center of a small crowd. Ben's stomach sank. Something told him those people hadn't gathered to admire the economy hatchback they'd driven from San José. He pushed through the crowd to discover someone had spray-painted *Gringo* on the side of the car, with the *o* drawn as a menacing skull and crossbones. Ben doubted the car rental people would believe the little hatchback had looked that way when he and

Miguel picked it up at the airport depot.

Miguel was already asking questions in Spanish. The onlookers were muttering among themselves and angrily gesturing at the car. Ben tightened his grip on the keys before he realized the crowd was furious with the vandal, not with either of them.

"They're really mad with the guy who did this. This isn't how *Ticos* treat their guests," Miguel said, using the slang term for native Costa Ricans. "I told them where we're staying. They'll let us know if they see anyone hanging around the car."

Ben rubbed at the paint. Dry. It must have been sprayed some time ago. He'd seen the car on their way back from the bar last night, but hadn't noticed any graffiti. It made sense for a vandal to strike when most people are asleep, but who tags a car at four in the morning?

"I don't think this is a coincidence," Miguel said, putting Ben's thoughts into words.

"Me neither." He stared at the skull and crossbones. It was the second threat in less than twenty-four hours. Third, if he counted Vasquez's not-so-subtle insinuations. That was three more threats than he'd expected on this particular holiday.

With utter disregard for his spotless clothes, Miguel lay down on the ground and slithered beneath the hatchback. The crowd's muttering grew as various pings and rattles echoed from the undercarriage. Miguel finally slid back out, drenched in sweat and caked in dust.

"The brake lines are intact and no one planted any explosives or tracking devices." He rubbed grease from his hands.

Ben was shocked. A threatening letter was one thing. A bomb planted beneath your car was a whole other level. "Don't you think you're being a little bit paranoid?"

"It's not paranoia if someone's actually out to get you." Miguel's gaze was distant.

Ben couldn't argue with that. He was struck by a sudden

nostalgia for his comfortable, predictable life in Oakville, where he only ever looked under his car to check that his neighbor's cat wasn't sleeping underneath. Still surrounded by the small crowd, Miguel hopped into the driver's seat and turned the key. Despite himself, Ben tensed.

Nothing happened.

"Battery's dead. We'll need a bump start," Miguel said.

"Do you think anyone here has jumper cables? Because we don't."

"No, a *bump* start. The car is a manual. If these guys give us a push, I can pop the clutch and get the engine spinning."

Miguel explained the problem to the onlookers. Within moments, they had bent to the task of pushing the car. The rental belched to life on the third attempt, tossing a cloud of gray smoke and gasoline into the air.

"Gracias!" Ben waved goodbye to the crowd as he slid into the passenger's seat. "Where on earth did you learn to do that?" he asked Miguel.

"Oh, you know. You pick these things up over the years."

Ben took the hint and dropped the subject. For once, he was glad to have a lengthy shopping list. It would give them time to recharge the battery.

Victoria walked along Tamarindo's main street, phone in hand. Her little blue dot drew ever nearer to the cartoon push pin that marked the Pacific Park building, home of Castillo, Arias and Associates. She silently cursed the beautiful weather roasting her in her woolen suit. One last errand to run before she could pack it away. Until she landed in Toronto, at least.

She felt a pang. It wasn't right, leaving Ben behind like this. But business was business. Even so, a small part of her wondered whether Mansion had engineered an excuse to drag her back into the office before she grew accustomed to freedom from indentured servitude. Or wearing sundresses.

She turned right, surprised to find herself strolling alongside a rutted dirt road. A bank plaza and an upscale Asian Fusion restaurant sat next to hostel bars and a parking lot crammed with the reprobates that made up the local fleet of unregistered taxis. That, or a not-at-all underground street racing club. You could almost touch the high water mark where the last financial crisis had halted Tamarindo's development. The gleaming white Pacific Park tower came into view once she passed a barbeque joint. The sign out front promised new, lower prices. Lower than what?

She stepped inside the sprawling marble-coated lobby and glanced at the directory. Castillo, Arias and Associates. Main floor. Easy enough. Until she almost walked headlong into the law firm's locked door.

She pushed the buzzer next to the heavy wooden door and waited. Nothing. She pressed it once more. This time there was a faint murmuring from inside that sounded much like ". . . if we just stay quiet . . ." in Spanish.

Victoria cleared her throat. "I can hear you in there," she said through the door.

The intercom crackled to life. "Hello?" said a woman's voice.

"Is this Castillo, Arias and Associates?"

There was some hushed discussion. "Yes," the voice admitted.

"This is Victoria Holmes of Holmes, Holmes and Wright."

Another pause. "I am sorry, but we have no record of your appointment."

"If there's no record of it, how do you know I'm here for an appointment?" Victoria asked.

Silence.

"I hope your windows are wide enough for you to fit through, because I'm not leaving until I speak with one of your partners."

★ ★ ★ ★ ★

Ben and Miguel ran their errands without incident, save for the occasional shopkeeper's puzzled look at the car's graffiti, Miguel's dirty clothes, and Ben's ripening bruises. No one asked any questions. Ben couldn't tell whether they were being polite or simply didn't want to get involved.

He'd winced while signing for the expensive speakers and audio mixing equipment that Miguel insisted they needed to bring Enrico's music to life. Ben had suggested they use the speakers they already owned, but might as well have proposed serving vintage champagne in an unwashed coffee mug.

Most of their other purchases were reasonably priced, particularly the construction supplies. With a fresh coat of paint and some other minor fixes, two of the storerooms could accommodate their pretend-owners. Oscar had promised to tackle the repairs that evening after the kitchen closed, and Ana had agreed to look after the furniture, bedding, and finishing touches. No one would mistake the cantina for a boutique hotel, but it would be comfortable enough for a man who'd spent half his life on the road.

They arrived back at the bar late that afternoon. Ana met them outside, and the three of them started offloading the new audio equipment.

"Nice paint job," Ana said, opening the door to the back seat.

"Thanks," Ben replied. "It would make the car menacing, if there wasn't a hamster wheel where the engine should be."

She laughed. Then she saw Miguel. "What happened?"

"It's a new look." Miguel looked down at his dusty, grease-stained designer T-shirt. "Haute Hobo."

"Very funny." Ana grabbed the heavy audio mixer and started up the path. "Notice anything new about the place?"

Ben looked up. Antonio's old sign had been replaced with a

hastily carved wooden plaque that read, "Enrico's." Beneath it, a smaller wooden oval read, "Industrias Cantina en la Playa." His face broke into a huge grin.

"Bar on the Beach Enterprises." Miguel shook his head.

"I am sorry about what I said earlier. It really is a good idea," Ana said awkwardly. "*Ta bueno?* It's okay?"

Ben smiled warmly, his eyes shining. "Thanks, Ana. The signs look great."

After a couple more trips, Ben, Miguel, and Ana had successfully emptied the hatchback, depositing the construction supplies in one of the storage rooms and the audio equipment at the edge of the dance floor. Ben gazed at the pile of electronics and wires, trying to figure out how they went together. He might as well have tried to build a time machine.

"Do either of you know how to hook this thing up?" he asked.

"I booked a DJ for later tonight," Ana replied, her arms wrapped around the last bag of drywall compound. "He will set up the system and try it out for us."

Ben gladly walked away from the jumble of electronics.

When they'd stashed everything, they staggered to the lounge area for a well-deserved breather. They had only thirty minutes before the bar opened and each of them would be on their feet for the next seven hours; longer, if they hoped to reverse the tide of money flowing from the bar.

Ben tried to pour a pint of beer, but managed only to produce a glass overflowing with foam. Ana nudged him out of the way and filled a pitcher for the three of them. Ben took a sip. Ana was right—the beer was getting warmer by the day. Two steps forward, one step back.

Victoria walked in as they were sitting down, her high heels clicking on the tile. Ben wondered why on earth she was in her business suit before realizing she must have come straight from the meeting at the nearby law office to hand over his case. Hopefully the new lawyer would keep him on as a client for more than a day and a half before ditching him for someone more important. Or solvent.

He knew he was being petty, but it seemed that was the way it went with Victoria these days. It had been so different, back when they were at university. They'd met in one of Ben's electives in economics and become fast friends, staying up late together to work through assignments, talk politics, and discuss the personal hygiene of the more eccentric professors. But that was a long, long time ago, before Victoria became a lawyer and he went off to make something of himself, only to end up making databases at Tara's uncle's IT firm.

Perhaps when you billed by the minute, you started to tally up how much all those minutes were actually worth.

She looked poised as always, if flushed from the heat. She gave the pitcher of beer a disdainful glance and strode to the back of the bar without breaking stride. To Ben's surprise, she emerged with a glass full of ice and a bottle of amber rum.

"Rough day at the office?" Miguel asked, eyes locked on the bottle.

Victoria dropped her briefcase to the ground, flopped into the chair, and filled the glass. "How could you tell?"

"Let me guess," Ben said. "They're not going to take my case?"

"I stopped in at both law offices in town. Neither is accepting new clients," Victoria said. "At least, that's what they told me through drawn blinds."

"They wouldn't even meet with you?"

"Eventually. It took some persuading." Victoria took a long drink from her glass. "They all looked terrified. Oh, the lawyers were polite enough, but they rushed me out the door as fast as possible. They would have rather turned off the lights and hidden under the boardroom table than meet with me."

Ben frowned. "Does this make any sense to you, Ana?"

She shook her head. "The lawyers around here deal with real estate and business, mainly. I have never heard of anyone turning away a new client, even a criminal."

Ben resented—and resembled—that remark. "Makes me wonder if they received some fan mail of their own." A crystal-clear image of last night's death threat flashed into his mind, unbidden.

Victoria rolled her eyes. "Don't tell me someone would actually be scared off by some third-rate arts-and-crafts project."

"It depends," Miguel said. "What if the threat showed up in their kids' school bags?" His words hung in the air. Ana shivered.

"We have enough problems right now without letting our imaginations run wild," Ben said, his imagination running wild.

"Speaking of imagination," Victoria said, "I quite like what you've done with your rental car. Personally, I prefer half-naked women clutching flaming swords atop unicorns, but it's a solid first effort."

Ben explained what had happened. Ana's eyes widened when he mentioned Miguel had crawled under the car to check for explosives.

"You think this is related to Antonio's murder, don't you?" Victoria said.

Ben and Miguel both nodded.

"I am not so sure. I do not know what it is, but there is something familiar about that graffiti. I think it is . . ." Ana paused. "Sorry, I cannot place it."

"Let me know if it comes to you," Ben said. "Anything new from the police?"

Ana shook her head. "The coroner's report should be ready tomorrow. As for the officers, they still think it's a robbery, except for Vasquez—" She stopped abruptly.

"—who thinks Ben killed Antonio," Victoria finished.

"Yes." Ana studied the floor.

"Did they say anything about the letter?" Ben asked.

"No one mentioned it. Now I think of it, I am surprised they didn't."

Ben sighed. "Who knows if Captain Reyes even turned it in? He might well have tossed it in the garbage the moment he left the bar."

"Sometimes I think the police are just waiting for the murderer to turn up at another bar down the coast, pockets stuffed with bloody *colones*," Ana said.

"What?" Victoria asked. "Bloody *cohones*?"

Miguel snorted beer. "*Colones*, Victoria. The Costa Rican currency?"

"Close enough," she muttered. "This whole situation is bollocks."

Ben glanced down at his bare wrist before he realized he needed to pick up a replacement watch, preferably one that hadn't been pre-smashed for his convenience. He glanced up at the wall clock instead. "Ten minutes till opening. We need to get going. If anyone needs me, I'll be in the office weeping into a stack of unpaid bills."

Miguel and Ana agreed to finish setting up the bar.

"I'll come with you," Victoria said.

On his way to the office, Ben gave a nod to Oscar, who'd emerged from one of the storerooms with paint brush in hand. Most of their exchanges had been limited to grunts and gestures—Oscar spoke little English, and Ben little Spanish—but he seemed to be holding up well after Antonio's death. Ben made a mental note to speak to him about the cooking, though. The sauce on Ben's last burrito had the flavor and consistency of glue. He was afraid to check behind the wallpaper in the guest rooms.

Ben slid behind the massive wooden desk. He'd managed to

clear room enough for a notebook and a pen, but no more. Ana had taken down the photos of Antonio grinning, leaving the walls bare and lifeless.

Victoria sat down on one of the wicker chairs, still clutching her glass of liquor.

"Any change in our financial situation?" Ben slid the cap off his lone pen.

"Don't start with the money." Victoria gazed into her near-empty glass. "That conversation has a three-drink minimum."

Ben laughed mirthlessly. He grabbed a bottle of rum from the desk drawer and poured a healthy splash into her tumbler. "Is it really that bad?"

She shrugged. "No worse than it was this morning, but that's bad enough." She took a sip. "There's something else. I asked the firm to look into the price of property in Tamarindo. Ana's right—sixty thousand is less than the bar is worth. It should have been ninety thousand. Not quite the hundred grand Antonio wanted, but more than you paid for it. And that's in its current state of disrepair."

"So, Antonio decided to sell the place cheap," Ben said. "I think he knew someone was coming for him."

Victoria wasn't convinced. "Or someone wants it to look that way."

"You still think Ana might be involved?"

"I had the firm run a credit check on her. She's heavily in debt to her bank. More than fifty thousand dollars, in fact."

"How on earth did she dig herself that deep in the hole?"

She shook her head. "I don't know. The credit report didn't say. My guess is that someone co-signed her loan."

"Antonio?"

"Could have been. Or someone who knew they could get the money from her—one way or another."

Ben scratched his nose, resisting the urge to reach for the

bottle resting on his blotter. He could hear the faint sound of Ana's laughter.

"You need to talk to Miguel. He's getting too close," Victoria said.

"I will. It's only . . . never mind. I'll talk to him. Soon."

They sat in silence for a few moments. Victoria tugged at her wool skirt.

"What time's your flight tomorrow?" Ben asked.

She gave him a sad smile. "Ten in the morning. I'll have to leave at dawn to make it back to Liberia in time to clear security."

Ben ran his hand over his empty pocket, in case his passport had magically reappeared. Oh, for the days when he could complain about an early departure. As it stood now, he had a better chance of boarding a ski lift in Hades than next week's return flight.

But that was his problem, not hers. "Thanks for everything. I really appreciate it," he said.

"I wish I didn't have to leave. Or that I'd at least found another lawyer for you," she said. "I hate leaving this unfinished."

"You're only a phone call away. Even a thousand miles from here, you're still twice as much lawyer as anyone in Tamarindo."

"Thanks, Ben. I'll fly back in a week or so if this mess hasn't sorted itself out by then. Otherwise, I'll take my next holiday here." She swallowed the last of her rum. "Maybe I'll sign on as one of your clients."

"Sounds like a plan." Ben smiled thinly. How many years would it take Victoria to slot him in between trips to New York and Saint-Tropez? "Shall we head back out?"

"Sure." Victoria glanced at her watch, then down at her business attire. "No sense in going back to change. I'll need to call it a night in a few hours, anyway."

★ ★ ★ ★ ★

The din bombarded Ben's ears the moment he opened the door. The locals were out in force, mingling with surfers, tourists, and weekend boaters. Some of the regulars even recognized Ben and Miguel as the new owners. A few complimented Ben on the new sign, and he told them about the pretend-ownership scheme. Most said it was a great idea. No one asked the price.

He was chatting up a surfer girl from Maui when Miguel grabbed him by the shoulder and dragged him into a corner. "Ben, there's a drug dealer in the bar."

"Bloody hell. Did Ana point him out?" Ben glanced at the bar, only to find it untended. "Wait, where's Ana?"

"She stepped out for a few minutes. I'm covering for her." Miguel took a deep breath. "As for the dealer, I saw him hand over a bag of white powder to some *tourista* in exchange for a wad of bills."

Ben followed Miguel's gaze. In the middle of the bar area a short, wiry expat with long dreadlocks and a smirking, stubbled face slipped through the crowd, slapping backs and shaking hands, eyes searching for the next customer. Another baggie left his hands. Hard to get more conclusive than that.

"Here's what I want you to do," Ben said. "Get Victoria to cover the bar for you. Bring the dealer to my office in five minutes. Ask nicely, but make it clear you won't take no for an answer. Get Oscar to watch your back. Questions?"

Miguel shook his head once. "See you in five."

Ben slapped him on the shoulder and strode back to the office, the glimmer of an idea forming in his head.

CHAPTER FIVE

The office door flew open and banged against the wall. The dealer swaggered in, surveying the room. Miguel shoved him toward a wicker chair. The man settled himself as though there of his own accord.

Ben said nothing as Miguel slung his massive frame onto a low filing cabinet behind the dealer, who turned sharply at the creak of metal bending. Miguel loomed over him like a scowling Colombian gargoyle. The dealer turned back into Ben's stare.

"Yeah?" he asked. A thin bead of sweat trickled down his jawline.

Ben leaned back in his chair, and put his feet up on the desk. He smiled. "Hey buddy, good to see you again. How's it going? How's business?" he asked. Then he abruptly swung his feet down.

"Do I know you, man?" The dealer glanced back at Miguel and again at Ben.

"Oh, I certainly hope so," Ben replied cheerfully. His voice turned to gravel. "Otherwise, you would be a complete stranger doing business in my bar without permission. I'd hate to think anyone is *that* stupid."

Miguel growled for emphasis.

The dealer flinched. "I'm Chris. You're Ben, right?"

Ben gave a single nod. So, word was getting around.

"I believe you've already met my friend. He's an excellent bartender, but not many people know he's also great at trivia," he said. "Miguel, tell us an interesting fact about the human body."

"The pain caused by a single strike to the liver is a crippling, burning sensation, followed by dry heaving and complete loss of breath." Miguel's voice was flat, as though quoting a medical textbook.

"Now we're all introduced. That's a good start," Ben said.

Chris swallowed weakly.

"Listen carefully, Chris. I have an offer for you, and I'm not going to repeat myself." He planted his palms on the desk and leaned forward. "You can continue to visit this bar, but on one condition: you don't do business here. I won't have you harassing my customers, and I don't want to see another baggie leave your hands while you're in my establishment. Do we have an agreement?"

Chris licked his lips. Finally he said, "Okay, we have a deal."

"Good." Ben took Chris's hand and shook it. He opened the bottom drawer of the desk and brought out a bottle and a pair of glasses. "Rum?"

Chris nodded, surprised. Ben poured two healthy measures of the amber spirit and handed one over. Miguel glared daggers, which Ben ignored.

"Listen, man. I was sorry to hear about Antonio," Chris said. "I'm sure you heard there was no love lost between us, but I didn't want to see him clock out like that."

"Bad for business?" Miguel asked sarcastically.

Chris looked over his shoulder. "Anything that scares tourists away is bad for business. I know people who are pretty pissed that Antonio went down without their say-so. They expect to be told about jobs like that."

"Any rumors about what happened?" Ben asked.

"Maybe. Depends on whether you believe in supervillains," Chris said. "One of my regulars says he saw something weird,

75

like a guy in a cape walking out the front door right before the police arrived. Says the Caped Avenger killed Antonio." Chris smiled into his rum. "Not exactly a solid source, but that's what he told me."

"Did your source see his face?" Ben said.

"Nah, dude. Even if he did, that guy's pretty fried. He'd pick his own mother out of a line-up if it would score him some rock."

Ben exhaled heavily. Apart from the death threats and a murderer on the loose, he had crack addicts hanging around outside his bar. Wonderful.

Chris continued, "Said it was too dark to make anything out. Thought the guy was carrying a bundle or something, but that's it."

"Thanks, Chris. Let me know if you hear anything else. I'm sure we can find some way to show our appreciation." Ben ignored Miguel's growl.

"Yeah, dude." Chris drained his glass and set it down. "Thanks for the drink. I should head out." He bent his fingers into imaginary guns, which he shot at Ben with a cluck of his tongue. "It's been real."

Miguel rose from the filing cabinet and opened the door. Chris shuffled out of the office. Ben and Miguel followed a few paces behind, back to the bar.

Where they came face to face with Detective Vasquez.

Chris grabbed Ben's hand and pulled him in for a buddy hug. "Good talk, man. Glad we reached an agreement. See you real soon."

Behind Chris, Ben caught a glimpse of Vasquez's stony gaze. This looked bad. The drug dealer clapped him on the shoulder and turned to leave.

"Making friends already, Mr. Cooper?"

Chris gave Vasquez a smirk on his way past. The detective

glared back, but remained planted in Ben's path.

"Detective," Ben said. "How can I be of service?"

"You can start by not entertaining known narcotics traffickers in your office," Detective Vasquez growled, leaning in close. His breath reeked of coffee and tobacco.

Ben opened his mouth to explain, then shut it. He'd never make the detective understand. He shrugged instead. "Anything else?"

"Your safe. Open it."

"What?"

"Not so helpful after all, are you?" Vasquez snarled, "It is a simple request. Open your safe."

"Do you have a warrant?"

"Are you refusing to cooperate?"

"I need to talk to my lawyer before—"

"So, you are refusing the request."

"She's right there." He pointed at Victoria, who was busy muddling mint for a mojito. "It'll only take a minute—"

Vasquez cut him off again. "I have had enough of your games, Mr. Cooper. You will be hearing from me." He pushed a meaty finger into Ben's chest. "Given the company you keep, you are fortunate I do not shut you down right now."

Ben considered passing along what Chris said earlier about the murder: *Detective, an anonymous crackhead claims he saw the Masked Marvel leave the bar immediately after the murder.* On second thought, perhaps he'd keep that to himself for now.

"I'll see you soon, Detective. Best of luck with your investigation."

"Watch yourself, Mr. Cooper." Vasquez stalked off, disappearing into the crowd.

Ben exhaled. He hadn't even realized he'd been holding his breath. What was that about? Until moments earlier, he'd thought of the massive office safe as any other piece of furniture.

He shook his head and went behind the bar, Miguel in tow.

"Thanks, guys," Victoria said, tossing them each a dish towel. "This is exactly how I wanted to spend my last few hours in Costa Rica—doing the work of three bartenders while learning some of Tamarindo's finest pickup lines." She tilted her head. "I think my favorite was, 'I wish I could rearrange the alphabet, so I could put you and me together.' That guy paid five bucks for a glass of soda water."

"Where's Ana?" Ben asked.

"I'll look for her." Miguel slunk off to escape Victoria's glare.

"Why was Vasquez here? I'd have come over, but the bar fridge would've been stripped bare by the time I returned." She poured a pint and handed it to a customer.

"He wanted to see inside the safe. Without a warrant."

"That's strange. What's he looking for?"

"I've no idea. He was so busy accusing me of running a drug ring and threatening to shut down the bar, he forgot to tell me. What's in there, anyway?"

She leaned forward to take the next order, then opened the fridge to fetch a bottle of white wine. "Nothing out of the ordinary. I had it open earlier today. All I saw was a stack of legal documents and a box of cash."

"Anything to suggest Antonio might have been involved in something shady?"

"Not that I saw. It looked like a normal cash box, filled mainly with US bills. There's perhaps a few thousand dollars there, at most. Seems about right for a bar this size."

"What about the legal documents?"

"Standard bar bumf. Health reports, tax returns, that sort of thing."

Ben ran a hand through his hair. None of it made any sense.

Luis interrupted his reverie. "Ben, can we talk for a minute?" The busboy wore an immaculate white shirt beneath a stiffly pressed black apron, already splattered with grease. He held a tray full of dirty dishes in his hands.

"This isn't a good time. Can we talk later?"

Luis started to say something, only to be interrupted by the sound of a pint glass shattering. He disappeared around the corner to fetch the dustpan from the kitchen.

"He seems like a good kid," Ben said.

"He's certainly the most enthusiastic fashion designer-cum-busboy I've ever met."

Ben laughed. "I don't know what we'll do without you, Victoria," he said. "Sorry, that wasn't fair. Of course, you have to go."

"Relax, Ben." She rested a hand on his arm. "You've had a rough couple of days. I don't expect you to be fair right now."

He opened his mouth to say . . . to say . . .

Victoria looked over his shoulder, where Miguel was returning to the bar with Ana. She drew her hand back. Ben's skin tingled where her fingertips had been.

"Where were you?" Ben demanded.

"Sorry, Ben." Ana avoided his glare. "I had something to look after."

"Apologize to Victoria, not me. She covered the bar while you were gone."

Ana started to speak. "Ben, I need to—"

He cut her off with a glare.

"Sorry, Victoria."

"Apology accepted," Victoria said. She handed Ana her damp dish towel and poured herself another glass of rum.

Ben went to take the next order, but the counter was barren. He looked across the cantina. It had thinned out since last he'd checked, minutes earlier. He watched a group of customers leave half-finished drinks on a table and head for the exit, muttering.

Suddenly, Ben knew what was wrong. "What happened to the music? Where's the DJ?"

Ana sighed. "That is what I was trying to tell you. The DJ cancelled at the last minute."

"What? Why?"

Ana muttered something.

"Sorry, I didn't catch that," Ben said.

"He thinks the bar is haunted."

"We have no choice, then. We'll stick with the old speakers and the CD player until tomorrow, at least."

"It's Saturday night in Tamarindo, Ben. *Everyone* is out tonight, looking for the best scene. If we do not have a DJ, we will not have a crowd. And if we don't have a crowd, we do not make any money," Ana said. "Besides, those old speakers are done for. It is like going to a concert with a diving helmet on your head."

Ben had to admit the speakers were horrible. Yesterday, he'd asked Ana where she'd found that song with all the humming. She'd given Ben an odd look and told him that's how the speakers sounded when they weren't playing music.

Victoria downed the rum she'd poured herself and slammed the glass on the bar. "I've got this." She passed her hands over her hips, vainly trying to smooth out her wrinkled skirt.

"The new speakers are still covered in an inch of bubble wrap, Victoria. Getting it all hooked up is going to take hours. You barely have time to sleep tonight, as it is." He stopped himself from adding that a single bad connection could blow the entire system.

Victoria drew herself up to her full height. In heels, she stood nose to nose with Ben. "I've. Got. This." She spun around, snatched up her briefcase, and stomped across the dance floor.

What on earth . . . ?

Miguel whistled. "I didn't know you could stomp in high heels."

"I think that's something they teach you in law school," Ben said.

"Should I help her?" Ana asked.

Ben thought for a moment, then agreed. Ana was the only one of them who could tell the outlets that produced electricity from those that started fires. She tossed her towel to Miguel and followed Victoria across the deserted dance floor.

Ben grabbed a beer from the fridge, twisted the cap off, and offered it to his friend. "Thanks for having my back in there, Miguel."

Miguel looked at the beer with distaste. "Brother, you're lucky you didn't tell me the plan before we kicked off. If I'd known you were going to ply him with rum and give him the run of the bar, I'd have tossed him out by his dreadlocks when I had the chance." He took the bottle from Ben's hand. "What the hell were you thinking, anyway?"

Ben opened a bottle for himself. "Antonio tried to keep out the drug dealers, and all it got him was a cold slab in the coroner's office. We don't need any more trouble in our lives than we already have. Besides, it's not like I gave him a foot massage. I spent as much time threatening him as I did plying him with rum. More, even."

"Those were empty threats. I don't mind looming over punks like Chris—I'm good at looming—but I don't hurt people. Not . . ." *Anymore* hung in the air, unspoken.

Ben patted his shoulder. "I know, man."

Miguel nodded, his eyes unfocused.

"All I want is a fresh start," Ben said.

"Try telling that to Vasquez. He's not going to leave us alone until he puts the murderer behind bars." Miguel poured a round of tequila shots for a group of sun-scorched golfers, then turned back to Ben. "What if the dealer killed Antonio himself?"

"Why would Chris murder Antonio?" Ben asked. "The man has clearly sniffed too much sunscreen, but he's right—murder is bad for business."

"How do you think someone like that moves up the chain?" Miguel eyed him sidelong as he mopped up a spilled rye and ginger. "It's not for selling the most mint chocolate cookies, that's for damned sure."

"You think Chris killed Antonio to get a *promotion?*"

"You say that like it's the first time it's ever happened."

"But what about the witness? If Chris was going to invent a story, don't you think he'd come up with something better than a man in a cape?"

Miguel scoffed. "The main suspect's buddy claims he saw a caped crusader, and we spend the rest of the week chasing our own tails—sounds pretty convenient to me."

"It's not like Chris is the only suspect."

"Who else is there?"

Ben took a deep breath. He couldn't put it off any longer. "Ana."

"So much for a fresh start," Miguel muttered.

"What's that supposed to mean?" Ben said, anger creeping into his voice.

"Nothing, man. Forget it."

"No, seriously. What does that mean?"

Miguel turned to face him. "It means you're still a mess from what Tara did to you. You can't look at another woman without thinking of all the ways she could stab you in the heart. Ana's a good person, man. She's helping us get our bar off the ground, and this is how you repay her? By accusing her of murdering her own uncle? That's cold. Even for you."

"Damn it, Miguel. How hard is it to keep your pants zipped for a week?"

"For your sake, I'm going to pretend you didn't say that."

"Victoria told me—"

Miguel cut him off. "Victoria? Her idea of true love is finding shoes that match her briefcase." He shook his head. "No wonder you have trust issues—you're taking notes from a woman with a childish nickname for her own father."

The new sound system suddenly crackled to life, sending feedback screaming across the bar. The screech was followed by Victoria's equally awful cursing.

Ben continued, "I'm only saying . . ."

"You've said enough."

Ben took a deep breath, and pushed his anger down. He considered telling Miguel the rest of what Victoria had told him, but he'd be talking to a brick wall. Who knew the great Colombian heartbreaker would feel so strongly about some girl he'd just met?

Ben turned to say something—anything—to cut through the frigid silence that had descended between him and his best friend.

Then the lights went out.

He felt the music before he heard it. An unseen force reached inside him and seized him by the bones. The air in the bar seemed to jump two inches to the side. Then it leapt back, pushed off again, and stopped.

A single, pitch-perfect note washed over the cantina, gripping the heads of the remaining bargoers and spinning them toward the dance floor. Beams of blue light shone out, casting the lone figure behind the equipment in silhouette and sweeping across the bar, before splintering into a dozen rays that played across the crowd. The lone note became a simple, beautiful melody. The deep, booming bass rose up. Beams of pure white light started to flash in perfect time to the beat. One melody became two, which then fused in exquisite harmony. The hairs on Ben's arms stood on end.

He blinked twice. The dance floor was getting crowded, and if the counter hadn't been in his way, Ben's feet would have taken him there of their own accord. The tempo picked up speed, and the tune became irresistible. Ben had stayed off dance floors most of his adult life, but he found himself dancing behind the bar, head nodding and feet sliding to every note.

The stage lit up, and Ben was astonished to see it was Victoria up there, gliding between two massive turntables. She bobbed and weaved in time with the music, her wrinkled jacket undone, strands of hair spilling from her normally perfect bun. Her face was glowing, and she looked entirely unlike he'd ever seen her before. A wave of excitement crackled through the crowd as it danced and flowed as one. Complete strangers were smiling at each other in their euphoria.

People came pouring in from the street and up from the beach, summoned by the rhythm of the music. Within minutes, the cantina was bulging at the seams.

Ben collapsed on the beach, almost within reach of the lounge chair, and pressed the back of his neck into the blissful coolness of the sand. Hot air wafted from the cantina as the bar exhaled the steam of the hundreds of patrons who'd left moments ago.

He could hear a sizzle of damp leaves and wrinkled his nose at the scent of pungent, earthy smoke. The glowing red ember of a cigar burned through the darkness. Victoria lay in a lounge chair, savoring a thick *robusto* and swinging a shoe from one toe to a tune only she could hear. She blew a single smoke ring into the air, then exhaled with satisfaction.

"Hell of a night," she said, staring out over the ocean. The waves gleamed in the dim glow of the fading moon.

It was an understatement of Biblical proportions. Ben's body ached more than it had when he woke up in the holding cell.

Even after they cut the music at three in the morning, it had taken another hour to herd the last of the dancers out the door. By the end, Miguel and Ana could barely stand. Ben had offered to close up so they could go home and sleep. It was an offer he was now regretting. He had personally served over a thousand drinks in the past twelve hours. By the end of the night, all they had left to work with was vermouth, grenadine, and soda water. Miguel mixed the three together, dubbing it *The After Party.* They'd sold dozens.

Victoria's show had brought half of Tamarindo to their door. The melodies she played glided from one to the next seamlessly, moving across every era and genre of music. Their only common denominator was the ability to grip you, touch you, hold you, shake you. Sometimes all at once. Time simply vanished.

"I never knew DJs could do . . . *that,*" Ben said, words failing him. "I've always enjoyed live concerts, but that . . . tonight . . ."

"It's the crowd," Victoria said. "The music is just a gateway to becoming part of something bigger than yourself."

Ben nodded, though wasn't sure he entirely understood. Perhaps it was the hour. Which was what? A golden glow was slowly lighting the horizon. Dawn would be upon them in minutes.

"You're going to miss your flight," he said. "There's barely time for you to pack."

"I'm staying."

"What about—?"

"There's no *about,* Ben," she said. "No more dockets. No more motions. No more lawsuits and counter-counter lawsuits. No more late-night conference calls and billing by the half-minute. I'm staying here."

Ben dragged himself to the lounge chair next to Victoria.

"You're sure?"

"Positive."

"Then welcome to paradise," he said. "Where on earth did you learn to DJ?" It seemed an inadequate term for what she could do, like asking Michelangelo where he'd learned to chip away at rock. He still had to ask, though. They'd been friends for more than a decade, yet Ben had never seen her with as much as a set of headphones.

"I taught myself, mostly. We traveled a lot when I was younger, particularly in Europe—France, Italy, and Spain. Mansion didn't much care what I did, so long as I wasn't underfoot. When he was around, that is. As I grew older, it was mostly Mother and myself." She took a long pull on the cigar. "After a few glasses of wine, she cared less than he did. I started going to clubs and I . . . I took an interest, you could say. Bought myself a couple of turntables, a mixer. It was a harmless hobby. Until it wasn't.

"I knew enough not to let my grades suffer or to talk about it over dinner. But one day I refused to let them add yet another activity to my already loaded schedule—synchronized needlepoint, Korean gymnastics, something like that. Suddenly, my love of mixing was 'A Threat to My Future.' " The last she said in a singsong voice. "We couldn't have that, now, could we?"

"If it makes you feel any better, I've always thought of you more as a threatener than a threatenee," Ben said.

She smiled. "It does, actually." She looked out over the ocean. "That was the end of it, for a while. I started spinning tracks again in university. I even played a few shows at some of the local clubs. Mansion found out and one day he called, threatening to disown me if I didn't stop once and for all. I think he had a private investigator following me." Ben saw tears well in the corner of her eyes. He'd never seen that before, either. "He thought I'd choose my music over his law firm." She stretched in her lounge chair. "Looks like he had reason to worry, after all."

"You're certainly not out of practice," Ben said. "I couldn't believe the crowd. What was that they were chanting at you? Maestro Tequila?"

When they'd first tried to kill the music, the crowd had started chanting in Spanish until she returned. They erupted into applause every time she set foot back on stage.

Victoria turned red. *"Maestra de escuela."*

"Oh. What does that mean?"

She muttered something under her breath.

"Sorry, what was that?"

"DJ School Mistress. Ahem." She gave the cigar a violent tap, dropping a wad of ash into the sand.

Ben remembered her dancing behind the sound system in her business suit, the top few buttons of her blouse undone, sweat trickling down her neck, past her collarbone. He shook himself from his reverie. School Mistress, indeed.

"Brilliant. You even have a secret DJ identity. We can, uh, modify your costume slightly, and—"

"I won't join the legion of women who take off every legal scrap of clothing to make it in this business." Victoria shook her head. "DJ School Mistress is bad enough—if they want a cut of meat, they can visit the butcher." She tossed the cigar stub onto the beach. "Apart from my new *nom de guerre,* the only downside of staying in Tamarindo is that I won't get to see Mansion's face when he hears the good news. 'Father, I'm leaving the practice to become a DJ in Costa Rica.' "

"That *is* tragic," Ben said.

"It's all right. I'll ask his secretary to capture the special moment on camera." Victoria buried the cigar stub in the sand. "I've always wanted to try a cigar. Never have, until today."

"How was it?"

"Absolutely vile."

Ben laughed. "I'm glad you'll be here to help deal with Vasquez, and whoever wrote that threat."

Victoria folded her arms behind her head. "You'll have to avoid being threatened or imprisoned while I'm spinning, but I'm confident I can find somewhere in my busy schedule to pencil you in."

Ben drummed his fingers on the lounge's armrests. "Would you join as a full partner?"

A flicker of suspicion crossed her eyes. "I'm not going to solve your money troubles, if that's what you're thinking. Even if I wanted to be your sugar momma—which I don't—my assets aren't exactly liquid at the moment. I'll match Miguel's five thousand dollar buy-in, but not a penny more."

"If I'd wanted your money, I would have asked," Ben said in a weary voice. "Besides, I'm sure you've already given us five thousand dollars' worth of your time alone."

"Sorry, Ben. I'm just used to . . . never mind." She sighed. "I've dug myself into a bit of a hole with a real estate investment, and I've got a lease to break on a brand-new Range Rover. You know how it is."

Ben nodded sympathetically, though he doubted Victoria's tragic struggle would inspire a breakthrough made-for-TV movie. "So, does that mean you're in?"

She was silent for a moment, then held up a single finger. "One condition—you tell me what happened between you and Tara."

He groaned. "Really?"

"Curiosity aside, I need to know what skeletons are in the closet before I hop inside."

She would find out one day. Ben might as well tell her and get it over with. "Tara was cheating on me." He took a deep breath. "With some clown."

"I'm so sorry, Ben. Was he someone you knew?"

"Sorry?" Then he realized, Victoria had misunderstood.

Halfway to downtown Toronto, Ben had realized he'd left his phone at home. He had turned back onto their street in Oakville only to discover a van blocking his driveway. *Beeboo the Clown: Birthdays! Face Painting! Fun!* was plastered on its side.

"No. Not a friend," he spat. "A real clown. You know, the guys with creepy face paint who make bloody balloon animals at kids' parties? Tara has a . . . a . . . *thing* for clowns."

He waited for Victoria to make a snide remark. When none was forthcoming, he continued, "I came home early the night of my bachelor party. I walked into the bedroom in time to see Beeboo the Clown step out of the bathroom wearing nothing but face paint, a red nose, and a smile." And a profoundly disturbing balloon animal. "Tara screamed when she saw me. I froze. Beeboo grabbed his floppy shoes and a bathrobe—*my bathrobe*—and was halfway to his van before I even knew what had happened.

"Me and Miguel carried on with my 'bachelor party'—in the truest sense of both words, much to my liver's regret—when he suggested we make use of the nonrefundable executive class tickets to Costa Rica that I'd bought for the honeymoon.

"I figured, why not? It wasn't as if I had work to worry about. Tara and my job at her uncle's company were kind of a package deal. So I quit my job, spent a week on Miguel's couch, flew down to Costa Rica, bought the bar, and landed myself in jail," Ben said. "It seemed like a good idea at the time."

A pair of passing surfers gave them a strange look. Apparently, they didn't often see a schoolmistress and a beating victim enjoying a beachside sunrise together.

Victoria sounded as if she were choking.

"Are you okay?"

She roared with mirth. "Thank heavens! I thought you'd stop

telling the story if I started laughing, but . . . Woooo . . ." She wiped tears from her eyes. "Seriously? *Clowns?*"

"Yes. Seriously. Clowns." He glared at her. "Do you need a tissue?"

"No, no . . . I'm fine . . . You know how it goes with tissues, take one out of your pocket and before you know it, you're pulling out a whole stream of them, all tied together." She gave in to a fit of giggles.

"Have you gotten it out of your system?" he asked after a minute.

"I think so, yes." She wheezed. "And do you? Feel better, that is."

Ben picked up a handful of sand and let it fall through his fingers. "I can't say I much liked waking up in prison, and I'm not a fan of the death threats. But, otherwise"—he smiled—"I'm having a really great time."

"You sound surprised."

"I didn't realize it until now," he said. "We've been so busy, I didn't know I was enjoying myself."

"Me too." She yawned, stretching her arms. "But I'm going to pass out on this lounge chair if I don't get back to the hotel. Enrico arrives at the cantina at three o'clock, right?"

"That's right. See you then."

"Good night, Ben."

"Good morning, Victoria."

As his new partner padded off along the beach, Ben thought about what had happened between him and Tara after Beeboo took off in a billow of bathrobe and tire smoke. The part he hadn't told Miguel and Victoria.

The part he wouldn't ever tell anyone.

First, there was shock. Tara tried to convince him that he had the wrong idea, that it wasn't what he thought it was. Ben countered that there was nothing else it could possibly be. She had no answer for that.

Next came the tears. They ran endlessly down Tara's face in rivers of mascara. After Ben had packed a suitcase with his most prized belongings, she confessed she had a clown fixation—*coulrophilia,* as she had put it so clinically—but that it did not change her feelings for him. Ben tried to ignore her, but the rawness of her voice gave him pause.

His packing slowed, then stopped. He sat beside her on the bed to talk. Twenty minutes later, he was in the bathroom, putting on face paint.

As he finished, Ben's eyes locked with those of his reflection. His hand froze as it reached for the oversized novelty bow tie that Tara had produced from her bedside drawer. Ben saw a profound sadness in his reflected eyes. It reminded him of a time long ago, one he thought he'd left behind.

He scrubbed the clown face off on one of their fine Turkish towels. He stepped out of the bathroom, grabbed his suitcase, and, without a single word to his fiancée, strode out of their bedroom and into the night.

From his lounge chair in Tamarindo, it seemed to Ben to have happened a lifetime ago. It was the first time he had thought of that evening without feeling ashamed or depressed. He simply felt relieved.

He walked down to the ocean and let the cool water wash over his toes. He watched the rising tide crash against the dark volcanic rocks that punctuated the soft sand beach. The surf tugged at the shore, a miniature sandstorm whirling beneath the liquid pane. All he could hear were the cries of the seagulls and the cheers of the first surfers to reach the waves. A warm breeze stroked his cheek.

He couldn't imagine a better place for a fresh start.

CHAPTER SIX

The sun sparkled off freshly shattered glass. Miguel could feel the heat from the burning car scorch his back. A lone piece of blood-splattered paper lay before him. He reached for it, but his arms were like lead. No matter how hard he tried, he could not move. This was the end. Because of him, all of them would die.

He woke suddenly, his heart hammering and his body awash in sweat. The sheets lay in a damp, tangled knot at his feet. He glanced around the room, straining to hear anything above the thumping in his ears. He was pretty sure he hadn't woken up screaming. He'd even got four full hours of sleep. Best night all week.

He rolled out of bed, splashed water on his face, and studied his reflection. He even recognized himself in the mirror this time. He dressed in a pair of gym shorts and a crumpled T-shirt, then headed out for a run. The woman at the front desk smiled as he jogged through the open-air lobby and past the pool.

He ran barefoot along the beach, as he had every morning since he'd arrived in Tamarindo. He felt better when he ran, especially once he left the surfers behind and it was just him and the beach. If he ran hard enough and far enough, he could reach the point where all he thought of was the next stride.

He ran until his lungs burned and his legs turned to rubber, then he sat down heavily on the warm, soft sand and looked over the sprawling bay, struggling to catch his breath. With it returned his problems.

He scolded himself once more for allowing himself to be taken unawares by the panic attack in the crowded café, days earlier. He still wasn't sure what had triggered the event, but suspected it was the shock of seeing the bloody piece of paper—so similar to the one that haunted his dreams—and Ben's signature on the deed to the bar. It wasn't the first time his heart had hammered in his chest while he struggled for breath, but it was the first time such an incident had overcome him with witnesses around. It was clearly tied to shock and stress, and his new life in Tamarindo was growing more stressful by the minute.

With every fiber of his being, Miguel wished his invisible foe had a physical form; that it was one more enemy to be laid to waste with instinct and brute force. He was so very good at brute force. But he hadn't the first idea how to fight what lurked inside and thrived on darkness.

He had hoped their trip to Costa Rica would help Ben get back on his feet. Instead, Miguel's friend had stolen a large sum of money from his ex-fiancée and her parents and landed himself squarely in the middle of a murder investigation.

How their lives had changed because of his ridiculous suggestion to come here. Perhaps Antonio would still be alive if he'd kept his idea to himself. It seemed all he did was leave bodies in his wake.

And how could he have left Ben drunk and alone in a foreign country? Foolish. What on earth had he been thinking?

He'd been thinking about Ana.

There was something there, between the two of them. It was too early to put it into words, but Miguel hadn't felt this way about a woman in a very long time.

But then something changed. One minute, Ana was laughing at one of his bad jokes and asking him to teach her how to spin bottles in midair. The next, she vanished. He'd finally found her in one of the storage rooms, taking an inventory she'd already done earlier that morning.

Perhaps it was better this way. How could he get a fresh start with Ana when he still carried so much baggage? He didn't know where to start unpacking it all, or what would happen if he did. It would be easier this way, to be another shallow bartender, moving from one girl to the next.

He and his fellow close-protection operators had called themselves heartbreakers and life-takers. The reality was far less romantic: They were the doers of undoable deeds. Now Miguel had to live with that.

The truth was he didn't deserve happiness. Not after what he'd done.

He rose to his feet and started to run, sprinting harder than he had on the way out. He ran until his breath came in ragged gasps and sweat stung his eyes, but he could not find the peace of his outbound run. Even the pounding surf couldn't drown out the words repeating in his head.

Your debts are still unpaid. You should be dead.

Miguel returned to the hotel with barely enough time to shower, shave, and change. It was already close to ten, and he still had an errand to run before Enrico arrived that afternoon. Last night's crowd had demolished their bar stock, and they needed to replenish it. There were still a few warm kegs in storage, but they were completely out of liquor. He'd buy as much as he could find. He was sure Enrico would pack the cantina to the rafters, even more than Victoria had the night before.

His arms were still stiff from slinging bottles late into the evening—or early into the morning, he should say. In all his years as a bartender, he'd never seen such a crazy night. He wondered again how Victoria had learned to spin. With skills like that, it was almost a shame she had to fly back home today. Almost. He wouldn't mind her taking her wild accusations against Ana home with her.

He walked down the hallway, stopping to press an ear to Ben's door. Snoring. That, or he was trying to smother a hippo. He resisted the temptation to wake him and drag him along for the ride. Better to let the man sleep; he had a busy day ahead.

Miguel grabbed a banana from the fruit bowl at the front desk on his way out. The clerk behind the desk fluttered her eyelashes at him. He gave her his best winning grin, all the while noting that the shift change at the front desk had occurred at 9:00 a.m. as usual. One clerk left, one arrived. Both would be distracted for five minutes during the handover brief. Video security remained active throughout.

There was a time when Miguel had tried to stop himself from seeking vulnerabilities and weaknesses in everything he saw. Eventually, he accepted that he could no more stop searching for threats and tactical advantages than he could will his heart to stop. He tossed the banana peel in the garbage and strolled out through the front gate.

It was another beautiful morning in Tamarindo. Bright and sunny, but not yet hot. A gentle breeze rustled the palms. All along the main street, store owners were unlocking their shops and setting out sandwich boards advertising beach towels, manicures, surfboard rentals, and everything in between. Amazing how all of it seemed to be on sale, all of the time. Funny how that worked.

The peak of the season would soon arrive, and hordes of tourists along with it. He hoped the bar was ready by then. He and Ben would have to find a new place to stay sometime soon, but there was enough to worry about for now without giving up the comfort of the Diria. They needed to get Uncle Enrico settled in first.

He thought about searching for a humble apartment somewhere, but his musings ground to a halt the moment he saw the rental car. The driver's side mirror dangled limply from its wires.

He was instantly on alert, running through his mental checklist: *Inhale. Check at five meters. Look for freshly turned earth, protruding wires, signs of a pressure plate. Scan out to twenty-five meters. Look for graffiti or chalk marks. Check for unusual activity from the locals, anyone paying too much attention or too little. Traverse in a circle. Exhale.*

His scan complete, Miguel was satisfied that the risk of anti-personnel mines or improvised explosive devices was low. He spotted nothing worth noticing, except for an ancient grounds-keeper raking the dirt and a hand-lettered sign offering "Kittens for Rent" in a nearby apartment window. He allowed himself a small smile at that. If he ever lost his job as a bartender, perhaps he could find work here as an English teacher.

Miguel walked over to the groundskeeper and asked in Spanish, "Excuse me, friend? It seems someone damaged my mirror. Have you seen anyone else park here?"

"No, no. There have been no new cars for the past two nights."

"Do you think it could have been one of the staff?"

"We are always very careful. We let management know if we hit anything. It's happened before, and they are understanding, as long as we are honest. There is only the one truck here, anyway," the groundskeeper said. "Perhaps a monkey hit it with a coconut?"

Miguel looked up at the soaring palms, then back down at the groundskeeper. "A monkey?" It was possible. Barely.

The old man shrugged. "What else could it have been?"

What else, indeed? Miguel examined the mirror carefully, checking to see if it had been removed with a hammer, tin snips, or good old-fashioned blunt force. He spotted a few dark streaks running down the fender, above the wheel well, but nothing else was out of the ordinary. Yesterday, the mirror was attached to the car. Today, it wasn't. The hammering in his chest picked up once more. Ben was going to love this. At least with the "Gringo" tag, they knew they'd been vandalized. Now the car looked like a bizarre art project.

Miguel's heartbeat steadied as he slid behind the wheel. The battered rental started on the first turn of the key, a pleasant change from yesterday. He rolled out of the parking lot and took the road out of Tamarindo in search of a supermarket with the variety and volume of liquor needed to restock the bar. The dense palm trees near the beach soon faded from view, replaced by long stretches of waving grass and the occasional ancient tree reaching for the crisp blue sky.

The driver's-side mirror clunked against the side of the car as he drove, reminding him of all the loose ends that lay tangled at his feet. He didn't enjoy facing an enemy he couldn't see, particularly one that sent unsigned death threats. He preferred them signed. At least you knew where you stood with those. And the car mirror . . . It felt too random. Like someone was trying to get under his skin.

He turned on the radio and pressed its buttons, searching for music that would help him relax and enjoy the leisurely drive. It was a beautiful, sunny day, the wind was . . .

The wind caught the mirror, thumping it against the door in a frenzied rhythm.

. . . Damn it. Miguel couldn't relax, not with the mirror banging. That was when he noticed the vehicle tailing him.

It was a dark brown SUV with tinted windows. The first model-year for the Jeep Grand Cherokee, by the look of the grill. At first, it hung so far back that Miguel could barely see it. He might not have spotted it at all if not for the slow-moving truck that pulled out between him and the Jeep. The Jeep slid across the double yellow line, blasted past the truck, and slowly dropped back to its original distance.

Miguel slowed down, and the Jeep slowed down. Normal traffic didn't do that. No one needed to keep a ten-count behind the car in front. Not unless they were trying to stay inconspicuous.

Miguel's heart began pounding once more. His breathing turned shallow, and the inky darkness began creeping in. He couldn't let that happen, not now. He blinked twice and took a deep breath. His hands trembled, then went dead calm.

High-speed pursuit in a soft-skinned vehicle. Pursuers are likely unarmed. Even if they have weapons, they won't want to open fire on a major route. If that's how they are willing to play the game, they would have opened up already. No weapons, smoke grenades, or other countermeasures available to break off the pursuit.

He cursed himself for telling Ben not to waste his money on renting a GPS. The directions he'd written down on the back of a receipt would be of little use once he turned off the main road. It was a risk he'd have to take.

He wished he'd had the chance to get to the supermarket first. Then he could have improvised a Molotov cocktail from a bottle of 151-proof rum and a greasy rag. But he was getting ahead of himself.

He glanced down at his messy scrawl on the crumpled receipt. Inspiration struck.

A fork in the road appeared in the distance. To the left lay the road to the Guanacaste supermarket. To the right was the road to the Tamarindo airport. Miguel slowed the hatchback to a crawl and triggered the left turn signal. The Jeep's driver had two choices: either slow down, hang back, and make it painfully obvious they were tailing Miguel or finally close the gap. The Jeep closed in, its left turn signal blinking in Miguel's rearview mirror.

He accelerated sharply into the left turn lane, then, halfway through the curve, he pulled hard on the hand break and spun the wheel to the right. The emergency maneuver would have been dramatic in a faster car, but the hatchback simply looped lazily across the median. An oncoming minibus, its horn blaring, missed Miguel by inches. He slammed the car into second gear and sped off toward the airport.

The airport wasn't much to look at, little more than a tiny strip of asphalt and a handful of steel-roofed outbuildings. But it was guarded by the Ministry of the Interior. Miguel steered the car into the parking lot.

He hopped out of the hatchback and strode inside. Every move he made was measured—not fast enough to attract attention, but not a second slower than necessary. He checked the arrivals board, then wandered over to the information counter and picked up a brochure. He leaned against a wall by a window and read the pamphlet as though he were waiting for a flight to land.

Miguel's adversary was now faced with three options, none of them appealing. If they lacked subtlety or skill, they would tear into the parking lot at full speed, arousing the immediate attention of the guards. Unlikely, but possible. He had never ceased to be amazed by the poor decisions his foes made once their carefully laid plans started to unravel.

Their second option was to take up a vantage point along the road to the airport and pick Miguel up again when he left. A bold but foolish move. It assumed that he hadn't called the police, caught a flight, or bypassed the airport entirely. The tail might opt for it if they thought themselves clever. But not clever enough to realize he could easily slip the net.

Last, his pursuer could break off the pursuit. This was the most dangerous option for Miguel for two reasons. Either the tail was patient and very thorough. Or worse, this whole episode could be a figment of his imagination. That would mean this threat, like his dreams, his panic attacks, and his obsession with

Ana, existed only in his head—the interest on his unpaid debt.

Miguel sat in the airport lounge, staring at the same brochure for almost an hour. When he finally left the airport, he saw no sign of the Jeep.

Ben's alarm beeped for several minutes before he finally woke up. He was having a rough time adjusting to being a night owl. He blinked twice and glanced over at the clock, his eyes laden with exhaustion. Almost noon. Better get going, if he didn't want to be late again. He sat up and looked longingly out at the Pacific sparkling in the distance. The inevitable surfers were barely visible between the folds of the waves. He hadn't even found time for a swim yet.

Or had he? Ben wondered, not for the first time, where else he'd gone the night of Antonio's murder. His clothing from that night hadn't been salty, nor had he found a starfish in his pocket or anything like that, but his failure to remember much of anything that happened that night still troubled him. What if the one clue that could crack this case had been washed away by a ninth shot of rum?

Ben knew what he ought to do: head down to the cantina, get Oscar to make him something to eat, and dig into the pile of paperwork threatening to envelop his desk and the nearby chairs. He gazed down at his white belly, soft from years of working behind a desk.

He reached for his shirt but grabbed his swim trunks instead.

Ten minutes later, he plunged into the surf headfirst, enjoying the silken slap of a wave breaking over his body. He wiped his eyes, his mouth tingling with saltwater. He could see why this stretch was so popular with surfers—every wave was almost the same size, as though forged by something more than tide and breeze.

Perhaps he'd sign up for surfing lessons. From what the surfers at the bar had said, Witch's Rock Surf Camp had a—

A surfboard sliced past his left ear, missing him by inches.

"Hey! Who the hell do you think you are?" He waved his fist at the surfer's back as he neatly turned the board and rode it onto the beach. Ben planted his feet on the bottom and waded over to give him a piece of his mind.

The surfer tucked the surfboard under one arm and turned to face him. She was one of the most beautiful women Ben had ever seen.

"Sorry about that nasty bit of bizzo," she said with a thick Australian accent. "You must've just hopped in. I checked this spot when paddling out, but not after I caught the wave. That was almost quite the bang-up." She shook the water from her short blond hair. Her tanned cheeks were flushed with the exertion of a hard morning spent riding waves.

Ben was suddenly very aware of his pudgy white torso and how his wet bathing suit clung tightly in some places and rode up in the others.

"That's all right," he said. "I'm Ben. Nice to meet you." He decided against reaching out for a handshake.

"Name's Jenni. You're the bloke who bought the bar, aren't you?" She flashed him a brilliant smile, then looked thoughtful. "I think I saw you the night Antonio died."

"You did? When?"

"About halfway through the night. You were standing on the bar, trying to pull a sombrero off the wall. Looked like you were having a hard time of it. I had no idea it was you who'd bought the place."

"That was me, all right." Ben scratched the back of his head.

Jenni planted her surfboard in the sand. "How's that doing so far? The bar, that is."

"It's doing rather well, actually." He explained the beach-bar-for-rent idea. "We have our first client coming in later today.

Enrico Morales. He's a famous bongo drummer." The words still sounded awkward to Ben, but he had faith Miguel knew what he was doing.

"Can't say I've heard of him, but I do enjoy a good show." Jenni checked her sport watch. "I should get back out there. I'd love to hear the full yarn about how you bought the bar, though. Mind if I stop by later tonight?"

His voice seemed to speak of its own accord. "I'd like that."

"Ace! See you tonight, Ben." She flashed him another million-watt grin, then splashed back into the surf.

Had that conversation actually happened? He turned to gaze at Jenni as she paddled back into the surf. It had. Things were looking up.

He swaggered back onto the beach, where he discovered his sandals and towel had been stolen. He did what he could to dry himself with his T-shirt, then made his way back to his room, his swim trunks dripping a trail of water as he went.

Miguel closed the lid to the hatchback, the last of the boxes of liquor loaded safely inside. The rear of the car sagged beneath the extra weight.

He should have been glad to be headed back to town, his errand almost done, but was still on edge. By the time he had reached the supermarket, he was convinced he'd imagined his pursuer. Still, he'd kept glancing in the mirror to see whether he was being followed. He couldn't shake the feeling that he was being watched. *This has to stop,* he told himself. It was all in his head.

He took a deep breath and smiled at an elderly couple, who squinted at Miguel and his graffiti-covered hatchback. They probably wouldn't approve of the hundred-odd bottles of booze in the back, either. He settled into the driver's seat and turned the key. The hatchback sputtered back to life.

He eased himself from the parking lot, careful not to bottom out the laden car. It was quarter to one, according to the dashboard clock. With luck, he would get back in time to grab a late lunch and finish setting up before Uncle Enrico arrived. The roads were quiet and he was making good time.

Ben was right. Miguel was being paranoid. He took a deep breath and tried to enjoy the drive as a scenic trip, not a series of choke points and kill zones.

His nerves aside, the errand had gone surprisingly well. He had found everything on his list, as well as a few choice bottles of Scotch, rum, and tequila. He smiled as he pictured Ben's reaction to the expensive bottles of aged tequila. Ben hated tequila. He said he'd rather drink the gasoline that floated to the top of rain puddles. More for Miguel, then. He'd acquired a taste for it while he was on exchange in New Mexico—the good stuff, the kind made from pure agave and aged in barrels, not the paint thinner served by most bars.

The long drive to the supermarket had given him time to think about last night's disagreement. Miguel had a hard time carrying a grudge. He'd eventually decided that, as long as Ben went back to minding his own business, the two of them would be all right. The tequila would serve as Ben's apology.

Miguel eased the hatchback onto the long, winding road back to Tamarindo. He was looking forward to seeing Uncle Enrico again, and—

He glanced to the right as a pair of headlights smashed into the side of the hatchback. The world went dark.

CHAPTER SEVEN

Ben strolled in through the beachside entrance to the cantina, whistling. Victoria and Ana sat at one of the tables, waiting for him, the bar's ledger at the ready. Victoria seemed more comfortable in a floral skirt and pale blue tank top than she had in the business suit earlier that morning. Ana tapped her pen on a pad of paper. The two seemed to have reached an uneasy truce. Whether they were united by a desire to see the bar stay open or a mutual fondness for sangria, Ben hoped it would hold.

"Where have you been?" Ana asked. The top sheet of her pad was covered with a lengthy checklist, written in cramped writing.

"And why are you whistling?" Victoria's eyes narrowed. "The last time you whistled was after you met Tara. And we all know how well that turned out."

He'd forgotten Victoria was the first friend he'd told about Tara, whom he'd met near the end of university. She hadn't approved then nor forgotten since, apparently.

"I went for a swim," he said. "My whistling is hardly a sign of impending apocalypse."

Victoria's eyes stayed narrowed. "And?"

He opened up the draft tap and filled a mug with foam. "And I met a girl."

"Told you." Victoria poured fresh glasses of sangria for herself and Ana.

"Who is she?" Ana asked. She frowned at Ben's feet as he walked from behind the bar. "Why are you wearing bright orange flip-flops?"

"Someone stole my sandals."

"A modern fairy tale," Victoria said. "She stole your heart—and your shoes."

"She didn't . . . Never mind." Ben flopped down in a chair next to them. He took a sip of warm beer and grimaced. "Is that new draft fridge ever going to arrive?"

"Tuesday," Ana said. "And only if we have money to pay for it." She looked at Victoria.

"The money's there. For now." Victoria flipped through the ledger. "Last night's take was quite large, but we're going to take a hit restocking the bar. It'll take time to make that back."

"Miguel is buying more bottles this morning," Ana said.

He looked up at the clock. "Really? It's already the middle of the afternoon."

"Says the man who just arrived at work," Victoria said.

Ana glanced down at her watch and frowned. "I will call him in a few minutes. I am sure he got held up somewhere."

Ben looked around the bar. They hadn't gotten all the grime, but most of the place gleamed. If you didn't look too closely. They'd also taken down the girly posters, though there were strips of ripped paper where the glue had proven particularly stubborn.

"The place looks nice," Ben said. "Anything else we need to do to get ready for Enrico?"

Ana tapped her checklist. "The extra storage rooms have been turned into bedrooms, and we will have liquor to sell. That's my list for today."

"What's he going to use for a bathroom?" Victoria asked.

"Oscar put a rain barrel up on the roof and hooked it to a watering can. That will be his shower," Ana said. "For the rest, he can use the men's bathroom."

"The same bathroom that was torn apart during a brutal murder?" Victoria asked. "Charming."

Ben recalled the smashed plaster and shattered mirror. Victoria's description was closer to the mark than he wanted to admit. "How's that bathroom looking, anyway?"

"Better," Ana said.

"Is that the same as good?"

"Not really." She took a long sip of sangria.

Ben envisioned a tall, manicured musician in silk pajamas, daintily stepping over passed-out surfers so he could brush his teeth above the daiquiri and phlegm-encrusted sink. He sighed. "We'll do the best we can with what we have for now. If we sign some clients, we can ask Oscar to put in another bathroom."

"We could change over one of the last two storage rooms," Ana said. "They are all filled up right now, but there is a lot of junk we can throw out."

"Good thinking," Ben said. "Anything else?"

"Miguel tried to get in touch with Enrico to see if he has any special requests, but he could not reach him," Ana said.

Ben shrugged. "He is on tour, after all. With all that traveling, I'm sure he'll be glad to have a bit of a break. Maybe hand out a few free drinks."

"We'll cross that bridge when we come to it," Victoria said. "Preferably, sometime after we tell him he's going to have to fight the monkeys for use of his shower."

Ben's lips flattened into a thin line as he looked over at Ana. "Any new developments on Antonio's case?"

"The coroner's report is back. No surprise, Antonio was beaten to death. There was only one strange injury, the bone that was broken here," she said, touching her collarbone. "They think it was maybe caused by a second weapon. A thinner one."

"A thinner one?" Victoria asked.

"It is difficult for them to know for sure. It was the baseball bat that killed him, though." She stared into the pitcher of sangria, but her eyes were dry.

She seemed oddly unaffected by her uncle's death. Or perhaps she had cried herself out some time ago. "I'm sorry, Ana," he said.

Ana nodded wordlessly.

The three sat in awkward silence for a time. Victoria's curiosity eventually won out. "Do they have any theories as to what the other weapon could have been?"

"One officer thought it might have been a pool cue . . ."

Ben tensed. He'd played a round of pool with Miguel in the cantina late yesterday afternoon.

". . . but we are not missing any of ours, and they already check the ones that are here," Ana finished.

"Strange." Victoria clicked her pen over and over.

"When do we meet the new girlfriend?" Ana asked, changing the subject.

"She's stopping by later tonight. She wants to hear the rest of the story of how I—we—bought the cantina. She already knows the part about me and the sombrero." Ben made a face.

Ana laughed. "I think half of Tamarindo knows that story by now."

"How did you meet her?" Victoria asked.

Ben took another sip of beer. It wasn't too bad, now that the foam had finally subsided. You just had to think cold thoughts. "You know, the usual story. Girl almost kills boy with her surfboard. Boy yells at girl until he realizes she is a girl. Girl invites herself to boy's bar for drinks later," he said. "Assuming she finds time to stop by. It sounds like she spends half her life out on the water, so who knows if she'll show."

Ana tilted her head to one side. "Is she Australian?"

"How'd you know?"

"That is Jennifer Walker. She teaches surfing. She competes, too," Ana said, "I am surprised she almost hit you."

"Could be the surfer equivalent of dipping your pigtails in the ink well," Victoria said.

"I'll admit, I was surprised when she asked if she could swing by. She's a gorgeous surfer and I've still got a face like a tie dye T-shirt."

"Everyone in town is talking about you and the cantina, Ben," Ana said. "You were in town for twenty-four hours and managed to buy a bar from a man who was soon murdered. Then you got arrested and have a lawyer fly halfway around the world to get you released on bail. There is even a rumor that you are here with the CIA to—"

Victoria snorted sangria out her nose. "Ana, not while I'm drinking." She wiped her face. "Augh. I think I lodged a lemon seed in my sinus."

"You should not be too surprised if women are interested in you," Ana finished, her face deadpan.

Ben was skeptical. And he planned to remain so until an entire evening passed without Jenni asking him to buy into a pyramid scheme or convert to Zoroastrianism.

Victoria glanced at her watch. "I'd like to get some lunch. Is there anything else we need to cover?"

Ana shook her head. "Not until Miguel gets back."

"Victoria, can I borrow your phone for a few minutes?" Ben asked.

"Again?"

"Again."

Heat billowed from the office the moment Ben opened the door. He had to move quickly if he wished to remain undetected. He pulled Victoria's phone from his pocket and dialed the fateful number.

"Greater Canadian Financial, how may I help you?"

"Hi, I'd like to try and access my account."

"Hi Ben, it's Miranda. I took your call yesterday."

"Hi Miranda. I don't suppose you could give me a hint, could you?"

"Sorry. I can't give you any hints, Ben."

Why on earth was she saying his name so often? Must be something they teach you in customer service school to calm frustrated clients. "Just thought I'd ask."

Miranda sighed. "Ready when you are, Ben."

"A ninja?"

"No, Ben."

That exhausted his childhood dream jobs. What had Ana said? "An international man of mystery?"

"No, Ben."

Last chance. Time to think outside the box.

"A grizzly bear?"

"Sorry, Ben. You've been locked out of your account for another twenty-four hours."

He clicked off the line. It was unlikely he could stop payment at this point, nor would he back out after dragging his best friends into the deal. But it would be nice to have access to his bank account again. If he played his cards right, he might even have money to put in it, one day.

He relented to the heat and switched on the ceiling fan. It stirred the air lazily, scattering a few stray papers from the top of his desk. He picked up a sheet that could either be a useless flyer or his liquor license, for all he knew. He would have to learn Spanish. Until then, though, he was going to have to ask Victoria to—

A ring broke the silence. At first, he thought it was Victoria's phone, but then he realized it had come from beneath the pile of paperwork. After a short but furious archaeological dig, he unearthed the bright red receiver. It was the kind of phone that, many years ago, a major world leader would have reached for to prevent the outbreak of thermonuclear war. The phone pealed once more.

"El Cantina, Ben speaking."

There was a flurry of Spanish on the other end of the line.

He glanced at the open doorway, hoping either Victoria or Ana was close enough to translate. No such luck.

"Hob-laz on-glaze?" he asked.

"Of course," said the woman on the other end of the line. "May I speak to the owner, please?"

"Speaking."

"This is Carmen at the *Tamarindo Gazette*. How are you?"

"I'm well, thanks." Ben leaned forward in his chair. He hadn't thought to talk to the local media about his business plan, but any coverage they could get would go a long way toward drumming up more pretend-owners.

"Great. You left us a message earlier about a classified ad for a new busboy. Are you still interested in running it?"

"Uh . . ." Ben's mind raced as he groped frantically for a pen. "Would you mind reading it to me?"

Carmen starting reading the ad in Spanish.

"Er . . . in English."

"Are you *really* the bar's owner?"

A bead of sweat slipped down his forehead. "Look, Carmen, you called me, all right? If that's the way you're going to be, there are plenty of other ways I can advertise this new position." Not that he could think of any. Ben was surprised Tamarindo had its own newspaper.

"Okay, okay," Carmen said. "It says, 'Wanted: Busboy at Antonio's. Immediate start. Must follow directions. Fashion designers need not apply.' I am a little confused by the last part."

Ben's blood ran cold. "I need time to think about it." He hung up before she could object.

He sat motionless beneath the whirling fan, lost in thought. Had Antonio fired Luis? He could hear the clatter of dishes from the kitchen, as Luis and Oscar started making lunch. If so, why? And why was Luis still here?

A sharp knock at the door brought him back to reality.

Ana leaned in. "Enrico will be here any minute."

"Any minute" is a flexible measure of time in Costa Rica. After they had waited close to an hour for Enrico to arrive, it began to seem literal. They could choose any minute they liked from now till eternity, and Enrico was equally likely to arrive during any one of them.

"Perfect in every way, but she insists on blending all of her food before she eats it." Victoria was putting the finishing touches on a paper airplane folded from a page torn from her ledger.

"You mean, at home?" Ben asked, trying not to wonder whether he'd been stood up by a bongo drummer. Correction: A world famous bongo drummer. He wasn't sure if that made it better or worse.

"No, everywhere. You're at a three-star Michelin restaurant and, after ordering the filet mignon stuffed with lobster and foie gras, she asks the waiter to 'put it all in a blender and set it on high for a few seconds.' " Victoria tossed the airplane in the air. It executed a perfect loop and landed back in her lap. She started tearing a set of wing flaps.

"No way." Ben shook his head. "I couldn't do it." They had been playing this game for close to an hour. If it went on much longer, Victoria was all but certain to start making clown jokes. "Your turn. Perfect in every way, but he has an imaginary friend who goes everywhere with him."

She stared up at the thatched ceiling. "Everywhere?"

"Everywhere. You'll ask, 'Want to go see a movie?' and he'll say, 'That sounds good. Mr. Wibbles, do *you* want to see a movie?' Then he'll go ahead and answer himself in a high, squeaky voice, 'Golly gee, that sounds like fun!' "

She laughed, shaking her head. "No, no! A thousand times, no."

Ana walked out of the back hallway. "Miguel is not answering his phone. I am getting worried." She glared at both Victoria and Ben, both of whom were still laughing. "It is good to see you are both *so* concerned for your friend," she said, her voice dripping with sarcasm.

Ben said, "We're playing 'Perfect in Every Way.' We each imagine our ideal woman or man. Then we take turns introducing a single critical flaw."

Victoria added, "We play it when we're bored."

"That sounds nice." Ana smiled thinly.

"Here, you try," Ben said. "Close your eyes."

"I do not think—"

"C'mon, give it a shot."

"You are the boss." Ana sighed and closed her eyes. "What now?"

"Now imagine your perfect partner. Everything you're looking for physically, but also with a wonderful personality. Got it?"

"All right." A small grin appeared on her face. "Fine, I think of him."

"Okay." Ben looked across at Victoria, who raised both palms and shrugged. No help there.

He thought fast. "Now imagine that, wherever he goes, he says 'Left foot! Right foot! Left foot! Right foot!' whenever his feet hit the ground."

Ana laughed and opened her eyes. "I would keep him. It is

kind of cute, really."

Victoria shook her head. "There's no accounting for taste. My turn. Perfect in every way, but—"

"Excuse me, Victoria, Ben, I really am worried for Miguel. I keep calling him, but I only get his voicemail," Ana said.

"I'm sure he's fine," Ben said. "I can't imagine him ending up anywhere he couldn't either talk or fight his way out of. Now, forgetting to charge his phone? That I could see." He had already lent his charger to Miguel, who had forgotten to bring his to Costa Rica. On the other hand, it wasn't as though Ben had a phone to charge anymore.

"But—" Ana was interrupted by the rumble of engines as a pair of cars pulled into the parking lot.

"See?" he said. "That's probably Miguel and Enrico right now." Ben planted his hands on his knees and rose from his chair. After a quick look at his shirt for stains, he strode to the front entrance to meet their very first client, Ana and Victoria at his heels.

He found himself staring at a search warrant instead.

"I will see that safe now, Mr. Cooper. And the rest of this bar," Detective Vasquez said.

Ben gritted his teeth. With everything that had happened yesterday, he'd forgotten Vasquez was determined to see inside the safe.

An officer came up and spoke to Ana in Spanish. Ben opened his mouth to tell her not to give in, then closed it when he spotted a second officer holding an acetylene torch. Ana recited what sounded like a stream of numbers. Perhaps giving the detective the combination wasn't such a bad idea, after all.

An officer herded the three of them back to the lounge area. Victoria looked daggers at Ben, as though willing him to ride this out. He met her gaze and gave her a small nod.

They were joined moments later by Luis and Oscar, both visibly shaken. Luis was still wearing soapy gloves. Perhaps even more surprising, Oscar was without his ever-present tool belt. They sat down next to Ben and the rest and studied the floor intently.

Vasquez shouted something from Ben's office. Their guard glared at each of them in turn, barked a few words at Ana, and disappeared inside.

Ana stared at the table, her face grim. "He say that if we move, we will be sitting on the floor in handcuffs instead of in these nice, comfortable chairs."

Ben raised both eyebrows but said nothing. He had searched the safe himself late last night, but found only what Victoria had already described. What on earth was Vasquez looking for?

Victoria slowly turned her head, stealing a glance at the office door. She then gradually undid the latch to her purse and began sliding out her phone.

Ben heard footsteps coming up the front path. "Psst!" he whispered as loudly as he dared, and gestured toward the main entrance with his head.

She snapped her purse closed. An older man, short, rotund, and with half a head of curly gray hair, wandered over to them. Dressed in a rumpled brown suit stained with coffee and fast food, he looked every inch a burnt-out detective.

Ben snapped. "Who the hell are you?"

The man took a short, sharp breath and drew himself up to his full five feet, five inches. "Who am I? Who am I? *I* am Enrico Morales, and this is *my* bar."

CHAPTER EIGHT

The cantina was an utter disaster. Most chairs had been knocked over and their cushions cut open by the police during their search. All of the bar's drawers had been pulled out and their contents dumped on the floor. The newly painted and prepared storerooms had been turned inside out, and even the already wrecked men's bathroom was in worse shape.

What concerned Ben most, though, was that Detective Vasquez had walked out the front door clutching an evidence bag wrapped around a crowbar. He looked angrier than usual, were that possible. Enrico's eyes had grown to the size of dinner plates at the sight of the fuming detective, evidence clutched in his massive hands.

It was not the welcome Ben had planned for their first client. A relaxing drink in front of the ocean, perhaps. A leisurely tour through the tidied office and freshly painted bedrooms, yes. But had Ben been asked to rank all possible welcome activities, a vindictive police raid would have ranked near the bottom, right between a bout with dysentery and a jaguar attack.

A line of customers was already out front, eager to see the great Enrico Morales in person. Enrico Morales, on the other hand, seemed only interested in seeing the bottom of a rum bottle. And the bar was due to open in fifteen minutes.

Enrico took a long pull from his glass and glared at Ben. "Where is my nephew? What have you done to my bar?"

Ben bit back a retort. This was what clients were paying for.

Would be paying for. With luck. One day. Apparently, some would take their pretend-ownership seriously.

Instead, he took a deep breath and said, "We seem to have lost Miguel."

Enrico's eyes narrowed. "What do you mean, *lost him?*"

"We've looked everywhere, but we can't seem to find him anywhere."

"I'm familiar with the concept of losing something, Mr. Cooper. No, I'm curious as to how *you* could manage to lose a *person.*" He sneered. "Particularly someone as large as Miguel."

Ben found himself at a loss for words.

"They didn't really lose me. I was just . . . misplaced for a bit," Miguel said from the doorway. All eyes turned to him.

"Miguel!" Ana cried. She gasped, then covered her mouth with her hands. "*Diay!* You look worse than Ben!"

Even Ben nodded in agreement. Miguel's right eye had turned a nasty shade of purple and the front of his neck was covered with angry red welts. His upper body was dusted in a fine, white powder. He seemed to be trying to keep his weight off his right foot, favor his left shoulder, and look nonchalant, all at the same time. He was doing a pretty poor job of it.

"What on earth is that white powder?" Ben asked.

"Airbag dust. There was a small accident. Can someone help me bring in the boxes from the car?"

They all got up to help, but Miguel held out the flat of his bruised palm to stop Victoria and his uncle. "Victoria, would you mind showing Enrico his office? We can handle the grunt work ourselves." Miguel's look urged her to play along; she nodded in reply.

"But I haven't even had the chance to greet my favorite nephew." Enrico strained his arm upward and pinched Miguel's bruised cheek.

The former soldier winced, but managed a small grin. "I'm

your only nephew, Uncle."

"Even if I had a dozen, you would still be my favorite." Enrico gave him an indulgent grin.

Miguel gestured toward the crowd outside. "We need to open, Uncle. There will be plenty of time to catch up later." After a few false starts, he managed to give Enrico a broad smile.

"Mr. Morales, if you would come with me, please?" Victoria's voice was soft as velvet.

"I never could say no to a beautiful woman," he said with a shrug, then followed her into the ransacked office.

Miguel fell to his knees the moment his uncle turned the corner.

Ana rushed to his side. With Ben's help, they managed to drag him to the lounge area and lower him into one of the few undamaged chairs. Ana fetched a bag of ice.

"What happened?" she asked, handing it to him.

Miguel gasped as he placed the ice on his right knee. "First you need to get outside and empty the hatchback. What's left to unload, at least."

That didn't sound good. Ben tried not to think of how many thousands of dollars of bar stock Miguel was supposed to purchase that morning. And now there was the massive cost of repairing the damage inflicted during the raid to add to the tab. Did they still have enough to pay for the new fridge? What about operating costs for the next six weeks?

Ben snorted, disgusted with himself. His best friend had almost been killed in a car accident and here he was, counting pennies.

He and Ana went out to the car. He expected to have to push through a thick crowd of customers, but the line was almost nonexistent. Then he noticed that the crowd had gathered in the middle of the parking lot. Again.

They shouldered their way through and had a look at the

rental car. "Baskets of bastards," Ben said, breathless.

The poor hatchback looked as though it had gone through a drunkards' demolition derby. The driver's-side mirror dangled by a single wire. The passenger-side panels were completely crumpled. A deflated airbag hung from the steering wheel. The windows—those that weren't shattered—were rolled down, and the car reeked of liquor. Only the graffiti remained intact.

Ben covered his face with both hands. "*What* is that smell?"

Ana wrinkled her nose. "Tequila."

He tried valiantly to tame his lurching stomach, plugging his nose as he threw open the back of the hatchback to reveal a mess of soaked cardboard and shattered bottles. He thrust his head back inside the vehicle once more, then drew back in disgust. The stench of hard alcohol mingled with the stink of airbag gunpowder. The miracle was not that Miguel had survived the car accident, but that he had driven the rental back to the cantina without suffocating.

Ben took a deep breath of fresh air before leaning in to help Ana sort through the mound of glass for intact bottles. He kept an eye on the curious onlookers as he worked. They seemed content to stand back and watch while he and Ana unloaded unspoiled boxes from the hatchback. Were it later in the evening, he'd worry about some enterprising bargoer trying to squeeze one of the floor mats into a shot glass. Not that they would be serving better drinks if they couldn't salvage a few more bottles.

In the end, the damage seemed worse than it was. Most bottles were wet but unbroken, particularly the more expensive spirits. Ben sighed with relief when he found that the bottle of fifteen-year-old Macallan Highland single malt was still intact, though he wondered what Miguel was thinking when he bought a hundred-dollar bottle of Scotch. Then to his shame he remembered last night's argument. Miguel was likely still angry with him—which would also explain the heavy crystal bottle of

Patrón next to the Macallan. Ben's eyes narrowed. Fair enough, he supposed. This time.

Ana stood guard as Ben used a dolly to shuttle the bottles back behind the bar. It took four trips.

"That's the last of it," he said, stacking the final two damp boxes. The crowd was starting to mutter about the delay.

Ana gestured angrily at the rental car. "Are you going to call the police?"

"If Miguel hasn't already called, he's got a good reason for it. Let's hear what happened first." He lifted the boxes. "Listen, Ana—I know you're worried, but we need to open *now* or we're sunk. Can you run the bar while I figure out what's going on?"

"I can do that, if Victoria can bring the spare cushions from the storage room and clean up the mess," Ana said. "Will you make sure he sees a doctor tonight? He needs to be checked out."

"I'll drag him there myself if I have to."

Ana strode up the walkway to the front entrance, Ben close behind. She flipped the wooden sign to "Open" as she passed, and the crowd surged past them into the bar.

He put the final boxes down behind the bar and glanced at Miguel, who looked as though he was going to fall asleep in the chair, even with the bag of ice on his knee. Ben clenched his hands.

A swarm of patrons was already three deep at the bar. He let out an exhausted breath. With Miguel out of commission, he'd have to get behind the bar himself tonight. First things first, though. He grabbed one of the new bottles and a couple of glasses from the bar, took them over to Miguel, and poured a healthy measure into each glass.

Miguel roused himself and picked up the amber tumbler of Patrón. "Have I gone to heaven?" he said with an attempt at a smile. "Or have you? You always said we'd share a glass of tequila over your dead body."

"I'm starting to regret my choice of words," Ben said. "Any particular reason you sent Enrico off with Victoria?"

Miguel took a healthy swallow of tequila and breathed a heavy sigh. "I didn't want him to see the car. He'd worry."

"*I'm* worried," Ben said. "What happened?"

"I think I was being followed." Miguel winced as he shifted his weight in the chair.

Ben gazed at the smashed car. "Looks like they followed rather closely."

"I let my guard down. It won't happen again." He told Ben about his trip, up to the point where he was sideswiped.

"The driver sped off before I could get a look at the license plate," Miguel finished.

"You think it was the Jeep that followed you?"

"Maybe. I'm not sure."

"Now's not the time to second-guess yourself, Miguel. I trust your instincts."

"That's good. One of us should."

"This isn't your fault."

Miguel put his glass down. "The bar isn't ready for Enrico. Half of the bottles are broken. We're short a bartender and our rental car is a total write-off. It won't even go above first gear. If this isn't *my* fault, whose is it?" Miguel scoffed and his expression darkened. "What does Victoria like to say? 'Success has many parents, but failure is an orphan.' "

"Don't you think you're being a bit hard on yourself?"

"This *is* my fault, and I'm going to handle it." Miguel closed his eyes and sighed. "We don't have insurance on the rental, do we?"

Ben shook his head. Miguel had argued for the coverage, but he had insisted they save a whole ten dollars a day. On the bright side, that didn't qualify as his worst financial decision of the week; it would be hard to top buying the cantina in the first place.

"More tequila?" Ben tilted the bottle toward Miguel's empty glass.

"Please."

Ben refilled both glasses. "Did you call the police?"

"I was going to. Then I smelled the broken liquor bottles in the back. If Vasquez took the call, I'd have been arrested for drunk driving. Not that I could have called them if I'd wanted to. The crash wrecked my phone, too."

Ben rubbed his forehead. "We can't pretend this never happened, Miguel. If nothing else, we can't afford to keep renting a wrecked car for the rest of our lives. We need to tell the police about this."

"Are you sure?"

"Not at all," he admitted. "But I'm sick of digging ourselves deeper into the same hole. For all we know, the whole point of this hit-and-run was to rattle your cage and put us at odds with the police."

"Mission accomplished." Miguel poured himself another slosh. "I'm feeling pretty rattled right now."

"We'll get Captain Reyes to come out and have a look first thing tomorrow." Ben slid the bottle back a few inches. "That meeting will go better if you're not sweating tequila."

"How do you know he won't send Vasquez?"

"I don't." Ben exhaled heavily. "We'll find a way to make sure it's Reyes who comes out. I can tell him I have some more information about the death threat, that it's something I need to talk to him about in person. He'll understand, once he sees the rental."

"Sounds good." Miguel raised an eyebrow. "Was Victoria's flight cancelled? I thought she was leaving this morning."

Ben told Miguel about his conversation on the beach with Victoria.

"She really said that, about the tissues tied together?" Miguel laughed, then clutched his side. "Oh . . . ow . . . my ribs!"

"You don't mind that I made her a partner without asking you first?" Ben asked. "That's your decision as much as mine."

Miguel held the glass up to catch the sunlight glinting off the Pacific. "When someone smashes into the side of your car and leaves you for dead, it tends to put things in perspective. I trust you, Ben. I hope you trust me, too."

"I do."

Miguel met his eye, and they buried last night's disagreement with a nod.

Enrico and Victoria stepped out of the office. At least, Ben assumed Enrico was with Victoria; presumably she wasn't holding the door open for an imaginary friend. Then a bushy tangle of gray hair appeared above the bar. That was Enrico, all right. Even though Victoria towered over him, she had to lengthen her stride to keep up. He and Victoria fought their way through the growing crowd and sat down next to Ben and Miguel.

"How are you settling in, Enrico?" Ben asked.

"It is good to be back, Mr. Cooper." He frowned. "I must say, though, I am not at all pleased with how you managed the bar while I was away." He looked around the cantina before shaking his head. "The cantina is a complete disaster. Very bad for business."

Ben bit his cheek. It had taken him the past few days to get used to being the bar's owner, and now he had to play the role of Enrico's obsequious assistant. "I'm very sorry, Mr. Morales. I am sure our situation will improve with you back at the helm."

Enrico smiled. "I think so."

"Has Victoria shown you to your room?"

The smile quickly disappeared. "Not as such. Ms. Holmes

did show me *a* room, but not *my* room. *My* room will be at the Tamarindo Diria." He grabbed Ben's glass of tequila and knocked it back. "I hear they have such wonderful amenities there these days. Running water, for instance." He raised an eyebrow and waggled the empty glass in front of Ben.

Ben sighed as he picked up the bottle of expensive tequila and refilled his former glass. This was not going as planned. Not at all.

Enrico smiled. "Besides, I will need some space to think if I am going to solve the murder of my former bartender." He gave Ben a wink.

Ben squinted at his client. "Uh . . . pardon?"

"You know, the murder?" He winked again.

Victoria was raising both eyebrows up and down repeatedly, as though trying to transmit a vital message via eyebrow semaphore.

"Yes . . . of course . . . the murder," Ben replied slowly.

"Very good." Enrico winked at him once more. "If that's all, then, I'll go and see if Ana needs a hand behind the bar. Mr. Cooper, see that my bags make it to the Diria, will you? They're in the red Mercedes parked out front. Victoria has the keys. I'll be back in a few minutes to have a drink with my favorite nephew." He slapped Miguel on the back, spilling tequila in the process, then made his way to the bar, taking his glass with him.

Ben glanced at Miguel, who seemed as puzzled as he was. So he turned around and asked Victoria what the hell that had been all about.

It was the first time Ben had seen her blush. "Enrico was getting a bit anxious about the state of the bar. And the office. And the murder. And Miguel." She took a deep breath. "I may have hinted—hinted, mind you—that this was included in his ownership experience. Part of the game, as it were." She deflated in her chair. "Is there any tequila left?"

Miguel's mouth dropped open, but no sound came out.

"Are you kidding?" Ben asked. "We have a murderer running loose, and you convinced Miguel's uncle that he's playing cops and robbers?"

"I didn't exactly have a choice. He was ready to walk out the door, but not before he tried to call Miguel's grandmother. He had the phone in his hand and had started to dial." She glared at him. "I did what I had to do."

Miguel paled. "He was calling my *abuela*?"

"So?"

"You don't understand, Ben. You're my best friend, and I would face an army for you. But not my *abuela*. A man has limits."

"She can't be that bad," Ben said. He had only faint memories of his own grandparents, but surely Miguel was exaggerating.

"A police officer once tried to give her a ticket for jaywalking. *Tried.* She grabbed him by the ear and dragged him back to his *abuela* for a tongue-lashing." He poured another measure of tequila into his glass and knocked it back.

"See? I made the right call," Victoria said. "Who knows? Perhaps Enrico can help us solve Antonio's murder."

"I wouldn't count on it." Ben looked over at the bar, where Enrico was re-teaching Ana how to make a vodka and soda. She smiled politely, her hands so tightly balled it seemed her knuckles might burst. "The man looks like he's well on his way to getting murdered himself."

"Hey, man. That's my uncle, remember?" Miguel said.

"Right. Sorry, Miguel."

Victoria hadn't finished. "There's more bad news. There's no room at the Diria. I tried to extend my own reservation, but they've got a large wedding party this week. There's no way you'll get a booking for Enrico."

Ben sighed. "All right. I'll move in here, then. Enrico can have my room." He glanced down at his wrist where his watch used to sit, then up at the wall clock. "I'll need to make time to pack my bags and move them over."

Victoria flipped open her agenda to jot down a few notes. "Oscar looked as though he's almost finished with the worst of the clean-up. I'll have him look after it."

So much for his last few days of luxury. "Thanks, Victoria. What about you? Where will you stay?"

She shrugged. "I haven't decided yet. I suppose I can move to the cantina as well. We do have a second bedroom, after all." She couldn't hide her disdain. To Victoria, lack of indoor plumbing was the third circle of hell.

Miguel let out a deep sigh. "You can take over my room at the Diria. I'll move in here with Ben."

"Are you sure?" Victoria asked, genuinely surprised.

"Might as well. You seem to be the only one of us who can handle Enrico, so it might help to have you nearby if—when—something comes up." He rubbed an aching shoulder. "Besides, Ben and I seem to have targets painted on our backs. We might as well stick together."

Ben started to say something sarcastic, but Miguel was right. Splitting up would only endanger the others and make each of them more vulnerable. He silently cursed himself for involving his friends in this mess. Miguel looked over at him. Ben nodded in reply.

"Now that's settled, did I miss anything while I was out?" Miguel frowned as he looked around the bar, noticing the damage for the first time. "Were we robbed?"

Ben told him about the coroner's report, Vasquez's surprise visit, and the crowbar he had taken into evidence.

"If the crowbar looked clean, what made him think it was evidence?"

Ben shook his head. "Vasquez came out of nowhere, tore the place to bits, and left as quickly as he arrived. I still have no idea what he thought was in the safe, or why he ripped the cantina apart. No wonder Enrico thinks this is all part of a game. I want to believe that so badly myself, I can almost taste it."

Miguel gave him a weak smile. "I think that's the tequila."

Ben looked back at the bar. Enrico was chatting up one of the surfer girls, studiously ignoring the crowd that was clamoring to be served. Ana raced from one customer to the next, scarcely making a dent in the line.

"Victoria, can you grab the spare cushions from the storeroom?" Ben rose from his seat with a sigh. "This is going to be a long night."

CHAPTER NINE

Ben had looked after a child only once in his life. One weekend, Tara's sister left her two-year-old son, Zenon, with them while she went shopping. It was toddler mayhem. Ben spent the afternoon racing after Zenon as he pulled books off the shelves, shattered treasured keepsakes, and smeared the walls with blueberry jam. Handing the kid back to his mother was one of the best moments in Ben's adult life. If he concentrated, he could almost hear the click of the front door and the wondrous silence that followed.

At the time, he had cursed every minute of those four exhausting hours. Now, those memories were his best and only weapons in his battle with Enrico. Unfortunately, Enrico was both larger and stronger than a two-year-old and even less inclined to listen to reason. Ben's only advantage was that he was slightly more nimble than the chubby musician.

In some ways, it would have been easier if Enrico was actually trying to be destructive, but he simply didn't know any better. He just wanted to mix a rum and Coke—how was he to know that the vermouth bottles looked like the rum bottles? And why were they kept next to each other, anyway? And what's the harm in offering tequila shots for twenty-five cents each, offer valid only for the next two minutes? If Miguel didn't want to be trampled, he should sit somewhere else. It didn't get any easier as the night wore on, either. At least Zenon hadn't managed to down the lion's share of a tequila bottle during his visit.

"No, Enrico," Ben said firmly, "we are not ordering new uniforms for Ana and Victoria. That is final."

Enrico drew himself up on his toes. "Mr. Cooper, I think you forget yourself. I am owner of this establishment, and I think that a tropical-themed costume—"

"Tropical-themed?" Ana snorted. "A pair of coconut halves and a grass skirt are the kind of uniform you would give a—"

"Mr. Morales," Victoria interjected, "you are quite right, you are the owner and this is indeed your decision. I will make a few calls and get back to you."

Enrico smiled. "Please, Ms. Holmes."

Victoria returned a less-lecherous version of his smile, then went into the office.

"At least one member of the staff has some respect for their employer." He scowled at Ben. "Keep this up, Mr. Cooper, and I'll dock your pay."

He watched helplessly as Enrico grabbed a bottle of tequila and tried to inveigle two bikini-clad Swedes to do a round of body shots. On the house, of course.

Ben wondered how much to charge future pretend-owners to make it worth this abuse, but stopped once he realized he needed a calculator to handle such sums.

Victoria came back a few minutes later. "I have good news, Mr. Morales. I've talked to our supplier, and he'll be able to send us the new uniforms in seven business days. I've gone ahead and placed the order. Will there be anything else?"

Ben suppressed a grin. Brilliant. That would be three days after Enrico's pretend-ownership came to an end.

Enrico grinned until the math caught up with him. "That's all for now, Ms. Holmes." He turned back to the bar and took another order.

"Thank you," Ben mouthed silently to Victoria.

She caught his gaze and smiled. It was a warm, genuine smile and it lit up the room. He hadn't seen that smile for a long time. It was nice. Even if it was her gloating over outwitting a lecherous musician.

"Ben?"

He turned around and found himself gazing at Jennifer Walker, her hand resting lightly on the bar. She was wearing a flowing red sarong that hinted at her athletic, feminine form. Strands of hair, whitened by the sun, fell across her temples. She wore the faintest hint of mascara and lipstick. She looked like every carefree summer Ben had never had.

"Uh . . . hi, Jenni," Ben said. Out of habit he asked, "What can I get you?"

A corner of her mouth turned upward. "Sauv blanc, if you have it."

"No problem. Back in a minute."

He had no idea if they had any sauvignon blanc, but he knew who would.

He walked over to where Victoria was mixing a gin fizz. "Where did you hide the good wine?"

She shot him a look. "Ben, I resent that remark—"

He glared back.

She sighed, waving at the bar fridge. "Bottom left corner, behind the diet ginger ale. Restock the fridge once you're done plying your floozy."

"Thanks." Ben smiled. "I'll keep us in good supply. I know you start breaking out in human emotion if you're not kept well medicated with grape."

She scoffed, but Ben thought he saw her smile faintly as she fixed the last of her order.

Luis poked his head out the pass-through to the kitchen. "Ben, do you have a minute?"

He closed his eyes and let out an exhausted breath. "Luis, I have even fewer minutes now than I did yesterday. Is the kitchen burning down?"

Luis shook his head.

"Then it can wait," Ben said.

Luis ducked back into the kitchen.

Ben rummaged through the fridge for a few moments, finding a few bottles of decent wine that had survived the onslaught on the bar stock. He was surprised Antonio had such good taste in wine. More likely, Victoria had done some shopping of her own. He settled on a bottle of Cloudy Bay.

He returned to the bar with the misted bottle of wine and two wine glasses. "It's from New Zealand. Hope that's all right."

"Well, I'll be cross if it makes me go blind." She smiled. "To be perfectly honest, I'm surprised you have wine that comes in a bottle. I think most of what Antonio served came in cardboard boxes."

Ben laughed. "I'd never thought of that. We could save some money if we put a few juice boxes out in the sun for a day or two. Might solve our financial troubles." He filled both glasses.

Jenni picked hers up by the stem. "Shall we toast?"

Ben picked up his own glass. "To . . . crossing paths."

"And uninjured swimmers."

They clinked their glasses and Jenni eased herself onto one of the bar stools.

"This *is* nice wine. Don't tell the Kiwis I said that, though." She took another sip. "What was that about financial troubles? It's not as bad as that, I hope."

"Pretty much." Ben took a large swallow of his wine and winced. Everything still tasted like tequila, and probably would until after Enrico left. "Even with Miguel and Victoria buying in as partners, we still only have enough cash to make it through another couple of weeks. That's why we started the pretend-ownership business."

Jenni looked sympathetic. "How's that going for you so far?"

Across the bar, he heard Enrico shout, "Watch this!" Glass shattered.

"About as well as it sounds."

Jenni rested her hand on his. "I'm sure you'll figure something out."

Ben raised his gaze to meet her eyes. "I . . ."

He trailed off as he spotted over her left shoulder the drug dealer, Chris, passing a phone to a tall, lanky beach bum in a ragged T-shirt. On the back of the phone was a small but familiar red maple leaf. The phone disappeared from the dealer's hand in exchange for a wad of dirty bills, which he stuffed into his pants pocket.

Ben's stomach twisted into knots. That was *his* phone.

"Sorry, Jenni. I'll be back in a minute."

He glanced over to where Miguel was sitting, only to find his friend gently dozing in his chair. Ben walked through the lounge in search of Victoria. When he found her, Enrico was grilling her about the murder.

"Did the police find any guns?"

"No."

"Victoria," Ben said between clenched teeth.

"Candlesticks?"

"What? No."

"*Victoria.*"

"Hmmm . . . a revolver?"

"A revolver is a type of gun, Enrico."

"Victoria!" Ben shouted.

"What is it, Mr. Cooper?" Enrico flapped his hands in annoyance. "Surely whatever petty business you have with Ms. Holmes can wait. We *are* trying to solve a murder, after all."

There was no way Ben could drag Victoria off to deal with Chris and leave Enrico to his own devices. The bar would burn to ashes in minutes.

He put a hand on Enrico's shoulder. "Mr. Morales, there is a matter that requires your urgent attention. There is a dangerous man in this bar, and only you can find out the truth of what he knows regarding Antonio's murder. Please wait for me in your office. I will bring him to you."

Enrico rubbed his chin. "I see, Mr. Cooper." A faint flicker of doubt crossed his eyes. "But why should he listen to me?"

Victoria cleared her throat. "He will not want to run afoul of someone with your . . . uh . . . ties to the criminal underworld."

Ben's stomach sank. She would say that, wouldn't she?

Enrico's eyes gleamed. "Of course. My ties to the criminal underworld. As you say. Bring him in immediately, Mr. Cooper." He straightened his tie and swaggered off to the office.

" 'Ties to the criminal underworld'?"

"You didn't give me much time to think. Who's he going to speak with?"

"Chris. The drug dealer. You know, the one with *real* ties to the criminal underworld."

"Oh. Want me to call it off? We can find something else for Enrico to do that won't pose a risk to the cantina."

"Like what, duct taping him to one of the pillars? Otherwise, the idiot would probably lock himself inside the walk-in freezer." Ben shook his head. "There's no time. Let's go."

Victoria close behind, Ben waded through the crowded bar to where Chris and his lanky customer were trading jokes over a couple of empty beer bottles. He held out his hand. "I'll take that phone. Now."

"Dude, you're too late," the beach bum said. "It's mine. Bought *and* paid for."

Ben snapped. He grabbed the man by his T-shirt and pulled him nose to nose. "It's stolen property. *My* stolen property." He let go of the man's shirt and turned to Chris. "Give him back his money."

"Hey man, no refun—"

Ben stabbed his index finger in the drug dealer's chest. "Chris, remember our little chat last night?"

"Yeah, man." Chris bobbed his head. "You said no . . . uh . . . special merchandise."

"I said no *business*. None. And that goes double for anything that used to belong to me."

"That's *your* phone?"

Ben exhaled slowly. Could Chris really be that dense?

"Didn't you turn it on? The background has a picture of me and my . . . my friend on it." He hadn't changed his background from the photo of him and Tara in Mexico a few years earlier. He'd thought about changing it after they'd broken up, but there was the trip and . . . well, it would have been yet another change in a world turned upside down.

He glanced back over his shoulder. Jenni was nowhere to be seen.

"Oh . . . what? That's *you* in the picture with that smokin' hot chick on the beach?" Chris squinted and leaned in toward Ben. "Not a good likeness, dude. With your round face, you should really go for, like, a two-thirds view." He nodded to himself. "Yeah, definitely. Two-thirds with a downward angle."

"Skip the photography lesson," Ben said. "I just want my phone. Give this guy his money back."

"Oh, right." He handed the money back. "Sorry for the confusion, dude. Got the phone from one of my regulars for half an ounce. Said he found it on the beach. I wouldn't have touched it if I'd known it was yours. I like my liver where it is, if you catch my drift."

The guy shrugged, pulled the phone from the pocket of his filthy jeans, and handed it to Ben.

He wrapped his fingers around the phone, savoring its weight in his hand. "Chris, how would you like to earn back your bar privileges?"

The door to the office flew open, the handle smashing into the freshly plastered wall. Ben pushed Chris into the room and pointed at the same seat he'd sat in the night before.

The office was perhaps in the worst shape of all the rooms in the cantina, having taken the brunt of the damage during Vasquez's search. One of the filing cabinets had been tipped over, and the contents of the other cabinets were now a thick carpet on the floor. Holes had been punched in the drywall, seemingly at random, and even some of the electrical outlet plates had been removed. Only the desk was immaculate. Victoria sat in the other visitor's chair, rum in hand. No Enrico.

As though on cue, the heavy leather office chair slowly swiveled to reveal Enrico Morales, maestro of the criminal underworld. His elbows rested on the armrests. He pressed his fingertips together and fixed Chris with an expressionless glare. "Mr. Cooper, please tell me why you have brought this *gentleman* to my office."

Ben sat down on one of the filing cabinets, as Miguel had the night before. "Chris has some information that might interest you."

"Uh . . . right," Chris said. He repeated what he had said earlier about the caped man carrying a bundle the night Antonio died.

"And what do you think was in the bundle?" Enrico asked.

"My guy didn't say. Like I told you, he was pretty fried."

"I did not ask you what your customer thought was in the bundle, Mister . . . ?"

Chris glanced at Ben as though asking for help. "People don't usually ask for my last name."

"I will be the exception, then."

134

"And, what if . . . like . . . I wanted to remain anonymous?"

"That would be very unfortunate, Chris. You see, I only address my friends by their last names. First names are reserved for people I care *nothing* for." He paused. "You are aware that I am a man who knows people?"

Chris swallowed. "It's Christianson."

Enrico raised an eyebrow. "Chris Christianson?"

"Yeah, man. My parents didn't like me very much, okay?"

"Fine, Mr. Christianson. I did not ask what your 'guy' thought was in the bundle. I asked what *you* thought was in the bundle."

Ben's back stiffened. Why hadn't he thought of asking that?

Chris opened his mouth to speak, and then paused. "You know, I never really thought about it."

Enrico gave him a small, patronizing smile. "Take your time."

"Well, he probably wouldn't have stolen anything, because the police or, like, Ana would have noticed stuff was missing," Chris said, thinking hard. You could practically see the steam coming off his dreadlocks.

"Go on," Enrico said.

"Maybe he tried cleaning up after himself? The bar has cleaning supplies, right? He could have been, like, trying to cover his tracks." Pleased with himself, Chris smiled broadly.

"Very good, Mr. Christianson. That is all I needed to know." Enrico swiveled the chair around, signaling the end of the interrogation.

Ben was puzzled. So what if the killer cleaned up, and took the supplies with him? It was a new wrinkle, but what did it mean?

After few moments, Ben whispered in Chris's ear, "That means you can go."

They left together, and once Ben had closed the door behind them, he said, "Good job, Chris. I think Enrico felt sufficiently intimidating."

"Thanks, dude. He was pretty real. If you hadn't told me it was an act, I totally would have bought it. All that swiveling scared the hell out of me."

"Quick thinking on making up a last name, by the way."

Chris looked at him blankly. "Who said it was made up?"

Ben glanced at the bar's wall clock. 6:23 p.m. Surprisingly early, given all that had happened in the past few hours. The sun had disappeared over the horizon, leaving a faint red band above the Pacific. A large crowd sipped and chattered beneath the strands of multicolored lights that crisscrossed above the lounge and dance floor. Not bad for a Sunday night. He looked for Jenni at the bar, but saw no sign of her.

Miguel had roused from his nap while Ben was in the office and somehow managed to find a pint of beer. Now he was deflecting the ministrations of some local girls, who seemed to want to be nurses when they grew up. They wore neon tank tops and jeans so tight they looked painted on. Miguel laughed and shook his head, as though downplaying his injuries. He never was one to seek the spotlight.

Ben tapped him on the shoulder. "Can you spare a minute?"

Miguel said something in Spanish to the girls. They giggled as they stood up, waved goodbye, and headed back to the bar.

"Thanks for the rescue." Only Miguel would thank you for ridding him of attractive young women.

Ben handed over his phone. "Can you look at this and see if there's anything of interest on it? Chris has had it for the past few days, and I'm wondering if he made any calls or took any photos that might help us figure what's going on around here."

Miguel took the phone and raised a gashed eyebrow. "You know it's a long shot, right?"

"I do, but I still think it's worth a try. This is bigger than

Antonio and his cash register."

"I'm feeling that too," Miguel said. "Anything else I can do to help?"

"The Diria keeps a doctor on call. He's on his way here to check you out. Use your new room, if you'd like."

"Are you sure?" Miguel scanned the bar. "I don't think we're out of the woods yet."

"Me neither. But you're no good to anyone if you have a concussion, or worse," Ben said. "See the doctor. Get some sleep."

"Thanks, Ben." Miguel started fiddling with the phone.

Ben stood up and strolled through the half-demolished bar, catching snippets of conversation as he went.

". . . think Enrico will play?"

". . . murder this week."

". . . glass everywhere."

". . . third warm beer tonight."

". . . glad that's not my car."

". . . see DJ School Mistress around."

By the time he reached the bar, it was clear no one knew what was going to happen at the cantina next, but they'd be damned if they would miss any of it. He was reminded of the Chinese curse: *May you live in interesting times.* It wasn't the reputation Ben had wanted for the bar, but so long as it boosted beverage sales . . .

The lone bartender was crouched down, rummaging in the fridge.

"Ana, did you see what happened to Jenni?"

The bartender turned around.

"You're not Ana," Ben said.

Luis smiled and pointed toward the ocean. "I think she's in the beach lounge with your lady friend. I watch the bar while she is away."

"Uh . . . thanks. Good work, Luis. Keep it up."

He took his half glass of warm wine from the counter and made his way through the tables, past the dance floor to the strangely empty beach lounge. Above the darkening red band of sunlight, the first of the stars flickered beside an orange moon. The din of the cantina gave way to the wash of waves and the chirp of crickets.

"Over here, Ben," Jenni waved from one of the lounge chairs. She turned to Ana in the chair next to hers. "Did he really take the cap off the bottle without an opener?"

The bottle of sauv blanc rested in a silvery ice bucket between the two lounge chairs, flanked on either side by flickering Tiki torches. A gentle breeze rolled up from the surf, bearing the scent of salt and damp cloth. Ana had done well. Very well, indeed.

Ana rose to her feet as he drew near. She leaned over to freshen Ben's wine, her voice dropping to a whisper as she flooded the glass. "Watch yourself," she said, and went back inside the cantina.

Ben struggled to keep his face impassive as he looked down at Jenni. Firelight danced across her delicate features, but her eyes shone with a strange intensity. It seemed as though her world began and ended within the arc of these torches. It was at once intoxicating and terrifying.

"Ana was explaining how you ended up with such a fine little boozer," Jenni said, shaking him from his reverie.

Ben sat. "Who? Our other partner, Victoria?"

Jenni laughed. "No, Ben. 'Boozer' is Aussie slang for a pub."

"Ah, right." Ben leaned back in the lounge chair, Ana's warning echoing in his ears. "Sorry about dashing off like that."

"No problem," she said with a smile.

You'd never know Ben had kept her waiting for half an hour while Enrico practiced his sinister swiveling.

Wait, why *had* she stuck around?

Enough. As much as it pained him to admit it, Miguel was right. Ben couldn't look at another woman without imagining the many ways she could crush his heart beneath her heel. He needed—

"Everything all right?" Jenni asked.

"Pardon?"

"Back inside," she said. "You looked like you were about to get into a brawl."

"I wish you hadn't had to see that. You must think I'm some kind of goon," he said. "Believe it or not, I'm usually a very agreeable person. I can't even remember the last time I got into a fight." Not entirely a lie. After all, most of his earlier fights took place when he was in no state to remember his own name. And it'd been a long time since then, anyway.

"Really?" Jenni asked.

"You don't have to sound quite so surprised."

"You're doing better than I am, for one." She spun the wine around in her glass, watching it catch the torchlight. "So, why did you decide to abandon your life of pacifism?"

Ben searched for some sort of articulate argument as to why he'd accosted Chris and his customer, finally settling for: "They had my phone."

"That does take a lot of cheek, stealing your phone and selling it in your own bar."

"It wasn't exactly stolen. Someone found it on the beach. I was a bit . . . spirited that evening." Also not untrue. He had been full up of spirits that night, rum among them. "Woke up in the police holding cell, thinking I'd been tossed in the drunk tank. Then Victoria walked in and told me I'm the lead suspect in Antonio's murder.

"I still can't remember what happened that night, but sometimes there are . . . echoes. When I saw that phone, I could feel that it was important. So I did what I had to do to get it back."

He looked over at Jenni. She gazed at him intently, the low flicker of torchlight accentuating her natural beauty. "That sounds ridiculous, doesn't it?" he asked.

She rested a hand on his forearm. "It sounds brave."

"Thanks." He smiled.

"No, really," she said gently. "The last fight in Tamarindo ended with one of the guys getting stabbed."

Time to change the conversation. "We've been talking about me all night. How did you end up in Tamarindo?"

Jenni cocked an ear toward the cantina. "Oh, I love this song."

"Would you like to dance?"

Ben couldn't remember the last time he'd danced at a club. Two years? Three? Pubs were more his style. You could talk to people in pubs without shouting, and there was none of this . . . moving, and such. Ironic that he now owned a dance floor. At least he could keep the volume at a halfway decent level, if he wanted. Admittedly, the holes in the roof did help with noise control.

The truth was he'd enjoyed dancing, at least before he'd settled down and become respectable. Until yesterday, he'd been unwilling to set foot on his own dance floor. He hadn't been able to shake the feeling that it was a bit silly for a thirty-something man to bust a move in public.

But Ben didn't *feel* silly. Not even in his orange flip-flops. Not with Jenni leading him by the hand onto the cantina's dance floor.

He could feel the bass thudding through the floor, the melody tugging at his muscles. She was right. This *was* a good song. He started moving with the rhythm. He found himself relaxing, losing himself in the music. Green spotlights wheeled across the bar, then converged on the DJ booth. Victoria stood behind the decks, wearing her business suit, looking poised but flushed. It seemed she was stuck with DJ School Mistress as her alter ego. Perhaps she would feel more comfortable once she picked up a lighter-weight suit. She should have a spare one anyway, if only so she didn't find herself delivering a closing argument in a jacket stained with coolers and glow-stick fluid.

Ben felt a jolt run through his body. If Victoria was spinning, then who was minding Enrico? Jenni executed a flawless spin, moving in perfect time to the beat. In one flash of light, he saw her white-blond hair flit across her eyes. The next, her smile drawing him in. Ben was suddenly aware of the stress he was carrying, the endless concerns that had thrust themselves on him, blinding him to this paradise. He needed to live in the moment, if only for a moment.

Ben cleared his mind of the death threat, Miguel's accident, and the damaged bar; and pushed back thoughts of Tara, his debts, and the criminal charges. He even forgot the cheap flip-flops chafing his feet. Time blurred.

A deafening screech of feedback shattered the music.

Silence.

Next, a few gentle taps on the microphone.

"Ms. Holmes?" Enrico gave a dry cough and cleared his throat. "Ms. Holmes, that is *quite* enough. Leave your music boxes alone. There are important matters that require your attention. I shall see you in my office."

The speakers crackled, then flooded the cantina with generic Latin jazz. The usually unflappable Victoria was consumed with rage. She shoved a stack of albums to the ground and shouted something in Spanish. Ben had never seen her this angry.

But then, she had been dealt the ultimate insult—to have her music interrupted mid-set and replaced with something else. To be interrupted by another DJ would have been bad enough, but to be supplanted by the kind of music you'd play in the waiting room of a Costa Rican dentist was unconscionable. This meant war.

The dancers stood transfixed. Victoria's hands darted across the console, twisting knobs and flipping switches. Then she paused, checked her work, and stabbed one last button. The jazz died and her turntables spun back to life. Her music resumed, louder than before, and so did the dancers, as though they had never stopped.

It took all of Ben's willpower not to rush to the office and lock Enrico in the safe, where he would no longer pose a threat to himself or others. Mostly himself. Because suddenly homicide no longer seemed so extreme an option. Ben peered about the cantina, straining to hear above the music, waiting for the other shoe to drop. He could have sworn he saw Enrico in the flicker of lights, never in the same place twice.

The speakers cracked again—once, twice. Then, the same dry cough in the microphone. A graveled throat cleared itself. Ben braced himself for another admonishment.

Instead Enrico said, "Very well, Ms. Holmes. If you wish to learn about music, then I shall teach you."

The lights spun round once more to the other side of the dance floor and converged on the great Enrico Morales. How had he managed that? In the span of minutes, he had somehow erected a small mountain of receivers and microphones alongside his famed bongo and conga drums.

Enrico launched himself into his music, his hand skimming across the drums, tapping out an impossibly intricate beat. Every inch of the seven drums seemed to have a different sound, with each of Enrico's fingers drawing out a different tone. Victoria's music raised the hair on your arms, but Enrico's had a direct line to raw emotion. People poured onto the dance floor, the crowd shaking in time to the beat.

Victoria stood behind her decks, eyes narrowed. The dancers took no notice as she put her headphones back on and started to spin dials and slide bars. Enrico's drumming built to an impossible crescendo, and then crashed to a finish. The silence rang in their ears.

Enrico's voice through the speakers. "Your move, Ms. Holmes."

His own music came back at him, remixed to create an entirely new sound and feel. Victoria had taken a recording of what Enrico had just played and, in minutes, crafted it to her own design. It could have been done to insult, but it wasn't—it showcased his remarkable talent like an aural pedestal. The hair on Ben's arms rose once more.

The dancers turned back to the famous bongo drummer, awaiting his next move. Enrico started to drum alongside the recording of himself, a massive smile on his face.

The battle raged on throughout the night. Enrico played until his hands bled, Victoria until she all but collapsed from dehydration. The overflowing crowd savored every moment.

Miguel posted Oscar outside the bar as a bouncer to prevent the line of waiting customers from storming the cantina. He warned them repeatedly that the odds of their getting into the bar that night were exactly nil, and when they got the message, they moved over to the parking lot, content to stay within earshot and dance in the dust.

Ben and Jenni danced for hours. She finally excused herself around midnight—she had a surfing competition coming up soon, and needed practice on the early morning waves. While he dithered about kissing her goodnight, she leaned in and pressed her lips to his cheek. "See you soon, Ben," she said.

After she had gone, Ben helped Luis collect the filthy glassware covering the tables. If this kept up any longer, they'd need to hire more staff, assuming they could pay more than promises. One more day until the bar closed for Antonio's funeral, earning them a brief reprieve from grueling shifts that stretched until sunrise.

Ben filled his tray and headed back to the bar with another load of glasses. Everyone had swarmed onto the dance floor for the finale, thinning the crowd at the bar. They would return with a vengeance once the last set came to an end. If he didn't move quickly, he *would* be serving vintage champagne in unwashed coffee mugs.

A customer leaned across the bar to get Ana's attention. The man was young, tall, and powerfully built, clad in a denim jacket, black T-shirt, and faded jeans. He must be a local—no tourist would wear that much clothing in a tropical bar. He did not look happy.

Ana stepped back from the bar, pressing her spine against the wall of bottles. Denim Jacket shouted at her in Spanish. She yelled back, her hands balled into fists. The music reached a fever pitch, and few noticed what was happening at the bar. Those who did pretended they hadn't.

Ben didn't have that luxury. He set down the tray of glasses and stepped into the fray. Denim Jacket turned and glared at him, eyes filled with rage. Before Ben could intervene, he stepped back from the bar, shoved Ben with his shoulder, and barked out a few parting words. Whether they were meant for him or Ana, Ben couldn't tell.

"Are you all right?" he asked her, his heart thudding.

Ana nodded and wiped her eyes with a shaking hand. Her other hand was hidden behind her back, but not so well that Ben couldn't see her fingers gripped around the handle of a paring knife.

"Mr. Cooper." Enrico tapped his shoulder. "I need you to come with me."

"Mr. Morales, this is the worst possible moment—"

"It's important, Ben. It's about the murder."

It must be important, if Enrico was addressing him by his first name. Only then did Ben realize the musical battle had ended and a wave of customers was poised to envelop the bar. He turned back to Ana. "You don't have to stay here if you don't want to."

She sniffed. "You go with Enrico."

He turned back to Enrico. "Let's make this quick."

Enrico led him to the bar's back door. He raised a finger to his lips before opening the door a crack, scarcely enough to see outside. There, Luis was hauling garbage bags from the kitchen to the cantina's dumpster. Once the last of his bags had been flung inside, he stretched his back and brushed the dirt from his apron.

Backlit by the street lights, Luis looked as though he was wearing a cape.

Chapter Ten

Ben struggled to make sense of Enrico's revelation as he walked back to the bar.

Could Luis have murdered Antonio?

He hadn't thought of the call from the *Tamarindo Gazette* since Miguel walked in the front door of the cantina, covered head to toe in bruises and airbag dust. After all, who would kill a man over a job rinsing dirty margarita glasses?

Then again. If the meager income from busing at the cantina allowed Luis to pursue his dream of fashion design, he might have been angry if Antonio tried to take that from him. Perhaps angry enough to kill. He'd have to talk to Ana about it. She was the only one of them who had known Luis for more than the past few days.

At the bar, people were lined up five deep to buy one last drink, blocking the way behind the counter. He'd have to go around to the far side if he wanted Ana's attention.

1:38 a.m. There'd been a time when he could make it through an entire weekend on four hours' sleep. Now he wanted nothing more than to grab a blanket and a mug of tea and curl up on the nearest horizontal surface not covered in a thin sheen of beer. He gazed longingly at the last intact couch in the lounge, then realized he was staring at a pair of retirement-aged tourists locked in the mother of all make-out sessions, their beige fanny packs grinding in time to the Latin dance music. Perhaps he'd find a chair instead.

Ben turned from the spectacle and winced. He'd caught a glimpse of who was behind the bar. Victoria was bartending. By herself. Again. Bloody hell. Where was Ana?

He swallowed his annoyance and reminded himself what his head bartender had so recently gone through, both that night and since the death of her uncle. If anyone deserved a coffee break right now, it was Ana Guiterrez.

He caught Victoria's eye, but it still took awhile for her to finish pouring a line of shots four feet long. The customer cheerfully handed over a thick wad of bills and began handing out shot glasses to a mob behind him like candy on Halloween. Ben smiled. *That* was the kind of questionable decision he could live with.

He looked back at the couch. Still going at it.

"You rang?" Victoria asked.

"Hey, baaaby . . ." slurred one of their more lubricated patrons, "Why duh . . . does he get served first? I'm nuxht . . ."

Victoria poured a glass of water and handed it to the drunk. "Have a vodka. On the house."

"Ruh . . . right on," he yelled, running away with his prize.

"Your understanding of human nature never ceases to amaze me," Ben said.

"Thank you. But I imagine you have something else to discuss? Otherwise . . ." She hiked a thumb back toward the thronging bar crowd.

"Where's Ana?"

"I haven't the foggiest. By the time I finally packed my equipment away and changed out of that damned business suit, the back of the bar was deserted and some moron was trying to drink straight from the draft tap."

"For crying out . . . Were you able to stop him?"

"Let's say he realized the error of his ways."

"Sorry?"

"He ran to the bathroom when foam started coming out his nose."

"That works," Ben said. "So, no idea where Ana might be?"

"None at all." Victoria turned back to the growing crowd. "Send her back when you find her. Assuming she doesn't have something more important to do, like painting her nails or teaching herself Mandarin."

Ben gave way to the press of patrons behind him and headed for the back hallway. He should have asked Victoria for a drink. This was shaping up to be another long night.

Ben began to push his way inside the storeroom but froze when he heard sobbing. This part of the job should have fallen to Miguel. It would have, if he weren't busy sleeping off a car accident. Only Ben could help Ana right now, and yet he couldn't shake the feeling he was wading into something that was none of his bloody business.

"Who's there?" Ana called in a trembling voice.

Now or never.

He pushed the rest of the way inside, blinking till his eyes adjusted to the dim glow of a single ancient bulb. Ana sat on a wooden crate, surrounded by musty cardboard boxes. "Hi, Ben. I am just . . . doing the inventory." She wiped her cheeks.

That would make this the third inventory in two days. He dragged a second wooden crate across the floor and sat next to her. They were silent for a moment.

"What are you doing here?" she asked.

"I thought I'd give you a hand," Ben said. "I've been doing a lot of inventory of my own lately."

"I can do this by myself."

"Should I get Miguel instead?"

"No!" She took a breath. "I mean, there is no reason to wake him up. He has gone through so much today already. I will be fine. Really. I miss Antonio, that's all."

Behind Ana's watery brown eyes, there was an unmistakable coldness. Ben was on intimate terms with grief. He knew every twist and turn of that long, dark road. Whatever Ana was feeling, it wasn't grief. It was rage.

Without another word, she rose to her feet and walked from the storage room, slamming the door behind her as she went.

Two in the morning. Ben had a mental list of suitable activities for this time of night. A last drink with friends. Contemplating the moonlit ocean. Getting to know Jenni. Curling up in a nice, warm bed. Definitely not skulking in the bushes while tailing his sobbing, enraged bartender down the dark, dusty side streets of Tamarindo. He might as well stab himself and call it a night. That would save everyone a lot of time and energy.

Where on earth was she heading? Ben still hadn't learned his way around the town, small as it was, and wondered if they hadn't passed that particular tree before. He listened intently, trying to sense what sort of trouble might await, but there was only the dull rustle of palm fronds, the faint music from another beachside bar, and the distant crash of the surf, now joined by the low rumble of a truck speeding along a dirt road. It seemed a peaceful night.

Ana pulled out her keys as she neared a low-rise apartment building on a dead-end road. Ben rolled his eyes. So much for trying to help. All he'd done was to trail her back to her place. There was a fine line between gallant and creepy, and Ben was on the wrong side of it. He crouched down in the bushes, trying to recall the way back to the cantina.

Then Ben saw him. Denim Jacket lurked by the entrance to the apartment building, smoking the damp stub of a hand-rolled cigarette. He stepped into the light as Ana fumbled with her keys, the corner of his mouth curled in an unmistakable smirk.

He flicked his cigarette into the bushes, a few feet from where Ben was crouched, and lunged for Ana. She dropped the keys as Denim Jacket seized her by her wrists. She tried to pull away, shouting. Ben couldn't understand their Spanish.

Denim Jacket let go of one of Ana's wrists and leaned over to pick up the keys. Even in the face of Ana's withering barrage, and now also shouts coming from a second-story window, his smirk never faltered. He selected a key, slid it into the lock, and began to drag Ana inside. That Ben understood.

He hadn't realized he'd picked up a rock, and he certainly hadn't planned to throw it. It just happened. The breath that followed was a humble prayer that it wouldn't hit Ana in the back of the head. Instead, he scored a direct hit on Denim Jacket's cheek. Ana's keys clattered to the pavement once more.

Then the knife came out.

Ben rose to his feet, hoping they'd say something nice at his funeral.

Denim Jacket locked eyes with him, brushed Ana aside, and started down the path, the naked blade gleaming in the street-light. Blood trickled down his face.

Ben might well have died on the streets of Tamarindo that evening but for an engine's rumble. Denim Jacket was bathed in blue and red light as a police cruiser rolled past, on routine patrol or perhaps in response to a call from the apartment above—he would never know. The knife vanished as quickly as it had appeared, and Ben crept noiselessly behind a dense hibiscus hedge.

Ana had disappeared.

Ben finally found his way to the cantina, only to discover that Ana had beaten him back. She'd pulled a stool down from the top of the bar and sat staring into nothing. Strands of hair spilled from her usually tidy bun and clung to her neck, damp with sweat. Her only concession to the oppressive nighttime heat had been to loosen another button on her plain black work shirt. A heavy tumbler filled with clear liquor sat before her. She hadn't bothered to put the cap back on the bottle.

"Leave, Ben," she said when she heard his flip-flops echo through the empty lounge.

"You do know this *is* my bar, right?" he asked gently.

"*Diay!* Everything is a joke with you." She took a long drink from her glass. "This is my problem, not yours."

Ben pulled down a stool and sat next to her, then reached over the bar and took another tumbler from the drying rack. He gripped it tightly, hoping to stay his trembling hand. He had to force his gaze away from the chef's knives drying beside the sink.

He filled his glass and weighed his words. "Ana, I really do want to help you."

"And how will you do that? By going back to my apartment, so Juan can stab you and you can bleed on him until my problems go away?"

"It would save him a trip to the bar." Ben regretted the words as they left his lips.

Ana slapped her hand on the counter. "If you will not leave, just let me drink in peace."

"Look, Ana . . ." He took a deep breath. "You're right. It's none of my business. And I'm sorry. For following you."

Her slight body slumped on the stool. "No, Ben. I was lucky you were there tonight." She took another gulp.

Ben reached for the open bottle by her elbow, wrinkling his nose at the fumes. Whatever it was, it wasn't rum. The label read *Cacique Guaro* and there was a picture of an Incan tribesman on the front. He filled his glass and took a sip. Definitely not rum. Or tequila, thank heavens. "What is this stuff?" Ben asked.

"*Guaro.*" She sounded sad. "It's made from sugar cane. To us *Ticos,* it is like mother's milk. Antonio made his own, a long time ago. We would have a glass, after the bar closed." She closed her eyes.

Ben was silent for a while. Then he found himself saying, "My mother died when I was six."

Ana's glass froze midair.

His voice caught. A crash. The smell of burnt cinnamon. A telephone held in small, shaking hands.

"What about your father?" Ana asked.

"He wasn't in the picture by then." Or ever. "It gets easier."

She gave him a small smile. "Thank you."

"You're welcome," Ben said. "And thank you for all your help this week."

"It was better than doing nothing." She paused. "Do you really want to help?"

"If you'll let me."

"Will you promise not to tell Miguel?"

Ben faltered. That was a lot to ask. "I . . ." He looked into Ana's eyes and saw the hope fading. "One condition. You tell him yourself. When the time is right."

"All right." She drained her glass. "Juan is my last boyfriend."

"Last boyfriend? Does that mean . . . ?"

"The last boyfriend I had, before now. Not my last boyfriend ever." She fixed Ben with a withering look, then continued, "I met Juan at a club in San José two years ago. He seemed dashing and handsome. I came back to Tamarindo, and one day he showed up at my place with flowers." She shook her head. "I knew it was a bad idea to move so fast, but before I know it he is staying at my place with me. He . . . moved in.

"I gave him some money, until he could find a job. He find

jobs but never keep them. A few days later, he asks for money again. I got so angry at him for smoking pot, for leaving my apartment a mess, for sleeping half the day away. I would threaten to kick him out, and he would turn on the charm.

"All of my friends know it was a mistake, but I do not listen to them. Eventually, they got tired of watching me ruin my life with Juan. By the time I knew how bad things really are, all of my friends are gone and I am deep in debt, thanks to him. Antonio helped me get a loan from the bank. I tell him it was so I could go back to school. He knew it was a lie.

"There was a time when Antonio treat me like his daughter. But things changed between us, after the money. He never ask anymore, he only give orders. And he make me come back every night to help close up, so he can keep an eye on me. Then he start to look at me the way he looked at all the others who owed him. It only pushed me and Juan closer.

"Eventually, I find out Juan left San José to escape gambling debts. I stop giving him money, but he take it from my purse. Or sell my things. One day, I come back home and the television has disappeared. And there is Juan, with big puppy eyes, saying it was already gone when he return from the corner store.

"When the money finally run out, so did Juan. He would come to my apartment only when he needed a place to stay, or food to eat." She looked up, and the fire returned to her eyes. "One day—the best day of my life—I change the lock. Juan came to the bar to threaten me once, but Antonio chase him away with his bat."

Something clicked. "Do you think Juan might have gone after Antonio?" Ben asked.

Ana thought a moment, then shook her head. "Juan is just a bully. He did not mind pushing me around, but Antonio was different. If he get the excuse to teach Juan a lesson . . . well, I do not think Juan would be here to cause problems."

Ben wondered if Ana meant here in Tamarindo or here, period.

She continued, "Juan went back to San José months ago, and left me alone since then."

"Until now."

"Juan hear about Antonio's death, and my inheritance. He wants it for himself. I tell him there is no more money, only enough to pay back what he has taken already." She took another gulp. "Juan does not care. He . . . he . . . threaten to . . ."

Ben rested a hand on her shoulder. "Take your time."

She took a deep breath. "Juan has *pictures* of me."

"Pictures?" he asked. Then he understood. "Oh. *Pictures.*"

"*Si*, Ben. *Pictures.*" Ana scowled. "Juan threaten to put them on the Internet, and email them to my family and friends." She shook her head. "I still do not know why I am telling you all this."

"I . . ."

A car pulled into the parking lot. Its horn honked twice.

"I have to go. My cab is here." She downed the last of her drink.

"You're not going back to your apartment, are you?"

"My friend Jacqueline says I can stay at her place. Juan will not find me there. Good night, Ben." She flipped her stool up on the counter and left without another word.

He watched in silence as she walked away. A small, selfish part of him wanted to break his promise. But he didn't need Miguel's help on this. He knew exactly how to stop Juan.

CHAPTER ELEVEN

Sunlight streamed through the windshield of the black SUV. In the back seat, the principal delivered his opening address via Bluetooth headset. He rested a pad of paper on his lap and jotted notes in indecipherable handwriting, paying no heed to the tumble-down buildings rushing past the passenger window.

No matter how many runs they did in a day, the principal's suit remained pristine. Today he was wearing the charcoal one, and his favorite cobalt blue tie knotted in a double-Windsor. His face held the same look of vague annoyance that it had for each day of the three years Miguel had provided close protection. Today was different, though. It was Miguel's first run as team leader.

He rested his thumb on the safety of his MP5 submachine gun. He had already chambered a round, before they got in the SUV. This was not a nice part of Bogotá. They were skirting the outer *barrios,* where makeshift houses were built on top of each other and capped with corrugated metal. Carjackers here were typically better armed than the *Fuerzas Armadas Revolucionares de Colombia* or their countless splinter groups.

And so he scanned. Windows. Doors. Traffic. Near. Far. Over and over.

Glass shattered.

Miguel woke as the shards hit the ground. Then came the crunch of glass being crushed against the floor. He sat bolt upright in bed. Someone was in the cantina.

155

He slid his feet to the ground and dressed himself sound-lessly, all the while reminding himself, *Slow is smooth, smooth is fast.* He thrust his feet into sandals and pulled on a pair of socks over them to muffle his footfalls. Going barefoot would have been quieter still, but he couldn't risk the broken glass.

He reached for the assault rifle leaning against his bedside table. His hand closed around empty air before he remembered there wasn't one. He hadn't had a firearm within arm's reach for almost a decade, but his dream left him feeling naked without the heft of cold steel in his hands and the comforting weight of body armor and an extra hundred rounds of ammunition on his chest.

He scanned the room for anything he could use as a weapon. Nothing. Perhaps that was for the best. Stepping outside with a weapon would either lull him into a false sense of security or put another body on the ground. Better to be cautious.

He gently turned the doorknob. The click of the bolt sliding back echoed in his ears. He put his eye to the gap between door and frame and slowly pulled the door open. Moonlight spilled in from the bar, bathing the corridor in liquid silver. Miguel peered down its length and saw the beam of a flashlight slice across the end of the hallway.

The door across from him opened. Ben staggered into the corridor, his eyes bleary with sleep. Miguel held a single finger to his lips and pointed sharply at the room behind Ben, then at the door handle. He mimed turning a key. Ben nodded once, stepped back inside his room, and quietly locked his door. Miguel released the breath he'd been holding. If only he could have mimed a way to tell Ben to call the police if he wasn't back in five minutes. Miguel hoped his friend could handle himself if the worst came to pass.

He crept down the hallway, keeping close to the wall. As he drew near the kitchen, he could hear the intruder walking behind the bar. Either the burglar didn't know how to muffle his footfalls, or he simply didn't care. The man moved as though he owned the bar. Miguel knelt at the end of the corridor, his back tight to the wall, and peered out from the doorway.

The intruder was on his hands and knees, going through the cupboard under the sink, tossing buckets aside and tearing open cleaning supplies. His clothing was dark, the kind of filthy gray that met the shadows in the way black never could. His face was masked with a balaclava of the same color, and a flashlight sat tucked under his arm. The light was barely visible. The beam had been dialed low, and there was a red filter on the end. That meant military or paramilitary, the type Miguel had served beside a lifetime ago. A rip-stop nylon pouch hung from the intruder's hip. There was almost certainly a weapon inside.

The intruder rose from the sink cupboard and reached for the bar shelves. He took down glasses and bottles and tossed them across the cantina, methodically shattering each in turn with the urgency of a man ironing his shirt. If he had been searching for something, he'd changed his mind. Now he was covering his tracks with an act of random destruction.

Miguel rose stiffly, silently cursing the car accident for leaving him slow and weak. Normally, he would have sprinted into the bar and disabled the intruder with a single blow. But if that pouch held a Taser, he'd end up on the floor. If it held a switchblade, he'd end up in the morgue. The doctor had taped his ribs well, but tape could only do so much.

He had but one advantage—surprise.

Miguel reached up and pulled the fire alarm. Lights flashed, and there came an ear-splitting wail. A recorded voice repeated *"Peligro! Fuego!"* between the siren's squeals. He stepped around the corner. The intruder looked frantically about the bar, trying to spot the source of the alarm. Fortune smiled on Miguel. His target still held a pint glass in his hand. One more item to drop before he could reach for a weapon. Miguel's hands closed around the neck of a wine bottle. It wasn't a rifle, but it would do. Nicely.

The first swing of the bottle struck the intruder a glancing blow on his chest. The glass fell from his hand. Miguel wound up and swung again, harder and farther than before. But instead of dodging or blocking, the intruder stepped into the blow and kneed Miguel in the stomach. He doubled over and the bottle flew from his hand, shattering on the ground.

Miguel braced himself for the final blow. It never came.

Dawn crept into the cantina, casting the wood and thatch in a pale glow. The firefighters had already been and gone. They hadn't been pleased to arrive at the scene of a fireless fire, though they were somewhat sympathetic once they saw the state of the place. Shattered glass littered every inch of the lounge and dance floor. The space behind the bar looked like a science fair gone awry. Bottles of cleaning fluid and rags of every description lay in a saturated heap that leaked vilely. The police were due any moment.

As soon as the firefighters left, Victoria rounded on Ben and Miguel with her usual empathy.

"You're both idiots," she fumed. "I don't know what I was thinking, leaving the two of you here without adult supervision."

"Victoria . . ." Ben pleaded.

"Don't you 'Victoria' me." She looked over her shoulder. "Enrico, get away from there. It's a crime scene. You'll destroy evidence, then cut yourself and die of tetanus. Do you want that to happen?"

Enrico pouted.

She stared him down. "Do you?"

"No, Victoria," he mumbled. He lingered long enough to

make it seem like he was making his mind up for himself, then went back outside.

Ben lowered his voice. "Did you have to bring Enrico?"

"Where else was I supposed to put him? The hotel daycare doesn't open until nine."

"Ha," Ben said mirthlessly.

"Would you rather I left him at the hotel, unattended?"

"Good point."

"What a bloody disaster." Her eyes swept across the shattered cantina. "What were you thinking, Miguel? Didn't you break enough ribs yesterday?"

"Are you blaming me for what happened to the car?" Miguel asked.

"Of course not," she said, "but I'd hoped the crash had knocked some small sense of caution into that thick skull of yours."

"If it makes you feel any better, I asked myself what you would do before I pummeled the intruder with a bottle of wine." He sat at an awkward angle in one of the lounge chairs, trying vainly to keep the pressure off his side. He took a sip from a steaming mug of coffee, grimacing as he swallowed.

"You did no such thing," she said. "I would never waste wine like that. This—"

Victoria stopped when she heard a car pull into the parking lot.

Ben went to the entrance to see who had arrived. "Vasquez. Wonderful."

The detective walked up the front path and knocked twice on the archway.

"Yes, Detective?" Ben asked, furious. "What can we do for you today? Would you like to strip search my employees? Look in the attic for Communists? Have a nice quiet conversation, just you, me, and the thumb screws?"

"Ben . . ." Victoria said.

"No, Ms. Holmes," Detective Vasquez said, "Mr. Cooper is quite right. I owe him an apology." He extended a massive hand in Ben's direction.

Ben hesitated, then shook the detective's hand. "Why the sudden change of heart?"

The detective frowned as he peered about the cantina. "Whatever your motives, Mr. Cooper, I do not believe you would do this to your own bar." He pulled out a notepad. "What happened here last night?"

Miguel recounted the night's events. Vasquez walked through the bar, jotting down notes on what little evidence there was.

He tapped his pen on the pad. "The car outside. It belongs to you, correct?"

Miguel opened his mouth to speak, but Ben silenced him with a look. "It's our rental car," he said. "There was an accident yesterday. We had intended to report it, but we had reasons for waiting." Including you, he added silently.

"Did the incident take place near the supermarket?" Vasquez asked.

Miguel nodded, surprised.

"What happened?" Vasquez asked.

Miguel told Vasquez about the hit-and-run, and his suspicions regarding the early model Jeep Grand Cherokee.

"That is what I suspected," Vasquez said. "We found a Grand Cherokee by the side of the road. It was badly burned. We tried to identify it, but the Vehicle Identification Number had been removed. *Completely* removed."

He paused as though to let that sink in. Ben remembered reading that a vehicle's VIN could be found in several different locations, not just the dash. Few knew where to find all of them.

"Do you think the cartel may be involved?" Victoria asked.

"I cannot say that for certain, Ms. Holmes."

Enrico stepped into the lounge from where he'd been listening in the office. "You have no other suspects? None at all?"

"And you are . . . ?"

"Enrico Morales. At your service." He took a small bow.

"Well, Mr. *Morales,*" Vasquez said, as though pronouncing a dirty word. "I suggest you leave this to the police. The people we deal with are not fond of amateur detectives."

Enrico shrugged. "Suit yourself."

"I do not mean to seem harsh, Mr. Cooper, but there are some very dangerous people in Tamarindo. They have no regard for law and order. You and your friends are in peril."

"I'm aware of that." Ben looked at the stain where a bottle of red wine had smashed against a wall in an echo of the brutal crime that claimed Antonio's life. "But what can we do?"

"Leave town," Vasquez said. "I spoke with Captain Reyes yesterday. We both agree that you are no longer a suspect in the murder of Mr. Antonio Guiterrez." Vasquez handed Ben an envelope. "Here is your passport."

Ben felt a surge of relief. He hadn't realized how much his freedom of movement meant to him until it was taken away.

Vasquez continued, "I have arrested some of the most dangerous drug dealers, enforcers, and gang leaders in Costa Rica. I will do everything in my power to keep all of you safe. Your lives are yours to spend as you will, but make no mistake—you are in danger right now. You may have strong feelings about this bar, but you need to ask yourselves whether those feelings are more important than life itself."

Ben glanced over at his friends. Miguel's expression was inscrutable. Victoria's was defiant. Enrico rolled his eyes.

"Thank you, Detective," Ben said. "We'll think about it."

"You are welcome, Mr. Cooper." He turned to leave, but hesitated. "Do I have your permission to return to the bar if I need to gather more evidence?"

"What do you think, Victoria?"

She weighed her words carefully. "We'd ask that you avoid coming by when the bar is serving customers, unless strictly necessary. And we reserve the right to withdraw this invitation."

"Fair enough, Ms. Holmes." He shook hands with Ben. "Be careful who you trust, Mr. Cooper. The cartel has a very long reach."

The four owners—pretend and otherwise—sat in silence for a long time after Vasquez left. Ben struggled to think of something inspiring to say, but managed only to rouse himself to brew another pot of coffee.

"Thoughts?" Ben finally asked, watching the creamer swirl into miniature hurricanes.

"In case I wasn't crystal clear, I don't think it's the cartel," Enrico said.

"Why's that?" Miguel asked.

Enrico described how Luis, backlit by the sparse lighting outside, had looked as though he was wearing a cape.

"I'm not sure that means anything, Uncle," Miguel said. "Anyone wearing an apron would have looked like that. Even . . ."

Ana. Ben wondered if it was she who had derailed Miguel's train of thought.

He considered mentioning his call with the *Tamarindo Gazette* and Luis's surprise termination, but had reached the same conclusion as Miguel: an apron alone wasn't enough to cast blame on any one person. They needed more.

Besides, that second clue could well be enough to make Enrico set up camp outside Luis's bedroom window. Though the idea had its appeal; if nothing else, it would keep their first pretend-client from charging about Tamarindo in search of the cartel.

Over Enrico's shoulder, Ben watched Ana walk in through the front entrance. She looked as though she'd scarcely slept. He cleared his throat, but to no avail.

"The cartel doesn't go in for aprons in the moonlight," Enrico said. "They go in guns blazing, kill their target and the family along with them. They send a message." He frowned at Ben. "Do you require a lozenge, Mr. Cooper?"

"Can I talk to you for a minute?" Ana asked Ben. If Enrico's comments upset her, she gave no outward sign.

"Of course."

They made their way back to the office in silence. Ben hated to admit it, but Enrico had a point. If the cartel had tried to send a message, he had no idea what it was.

"I want you to forget what happened last night," Ana said once they were inside.

"It's a little late for that, don't you think?"

"I don't want you involved in this."

Ben's smile disappeared. "I got involved the moment Juan walked into my bar. You *knew* he was coming, but you chose to bury your head in the storeroom. If you'd said something earlier, perhaps we could have dealt with this little problem before I found myself on the wrong end of your ex-boyfriend's knife."

"I—"

"I'm not finished. I'm not just some daft sombrero-stealing gringo. I'm your boss. And if I'm going to continue to be your boss, you need to trust me."

Ana gazed at the faded patches of wall where the photos of Antonio had hung until a few days earlier. "Now are you finished?" she asked.

He remembered, belatedly, that he was berating his head bartender the day before she buried her uncle. "Yes."

"I know, I should have told you sooner." Tears welled in her eyes. "But I was ashamed. Do you understand? Do you have

163

any idea of what it's like to feel that way?"

The white van parked outside the clapboard house. Tara, crying. Putting on face paint. A week and a lifetime ago. "I do."

"Can we start over?"

"One condition," Ben said. "You forget about the damned sombrero. Deal?"

"Deal." She laughed despite her tears. "And I would like your help, if you are still willing to offer it."

"God, yes. All I need is one piece of information."

"What do you need to know?

Ben was about to cross a line beyond which there was no guarantee of safe return.

"His email address."

Miguel, Ana, and Enrico were still discussing legendary cartel assassinations by the time Ben returned from the office.

". . . then they cut a large 'Z' in the middle of the roof," Enrico finished.

"You're thinking of Zorro, Enrico," Victoria said, turning to Ben. "How's Ana doing?"

"She's fine," Ben lied, distracted. His conscience tugged at him, but it had nothing to do with their head bartender. "Mr. Morales, I'm afraid we haven't been entirely honest with you," he said. "You were led to believe that we invented Antonio Guiterrez's murder to make your ownership experience more exciting. But Antonio really was murdered, here in this bar. Detective Vasquez was right. Everyone who remains at the cantina is putting their life in danger."

The musician only smiled. "I had deduced as much, Mr. Cooper." He waved at the shattered glass that still littered the floor. "This is all rather more elaborate than the kind of community theatre I'd expected of being a pretend-owner. Apart from Vasquez. That man is the most wooden performer I've ever seen."

"And you still want to stay on?"

"I do." He smiled at Victoria "I could never abandon a fellow musician in a time of need. And don't worry, nephew. I will not call your *abuela*. Not until we have the enemy cornered."

Ben looked at Victoria and Miguel in turn. "Are either of you having second thoughts about staying on? I wouldn't blame you if you did."

"And let you have all the fun? I think not," Victoria scoffed. "Besides, I'd rather face the cartel than go back to Mansion with my tail between my legs."

"I want to see this through," Miguel said. "Besides, I don't think they'd let me through security looking like this."

Ben smiled. "Thank you both. It's a brave decision. Or foolish. Either way, I'll do what I can to make sure you don't regret it."

"What about you, Ben?" Victoria asked.

"What about me?"

"You have your passport back. You can leave now, if you want."

He shook his head. "There's nothing for me back there." As strange and exhausting as the past week had been, he couldn't imagine returning to the life he'd left behind. "So, what now?" Then he cursed inwardly. His not-so-rhetorical question might as well have been an engraved invitation calling upon Enrico to swivel Tamarindo's criminal elements into submission.

"What's everyone looking at me for?" Enrico asked. "I'm not going to go off half-cocked, if that's what you're worried about. I enjoy a good mystery as much as the next guy, but we've nothing to go on. We have to stick it out and see what happens next."

Ben breathed a sigh of relief.

"In that case . . ." Victoria opened her notebook. "I think it's time we discussed your ownership experience."

Ben waited in line at Café Tico, a diminutive coffee shop tucked along one of Tamarindo's meandering side streets. The din of conversation and music, grinding beans, and clinking dishes proved a welcome distraction from the squeal of sirens and the crack of shattered glass.

He stared at the menu, thinking instead of reading. The conversation with Enrico had been . . . enlightening. He'd known their pretend-owners would have some unusual requests but, well, this one had come as a surprise. Ben had no idea where he would find—

"Sir?" the barista asked, snapping him from his reverie.

"Uh . . ." He looked up at the chalkboard once more. What was the difference between a mocha and a macchiato, anyway? The hell with it. It would take more than a choco-latte mocha-something to pay the interest on his sleep debt. "Triple espresso, please."

The cash register chimed. "Would you like anything else?"

"No, thanks." An idea struck Ben. "Actually, do you know where I could find . . ." He leaned forward and mentioned a few of the more esoteric items on his shopping list.

She took a step back. "I have no idea where you get those, sir."

Worth a shot. He paid for his order and waited near a decadent array of baked goods, wondering where on earth he could find those supplies. He hated to even consider it, but Chris Christianson—

"Hiya, Ben," said a familiar voice over his shoulder.

He turned and saw Jenni at the end of the lengthening line. "Hey, you. You following me?" he asked with a relaxed smile.

"Following you?" Her entire body tensed. "Why would you say that?"

"Never mind. It was a joke," Ben replied. And a great one at that. Everyone knew the best jokes were those you had to explain.

"Ha ha ha ha ha!" Her laugh, so charming the night before, was now that of an electronics salesman attempting to unload his last VHS player.

"So . . ." Ben said, struggling to change the subject. "How was practice?"

"Practice? Oh. Right. Practice. It was good. Lots of waves and such." She checked her watch. "Would you look at the time? I've got to head off. All right if I swing by the cantina later?"

"Sure, I guess . . ."

Jenni left the coffee shop without another word.

Bizarre. Was Jenni some kind of stalker? Was that what Ana had been trying to warn him about? And why had she left the coffee shop without ordering anything?

Something grazed Ben's elbow. He spun in place to find his triple espresso and a nervous barista.

Ben pushed Jenni from his mind. He had some shopping to do.

"Did you get it?" Miguel asked, a frantic look in his eye.

"Most of it." Ben set the heavy, brown paper bag down on the bar counter.

"Most of it?" Miguel echoed, peering inside the sack. "I don't think 'most of it' is going to cut it for Enrico."

"You saw the list, Miguel," Ben said. "You know what I'm up against."

"Yeah, but . . ."

Victoria stuck her head out the pass-through. "What's taking so long?"

"Ben didn't get everything on the list," Miguel said.

"What?" Victoria ducked back out of sight and then came over to the bar. "Enrico was very particular about that list."

"I know, Victoria," Ben said. "I was there, remember?"

"I doubt I'll ever forget." She sighed. "What's missing?"

"See for yourself." He gestured toward the bag.

She began rifling through the supplies.

"Where did you find all that, anyway?" Miguel asked.

"One of the concierges at the Diria put me in touch with his supplier," Ben said. "The address alone cost me five thousand *colones.*"

"A bargain at twice the price, brother."

"What about Enrico's other request?" Ben asked.

"Luis knows a guy that can help us out," Miguel said. "He'll be here at seven."

"He knows what's required of him?"

Miguel nodded. "He even has his own equipment."

"Perfect."

Victoria finished her inventory. "We're close. Very close. Perhaps if we substitute dry ice for the liquid nitrogen, we can—"

They turned at the sound of footsteps. Enrico stepped from the back hallway, clad in a splattered apron, elbow-length gloves, and a dust mask. "Where are my ingredients?" he demanded.

Luis followed a few steps behind, clutching a cardboard box filled with forgotten gadgets pillaged from the storeroom.

"Right here, Mr. Morales," Ben said.

Enrico stepped forward, holding his gloved hands skyward like a surgeon bound for the operating theatre. He nodded toward the bag. Ben withdrew each item in turn.

"No sparrows' eggs?" Enrico asked between the gold leaf and

the rosemary syrup.

"Out of season. But I was able to procure three fermented cones from the monkey-puzzle tree." He withdrew the spiked bulbs from the bag, each the size of a large softball.

Enrico judged the haul in silence for a few heart-rending moments. "You've done well, Mr. Cooper," he said. "Luis, bring them to my laboratory."

Luis dutifully gathered the ingredients and followed Enrico into the back hallway. Ben looked at Victoria, puzzled. She mouthed the word *kitchen*. He would have preferred something at a safer distance—Guatemala, perhaps—but at least Enrico was conducting his experiments somewhere well ventilated. The fire extinguisher wouldn't hurt, either.

"How's it going so far?" Ben asked in a low voice.

"He's created two concoctions already," Victoria said.

Ben raised his eyebrows. "Not bad for a few hours' work."

"On closer inspection, they proved to be a Blue Hawaiian and a French 75."

Miguel shrugged a shoulder. "We did tell him that inventing a new cocktail was harder than it seemed."

"We certainly did," Ben said. "And that's when Dr. Jekyll handed us that bloody grocery list."

Enrico's voice echoed from inside the kitchen. "Luis, did I ever tell you that I started my entertainment career as a juggler?" A hollow crack unleashed a rancid aroma not unlike blue cheese wrapped in gym socks.

"Do you think we should, you know, give him a hand?" Ben asked with no small amount of reluctance.

Victoria shook her head. "I tried that already. He said my presence was 'impeding the creative process.' "

Luis dashed down the hall toward the dumpster, garbage bag in hand.

"Heaven forbid," Ben said.

He and his friends retired to the lounge. "I almost forgot." Miguel reached into his pocket and pulled out Ben's battered phone. "I found something interesting last night."

"Let me guess," Ben said. "A video of me trying to steal the sombrero off the wall?" He almost hoped that was the case. They could post it on YouTube and live off the royalties.

"Even better."

"Was there another article of clothing? A pair of socks nailed to the ceiling, perhaps?"

"You were dictating some of your bright ideas for the bar into the voice recorder."

Victoria clapped her hands together. "I'm so glad they were recorded for posterity's sake."

"Yes, I was quite the posterior that evening." Ben sighed.

"I'll play it for you." Miguel tapped the screen and set the phone down so everyone could hear.

Ben's slurred voice came over the phone's tinny speaker. "Note to self. Monkeys. Costa Rica has lots of monkeys. What about a bar with monkeys? And what if they wear little tuxedos? Monkey butlers. What would someone pay to rent a bar with monkey butlers?" There was a brief silence, then the sound of ice cubes tinkling in a glass. "Another rum!"

"Right away, Mr. Cooper," said a faint, heavily accented voice.

"Was that Antonio?" Victoria whispered.

It was. This all felt uncomfortably familiar.

His past self continued, "Note to self. We need a mascot. What kind of mascot? Larry the Lizard? Bloodbeard the Pirate? Toby the Dancing Sloth? Toby the Dancing Sloth. Contact tailors for pricing on a costume. One size fits most." There was a scuffling noise, as if the phone were being put down clumsily.

"Here you are, Mr. Cooper." There was the faint sound of liquid splashing into a glass, then a brief pause, and the further burble of booze. Antonio had a very generous pour.

"Thanks, Antonio." A pause, then the thud of a glass on the bar. "I love you, man. You're . . . you're . . . like . . . amazing." A belch. "I don't feel so good."

"It's a nice night, Mr. Cooper. Why don't you go for a walk and clear your head? Take the bottle with you. On the house."

"Hey . . . thas . . . that's a great idea."

Glass slid against wood, a cork popped. "A doast!" Ben could almost hear himself swaying on unsteady feet. He wished they'd recorded him trying to steal the sombrero instead. "What should we doast to?"

"To dreams coming true."

"To the teams drumming crew."

Ben closed his eyes as he listened to himself stagger off across the tiled floor.

"I must have—" he began.

Miguel held up a finger, shushing him. There were a few seconds of silence, then a series of faint tones. Someone dialing a cell phone. Antonio started speaking Spanish. Miguel translated, " 'Hello.' 'It's Antonio.' 'Never mind that. I need to return some bottles. Quickly.' 'Tonight.' 'No.' 'Not rum or gin. This is different. Trust me, it's worth your time.' 'Fifteen.' 'Your place in an hour?' 'See you then.' "

Miguel stopped the replay. "Ana returns to the bar a few minutes after the call and the recording cuts off. I think your battery died." He looked grim. "I hate to say it, but Vasquez could be right."

"About what?" Ben raised an eyebrow. "That the cartel is branching out into bottle returns?"

" 'Bottles' sounds like a code word," Miguel said. "I think Antonio was trying to unload drugs or stolen goods. Maybe even weapons. It wasn't the first time, either. 'Rum' and 'gin' were whatever he usually sold. Whatever these 'bottles' were, they were different."

"And 'fifteen?'" Victoria asked.

"I don't know. It could have been the number of bottles, or something to do with the price. Either way, I think he was trying to clear out those goods as fast as possible."

It was bad enough if the murder was a robbery gone wrong; far worse if it involved a far-reaching crime syndicate. "So much for Antonio steering clear of the cartel and pushing out the drug dealers," Ben said. "It sounds like he was more concerned with keeping the competition at bay than with keeping drugs out of his bar."

"We shouldn't jump to conclusions," Miguel said. "I have no proof of any of this, only my gut feeling."

"Perhaps Antonio loved recycling?" Victoria turned to Ben. "Whatever his plans, it's clear he wanted you out of the bar as quickly as possible."

Ben hadn't considered that. He was still coming to terms with how different the Antonio on the recording was from the man he had imagined, or the uncle Ana had described.

Inspiration struck. "Did you find anything on the phone about what I want to be when I grow up?"

"What?" Miguel asked.

"Never mind," Ben said. "Did Chris make any calls with it?"

Miguel shook his head. "Nothing from Chris, but Tara called last night. She left you a voicemail message. I don't think it's the first one, either."

Ben had checked his voicemail for the first few days after his phone was stolen, but forgot about it entirely when the cantina started to take off. "I'll deal with that later." He coughed. "I'd rather face the cartel right now, to be honest. Any other thoughts about the recording?"

"Toby the Dancing Sloth? Really?" Victoria asked.

"Any *other* other thoughts about the recording?"

"Only the obvious one—whatever Antonio was selling, it's still here."

CHAPTER TWELVE

"Perfect in every way, but she has flamethrowers for hands."

"I don't think that is the way the game works, Enrico," Ana said, pulling a bottle of wine from the fridge.

She held the bottle up for Miguel, who retrieved it without looking. He passed back a dampened margarita glass, which she rimmed with salt and filled with tequila moments before he poured the rest of the mix inside. No wonder the two barely spoke to one another. They didn't have to. And they still did the work of five bartenders.

Leaving Ben free to entertain Enrico.

"Well, Mr. Cooper?"

"No, Enrico," Ben replied automatically, having already rejected almost-perfect women with robot husbands, scurvy, and "laser skin," whatever that was. "She'd have a hard time bathing our future children, for one."

"But not drying them off afterwards," Enrico pointed out.

He had Ben there. "Perfect in every way, but she only has eyes for her knight in shining armor," he said. "Literally."

"A difficult proposition for a drummer," Enrico mused. "On the other hand, a fine set of chain mail can be quite practical in day-to-day life. Back when I was working at an archery club in Sacramento . . ."

Ben zoned out as Enrico debated the relative merits of different types of gauntlets. It had proven a quiet day at the cantina, giving them time enough to clean up the rest of the mess from last night's unwanted guest. And consider the implications of the recording on Ben's phone.

He'd wanted to go to the police. Then Victoria had explained how much money they'd lose if they closed the cantina while Tamarindo's finest tore the place apart looking for whatever it was Antonio had hidden.

Assuming it was still here. Those officers could go through a lot more drywall before they decided it wasn't.

On the bright side, Enrico's drink experiment had been a success. So he claimed, at least. He'd sealed up the mixture and placed it in the storeroom to allow for "secondary fermentation." Ben didn't like the sound of it—neither the words themselves nor the angry burbling emanating from inside the jug—but Miguel had assured him the experiment was unlikely to cause a fire. Mass blindness, on the other hand . . .

Ben's phone buzzed once as a reminder. 6:45 p.m. Fifteen minutes until Enrico's next pretend-ownership experience kicked off. He let out a measured breath, readying himself for what lay ahead.

Enrico continued, ". . . and then there are the practical matters of romance to consider. If the suit of armor must always be *complete,* for instance . . ."

A lanky Latino in a plain white T-shirt walked into the bar. He gazed about, searching, then caught Luis's eye. The two exchanged a few words before Luis once again vanished into the dining area to collect the plates from a recently deserted table.

That was their man.

Grateful for an excuse to interrupt, Ben turned to Enrico. "The crow flies at dusk. His white-tipped wings do not disturb the leaves."

Enrico froze. Ben wondered if he'd somehow garbled the secret phrase. He bloody better well not have, after all the time he'd spent practicing in the men's room, much to the confusion of the customers.

Enrico spotted the man in the white T-shirt and replied, "The eagle sees the crow and readies himself to plummet through the clouds."

"If you'll excuse me, Mr. Morales, I need to go fold some napkins."

Ben seated himself at a nearby table and waited for their man to approach Enrico. White T-Shirt studied the menu pinned by the entrance as though—

A hand touched his shoulder. Ben spun and found himself face-to-face with Jenni. "Is everything okay?"

"Just fine, thanks," he said, eyes twitching back toward the drama ready to unfold. "How are you?"

"Parched," she said with feeling. "Can I get a drink?" She took a step toward the bar as White T-Shirt made his approach.

"No," Ben said, louder than intended. They'd warned their other patrons, but Jenni must've arrived after Miguel made his rounds. "I mean, it's a nice night. Why don't we just enjoy . . . this table?"

"Are you sure you're all right?" she asked. "You're acting really odd."

White T-Shirt said a few words to Enrico, then reached into his pocket.

"You might want to stand back a bit," Ben said.

Enrico wasted no time. He leaned forward and grabbed White T-Shirt by both shoulders, dragging him across the bar and plunging his head into a sink full of ice. Angry Spanish filled the air and, for once, Ben understood a few words. Mainly the swearing, but it was a start.

"Nobody move, this is a robbery," someone shouted. Another man in a white T-shirt stood near the bar, clutching what was obviously a rubber knife.

Uh-oh.

The bar went silent, but for the clatter of ice sliding into a head-shaped void.

"Oh, the hell with it," Enrico said, vaulting over the counter and onto the second man's shoulders.

Jenni really had disappeared this time. Ben wasn't sure exactly when. Sometime after their table was upended, but before Enrico conked two brawlers' heads together like coconuts.

Ben had made peace with her departure. Then he barricaded himself in his office in the hope that he might, for once, enjoy a quiet night.

There was a knock on the door. He considered playing dead, then relented and muttered a greeting.

Ana pushed inside and sat in one of the visitor chairs, beer in hand.

"Everything all right?" Ben asked.

She nodded. "I just want a few minutes' break."

"Here?"

"I use the storeroom, before. Now all of you know to look for me there."

Point taken. Besides, there was room enough here for two to escape the outside world.

"I thought Luis's business partner was a good sport, all things considered," Ben said. Marking their faux robber with a plain white T-shirt wasn't the best idea they'd ever had, even if it was Enrico who'd ultimately jumped the gun. Jumped the knife?

"Luis and Ramon have a fashion show in a few weeks. The word-of-mouth advertising alone is worth a few bruises," Ana said. "Besides, I think Enrico will buy some of their line-up. So there are no hard feelings."

That might be for the best. If any man could use a wardrobe makeover, it was Enrico. Even his undershirts were beige. Ben just hoped Luis's slacks wouldn't burst a seam in the middle of the next bongo performance. No one wanted to see that.

Not that it was much of a bar fight. Even when a few unruly sorts decided to get in on the action, Miguel and Enrico ended the kerfuffle before it got out of hand. Amazing what a sink full of ice could do to cool tempers.

"It's a shame the fight scared Jenni away," Ben said.

"Scare Jenni away?" Ana said. "I thought that was why you hide in the office. She is looking all over the cantina for you."

"I'm not hiding—" Ben said, annoyed. "Wait, what? Jenni's *still here?*"

"I think you need more than a little bar fight to get rid of *her.*" Ana took a swig from her Imperial.

"Why would I . . . ?" Ben stopped, remembering the awkward conversation earlier that morning and her warning the night before. "I don't get it, Ana. You went to all that trouble to set up a romantic date for me and Jenni, then you warn me off. What are you worried about?"

"You are a good guy, Ben," Ana said. "But I am not as nice as you think I am. Jenni paid good money to arrange the Tiki torches and everything."

This was a new one on Ben. "That actually sounds kind of sweet," he said.

"You didn't see the look in her eyes when she ask," Ana replied. "She—"

Miguel burst into the office. "There's someone out behind the cantina," he said. "Stay here."

"The hell with that." Ben rose to his feet. "Where's Victoria?"

"Looking for Enrico."

Bloody marvelous. "Ana, can you mind the bar?"

She nodded and slipped out the door.

He fell into step beside Miguel, and they marched down the hallway toward the metal door leading out to the dumpster.

"Any idea what's going on out there?"

"None. But I know when someone's trying not to make noise."

That seemed like trying to imagine the sound of one hand clapping, but Ben trusted Miguel. If nothing else, Ben knew that if he'd been the one to investigate last night's disturbance, the intruder would probably still be there, playing pool and sipping a mai tai.

Miguel reached for the switch and plunged the hallway into darkness. The heavy steel door creaked and groaned as he eased it open. A razor of light from an outdoor bulb cut into the darkened corridor, widening as Miguel made his way outside.

He nodded toward the outdoors, and Ben joined him in the shadows. He saw little more than the usual motley array of insects orbiting a bare overhead bulb. He strained his ears for anything beyond crickets, the wash of waves, and the faint buzz of electricity in the wires overhead.

There was a rustling in the underbrush beside the dumpster. By the time the noise registered with Ben, Miguel was already three paces out, bounding toward the errant bush. Ben followed, then stopped as he spotted a flicker of movement toward the front of the cantina.

Then Enrico bore him to the ground.

"I've got you now, you—" Enrico began before recognizing his prisoner. "Oh. Good evening, Mr. Cooper."

Miguel emerged from the bushes, looking somewhat chagrined.

"Good evening, Enrico," Ben replied, doing his level best to ignore both the adrenaline flooding his bloodstream and the squishy dampness that had cushioned his fall. "You were expecting someone else, I take it?"

"I was," he admitted. "I was hoping to make the acquaintance of the gentleman Mr. Christianson told us about." Enrico rose to his feet, dusted off his stained suit jacket, and extended a hand.

Ben stood up on his own. "The crack addict?"

"Please, Ben. There are enough labels in this world."

"What should I call him, then? Chris didn't exactly make a full introduction."

"How about . . . an aficionado of recreational substances?"

Enrico seemed awfully concerned about the emotional well-being of a man he'd planned on tackling. Ben knew better than to try and argue the point. Tired as he was, his brain was busy manufacturing covers for a new magazine: *Crack Aficionado*. In this edition, an exclusive preview of next year's glass pipes. Next month—

"Over there," Miguel said.

Ben had almost forgotten that flicker of movement. He looked up once more and spied the silhouette of a tall, thin man in baggy clothing. Ben and Miguel dashed after him, but the man had disappeared by the time they reached the front of the cantina.

"The best laid plans of mice and drummers," Enrico said as they returned.

The rear door flew open, revealing the outline of the world's angriest businesswoman. "There you are," Victoria said to Enrico. "Do you have any idea how long I've been looking for you?"

"Just long enough to find me?" he asked sweetly.

"Uncle Enrico was searching for our eyewitness," Miguel said, positioning himself so as to prevent Victoria from permanently harming his uncle. "Until we scared him away."

Assuming that was even their eyewitness. Whoever visited the cantina last night clearly hadn't found what they were looking for. Perhaps they'd chosen a more subtle approach for tonight.

Enrico clapped Miguel on the shoulder. "Don't beat yourself

up, nephew. It was bad timing, plain and simple."

Ben stifled a yawn. "Do we have many customers left?"

"We're down to two incorrigible drunks and a trio of teenagers with ID issued by the Democratic Republic of Photoshop," Victoria said. "Your floozy left five minutes ago."

So much for figuring out what was going on with Jenni. "Enrico, do you mind if we shut down early?" Ben asked. "Miguel could use the time to heal, and I wouldn't mind getting some sleep myself."

Enrico looked at Miguel, who was swaying on the spot. "Good idea, Mr. Cooper."

"I'd like to rig some tripwires before we go to sleep," Miguel said. "Just in case anyone tries to enter the bar."

Ben nodded.

"Just make sure you clean up the bodies before the rest of us arrive tomorrow morning," Victoria said. "And you might want to lay down some plastic sheeting. It takes forever to get blood out of grout lines."

"Tin cans on a string, Victoria. Not spike pits or poisoned darts."

"Suit yourself," she said with a shrug.

Miguel disappeared into the storeroom to look for whatever it was you built tripwires out of, while Ben brought Victoria into his office.

"Can you make some kind of sign explaining that we closed early?" he asked. "I don't want anyone stumbling into the cantina later tonight." He grabbed a piece of paper and a marker from his desk and thrust them into her hands.

Victoria leaned over to write the sign, then froze. "Ben? We need to have another look at Luis."

CHAPTER THIRTEEN

Ben turned to face Victoria. "What?"

"This paper. It's a loan agreement," Victoria said.

"Doesn't it match up with what we know about Ana?"

"It's not her loan. This one's between Antonio and Luis." Victoria rifled through the papers on the desk and started pulling out individual sheets. "Brutal terms, an aggressive repayment plan, and an interest rate that puts the credit card companies to shame."

"Yikes."

"That's not the worst of it." Victoria looked up. "If Luis missed a single payment, Antonio would have gotten half the value of his clothing line."

Luis seemed like such a nice guy, but if there was anything he'd be willing to kill for . . .

"I'm going to go through the rest of these papers," Victoria said. "Looks like it's going to be another late night."

Ben slept late that morning. Apart from the hours spent climbing the mountain of papers, he was up half the night listening to tin cans in the wind. Then he spent the other half dreaming they'd found a secret passage full of cocaine beneath the pool table. When he emerged from his room, Victoria, Miguel, and Enrico were already hard at work.

"You see? It's a great idea." Enrico pointed at a sketch on the back of a napkin with the tip of his half-chewed pen.

Victoria sighed. "Enrico, I really don't think we should bother Ana with this today."

"It wouldn't hurt to ask."

"It might, actually."

"But if we just—"

"Enrico, I'm *certain* Ana does not want us to bring a keg of beer to her uncle's funeral."

"But think of the extra sales."

Ben took a seat. "Did you bring them up to speed?" he asked Victoria.

"Not yet. I was waiting for you."

"Up to speed on what?" Enrico asked.

Ben revealed what he had learned of Luis and Antonio, including the busboy's firing.

Victoria added, "I couldn't find anything else in that stack, but that doesn't mean we know the full extent of Antonio's racketeering."

"So, Antonio gets Luis to sign away his soul and then fires him?" Miguel said. "That's cold, man. Really cold."

"No wonder he wound up dead," Ben thought, then realized he'd said the words aloud. No one disagreed. Good thing Ana hadn't arrived yet.

"We should have a little sit-down with Luis," Enrico said. "When is he expected to return to the cantina?"

"Not till tomorrow," Ben said. "We're closed today for the funeral."

"Oh, I expect we'll see him sometime before then," Enrico mused.

Ben turned his head at the sound of tires rolling across gravel. A large van pulled into the parking lot. The driver honked twice.

"What now?" Ben asked.

"Tuesday, 9:00 a.m. Keg fridge delivery," Victoria read from her agenda.

At least they'd drown their sorrows in something cold. He walked over to the van and signed the delivery receipt without reading it, reminding himself again to work on his Spanish. For all he knew, he'd just purchased an industrial-sized pizza oven.

The deliveryman and his co-driver wheeled in a large, cardboard-wrapped fridge and unhooked its ancient counterpart from beneath the bar. It took them but a few minutes to load the old fridge onto the van and slide the new fridge into place.

Enrico called from the parking lot, "Mr. Cooper, I've found something that might interest you."

Ben joined his friends outside. The reek of tequila had faded during the night, but the smashed hatchback seemed even more pathetic in the light of day.

Enrico stood on the far side of the car, peering intently through a magnifying glass. *A magnifying glass?* Ben wondered. *Where on earth did he find a magnifying glass?* He shook his head. If this went on much longer, nothing would surprise him.

"What is it, Enrico?" he asked.

The musician pointed at the lurid *Gringo* tag on the side of the vehicle. Ben knelt in the dust beside Enrico, face to face with the skull and crossbones.

"I recognize this graffiti," Enrico said.

"You what?" Ben choked.

Enrico tapped the side of the vehicle. "It's all over Brasilito. I was on tour there a few weeks ago. A few owners of the bars I played had their places tagged. Apparently there's a local vandal who fancies himself quite the street artist."

Ben frowned at the neon-green paint on the side of the hatchback. He enjoyed street art as much as anyone else, but somehow doubted he could recoup his losses by selling the crumpled hatchback at an art auction. It had a certain character, but it lacked the poignancy of a protestor hurtling a bouquet of flowers. Hell, Banksy's tax return had more artistic appeal than that spray-painted skull.

He stood up. "We should look into this. We'll go to Brasilito after the funeral."

"How?" Miguel asked. "We can't take the hatchback. It tops out at twenty kilometers an hour."

"Is there *anything* you can do to make it go faster?" Ben asked.

"You might be able to get it up to thirty if you drove it down a really steep hill." Miguel shrugged. "I could try to fix the transmission, but that'd take days."

Enrico pointed to a sleek, bright red Mercedes-Benz convertible. "We'll take mine."

"Thanks, Enrico." Ben struggled to come up with some reason—any reason—for Enrico to remain behind and spy on Luis, but none came to mind. Worse still, this meant Ben would probably have to ride in the Benz's back seat, which looked like it could scarcely accommodate a four-year-old.

"There's something else." Enrico pointed at the dangling side mirror. Several thick, black streaks ran down the side of the fender. "I don't think your mirror was broken off."

Miguel stared at the streaks. "Really, Uncle?"

"It melted." Enrico ignored Ben's skeptical gaze and continued, "It's simple, really. The mirror was broken off and glued back on before you rented the car. That's what these streaks are—glue." Enrico failed to keep a smug grin off his face.

Victoria leaned in for a closer look. "I think he's right," she said. "I have an idea, Ben. Mind leaving this with me?" She took out her notebook and pen.

Ben agreed and they went back inside. Would a rental company really send out a car with a glued-on mirror? So much for nothing else coming as a surprise.

Ana arrived as the delivery crew finished connecting the draft towers. She wore a black dress, despite the sun and heat.

Miguel gave her a hug. "How are you doing?"

"I am okay," she said. Her eyes were raw and red, but dry. Eventually the tears ran out. Ben knew that well enough.

He took a pint glass from the shelf under the counter, held it beneath the tap, and pulled the handle. Foam overflowed the glass in moments. Bloody fantastic.

"Maybe the keg needs longer to cool down," Victoria offered.

"Perhaps." Ben wiped his wet hands on his pants. "Mind joining me in the office? I have a favor to ask."

Juan awoke to the clatter of pots and pans and the glare of morning light streaming through the window. He shielded his eyes and looked at the clock. It was only 10:35 and already the bitch was in the kitchen. Christ, what was wrong with her? He'd only been there for three nights, and this chick—Lara, Lena, whatever her name was—was treating him like a piece of her damned property.

If he could hold on here a few more days, he could get the cash from Ana and head back to San José, leaving this backwater behind for good. He cracked his knuckles in anticipation of the fun he'd have sending out all those naughty pics to her friends and family once the money was in his hands. That would teach her to lock him out of his own apartment.

Juan pushed off the covers and coughed, then reached through the empty bottles cluttering the night table to grab one of Lita's cigarettes. He lay back in bed, relishing his first drag of the day.

"Juan, honey, what do you want for breakfast?" she asked.

"Nothing, baby," he yelled back, then clamped a hand to his pounding forehead. All he wanted was some peace and god-damned quiet. Was that too much to ask? He'd need to have a little talk with Luna and tell her what he thought of being woken up at this ungodly hour. His head still throbbed from everything they'd done last night. Well, he knew how to fix that.

"Baby," he called. Then louder, "Baby!"

"Yes, honey?" She poked her head through the doorway and smiled. "Are you sure you don't want breakfast? I made eggs and toast."

Juan ashed his cigarette over the side of the bed. "Baby, are there any five-one-twos left?"

Her face fell. "No, honey. We popped them last night, remember?"

He didn't. He'd blanked out around midnight, after they'd shared his last line of blow. "Baby . . ." he wheedled. "Can you go out and get some more?"

Percocet and a cigarette. That was how to start the day on the right foot.

"Sure, honey. I'll hit up Carlos right after breakfast."

"Can you go now? Please? You know I get these really bad headaches if I don't have a couple of Percs when I wake up." He winced and put on a show of it. Chicks like Lana loved playing nursemaid.

"Well . . ."

"Thanks, baby." He handed her the bunch of *colones* he'd lifted from her purse the night before. "You're too good to me."

He pushed himself out of bed the moment the door shut behind her. Finally, some peace and quiet. Laina hadn't been a bad lay at first, but that was three days ago. A man has needs. He picked up his smartphone and opened his email. Time to get in touch with another one of his ladies-in-waiting, as he liked to think of them.

Nothing interesting in his inbox, just stuff he could ignore. *Blah blah paternity test blah blah.*

But then he spotted a message from a name he didn't recognize.

From: Carlita (carlitaxx69@jmail.com)
To: Juan (juandaman@jmail.com
Subj: Heyyy
Juanito,

   i got ur addy from my frend maria, at club vita. she says you like to party and known how too treat a girl rite. Hit me up next time ur back in San José.

XX Carlita

   Ps. heres my pic . . .

Carlita? She sounded like another strung-out party chick looking to score a cheap buzz. Juan shrugged. It never hurt to have another easy lay to hang with, especially when he was about to score some fast money. He tapped his finger on the attachment at the bottom of the message, but got an error message in return. Goddamned chick didn't even know how to attach a photo.

He tapped out a quick reply, "Hey baby, can u send another pic? Can't wait to see you, I'll be back in San José soon. XX Juanito."

He was about to pull up the photos of Ana when the front door opened with a creak. Juan switched off the phone, hopped back into bed, and reached for another cigarette.

Victoria's laptop dinged and a small envelope appeared in the corner of the screen.

"I don't like this, Ben," she said, "Not one bit."

"Quiet." His fingers flew across the keyboard. "I need one more minute."

"You do realize that what you're doing is a crime in Costa Rica *and* Canada, right? And that I could be disbarred if anyone could prove I helped you in some way? By lending you my laptop, for example."

"Stop worrying. There won't be any trace of this on your

computer. Besides, what's Juan going to do? Tell the police someone thwarted his blackmail attempt by erasing photos he took without permission?"

"You don't know he took those photos without Ana's consent," Victoria said. "You only have her word on this."

"That's good enough for me," Ben replied. An image flashed up on the screen. It was enough to confirm Ana had told him the truth. He closed the window, typed a command, hit enter, and waited.

Finally, the blinking cursor spat out a page of jargon. Ben scanned the log, then rebooted Victoria's laptop.

"What happened?" Victoria asked.

"It worked," he said. "I'm restoring your computer from the backup. Give me ten minutes, it will be like nothing ever happened."

"Not good enough. I need to know exactly what you did."

"Why?"

"That's the price of using my laptop to commit a felony. I need to ensure that, if I'm ever interrogated about your hacking, I know whether they've got real evidence or if they're just trying to shake me down." She sounded calm but resolute. "This clearly isn't your first time, and I doubt it will be the last."

The laptop spun up the disc he'd dropped in the drive and launched a full restore. "You don't want plausible deniability?"

"In for a penny, Ben."

In for a pound. Victoria was right. She deserved to know what he had done. And if she was willing to trust him with her computer and her profession, the least he could do was trust her with one little secret.

"Fair enough." Ben cleared his throat. "I sent Juan a message from a fake email address. It contained malware that opened a back door into his smartphone. I used that to identify and corrupt Ana's photos."

"You wrote a virus?"

"Borrowed. Tweaked." He shrugged. "Think of it as a tool in my toolkit."

"Until five minutes ago, I didn't even know you owned a hammer," she said. "What if Juan made copies of the photos?"

"His email password was stored in the phone. I fed the file parameters into my script, which hunted for the photos and replaced them with corrupted duplicates. The message is still there, but it's filled with garbage." That was the part that could land him in real trouble. Juan's email account was hosted by a major multinational. The server was on US soil, which meant his script had violated a half-dozen American laws in milliseconds.

If Victoria realized any of this, she didn't let on. "And what if Juan has the photos backed up on another computer?"

"My bet is he doesn't. The photos were valuable only as long as he could hold them over Ana's head. The more computers they were on, the greater the chance someone else would leak them. Even so, the virus will use any of the Wi-Fi passwords stored on the phone to scan computers on the network and perform the same kind of bait-and-switch routine it did with Juan's email account."

"Juan gets around, Ben. He could end up infecting half the computers in Costa Rica."

Ben shrugged. "The virus self-destructs after each find-and-replace operation."

"I'm still not comfortable with this."

"I know what I'm doing."

The laptop beeped to signify that the restore program was finished.

Victoria watched as Ben removed the disc, snapped it in half, and melted the remains with a butane lighter. "That's what scares me."

"Come on," Ben said. "We're late."

CHAPTER FOURTEEN

Candles placed on either side of the coffin cast a pale, flickering light on the shroud covering it. The priest's voice reverberated off the church's high ceiling, rising and falling in volume, washing over the congregation in waves. It was Ben's first Catholic funeral, and it felt longer than any of the others. Probably because it *was* longer. Funerals always made Ben feel morbid. Morbid and restless. It didn't help that he couldn't understand either Spanish or Latin. And he never knew what to do with his hands except clamp them to the funeral program.

The priest paused. Everyone stood up, Ben a half second behind the rest. There was a chorus in Latin (Spanish? Spatin?) but he stayed quiet. He could have mouthed the words, had he known which words to mouth. Surely he knew *some* Latin that could fill in the gaps. Plant names, perhaps? The congregation sat down, Ben last among them. The priest resumed his monologue.

Ben glanced up and down the length of the pew for the umpteenth time. Ana was staring at her lap, her cheeks still dry. Had she come to terms with Antonio's death or was there another motive behind her lack of emotion? There would be no eulogy at this service; instead, they would have a small, private ceremony on the beach at the cantina, after Antonio had been cremated. Miguel had told him they were going to empty Antonio's ashes there. It was fitting, if of questionable legality. Or could you get a permit for that? Better not rock the boat.

He tugged at his oversized collar. It was getting hot. He could feel the sweat trickling down the back of his neck, spreading through the suit he'd borrowed from Enrico. The jacket hung around him like a tent and every time he stood, he had to hitch up the waistband, which meant the pant legs stopped mid-calf. Still, it was better than attending a funeral in a T-shirt.

Stand up. "Ahem . . . *Caveat emptor. E pluribus unum, modus operandi.*" Sit down.

Ben stared around the church, searching for something to rest his eyes upon. His gaze turned to a marble statue near the altar. Even the most humble Catholic Church seemed to overflow with stunning works of art, but this statue was unlike anything he'd ever seen. The sculpture depicted a woman— Mary?—holding Jesus in a tender and loving embrace. The ghostly flesh seemed to want only blood to come alive.

How on earth had a sculpture like that found its way to Tamarindo? Brought in by a cartel leading light, perhaps. Someone hoping to salve his soul for some unspeakable crimes? Or was he seeing the hand of the cartel everywhere?

The mourners rose to their feet once more and began to shuffle out of their pews. Was it over already? The line started moving toward the front of the church to take Communion. Ben stood up to join them, but then Miguel motioned for him to stay put. Right. Not for the uninitiated.

Perhaps Victoria had the right idea. At the last minute, she had graciously excused herself from attending the funeral so she could tackle some outstanding accounting. For once, the notion of diving into a pool of paperwork rather appealed to Ben.

He wondered where they would find the money they—he—so desperately needed. His prayer was not for the dead, but that Enrico had one or two wealthy friends willing to shell out for a week or two of pretend-ownership. He had no idea what they could do, otherwise. Cold call some travel agencies? March around the streets of Tamarindo wearing a sandwich board? It might yet come to that.

He searched for something pleasant to think about. Perhaps Jenni would stop by again. Better yet, perhaps there was a reasonable explanation for her . . . enthusiasm. It had only been a week and change since Ben called off the wedding, and he wasn't quite ready for something this intense. He could go days without thinking about Tara, and then something impossibly small—a word, a gesture, even a smell—would bring it all crashing in on him, burying him alive. He had grown tired of digging himself out, over and over again.

Enrico cleared his throat loudly. Ben turned to his right. Everyone from his pew was neatly lined up, waiting for him to let them back to their seats.

No doubt about it. Whatever Victoria was doing, it was better than this.

A cockroach skittered across the floor and hid beneath the sagging bed, mere feet from Victoria. She chose to leave it where it was, having already learned that Costa Rican fauna did not die easily. She resettled herself on the battered wooden chair and picked up her binoculars. The target was still in place.

The upside of staying in a cheap hotel room in a tropical climate was that no one wondered why the window was open in the middle of the day. The downside was, well, there were *many* downsides, but cockroaches were the worst of them. She lowered the binoculars and double-checked the chair's distance from the window. About ten feet. Close enough to see what she needed to see, but far enough back that there would be no glare from her binoculars. The stink of mildew, the grunting noises coming from the room next door, and the crisp hundred dollar bill she'd slipped the clerk at the front desk were a small price to pay for this kind of concealment.

She checked her equipment once more. Her weatherproof, hardened laptop confirmed that the tracker's signal was still coming through strong. She extended the tripod on the parabolic microphone and pointed the dish at the small café framed by the open window. The target was still silent, but there were plenty of other people within range. Victoria chose a table with two catty-looking twenty-somethings and flipped the switch. ". . . going to happen when you're sleeping with a married man," she heard over her headphones.

"Can you imagine what his wife would say? She has no idea he's screwing her . . ." Clear as a bell. She switched off the mic.

Years earlier, Victoria might have been tempted to continue listening to such gossip, but she had done this too many times to risk her batteries running down or her primary target slipping away. She picked up her Canon SLR camera, attached the telephoto lens, and snapped a few quick photos of the backbiters. Victoria could barely hear the click and whir of the camera above the background noise of the hotel. She looked down at the camera's display to inspect the test shots. Perfect. Her checks completed, Victoria settled in to wait.

This was one of the reasons that her firm—Mansion's firm, that was—could charge two thousand an hour for their services. Once upon a time, they'd hired contractors for this sort of research, under the supervision of one or two promising associates. A few costly mistakes had persuaded Mansion to cut out the middlemen and train the associates to handle the surveillance themselves. Not only had that eliminated loose ends, it also meant the surveillance operators couldn't be made to testify if they inadvertently learned something compromising about one of their own clients. Solicitor-client privilege was a wonderful thing.

Even so, they mainly used the information gathered during these sessions to steer their more traditional lines of inquiry. It would have been poor form to use a lawyer's covert photographs in court. Some might consider it rather unethical, if not strictly illegal.

She raised the binoculars and brought the target back into focus. Jenni nursed the dregs of a stone-cold cappuccino at an isolated table on the far side of the café's patio. She kept her back to the wall and faced the street, watching people as they walked past. She was doing a very poor job of waiting for someone. Victoria pointed the parabolic microphone at her table.

Jenni started chewing a nail. That was her tell. She had done the same the past two nights, whenever Ben's back was turned. He hadn't noticed but, to Victoria, it was about as subtle as a brick through a window. So she'd slipped a small tracker into Jenni's purse when her back was turned. Who would notice a stick of lip balm?

If she were doing this by the book, Victoria would have conducted a full pattern-of-life analysis before trying to catch a meet. In as little as a week, she would have known Jenni better than she knew herself—from when she ate breakfast to how often she sped while driving. They hadn't had the time to do this, so Victoria had opted instead to set virtual fences around Jenni's apartment and the section of the coast where the pros liked to surf. Then she'd configured the system so she'd receive a text message whenever Jenni entered or left either of those zones. It had taken all of three minutes between sets to activate. She'd even had time to enjoy a glass of wine before getting back up on stage.

By the following morning Victoria had almost forgotten she'd placed the tracker. Then she'd received an auto-alert mere minutes before they left for Antonio's funeral. When she saw Jenni's dot heading for the outskirts of Tamarindo, she'd thought it might be worth checking out.

It was.

A large Hispanic man in sunglasses and a drab windbreaker stopped on the sidewalk in front of the café. He glanced at his watch, as though waiting for someone, then looked left, right, and left again. He looked at the windows of the hotel as he swung his gaze back for a third time. Victoria recognized a routine check for mobile and static surveillance. He could be their guy. Not his first rodeo, she surmised. She raised her camera, but his head was down by the time the shutter clicked.

He disappeared into the café, moving quickly, and emerged on the patio a moment later. He walked over to Jenni and said a few words. Asking if he could join her, Victoria figured, in case anyone was listening, making himself seem like any guy trying to hit on a pretty girl. He sat down next to her, then slid the metal chair so his back was to the street.

Victoria let out a frustrated groan. She dropped her camera and flipped the switch on the parabolic mic.

". . . so far?"

"Bugger all. He was running around the bar putting out one fire after the next. I barely had time to get to know him." She took a nervous sip from the empty cup. "What's the rush, anyway?"

"You will have to do better than that, Ms. Walker. It could go poorly for you, otherwise," he growled.

"Well, there were a few bits and pieces. The bar's skint, for one. He has no memory of what happened the night Antonio carked it. Oh, and he's got his phone back. Some drug dealer was trying to sell it. At the bar, if you can believe it." She went to bite her nail, but caught herself. "I can get you what you want, but I need more time."

The man exhaled slowly. Nervous? Excited? Victoria couldn't tell. She picked up the SLR and snapped a few shots. She still couldn't see his face, but at least she could prove Jenni was at the meet.

"Have any of them found something unusual at the bar?" the man asked.

"I don't know. Can't really ask him that, can I? You told me often enough what'd happen if he figured out what I was doing there." Jenni sounded tough, but her hands shook as she spoke.

Victoria snapped another batch of photos.

"See him again. Win his confidence. Find out what I need to know. I do not care how you do it." His voice grew gravely quiet. "You know what will happen if you fail to live up to your end of the bargain."

With that, the man rose from his chair and strode out of the café, looking to all the world like any other rejected suitor. Victoria tried in vain to get a single clear shot of his face.

Ben winced as the light struck his eyes. He walked down the stone steps, joining the growing crowd outside the small stone church, and waited for Miguel and Enrico to emerge. The sky was cloudless yet again. Wasn't this supposed to be the rainy season? He fanned himself with the damp program. There was a familiar face in the crowd—Captain Reyes, his neatly pressed dress uniform radiating authority. The group of mourners parted to let him through. He looked surprisingly comfortable in the heat and the press of the crowd. Then again, he would have attended more than his fair share of funerals over the years. He was the kind of person the community would turn to when the world stopped making sense.

"Mr. Cooper," Reyes said politely.

"Captain Reyes. Good of you to attend. I know it will mean a lot to Ana."

"I'm afraid I have other reasons for being here."

"Oh?" Ben suddenly felt cold. "Do you know who left that

death threat at the cantina?"

"Not yet. But we have received your blood work from the evening of Mr. Guiterrez's murder," Reyes said. "Your blood alcohol content was extremely high. It's a small miracle that you suffered no permanent effects."

That's debatable, Ben thought.

Reyes continued, "Mr. Cooper, there is no delicate way to ask. Do you take any prescription drugs? Or engage in casual drug use?" The words seemed to leave a bitter taste in his mouth.

Ben shook his head. "The occasional Advil when I have a headache."

"Nothing else? A small something for anxiety, perhaps?"

"No."

"In that case, I believe you were drugged that evening."

"Drugged?" Some of the mourners turned to stare. Ben kept forgetting how many of the locals spoke English.

Reyes moved a half step closer and lowered his voice. "Yes. Drugged. Benzodiazepine, it would seem."

"Benzodiazepine?" Ben asked, confused.

Reyes lowered his voice further still. "It is sometimes used as a substitute for Rohypnol."

"I was *roofied*?" Ben's stomach lurched. "Wait. Are you saying that I was . . . ?" He turned bright red as fear choked off his voice.

"No," Reyes reassured him with a gentle smile. "There was nothing to suggest that anything untoward happened to you while you were unconscious." The shadow returned to his face. "You're lucky that whoever administered the drug seemed to know what they were doing. They used a small, measured dose. My medical examiner informs me that if barbiturates, ketamine, or even GHB had been used, you would be dead right now."

"You say that as though I wouldn't be the first."

"You wouldn't."

Ben paled.

Reyes continued, "Do you remember anything else from that night?"

Ben shook his head. For a second, he considered playing the recording from the night of the murder for Reyes. Then he thought better of the idea and shoved his hands firmly in the pockets of his ill-fitting pants. They simply couldn't afford to shut down until the police found Antonio's enigmatic "bottles," assuming they were still in the bar. "I'll let you know if anything comes back."

Reyes leaned in. "Mr. Cooper, it is not my place to tell you this, but I feel a certain responsibility for your situation." His breath was hot on Ben's face. "I am no lawyer, but one might say this new development would help you convince a judge to overturn your contract to purchase the bar."

"Give up the cantina?" Ben balked. "Why are you telling me this?"

"Believe it or not, I value the tourists who come to Tamarindo. Yes, there are some who care only for the sun and the surf, but many grow to love this place and the people who live here. When I first met you, Mr. Cooper, I believed you were, at best, a mindless drunk. At worst, a murderer." He tugged the hem of his uniform jacket. "Now I believe you are a brave man with a good heart. But you are, without a doubt, the unluckiest person I have ever met. This may not be a bad time to cut your losses, as they say."

"I'll consider your advice, Captain."

"One other matter, Mr. Cooper. A Miss Tara Whitmore placed a call to our station, searching for you. Our desk sergeant informed her that we do not keep track of tourists and legal matters would need to go through diplomatic channels. She seemed very upset." He raised an eyebrow.

Ben weighed his next words carefully. Did Reyes know the

bar was bought with Tara's money? Was he trying to give him a way out?

Reyes clapped him on the shoulder. "I wish you luck, Mr. Cooper." With that, the captain disappeared back into the crowd as unhurriedly as he'd arrived.

Ben's phone beeped before he could make sense of Reyes's remarks. He steeled himself as he glanced at the call display, fully expecting to see Tara's number. He found an urgent text message from Victoria instead. *I have important news. Let me know when you'll be back.* She never had got the hang of texting in shorthand. The message was perfectly composed.

Ben texted a reply. *Bk soon. Off 2 Brasilito to chk out lead. Or meet 1st?*

There was a lengthy pause. Then: *No. It will wait. Enrico shouldn't see this. You'll need to keep him busy.*

Rgr. E can look 4 Luis.

Sounds good. Let me know when you'll be back at the cantina.

Ben slid his phone back in his pocket. Finally, he spotted Miguel's face in the crowd.

"Sorry we're late." Miguel kept his massive hands planted firmly on Enrico's shoulders. "Uncle Enrico wanted to say a few parting words to Antonio before they took him away."

"I have never seen such a shoddily built casket in all my life." Enrico struggled against his nephew's grasp.

"You didn't have to point out its flaws to the priest, Uncle. Not in front of Ana, at least."

"I thought the Father would want to know. He could have given an extra blessing or something to make up the difference. Those hinges!" He shuddered. "He didn't have to shoo us out of the church like that. The nerve of the man!"

Miguel eyed Enrico. "You pressed your ear to the casket, knocked on the top, and shouted that if it was real mahogany, then you were a French nun."

"I didn't shout, exactly," Enrico grumbled.

Ben had heard enough. "Where's Ana?"

"She was gone by the time we left the church," Miguel said. "She muttered something about having to sort through Antonio's effects. I think she's going to stop by the cantina when she's done."

"Shall we head to Brasilito and see if we can run down our missing vandal?" Ben asked.

Enrico led them over to the parking lot where his Mercedes waited in the sun. He popped open the door and slid into the front seat. Miguel opened the passenger door and looked apologetic as he tilted the seat forward so Ben could wedge himself in back. Even seated behind Enrico, he had to slide his knees up to his chin.

Enrico hit the Benz's start button, and the music picked up where it had left off, blasting at full volume. *"I'm on the highway to hell . . ."*

Miguel and Ben both stared at Enrico, mouths agape.

"What?" Enrico asked.

The Benz flew from the parking lot, shrouding the lingering mourners in a cloud of dust.

The red convertible cruised past the wooden and cinderblock shacks that lined Brasilito's meandering side streets, drawing attention from those who thought they had a pretty good idea of what men inside a slow-moving Mercedes were searching for in that neighborhood.

A thin man with long, greasy hair and stained linen pants approached the Benz. "Hey man," he asked with a predatory grin. "You looking for *anything*?"

Miguel smiled back, then fired off a series of short, sharp phrases in Spanish.

The thin man jumped as though slapped and backed away

from the car toward his herd of equally disreputable friends. Enrico tossed his head back and laughed.

Ben leaned forward from the back seat. "What did you say?"

"Nothing, really," Miguel said. "I told him we were looking for Kalashnikov-pattern rifles, 7.62 mm armor-piercing rounds, Dragon Skin bullet-proof vests, and night vision goggles. Oh, and three kilograms of Semtex plastic explosives. With detonators."

"Of course. Can't forget the detonators." Ben allowed himself a chuckle. "Could you imagine if he'd actually had any of that?"

"I don't know. It would have been nice if he'd had *some* of it."

Ben blinked. What exactly had Miguel done in the Colombian army? He'd always made it seem like he was simply another conscript, serving out his time. Yet, as far as Ben knew, most draftees couldn't casually order enough firepower to overthrow a small Central American nation.

"Look!" Enrico pointed at a ramshackle convenience store. Beneath colorful advertisements for beer and ice cream there was a small Gringo tag, barely visible from the road. To Ben's surprise, it actually looked like art. The vandal must have been practicing since he'd tagged their rental car.

He pointed to the side of a small Internet café. "There's another one over—"

His face bounced off the headrest as Enrico slammed on the brakes. He turned to his nephew. "Do you see? Third boy on the right, in the blue shirt." Enrico pointed toward a group of young men standing on the dusty street corner.

Miguel nodded and threw open the door. The youths turned and glared at him, then shouted something in Spanish. The vandal stood his ground for a moment, then broke from the group in a dead sprint. Miguel dashed after him.

"Hold on," Enrico said.

"To what?" Ben asked, rubbing his nose.

Enrico stomped his foot on the gas, unleashing a wail of rubber and a wall of tire smoke. Ben was mashed back into the leather upholstery as Enrico swung the heavy convertible around the corner.

An oncoming pickup truck blared its horn, flashing past them a split second after Enrico wrenched the convertible back into its own lane. To his right, Ben caught glimpses of the blue-shirted youth and Miguel sprinting under towering trees through the yards of haphazard houses. His head snapped forward as the Benz howled around another corner.

No sooner had he regained his sense of balance than his face bounced off the headrest once more. The squeal of brakes was replaced by silence, broken a moment later as the teenager cartwheeled into the back seat of the Benz, his head landing heavily in Ben's lap. Miguel caught up seconds later.

"Nice catch, Uncle." Miguel loomed over the side of the convertible, barely out of breath.

"Did he leave a dent?" Enrico asked, frowning. "I'd only hoped to slow him down for a second or two. I never thought he'd be stupid enough to run into the car."

"What do you want?" The youth struggled vainly against Miguel's heavy grasp. "I didn't do anything, man!"

Enrico leaned in. "We'll ask the questions here . . . *Gringo.*"

The youth swallowed hard, then glared back at Enrico. "What are you talking about? My name is George."

"Fine, *George.* If you are innocent, why did you run from Miguel?"

"Who *wouldn't* run if *he* was chasing them?"

He has a point, Ben thought.

"Well, then." Enrico chuckled. "You're a bit old for finger-painting, aren't you?"

Ben looked down at George's clenched hands. Despite the

vandal's best efforts to hide the evidence, the tips of his fingers were clearly covered in a rainbow of spray paint.

George—Gringo—turned defiant. "I want a lawyer."

"If I was a police officer, I would be glad to get you a lawyer." Enrico smiled sympathetically. "But I'm not."

"What?" George looked at each of them in confusion. "You're not cops? Why are you all wearing suits?"

The car's engine roared to life. "Let's take a little drive, shall we?"

"No!" George's eyes widened in terror. "Stop! I'll do anything!"

"Ready to come clean?" Enrico revved the engine. "Are you sure?"

George bobbed his head rapidly. Ben thought about confessing himself, if it would spare him another ride in the back of this damned convertible.

The engine cut out.

"All right. Start talking."

When they got back to the cantina, Ben found Victoria alone in the lounge with a glass of wine and a trashy magazine for company.

She didn't bother to look up. "Any luck finding the source of the graffiti?"

"We found Gringo, and he confessed," Ben said wearily. He went behind the bar and fixed himself a drink. A very strong drink.

"Really?" Victoria put down the magazine. "Did you just run into him by chance?"

Ben took a sip and grunted. That was either a potent drink or a mild drain cleaner. "I wouldn't say it was by chance."

Enrico walked in and clapped his hands. "Good news, everyone. I think the scuff Gringo left on the Benz will buff right out. All I need is some soap and a little bit of carnauba wax. Mr. Cooper, I require two of your finest chamois."

Victoria was aghast. "You ran him over?"

"Technically, he ran over us." Ben sat down in the chair next to hers, then turned his mind to Enrico's request. Unfortunately, he wasn't entirely certain what a chamois was, let alone which was his finest. "My regrets, Mr. Morales. The intruder destroyed all of our chamoises last night."

Ben might as well have cancelled Christmas. "Even the sheepskin from New Zealand?"

"Especially that one," Ben said, then told Victoria about the high-speed chase. Meanwhile, Miguel and Enrico fixed drinks of their own, then joined Ben and Victoria in the lounge.

"Who was he working for?" Victoria asked.

"No one." Ben leaned back in his chair and pressed the ice-cold glass to his forehead. "He was in Tamarindo visiting friends, got drunk, and decided our little hatchback was the ideal canvas."

"He said he was sorry," Miguel said. "That was nice of him."

"Nice? *Nice?*" Enrico fumed. "He leads you on a foot chase through the back streets of Brasilito and scuffs my beautiful car, and now he's *nice?*"

"Gringo did think we were trying to arrest him, Uncle."

"Apparently, he was disappointed with the quality of his work that night," Ben said. "He even offered to repaint the car. From what I could gather, he's something of a budding artist."

"We told him the car had bigger problems than a bit of graffiti." Miguel said.

"So, now we're back to Luis," Enrico said.

Ben leaned forward. "If Luis did murder Antonio, he's going to want to get his hands on that loan agreement. One of us should keep an eye on the office in case he breaks in to look for it."

"I'll do it," Enrico said. "If he does show, I'll lock him inside and we can question him at our leisure."

"Are you sure, Uncle?" Miguel asked.

"That burglar wasn't messing around," Ben cautioned. "You could get hurt. Or worse."

"I think I can manage to pull a door shut without getting myself in trouble, Mr. Cooper. Unless you're worried about me being in the kitchen alone with all those sharp knives about? Perhaps you'd like to put some plastic covers on the electrical outlets as well?"

Ben shrugged. "Yell if you need anything."

Enrico stomped off to the kitchen.

Miguel frowned. "I'm not sure how I feel about you leading my uncle around like a cat chasing a laser pointer."

"Enrico's a bit . . . zealous. If he's content to chase after Luis and leave the cartel alone, that's just fine by me. Who knows? He might even be right." Ben turned to Victoria. "What did you want to show me?"

"You're not going to like it," she said, pulling her hardened laptop out of her attaché case.

"If it's a new lead, then I'll like it just fine," Ben said.

"Hold on to that thought." She powered up the laptop and set it on the table.

There was something unusual about Victoria's computer. Its dark steel surface seemed rather more tank-like than the one he'd used earlier that day. "Is that a different laptop?" he asked.

"Consider it another tool in my toolkit."

Victoria opened the photos and audio of Jenni's meeting with the unknown man. When she had finished, Ben leaned back in his chair, his eyes unfocussed and his glass empty.

"Beer?" Miguel asked.

Ben nodded, then turned back to Victoria. "You *spied* on her?"

" 'Spied' is such a harsh term. I prefer—"

"Enough!" Ben yelled, slamming his hand down on the armrest. He lowered his voice. "I've heard enough."

Miguel returned with two pints of foam. "It's cold now, at least."

Ben set his glass down on the table to let it settle and stared at the streams of tiny bubbles, racing to the surface and bursting into nothing.

"What now?" he asked finally.

"That doesn't look or sound like Luis," Miguel said.

"What about his partner, Ramon?" Ben asked. He doubted any of them had paid much attention to Luis's business partner during the bar fight, except to make sure he wasn't badly injured afterward.

"Whoever he is, he gave orders for Jenni to get in touch with you," Victoria said. "When she does, we feed her some misinformation that should draw him out of hiding."

Miguel looked up sharply. "What if he realizes we're playing Jenni against him? He might kill her, too."

Victoria mulled that over for a moment. "What if we wait until Jenni makes contact, then we sit her down somewhere and tell her we know all about her little deal?"

Miguel looked skeptical. "She wouldn't make it as a double agent. You can tell from the recording that she doesn't have the stomach for it."

Ben took a deep breath. If anything happened to Jenni because of him, he wouldn't be able to live with himself. "Let's keep this simple. All we need from her is a name. The police can take it from there."

"And if she doesn't have a name to give us?" Victoria said.

"She'll have something we can use. A phone number. A birthmark. Something," Miguel said. "I'm with Ben on this. We've already tried to do too much on our own. There's a big

difference between running a white-collar surveillance operation
and trying to turn a cartel source."

Victoria thought about it for a few moments. "You're right,
Miguel. We haven't the time or the training to play spymaster.
After we've confronted her, we'll take this to Reyes or Vasquez
directly. Otherwise, we risk the wrong people getting wind of it.
Agreed?"

"Not that I'm objecting to the plan that's least likely to get
Jenni killed, but what if she dashes back to the mystery man
after we make our approach?" Ben asked.

"Then it's a good thing someone planted a tracker on her,
isn't it?" Victoria said.

"Good point," Ben said. "In that case, I agree with your plan."

"Me too," Miguel added.

Ben made a face as he sipped from a glass with more froth
than beer. "Whatever happens, it's absolutely vital that Enrico
knows nothing about this. I just don't trust him not to torpedo
our plans and put Jenni at risk."

Miguel and Victoria both nodded.

"So, what next?" Ben asked.

"We wait." Victoria picked up her trashy magazine.

"Why not approach Jenni now, while Enrico is occupied?"
Ben asked.

"We need to wait until she's here at the cantina." Victoria
flipped to a full-page advert for a product that promised longer
eyelashes and eternal youth.

"It's safer if Jenni is on our turf," Miguel said. "From what
she told her handler, she'll be back tomorrow. We can wait until
then."

Ben looked up at the clock. It was still early afternoon. That
was a long time to sit on his hands.

Miguel yawned, stretching gingerly as he rose to his feet. "I'll
be in my room, taking a nap."

Ben sighed. He'd been struggling against exhaustion most of the morning, but there was no way he could go to sleep now. He wasn't even enjoying his beer.

"I'm going to sort out the damned draft tap," he said.

Miguel eyed him with a mix of surprise and dread.

Ben rolled his eyes. "I promise not to break anything."

"I've heard that before. Be careful."

Ben headed over to the bar and opened the door of the new keg fridge. Everything looked as it should. Well, as far as he knew, at least. All the hoses were hooked up, and each of the gauges was in the green. Perhaps the keg had gotten shaken up? He switched the lines between the two kegs—creating a small lake of beer in the process—and tried the offending draft tap once more. Another pint of foam.

This didn't make any sense. Ben sat down on one of the bar stools. Before the new fridge arrived, they had warm, foamy beer. Now they had cold, foamy beer. The new fridge had fixed the temperature problem, but not the foam. He looked at the gleaming draft tower, a brass pillar secured to the counter with four screws.

Ben fetched a small screwdriver from the toolkit under the sink. He peered at Victoria, who was still immersed in her magazine. He listened for a moment, but heard no sound from Miguel's room. He had a pretty good idea how his friends would react if they saw him taking tools to their latest purchase, and most of the possibilities involved said tools protruding from his chest. Ben slowly removed each of the four screws and gently lifted the draft tower from the counter.

A small cloth bag dropped from inside the tower, spilling open on the counter. A gleaming emerald the size of a sparrow's egg rolled across the counter and into the sink.

CHAPTER FIFTEEN

Ben lunged after the emerald as it tumbled toward the drain. He exhaled sharply when it lodged safely between a lemon slice and a half-crushed martini olive. He picked up the jewel delicately and dropped it back in the bag, where it nestled amongst more than a dozen glittering stones of roughly equal size.

He slid the pouch into his pocket and glanced over at the pass-through into the kitchen. He couldn't believe his eyes. It looked as if Enrico was cooking. Surely not? There was a large pot of water on the boil and a range of utensils out, but together they made no sense. Why did he need a can opener, a rolling pin, and a garlic press? Then Ben realized that Enrico was trying to look at home in a kitchen, despite clearly never having made food for himself at any point in the past three decades. With no idea what any of the implements actually did, he'd simply chosen ones with different shapes and sizes.

Ben dashed over to where Victoria was sitting and grabbed her by the arm. "Come with me," he hissed. "No time to explain." The magazine fell from her hands, and she and Ben snuck past the kitchen and into Miguel's room.

Victoria blushed and clapped a hand over her eyes.

"Hey!" Miguel yelled. He was sprawled on the bed, naked but for a pair of well-worn boxer shorts covered in yellow smiley faces.

"Shhh . . ." Ben frowned. "Lower your voice. And put some

pants on, there's a lady present."

"This is my room!" Miguel said in a whisper with the force of a shout.

"Just let me know when I can move my hand," Victoria said.

Miguel dragged a pair of pants out from under his bed and put them on. "You can open your eyes now," he said. "What's all this about?"

Ben pulled out the bag of emeralds. He opened the drawstring and held one up to the light. Miguel sat heavily on the bed, his arms wrapped around his midsection. His breathing turned ragged.

Definitely a panic attack. Ben put a hand on his friend's shoulder. "Relax, man. You're all right. Take slow, deep breaths."

The reassurance only made matters worse. Miguel's eyes widened as his breaths devolved into rasping gasps. Ben's grip didn't waver. To their surprise, Miguel soon brought himself back under control.

"Quick thinking, Ben," Victoria said.

He almost didn't hear her. He was a thousand miles and decades away, struggling to comfort his cousin Emily after a shouting match between her and her father, the man who had become Ben's guardian.

The weight of the emeralds in his hand brought Ben back to the cantina. He blinked twice and saw in Miguel's eyes a desperate plea for silence. "The same thing happens to me sometimes, when I'm woken suddenly," he lied, removing his hand from Miguel's shoulder.

"Oh," Victoria said, puzzled.

Miguel took the bag of emeralds from Ben's hand. "These are bad news, brother."

"You're thinking this points to the cartel?" Ben asked.

"Fuerzas Armadas Revolucionares de Colombia."

"FARC," Ben said.

Miguel's eyes grew distant. "Or worse."

"Miguel, stop scaring Ben." Victoria plucked a stone from the bag and held it up to the light. "You realize how ridiculous this is, right? Where did you find them?"

"Hidden in the draft tower."

"Hell of a place to stash a small fortune in emeralds," she replied.

"No wonder the burglar couldn't find them," Miguel said. "I should have thought of that earlier. There was a kink in the line. That's why the beer was foamy."

"Antonio must've planned to collect them at the end of the night," Ben said.

"Sounds risky," Victoria said. "What if you'd come back later that night? It was your bar by then, after all."

Ben told them what Captain Reyes had said at the funeral about the benzodiazepine.

Miguel whistled. "That's one way to arrange some privacy."

"Except that someone who knew about these stones came by the bar soon after Ana left." Victoria put the emerald back in the bag and pulled out a larger one.

"Speaking of Ana, we need to tell her about this," Ben said.

"Are you sure?" Victoria asked. "What if she was involved?"

"Not this again," Miguel said.

"Ana deserves to know why her uncle died," Ben said. "Where is she?"

"I thought she was with you," Victoria said.

"She said she was coming back to the cantina," Miguel said.

"She probably got caught up with something to do with the funeral," Ben said.

"I'll give her a call." Miguel borrowed Ben's phone. "No answer," he reported a few moments later.

"She might have forgotten to turn it on again after the service. We'll try her again later," Ben said. "Right now, we need to figure out what we're going to do with these emeralds." He reached for the bag.

Victoria clutched the emeralds to her chest and glowered at Ben, then slowly handed them back. "In case you were wondering, these fourteen little green rocks would more than take care of our financial problems."

"You're not suggesting we keep them?" Ben was astounded. "After what happened to Antonio?"

"While we're at it, why don't we set up our own drug ring?" Miguel asked.

"The bar has a lost-and-found box, doesn't it?" Victoria said. "We'll put the emeralds there. If no one claims them after a month, they'll become the property of the cantina. Done."

"And if someone does claim them?" Ben asked.

"Then we have them arrested for Antonio's murder." Her face was the picture of innocence.

Ben laughed at the notion of keeping the emeralds in a ragged cardboard box between a pair of scratched aviator glasses and a baseball cap that smelled of sardines. "Tempting, but I think we need another plan."

"Suit yourself." She tapped a few numbers into her phone. "By my calculations, you only need to sell 350,000 beers to make up the difference."

He glared at her. "We need to catch this killer. I don't want him coming back here again, looking for these emeralds."

"I have an idea for how to lure him in, but we'll need to pick up some supplies," Miguel said.

"Like what?"

"I need a ski mask, ten pounds of ball bearings, a chainsaw, a tank full of helium, and thirty yards of marine-grade rope."

Ben stared at him blankly.

"Or we could call the police," Victoria said.

"That's probably a better idea," Miguel admitted.

There was a loud crash in the kitchen. "I'm okay!" Enrico shouted. Then, "Has anyone seen the first aid kit?"

"First, we need to take Enrico somewhere he won't hurt himself," Ben said above the racket of another crash. "Or the cantina."

The bar was unusually quiet as Ben paced the floor, waiting for the police to arrive. Even the rustle of the palms and the boom of the distant surf seemed strangely muted. Most days, the place would already be packed with chattering bargoers, backlit by the last rays of the setting sun. There would be no vivid sunset that night; the long-awaited clouds had rolled in from the Pacific, ushering in an early dusk. Heavy raindrops had already begun to patter on the thatched roof of the cantina and drip through its gaping holes.

He flipped on a light to boost his spirits. Miguel and Victoria had dragged Enrico back to the Tamarindo Diria, chasing yet another fabricated clue. He wasn't convinced they could hold the man's attention for more than a few minutes, but Victoria assured him she had the matter well in hand. Miguel had offered to stay at the cantina with Ben, but it made more sense for him to keep an eye on his uncle and keep trying to reach Ana.

He checked his phone. Nothing from Jenni. Maybe she—

There was a knock by the front entrance. Detective Vasquez.

"Good evening, Mr. Cooper." The detective stepped inside when Ben opened the door, brushing the rain from his suit jacket. "I am here for the emeralds."

"Are you sure this is a good idea?" Miguel whispered to Victoria while keeping an eye on Enrico.

"Do you have a better one?" she hissed.

Miguel shook his head.

"This is *fantastic*," Enrico said, pointing the parabolic microphone at some diners in the poolside restaurant. "Oh, you catty little minx." He clucked his tongue. "How could you say that about your very own sister?"

"Remember, Enrico, we're expecting Luis to meet with his supplier this afternoon. Make sure you don't miss him," Victoria said.

Miguel wasn't a fan of this little fiction, but it was safer than telling Enrico about the emeralds.

"Yes, yes." Enrico kept the binoculars firmly planted against his face. "You've told me that three times already. Luis is meeting with one of Chris's clients within the hour. He wants to buy a forged passport and escape to Nicaragua. Why even a fugitive would want to live in Nicaragua is beyond me." He exchanged the binoculars for Victoria's camera and took a rapid-fire series of shots. "So much for your 'secret' liaison, Mrs. Witherspoon."

The camera beeped twice. Enrico frowned at the black screen for a moment, then felt in Victoria's bag for a spare memory card, which he slotted in with the grace of a seasoned gunslinger. The camera beeped again. "Full already? I haven't taken a single picture." He pulled up the photo display with a press of a button.

"What have we here?" Enrico was staring at a photo from Victoria's stakeout earlier that day. "That looks like Ben's lady friend." He flipped through more photos, and then abruptly stopped.

Enrico shot Miguel and Victoria each a look of pure disdain. "Fun's over, you two. I need to see these on a proper screen."

"Would you like a drink, Detective?" Ben asked as they walked toward the office.

"Thank you, no." Vasquez scanned the bar as they went, vainly trying to avoid the streams of water that trickled from the ceiling. "Where are your friends?"

"We thought it best if I handled this on my own." Ben held the door open for the detective.

"That was wise. I am glad you are taking this seriously." Vasquez unbuttoned his sodden jacket and sat in one of the guest chairs. "Where did you find them?"

"The emeralds? Hidden inside the draft tap, of all places."

The detective leaned back in his chair, absently scratching his chest. "The draft tap," he said finally. "Yes. Yes, of course." His damp shirt clung to his skin where he'd scratched, revealing a lurid half-moon bruise beneath the translucent fabric. It looked to Ben to be exactly the shape and size as the wine bottle Miguel had hit the intruder with, two days earlier.

"Next. Next. Next," Enrico barked.

Victoria clicked slowly through the photos she'd taken during the meeting between Jenni and the unknown man. Enrico stared hard at each one, muttering, "Come on. Come *on*. Think, think, think."

He brushed Victoria's hand away from the laptop with a flick of his wrist, wresting control himself, and flipped through a few more pictures. Then he stopped. The hotel room was dark and silent, but for the patter of rain on the window and the hum of the laptop's fan.

"I know this man. I *know* him." Enrico leaned forward, squinting. "I can almost . . ." He grunted in exasperation and hammered a few more keys.

Victoria crossed her arms and glared at the back of Enrico's head, apparently having both second and third thoughts about letting Enrico touch her equipment.

"Did you notice anything in particular, Uncle?" Miguel asked quietly.

"Not really. It's only a feeling." He leaned closer to look at the next photo. "Well, you don't see one of those every day." Enrico zoomed in and pointed to a small black object hanging off the unknown man's belt. "See that pouch?"

"The intruder last night wore one just like it," Miguel said.

"It's a baton."

Miguel closed his eyes and let out a deep breath. He should have known.

Victoria squinted at the screen. "It can't be much more than six inches long."

"It telescopes. There are two or three sections inside. It's about two feet long, extended. Nasty bits of work, those."

"How do you know so much about telescoping batons?" Miguel asked.

"Life on the road isn't all rum and bongos, you know." Enrico glared at Miguel before turning back to the screen. "One of my musician friends carries one for protection."

"Didn't the medical report say Antonio had some strange injuries? A break that was too thin to be caused by a baseball bat?" Miguel leaned over and tapped on the screen. "A telescoping baton would do that."

Enrico clicked through the photos once more. "Now if we can figure out who it is . . ."

Victoria suddenly reached into her bag, pulled out her notebook, and began flipping through it.

"What is it?" Miguel asked.

"Something Ana said a few days ago." Victoria flipped through another half-dozen pages. "Here it is. 'Vasquez once broke a rookie's nose while teaching him how to use the baton.' "

"That's it!" Enrico slapped the desk. "It's his voice on the tape. I knew it. That bloody man never used a contraction in his life."

"We need to get back to the cantina." Miguel reached for the door.

★ ★ ★ ★ ★

"And where are the emeralds now?" asked the detective.

Ben leaned forward and rested his elbows on the desk, ignoring the question. "If you don't mind me asking, how do you plan to catch the murderer?"

"I *do* mind you asking!" Vasquez bellowed, his eyes gleaming with rage. He lowered his voice. "The less you know about police operations, Mr. Cooper, the safer you and your friends will be. Now, where are the emeralds?"

"They're in the safe," Ben said. "I expect you remember the combination from your earlier visit."

Vasquez glowered at Ben, then walked over to the safe, dented from years of use. He knelt down and started to twist the dial.

Ben rose from his chair wordlessly and reached for a clean glass from a shelf. "Are you sure you won't have a drink?" he asked.

Vasquez looked back and shook his head, then returned his attention to the safe.

"Back in a minute," Ben mumbled. "Need to get some ice." He walked out of the office, leaving the door open, and flinched as he heard the safe open with a mechanical thunk.

The light fixture beside him exploded in a cloud of flying glass. "Raise your hands and turn around," Vasquez shouted. "The safe is empty, Mr. Cooper. Where are the emeralds? Hand them over, and you may still get out of here alive. There will not be another warning shot."

Ben lifted his hands and slowly turned around, his ears ringing from the report. The detective knelt by the safe, his pistol trained on Ben's chest. He'd never make it out of the cantina; Vasquez would put a bullet in him before he got twenty feet. He stole a glance to his left, through the doorway to the kitchen.

As Vasquez rose to his feet, Ben dashed into the kitchen, tossing pots and pans from the counter as he ran. Even with his ears ringing, he could tell the detective was gaining on him. He had seconds at best.

He threw open the door to the walk-in freezer and leapt in, slamming the heavy metal door behind him and reaching for a lock that wasn't there. His hands closed on the emergency release latch instead. He pulled the lever as far away from "Emergency Open" as it would go, then jammed a metal tray between it and the wall.

The handle began to move.

CHAPTER SIXTEEN

Blood trickled down Ben's forehead and into one eye. He hadn't felt the cut until then; he must have been hit when the light exploded. He shivered in the darkness, and the frigid air burned his lungs as he struggled to catch his breath. He strained to catch some sound of Vasquez in the kitchen. Silence.

Ben touched a hand to his ears and then rubbed his fingers together in the dark. At least his ears weren't bleeding. It was small comfort. He leaned against the cold, heavy door of the freezer and patted the reassuring weight of the emeralds in his pants pocket, then reached to double-check the tray was still in place.

There was a series of deafening explosions, each joined by the shriek of metal being pierced. A horrifying noise that came again, and again, and again as Vasquez tried to shoot through the freezer's latch.

Ben found his breath. He screamed.

Miguel stopped sprinting about a hundred feet from the cantina, taking shelter beneath a large palm from the pouring rain. Enrico and Victoria caught up with him a few seconds later, after weaving their way around several rapidly growing puddles.

Miguel pointed to a shop across from the cantina. "Wait over there," he said. "I'll go inside the bar and—"

The repeated crack of gunfire cut him off. He ducked his head instinctively, while Victoria and Enrico froze for a few terrifying seconds. Then Miguel grabbed them each by the arm and dragged them around the corner of the shop.

Safely behind cover, Victoria shook herself from her daze and pulled out her phone. "I need to speak to Captain Reyes. Now," she said in Spanish. "No, only Captain Reyes." She listened. "Call him at home if you have to." Her eyes narrowed. "What's this about? It's about you spending the next six months of your miserable life hosing out the holding cell, if you don't get him on the phone in the next three minutes."

She turned to the others. "He's putting me through now."

Miguel motioned for her and Enrico to hug the wall. He leaned around the corner to assess the situation in the bar, but a torrent of rain obscured his view. He tried in vain to hear anything from the cantina above the drum of water on the shop's metal roof. Nothing. He slid back behind cover.

"Captain? It's Victoria Holmes. Shots fired in the cantina. It's Detective Vasquez." She paused. "No, *he* doesn't need backup. *We* need backup. *He* murdered Antonio." Another pause. "Good idea."

She turned back to Miguel and Enrico. "They'll be here soon."

"Who? Reyes?" Enrico asked.

"No. Everyone."

"How long do you think you can play this game, Mr. Cooper?" Vasquez's voice was muted by the freezer door.

Ben shivered. He'd never thought he'd feel so grateful for Enrico's ill-fitting wool suit, but it did offer some protection from the icy cold. His racing heart and the sudden rush of adrenaline had kept him warm for a time, but the effects were already wearing off.

How long before Miguel and Victoria began to miss him, he wondered. They hadn't thought to schedule a meeting, opting instead to message each other as the situation developed. Ben pulled out his cell phone. No signal. Apparently the thick freezer walls blocked more than bullets.

He used the glow from his phone to locate the light switch on the inside of the freezer. He flipped it on, but nothing happened. Right. That was another item on his never-ending list of repairs, somewhere between getting rid of the strange smell in the dishwasher and figuring out why the blender gave off purple smoke. He found the candle Ana had shown him, but had nothing to light it with. He clicked off his phone, plunging the room into darkness.

"You cannot stay in there forever. It is only a matter of time before you freeze to death or run out of air," Vasquez said. "Give me the emeralds. It is your only option."

"Not happening, Vasquez," Ben said. "You'll shoot me the moment the door is open."

"Do you really think I am that kind of man, Mr. Cooper?"

"Would you like an honest answer?"

"If I had wanted to, I could have killed you and your friends countless times over," Vasquez said. "All I wanted was for you to leave the bar so I could find my emeralds."

"*Your* emeralds? How many centuries did you save to buy those on a detective's salary?"

"You can believe what you wish, Mr. Cooper, but I have my reasons for what I have done. I do not expect you to understand, but some loyalties are more important than those represented by a badge."

"That's small comfort for Antonio."

The door of the freezer clanged as Vasquez struck it. "He made his choice!" he yelled. Then, more quietly, "You have no idea what happened that night, do you?"

"Enlighten me."

"Stalling for time will not work, Mr. Cooper. The police cannot help you."

"That's a risk I'm willing to take," Ben said.

"I do not care whether you hand me the emeralds or I take them from your frozen corpse," Vasquez said. "But are you willing to throw away Ana's life along with your own?"

"*This* is everyone?" Victoria fumed.

Captain Reyes had arrived minutes after her call with two squad cars and a single unmarked police car. Four officers fanned out around the cantina.

"Thank you for your concern, Ms. Holmes." Reyes looked grim. "Unfortunately, Detective Vasquez managed to dispatch most of my men on frivolous errands at the outskirts of our jurisdiction. I assure you, they will be here soon."

She waved at the massive gaps between the advancing officers. "In the meantime, Vasquez can drive a bus through this disaster you call a perimeter."

The captain's eyes narrowed as he turned back to face the cantina. He grabbed his handset, the radio cracking to life as he pressed the switch. "All stations, this is command post. Report. Over," he ordered.

"Alpha, no change. Over."

"Bravo, no change. Over."

"Charlie, in position. No sign of the target yet. Over."

"Delta, fifty meters out and closing. Over."

"Roger. Command post out." Reyes released the handset and raised his binoculars.

Victoria and Miguel exchanged a knowing glance. The rain had slackened off enough for them to see that the cantina's lounge and dining areas were deserted and that the windows in the office and the new bedrooms had been shuttered or blacked out. Vasquez knew police procedures and how to counter them each in turn.

Reyes grunted, lowering the binoculars. He leaned in the window of the unmarked car and asked the detective inside, "Have you been able to reach Vasquez on his phone yet?"

"Not yet, Captain."

"Keep trying."

"Yes, sir."

Miguel whispered to Victoria, "Distract Reyes. I'm going inside."

"Do you really think you can make it past Reyes's men *and* take Vasquez by surprise?" she hissed. "You heard those gunshots. He'll kill you."

"He'll try."

The freezer's compressor clicked off, leaving Ben in silence, except for the chattering of his teeth. It seemed a lifetime ago that he'd learned in Boy Scouts how hypothermia killed—first you were cold, then you felt warm and drowsy, and then you fell asleep. And never woke up. The cold and the dark were already starting to make him feel as though he was about to drift off. He had to stay awake at all costs.

"What have you done with Ana?" he asked.

"She is safe. For now."

"I don't believe you."

"You think you know what this is all about?" Vasquez asked. "You have no idea what you and your friends have blundered into."

"So you keep saying."

There was a long pause. "I have closed more cases than any three other detectives combined. I work all hours, day and night, but my wife understands. She knows this is my calling. Sofia never complained. Not even when she got sick.

"She has cancer of the liver. It is very serious, and not one of the doctors we have consulted thinks she can survive. Her cousin is a doctor in the United States. He told us there is an experimental procedure there that may save her life. I have spent the past twenty years keeping the people of this country safe. I have never asked for anything in return, except for this treatment. The Ministry of Health refused.

"I am not an evil man. I could have made a fortune working directly for the cartel. They could have had free run of the coast. They would have become unstoppable. Instead, I simply helped to remove some of their competition. Occasionally, I failed to follow up on a lead. Where was the harm? The men I arrested were all criminals. I never hurt anyone who was innocent."

"Except Antonio," Ben replied.

"Antonio." Vasquez's voice dripped with scorn. "I gave him the same generous offer that I have given to you. He made his choice, and he died by it."

Miguel quietly walked away from the police perimeter. The wind gusted, tearing fronds from the palm trees. Already soaked to the skin, he scarcely noticed the driving rain. He hunched his shoulders and assumed a steady walking pace. In the fading light, he was but another civilian shuffling from one place to the next, invisible in plain sight.

Once out of view, he turned back toward the row of bars and restaurants along the beachfront. The businesses all looked as though they'd closed for the storm, but he kept his eyes open for anyone still inside. Luck was with him; the seafood restaurant he entered was deserted.

He paused for a moment to take in his surroundings. The light was fading fast, but was still bright enough for his purposes. The restaurant's layout was similar to the cantina's, only smaller. He slid behind the bar and started opening drawers.

He carefully checked inside each one until he found what he was looking for. He wrapped his hand around the handle of a long, serrated utility knife and took a moment to gauge the knife's weight and balance. It would do the trick. He turned it in his hand and flipped it into a reverse grip, blade downward, then twisted it so the knife was hidden neatly behind his forearm. Openly carrying a weapon could lead to awkward questions.

He scanned the restaurant and the space between it and the next one. Most tourists never gave the gaps between the beach-front businesses a second glance. Some were separated by a wooden fence, others by a hedge or a few lanky weeds. Enough to keep customers from marching over to the next restaurant when their meals were a half hour late, but not enough to slow a former soldier.

Miguel leapt the fence with a single hop. He moved through the row of restaurants, clubs, and hotels, one after the other, knife in hand.

"What do you mean, you gave Antonio the same choice?" Ben's eyelids were growing heavier by the minute.

"Those emeralds are the only pension I will ever see. The one and only payment I will ever receive from the cartel for turning the occasional blind eye."

"You hid them in the bathroom."

"Antonio invited trouble into his life the moment he decided to steal them from me. My contact handed them off when I was in the bar on police business. I did not expect to be dispatched to a crime scene before I had the chance to put them away safely. I sealed them in an evidence bag and hid them in the tank of the toilet in the men's room."

"But Antonio saw you."

"He always did know everything that went on in his bar,"

Vasquez said.

"Who was your contact?"

"The cartel and I have a very delicate arrangement, Mr. Cooper. Revealing my contact would invite trouble into *my* life. And yours.

"I returned to collect the emeralds later that evening. When I saw they were missing, I confronted Antonio. I am a reasonable man. I simply asked that he return what he had stolen from me. I did not even draw my gun.

"Antonio was not reasonable. He said he would return the emeralds, but he reached for that bat of his instead. He swung at me, so I struck back with my baton. Even after I broke his collarbone, he still tried to kill me with the bat. He would have tried everything. I could see it in his eyes."

"So you took the bat from him . . ." Ben choked on the words.

"I did what I had to do, Mr. Cooper. For Sofia."

"What about the apron and that suspicious bundle? Why try to pin this on Luis?"

"How did you know I was wearing an apron when I left?"

Ben went silent, wondering if his curiosity had condemned some poor addict.

"It does not matter," Vasquez continued. "If you must know, I wore the apron to hide the blood on my clothing. As for the bundle, it held the money from the register, Antonio's effects, and the dish towels I used to remove all traces of my presence. I had no intention of trying to frame your busboy."

Pain enveloped Ben as he touched the cut on his head; when it released him, he found himself clutching a shard of glass. He remembered belatedly that he should have left it where it was, blocking the flow of blood. Too late for that. He pressed his sleeve to the wound before the trickle become a flood.

He cleared his throat, and said with hollow bravado, "Let Ana go. I'll give you the emeralds once she's safe." His sleeve was already soaking through.

"That is a touching offer, Mr. Cooper. But I am afraid you are on the wrong side of the door to make such a demand. Give me the emeralds, and I will release Ana in due time."

"You expect me to trust you?"

"As if your life depended on it."

Miguel crouched behind the fence between the cantina and the small hotel next door. He heard the faint crackle of a radio in the distance, followed by the occasional murmur from one of the police officers surrounding the place. He cursed the weather; he'd hoped the rain would last until he made it inside. Now his only camouflage was the gusting wind and rapidly darkening sky.

It occurred to him that the police might have night-vision goggles. If he were Vasquez, he would have disabled the night-vision equipment before heading to the cantina, but there was no way to know whether they were watching his every move. Miguel took a deep breath. The only way to find out would be getting a bullet in the back, long before he set foot inside the cantina.

All he knew for certain was that Vasquez had drastically weakened Reyes's position. The captain would need to wait until the other officers returned before he could mobilize a strike team and breach the cantina. If he tried to storm in with the handful of officers there now, Vasquez would almost certainly escape. Or kill Ben. Or both. The police could monitor the bar's doors and windows, but nothing more.

He slid through a gap in the plank fence and climbed atop a stack of discarded tires. He slid the knife into his belt and grabbed the narrow eave of the cantina's largest remaining storage room, a windowless cinder-block structure. Once he had hauled himself onto the thin metal roof, he lay motionless on his stomach for a count of ten. His heart hammered in his chest as he waited for the police to open fire, but there was only the rush of the wind. He had gambled that approaching the cantina via the one room without windows or an outer door would let him enter undetected. That bet had paid off.

He slowly rose on his hands and knees. There was less than fifteen feet of corrugated metal roof to cross, but he had to consider each movement carefully, or else risk making a noise that would draw the attention of nervous men with loaded rifles. With painstaking caution, he crossed the roof without a sound.

He held his breath as he crossed onto the thatched roof of the bar itself. Even if the rotten reeds held his weight, it would make noise as he climbed. Still, the sound of creaking thatch should blend with the noise of the palm trees whipping in the wind. He crawled until his pace count put him over the bar, then slid the serrated knife from his belt and began to saw.

He set aside the chunk of the roof, then gently lowered himself through the hole into the cantina, landing with a soft thud.

"We have movement." Captain Reyes lowered his binoculars and raised his radio. "All call signs, this is command post. Prepare to breach, over."

Victoria was shocked. "You don't have enough—"

Reyes cut her off with a wave of his hand. Each of his officers radioed back in turn.

He replied, "Command post, Roger alpha through delta. Hold assault positions and maintain radio silence until my mark, over." He turned to Victoria with barely contained anger. "Ms. Holmes, if you interrupt me once more, I'll have you tossed in the back of this squad car."

"What makes you think—?"

"Vasquez is the best detective I have ever worked with. He

knows our procedures better than I do. Right now, he believes he has delayed us for several hours. It is getting darker by the minute, and he will soon have free run of the cantina to do as he chooses. If we wait any longer, there is a very real chance my officers will walk into a death trap. I'm done reacting to Vasquez. It's time for him to start reacting to us."

Victoria opened her mouth to say . . . say . . . What could she say? Miguel is inside? He told me to trust him? He sounded really confident about it?

Reyes keyed his handset. "Breach."

Miguel checked the pass-through between the bar and the kitchen. A steel tray had been wedged into the frame to obstruct the view from outside. He sidled toward the kitchen door, his back brushing the shelves of liquor. He stopped and stared at the knife in his hand, then reluctantly set it down. A knife fight could only end one way, and he wasn't prepared to add another death to his conscience. He resumed his slow approach, the detective's voice growing more distinct with each step he took.

He rounded the corner to the hallway and peered through the kitchen door, leaning in until he glimpsed the back of Vasquez's suit. He pulled back. From the walk-in freezer to the countertops, every surface in the blasted kitchen was gleaming stainless steel. His odds of catching Vasquez unawares were now nil. On second thought . . . He slid back into the bar and looked along the cluttered counter. A beer cap. Perfect.

He tossed it down the hall. The cap spun through the air and landed between the kitchen and the bedrooms with a faint clack, not unlike the sound of two magazines full of ammo clicking against one another. He could hear Vasquez's footfalls as he moved to investigate the strange noise. Miguel counted the seconds. *One one thousand. Two one thousand. Three one thou—*

There was the faintest noise of metal rubbing against wood.

A second later, Miguel caught a flicker of movement in the doorway, then he heard the safety catch on Vasquez's pistol click. Miguel struck out as he spun in place, slamming Vasquez's arm against the doorframe.

He grabbed the pistol with both hands, but could not break the detective's grip. He slid his finger inside the trigger guard and squeezed. And squeezed. The bar filled with thunder and lightning. Then the slide caught on the pistol's empty magazine.

Reyes's radio crackled. "Shots fired. Say again, shots fired."

Victoria could hear the panic in the officer's voice. Reyes replied with icy calm, "Respond with all force necessary."

Miguel's grip tightened around the pistol as it slipped from Vasquez's hand. He had to get inside the kitchen. He rounded the corner into the hallway and turned to—

He stared down the barrel of a submachine gun and saw the wide-eyed police officer at the other end. There was a flash, and everything turned black.

CHAPTER SEVENTEEN

Ben swam on through the brilliant sapphire of the ocean. He propelled himself into the dark abyss, farther and farther from the surface, chasing a faint flicker of movement. The water grew colder as he swam, and soon he was shivering uncontrollably in the ocean void.

Still he drove himself onward, until he finally caught a glimpse of his goal: a rum bottle on a string, being trolled through the water. Ben looked up and saw a wooden hull far above him drift away and vanish.

He rose slowly to the surface, gasping for air, and found himself surrounded by a troupe of clowns riding miniature jet-skis. They raced around him, honking bicycle horns and dousing him with their wakes. Ben clawed frantically at the pitching waves around him, choking on the saltwater.

One of the laughing clowns tossed him a life preserver. Ben wrapped his arms around it, only to have it deflate with a flatulent trumpet. He sank back into the depths of the ocean, his eyes fixed on a lone clown floating above him, calling his name. "Ben . . . Ben . . ."

He knew that voice. That wasn't a clown. He slowly swam back to consciousness.

"He's waking up," Victoria said over her shoulder. She turned back to Ben. "How are you feeling?"

"Awful," he said. "What happened? I heard gunshots."

"Relax. You need time to warm up."

Ben looked down at his prostrate form. Someone had laid him on a couch in the cantina's lounge and covered him with a reflective survival blanket. He sat up slowly, cradling his bandaged head in his hands. He never thought he'd have a headache worse than the one he'd had in jail. But he did.

"Here, drink this." Victoria handed him a warm mug. "It's an old family recipe."

"Thanks." Ben took a sip and choked. "It tastes like camphor and death."

"I said old, not good."

He managed a smile. What a strange dream. The ocean was like a jewel, a sapphire . . .

He looked over Victoria's shoulder, finally noticing the hive of activity in the cantina. The bar lit up with a flash as a police officer snapped photographs of a long knife on the counter, behind crisscrossed streams of police tape. In the dining area, Captain Reyes and a detective Ben hadn't seen before were quietly jotting down notes while a stream of uniformed policemen delivered reports.

"How did you find me?"

Victoria explained how Enrico had helped them link Vasquez to the attack on Antonio. "Vasquez escaped. The police raided the bar and found you lying on the floor outside the freezer, unconscious. We're lucky they came in when they did. You were barely breathing."

"The emeralds . . . I . . ." Ben remembered opening the door, and then . . . what?

"Gone," Victoria said. "No one blames you, Ben. You did what you had to do to survive. If anyone doubts that, you can show them the eighteen stitches on your forehead."

A bottle of rum on a string, Ben thought. "Where's Miguel?"

"In his room. He managed to sneak into the bar and disarm Vasquez, but got caught in the middle of the police raid."

"Is he all right?" Ben tried to stand up but his legs didn't work quite the same way they used to.

Victoria gently pushed him back down. "A flash-bang grenade went off right next to him, but he'll be fine. Enrico is looking after him."

"How's that going?"

"He's putting Florence Nightingale to shame, I'm sure."

Reyes appeared behind Victoria's shoulder. "Mr. Cooper, it's good to see you awake again. Are you feeling well enough for me to ask you a few questions?"

Ben waved toward a nearby empty chair. The ocean was so cold . . .

Reyes settled himself and flipped open his notepad. He glanced at Victoria, then back at Ben. "I assume you want your lawyer to remain during your statement?"

"That's right."

"In your own words, please tell me what happened," Reyes said gently.

He told the captain everything that had happened from the moment Vasquez arrived at the cantina. Enrico quietly walked into the room and sat next to Victoria while Ben related what Vasquez had told him.

Reyes leaned back, tapping his pen against his notebook. "Did he give you any indication as to how he intends to leave Costa Rica?"

"None." A wooden hull disappearing into the distance . . .

"You gave him the emeralds in exchange for your freedom? All of them?"

Ben thought for a moment. "I must have. I don't remember opening the door, but there was no other way for Vasquez to get into that freezer." Or for Ben to get out.

"A Special Investigations Unit from San José will be called in to continue the investigation, but I will recommend that you be absolved of all responsibility for the theft of the emeralds." He closed his notebook and slid it back inside his pocket. "While Vasquez's actions are unfortunate, you were right to call the police when you did. Had you kept the gems, you might have faced charges for theft or even money laundering."

"What happens now?" Victoria asked. "My clients live here in the cantina, and have no other place to stay. How long will we be unable to use the bar?"

"I will leave Constable Andino here overnight as a precaution and to ensure the crime scene remains secure. Provided you do not go behind the bar itself or enter the kitchen, you may use the remainder of the cantina as you see fit. Barring any further surprises, we will finish processing the scene early tomorrow morning."

"Do you have any leads on Ana's whereabouts?" Ben asked. Clowns on miniature jet-skis, riding in circles . . .

"So far, we have been unable to locate Ana Guiterrez. If what Vasquez said is true, then I expect he will keep her as a hostage until he can make his escape. We are searching with every available resource," Reyes said. "If Vasquez is still in Tamarindo, we will find him."

"What if he's already left?" Enrico asked.

"Then we will have to hope he is a man of his word." Reyes stood up. "I suggest you all get some rest. Good night, Mr. Cooper."

He walked back to the dining area and dismissed the detective and all officers but one. The police gathered up their equipment and left, while Constable Andino took up a position beside the door to the kitchen.

Enrico drummed his fingers against the arm of his chair. "I think we should pay Miguel a visit." He looked at Ben. "Can you walk?"

Ben set his mug down on the table, glad to be rid of the foul beverage. He rose unsteadily to his feet but found himself growing sturdier as they went through the bar, past the lone policeman, and down the hall to Miguel's room. Victoria closed the door softly behind them. There was a faint smell of burn ointment in the air, but Miguel seemed fine. Better than fine.

"Ben," Miguel exclaimed. "It's great to see you. How are you?" He sat on the bed cross-legged, bouncing up and down.

"Is he okay?" Ben asked. A faulty life preserver . . .

"He's fine," Enrico said. "He's had a few cans of Red Bull, that's all."

"Red Bull?" Victoria echoed, aghast.

"How many is a few?" Ben asked.

"Four or five." Enrico looked down at his feet. "The medic thought he might have a concussion. I wanted to make sure he didn't fall asleep."

Miguel hopped off the bed and started doing jumping jacks.

"No risk of that," Ben muttered, easing himself into a chair in the corner of the room. Mouthfuls of sea water . . .

"Enrico, they changed that years ago," Victoria said. "Most doctors think it's better to let a concussion victim sleep. Unless Miguel is bleeding from the ears or has an open head wound, you're just supposed to wake him every few hours. That's all."

Enrico shrugged. "Oops."

"How are you feeling, Miguel?" He looked different, somehow, but Ben couldn't pinpoint why.

"Never better," Miguel said between jumps.

"How is he, really?" she asked Enrico.

"He'll be fine. He knocked his head on the floor and he has a few minor burns from the stun grenade. It'll just be a month or two before his eyebrows fill back in."

Ben looked at the singed stubble where Miguel's thick, dark eyebrows had once been. Well, that explained the change in his appearance.

"I have bad news," Ben said. "Ana's missing." He brought Miguel up to date on everything that had happened that night.

Miguel stopped jumping. "When are we going after Vasquez?"

"I don't even know where to start with this one," Victoria said. She looked at Enrico and Ben in turn. "Do either of you have any ideas?"

Enrico shook his head.

Sinking beneath the waves . . . Ben sighed. "I can't think straight. I had the strangest dream when I was unconscious, and I can't get it out of my head."

"What was it about?" Victoria asked.

"It was pretty ridiculous . . ." Ben said, then recounted every detail he could recall, from the rum bottle to the clowns.

"That *is* bizarre," Victoria said.

"Are you sure you didn't fix yourself a snack while you were trapped in the freezer? Perhaps a small sauerkraut and salami sandwich?" Enrico asked. "Sauerkraut always gives me the strangest dreams. This one time, I thought I was a hot air balloon pilot from Argentina, and I've never been to—"

"It doesn't make sense to me, either," Miguel said. "But there's something familiar about the boat."

"What could be more familiar than a fishing boat towing a bottle of rum?" Victoria said. "Perhaps I should check your pupils again."

"No, Miguel's right," Ben said. "Someone said something about a boat a few days ago. What was it?" He was so close, but he still felt foggy from his time in the freezer. Then something clicked. "It was a sailboat, wasn't it? Something about a sailboat."

"Not a bad way to leave the country," Victoria admitted. "The police will be watching the airports and the road crossings. But there are plenty of sailboats anchored off the Tamarindo beach, and they come and go as they please. No one would notice another one heading out to sea."

Miguel snapped his fingers. "Antonio had a boat. He used to run fishing charters. Ana told us he planned to spend his retirement sailing. She would have inherited it."

"The timing fits," Ben said. "We lost track of Ana after she left the funeral, when she went to deal with the rest of Antonio's effects."

"Well done, Miguel," Victoria said.

Enrico reached for the door. "I'll get Constable Whatshisname."

"Wait!" Miguel said. "We need to talk this through first."

"Miguel, I know you want to help Ana, but we've had enough excitement for one day," Victoria said. "We should let the professionals handle this."

"Hear me out," Miguel said, holding out both palms. "How do we know Vasquez doesn't have an accomplice in the police department?"

Silence filled the room.

Finally Ben said, "That would explain how he got word of the emeralds soon after I called the police. And how he sent so many officers on a wild goose chase."

"We don't know that for sure," Victoria said.

Miguel bounced up and down on the balls of his feet. "I bet Vasquez got his fellow officers out of some tight spots over the years. If he needs a favor, they might not ask any questions. And who knows how deep that loyalty runs?"

A chill ran through Ben. Suddenly, the presence of Constable Andino at the cantina felt far less comforting.

"We need to handle this ourselves. Tonight."

Flashlight in hand, Ben crept toward the water taxi stand on the shores of the river estuary. Heavy branches swung in the wind as he made his way along the sandy path. Though scarcely on the outskirts of town, the stand seemed on the verge of being swallowed whole by the jungle. The flashlight lit up flimsy wooden outbuildings and piles of carelessly stacked canoes. In the distance, he could faintly spot a handful of moored motorboats. No sign of Vasquez.

They had helped themselves to the flashlight—and some other choice provisions—from the tactical vest Constable Andino left unattended in the kitchen while he patrolled the perimeter. Stealing from the police had proven to be the easy part; more difficult was figuring out where Antonio kept his boat. They'd searched the office for over an hour before Victoria found a crumpled invoice wedged in the bottom of the desk drawer. The bill was for several hundred dollars, payable to Guanacaste Water Taxi. Ben might have missed its significance, but Victoria realized a bill that size meant Antonio was paying for more than the occasional ferry ride across the river.

Ben and his friends had snuck out of the bar with ease, then quickly made their way down to the estuary. It was only when he hopped out of Enrico's convertible that Ben noticed the police station was less than a hundred meters away. He was too tired to appreciate the irony.

He checked his watch, newly borrowed from Enrico: 12:38 a.m. Fewer than twenty minutes remained until the tide reached its highest, offering Vasquez his best shot at a clean escape. Ben kept going down the path.

A voice crackled in his ear. "Radio check," Victoria said through his tiny earpiece.

He steeled his nerves and cleared his throat. "Coming through loud and clear. Stand by for my signal." There was a lengthy silence. Ben hefted the flashlight. "Mark."

He played the beam of light over the fleet of water taxis—large fiberglass motorboats with thin canvas canopies—and then along the shore, looking for any sign of the sailboat. Finally, he spotted a flimsy dock built of rotten lumber beyond the water taxis. Tied to its side was a long, sleek cabin cruiser. He walked closer until he could read the name *Real de a Ocho* painted on the side. There was no sign of movement aboard, but the boat was rigged to sail.

"Vasquez!" he shouted. *"Vasquez!"* His words died in the cool night air. There was only the sound of water slapping against hull and shore, of the wind lashing the trees.

Then Ben felt the cold muzzle of a revolver on the side of his neck. A muscular arm stretched around his throat. "There is no need to shout, Mr. Cooper," Vasquez murmured in his ear. "Turn off the light, then drop it on the ground."

Ben clicked off the flashlight and let it slide from his hand.

"Did you come alone?" Vasquez asked.

"Yes."

"Forgive me if I do not believe you," he hissed. "Why are you here?"

"To make sure you keep your end of the bargain."

"I will release Ana as soon as I reach my destination. You have my word."

"That's not good enough."

Vasquez cocked the hammer and pressed the muzzle in harder. "It will have to be, Mr. Cooper."

"You won't shoot me," Ben said. "The police would be here in minutes."

"They would find your body and an empty dock."

A moment's lull in the wind betrayed rustling in the jungle beside them. Vasquez spun in place, keeping the revolver pressed to Ben's throat. "You may come out now, Mr. Valares."

Miguel stepped from the shadowed brush, holding up both hands before him. "It's over, Vasquez." He stared at the detective as he slowly sidestepped toward the dock. "You wouldn't shoot two unarmed men. You aren't a cold-blooded murderer."

Ben felt the pressure of the muzzle against his skin slacken. Then Vasquez swung the revolver to bear on Miguel.

"No!" Ben shouted. He clenched his eyes shut.

The flashlight at his feet exploded in a wave of light and sound. He fell backward, opening his eyes as Miguel bore a stunned Vasquez to the ground. The revolver arced through the air, landing beside Ben. He scrambled to his feet, picked up the weapon, and hurled it into the water.

Vasquez rolled atop Miguel and hammered his face with heavy blows. Miguel brought up his elbows and withstood the onslaught as best he could, then knocked the detective off balance.

They scrambled to their feet and slowly circled one another. Miguel lashed out with blistering jabs and crosses. Vasquez ducked, blocked, and countered with a heavy blow to the jaw. Miguel's head snapped to one side.

Miguel took a leaden breath and threw everything he had against Vasquez. The detective struggled for a moment, then slammed a heavy fist into Miguel's stomach. Miguel staggered back, then lashed out with a kick. The detective slid alongside the raised leg and struck Miguel's kidneys with a heavy elbow. Miguel dropped to his knees, and Vasquez drove his heel into the small of his back. He hit the ground with a muted thud.

Ben dashed forward. Vasquez turned, grabbed Ben's shoulders, and drove a knee hard into his diaphragm. He fell to the ground, fighting for breath, watching in horror as Vasquez fell upon Miguel once more, wrapped his hands around his throat, and began to choke the life from him.

"Ben!" Victoria shouted through the earpiece. "Ben!"

He couldn't speak. The only noise was Miguel's strained gurgle—

The *Real de a Ocho* roared to life. The harbor engine

thrummed and the navigation lights cast the shore in a vivid red and green glow.

Vasquez looked up for a split second. Miguel grabbed him by the jacket and yanked the detective down with all his strength. Their skulls connected with a lurid crunch. Vasquez collapsed, clutching his broken nose.

Miguel leapt on the wounded detective, tugged a pair of plastic zap-straps from his pocket, and secured Vasquez's wrists and ankles. He patted the man down for the collapsible baton, but it was nowhere to be found.

Ben tapped his earpiece. "Victoria?" he wheezed.

She stepped from the shadows, radio in hand. "What happened?"

"I think the plan actually worked."

Victoria smiled. "I still can't believe Miguel managed to turn a flashlight into a flash-bang." The flashlight's metal shell lay smoking on the sand, split apart by the force of the pyrotechnics.

Miguel grunted and rubbed his throat, but a huge grin split his face.

"Next time, can we make the trigger word something other than 'no'? I was sure I was going to detonate it by accident while it was still in my hand," Ben said. "That was some brilliant improvisation by Enrico, starting the boat up like that."

"It wasn't me." Enrico hobbled out of the jungle. "I twisted my ankle on my way down to the beach."

Miguel touched his forehead and winced. "Then who—?"

They turned to look at the *Real de a Ocho.* Ana beamed at them from the deck. *"Hola."* She raised her hands, bound at the wrist with thick marine rope. "Can one of you get this off me, please?"

Chapter Eighteen

Victoria leaned into the office. "It's time."

Ben glanced down at the voicemail icon on his cell phone. He'd already put off listening to the countless messages for days now. Another ten minutes wouldn't hurt. He rose from his desk, feeling every ache and bruise from his trying week. Enrico had proven to be a successful—if exhausting—owner. Better still, the cantina had been packed every night since the police raid, bullet holes and all.

Miguel had even managed to convince Enrico to give up his dream of becoming a world-class bottle spinner. In the span of a single night, the man smashed more glassware than Vasquez had while terrorizing the cantina. Enrico was briefly disappointed, but soon divvied the remainder of his time between chatting up the patrons, bossing Ben and his friends about, firing Oscar from no fewer than three jobs, and freestyling behind his bongos. It was one hell of a week, even if none of the reporters they'd invited ever showed.

Ben would never forget last night, when Enrico invited his band to join him in a full-on musical battle against Victoria and some of the top DJs in Tamarindo. The party had raged on until well after sunrise. Ben stifled a yawn. He would have taken time to sleep it off, but they had vital business to attend to.

"Good news," Victoria said. "Because of the problem with the glued-on mirror, the rental company has agreed to sell us the car for an even thousand dollars."

"Are you kidding?" Ben asked. "We have cases of empty bottles worth more than that blasted hatchback. It's not even drivable."

"It's the best we can do under the circumstances. We have a good shot at getting back the rest of the money from the police department as compensation for the damage done by Vasquez, but that's going to take time."

They walked past the kitchen, where Oscar was tending to a half-dozen pots while rolling a fresh coat of paint onto a wall scorched by the stun grenade. Ben looked at the freezer and shivered.

"Miguel seemed excited," she continued. "Apparently, he has something special in mind."

He shrugged. If Miguel wanted the hatchback, Ben would chalk the cost up to danger pay. "Works for me."

Victoria started whistling.

"You're in a good mood," Ben said. "Any word from Mansion?"

She smiled. "None at all."

"Then why are you whistling?"

"I've done a lot to anger Mansion over the years. Whether I was selling Mother's diamonds on eBay or dying my hair blue, I've always gotten *some* sort of reaction from him. Usually, he hires another private detective to babysit me or threatens to cut off my trust fund. He's never, ever been speechless before." Victoria grinned. "He must be absolutely furious."

Ben shook his head. He didn't think he'd ever truly understand Victoria.

Though they'd only just opened for lunch, the main lounge area of the cantina was already jammed with customers chatting happily, drinks in hand. Some of the regulars greeted them or clapped Ben on the shoulder as they walked past. Word of their showdown with Vasquez had quickly spread. The tale grew more fantastic with every telling.

Luis smiled at him from behind the bar, then began shaking another *Totales Morales,* the end result of Enrico's little science experiment. No one—least of all Enrico—knew what it contained, but the customers seemed to love it. It tasted like stale turpentine to Ben, which meant there was tequila in there somewhere.

Their busboy had been somewhat amused to discover he'd been the lead suspect in Antonio's murder, but still stepped up when Miguel took time to recover. By unanimous vote, he'd earned a promotion to bartender. And a day off for his fashion show.

Ben gazed past the stack of surfboards leaning against the timber doorframe, beyond the sand to the sparkling blue ocean. A line of waves swelled and crashed onto the beach, bathing the soles of smiling travelers. He would never tire of that view. He took a deep breath, savoring the smell of grilled meat and plaintains. A familiar figure walked through the front door, plucking awkwardly at his neatly ironed khakis and tucked-in Hawaiian shirt.

"Captain Reyes," Ben said warmly. "Always a pleasure."

"Mr. Cooper." The captain handed Ben a thin manila envelope. "I wanted to return this to you."

"What's in here? You've already given me my passport back."

"It is the deed to your bar, the one we took as evidence on the day you were arrested. *Mister* Vasquez has confessed to the manslaughter of Antonio Guiterrez and the hit-and-run against Miguel Valares, so we no longer require it." Reyes smiled. "I included the death threat as well. I thought you might appreciate a—what is the word?—a memento of your little adventure. You can put them on your wall of self-love."

Ben looked up from the blood-splattered deed that bore his signature. "My what?"

"Perhaps my English fails me. The wall that people have, where they hang their degrees and records of their accomplishments?"

"His 'I love me' wall?" Victoria asked.

"That sounds right," Reyes agreed.

Ben was genuinely touched. "Thank you, Captain. I'll hang them in our office."

"You're welcome." Reyes's expression darkened. "But do not take this as any sign that the Tamarindo Police approved of your interference in the apprehension of Mr. Vasquez."

Victoria snorted.

Reyes continued, "In light of the unusual circumstances, however, we are prepared to withhold charges. *This* time."

"Thank you, Captain," Ben said. "And the emeralds?"

"The emeralds will be kept as evidence in our ongoing investigation against the cartel." Reyes scowled. "Don't push your luck."

"Understood, Captain. Please let us know if we can be of any further assistance." He grinned broadly.

Reyes shook Ben's hand in an ironclad grasp. "Welcome to Tamarindo, Mr. Cooper. You should fit in well." He marched out the way he came in.

Victoria glanced around the cantina, then sighed. "Wait here. I'll go and get Ana."

Ben stepped behind the bar and tucked the envelope in one of the drawers, then slid himself onto a bar stool. They really needed to fix the hole Miguel had carved in the roof during his rescue attempt. Ana and Luis had taken to calling it the skylight, but when it rained—

He felt a hand on his shoulder. "Hiya, Ben."

He swiveled around. "Oh. Hi, Jenni." He gave her a small, awkward smile. "Long time no see."

She looked up at him with wide green eyes. "Look, there's

247

something I need to tell you . . ."

"Oh?" Ben did his best to sound surprised. She looked every bit as striking as he remembered, but whatever spark there once was had since winked out. He'd apparently have to add *pumping me for information on behalf of a crooked cop* to his list of deal-breakers, somewhere between clown fetishes and leaving wet towels on the bathroom floor.

"A few months back, Detective Vasquez caught me with a small bag of pot. He promised not to press charges, so long as I kept my eyes open for him." She lowered her gaze. "After Antonio was murdered, he asked me to spy on you."

"I see." Ben found himself wishing Jenni had arrived about four *Totales Morales* into the evening.

"I didn't tell him very much about you, but, well . . ." Jenni faltered under Ben's steady gaze, then pressed on. "I want you to know I hated every moment of it. And I never would have agreed if I'd known what Vasquez had done." She gave him a small, sad smile. "Or if I'd known what a great bloke you are. That's all. Bye, Ben." She started to walk away.

"Jenni, wait," Ben said. "There's something I want to tell you."

"Yes?" she asked, hope in her eyes.

"Victoria put a tracking device in your purse and followed you to your meeting with Vasquez. I didn't find out about it until later. I never would have approved, had I known. But if she hadn't, he might well have escaped with Ana and the emeralds. So, can we call it even?"

"She put a *tracker* in my *bag*?" Jenni grabbed her purse and started rummaging.

"Yeah. And she'd like it back, if that's not too much trouble. It's . . . There it is. That stick of lip balm."

Jenni shoved it into Ben's hand.

"If it makes you feel any better, she stopped tracking you

ages ago," he said.

"She—" Jenni fumed, then took a deep breath. "I suppose I deserved it."

"Can we start over?" he asked. "As friends?"

"I'd like that." She smiled, then suddenly threw her arms around him. "But you tell that hussy if she spies on me again, I'll wallop her with my surfboard."

Ben moved to return her embrace, but flinched when Victoria cleared her throat inches from his ear. Where on earth had she come from?

"We're waiting," Victoria said.

"Sorry," he said to Jenni. "Got to run."

Ben and Victoria walked over to where Miguel and Ana were standing outside the front entrance to the bar.

"Where is he?" Miguel asked.

"He'll be here any second," Victoria said. There was a crash over by the office. "Here he comes."

Enrico stepped through the doorway, towing a pair of massive leather suitcases and wearing the same cheap rumpled suit as when he'd arrived.

"That's everything," he said, his voice tinged with sadness.

After Vasquez was arrested, Enrico had insisted on moving into the cantina so Miguel could recover at the *Tamarindo Diria*. The rest of them suspected it was so he could wander the bar in the middle of the night, prowling for prowlers.

Ben cleared his throat. "Enrico Morales, on behalf of the staff and customers of Enrico's Cantina, I would like to thank you for your dedicated service as our owner. You are, without question, the best client we've ever had."

Enrico glared at him. "I'm the only client you've ever had, you *pendejo*."

Victoria handed him a thin package wrapped in brown paper.

"We would like to offer you this token of our appreciation to remind you of your time at the cantina."

He tore open the package. Inside was a framed picture of Enrico standing behind the bar, tossing a bottle of rum in the air. He had a huge smile on his face.

"Thank you," Enrico said. "It's . . . just . . ." He dabbed his eyes with a filthy handkerchief.

"Enrico Morales, speechless." Victoria shook her head in mock disbelief. "I never thought I'd see the day."

"You're ruining the moment." Enrico blew his nose. "Don't forget to keep some of your weekends open. I want you to join the band on tour later this year."

Victoria smiled. "I wouldn't miss it for the world."

"And if I ever need to borrow some of your surveillance equipment?"

She laughed. "Then you can pound salt."

Enrico shrugged. "Never hurts to ask." He stuffed the handkerchief back into his jacket. "Almost forgot," he said, pulling a crinkled envelope from the same pocket. "I know this was supposed to be a trial run, but I'd like to pay for my ownership. I didn't know how much you're planning to charge, so I took a guess." He handed the envelope to Ben.

Ben took the envelope and ripped it open. His eyes bugged when he saw the amount Enrico had written on the check inside. It was enough to pay for the car, to restock the bar, to . . . "This is fine," he said quickly, slipping the envelope into his pants pocket.

"I've told my friends about the cantina as well. I wouldn't be surprised if you get a few calls. And let me know if you ever need a loan to cover some repairs."

"Thanks, Enrico," Ben said, profoundly grateful.

"Thank *you*." Enrico held out a hand, which each of them shook in turn. "I haven't had this much fun since—"

"Take care, Uncle." Miguel gave him a hug to stall yet another long story. His bruises were starting to fade, but his neck was still mottled brown and purple from his collarbone to his ears.

"You too, Miguel. Try not to tackle any more gunmen." Enrico grinned. "That goes for the rest of you as well." He picked up his bags and pulled them over to his red Mercedes.

They waved until he disappeared in a cloud of dust and tire smoke. Ben turned back to the cantina, stopping when something flashed in the corner of his eye. He looked up at the sign that had said Enrico's until minutes ago. Now, the side panel of the rental car hung in its place, letting all the world know that Gringo's was open for business.

"Ana, did you do this?" Ben asked.

"Do you like it? It seemed . . . perfect."

"I love it."

"Me too," Victoria said. "Thank you, Ana. For everything." She cleared her throat. "I'm sorry for ever thinking you could have murdered your uncle."

"That is all right," she said. "I would have done the same thing, if I was in your heels."

They started toward the beach, but then Ana held Ben back by his arm.

"Yes?" he asked.

Her eyes were downcast. "Are you sure I don't need to worry about Juan? He keeps sending me text messages threatening to . . . and . . . and I do not think he will wait much longer."

"You have nothing to worry about. I'm sure." He smiled. "Come on, let's go."

They walked together down the beach to the crashing waves, where Miguel and Victoria waited for them. Ana picked up a small brass urn and stared out over the ocean. "Antonio Guiterrez spent his entire life in Costa Rica, and he loved it dearly. He was not a perfect man, but he was like a father to me. He helped me through some tough times in my life, even after . . ." She looked at Miguel and faltered. ". . . after others had given up. Some people will only remember him for stealing a small fortune in emeralds, for drugging Ben and attacking a detective with a bat, but I know . . . I know . . ." Ana stammered. She looked up at the rest of them. "I am not very good at this. Would any of you like to say something?"

Victoria, Miguel, and Ben looked at each another expectantly. Finally, Ben stepped forward and cleared his throat. "I've come to realize that the greatest people in life are those who help us change in ways we can't manage on our own. By that measure, Antonio was one of the most important people in my life. Thank you, Antonio. I hope you know peace."

Ana smiled. "That was nice, Ben. *Gracias.*"

"Well done," Victoria whispered as he stepped back.

Ana knelt in the rolling surf. She set the urn down, removed the lid, and stepped back from the water. A wave rushed over the urn, scooping up ashes as it passed. Within moments, Antonio Guiterrez was part of the Pacific. She picked up the empty urn and turned to Ben. "Do you mind if I go on break for a while?"

"Take all the time you need."

She walked along the beach, the empty urn tucked beneath her arm. Victoria looked at her watch. "When do you want us back here? An hour after sunset?"

"That's right. Mind giving Luis a hand with the lunch rush before you go? I need to make a phone call."

"No problem." She turned and headed back to the cantina.

Ben slowly lowered himself onto the sun-warmed sand and watched the surfers slice across the massive waves. Perhaps he could—He stopped himself. No, no more excuses. He pulled out his phone.

He brought up the most recent message from Tara. "It's me.

Again. I'd hoped we could settle this like adults, but it's already been more than a week. I want you to know that my parents and I have contacted our lawyer, and we intend to get back every penny, plus interest and damages. If you think you can hide from this in Costa Rica, I have two words for you— Extradition. Treaty."

Ben let out the breath he'd been holding. It was worse than he'd hoped, but not as bad as he'd feared. Despite it all, he was truly happy.

Something clicked.

He picked up the phone and dialed a number he hadn't called in almost a week.

"Canadian First Financial. How may I help you?"

"Happy!" Ben yelled. "I want to be happy when I grow up."

He waited, heart hammering in his throat.

"I'm sorry, Ben. That's not the correct answer," Miranda said.

"Dammit, Ben," he muttered to himself.

" 'Ben' is the correct answer. Your account is now unlocked. Would you like to make a transaction?"

Elation washed over him. "Not today. Thanks." He clicked off the line.

Ben. He wanted to be *Ben* when he grew up. It made sense, in a Drunk Ben kind of way.

Luis appeared at his side. "Ben, there's someone on the phone for you. It's a reporter."

"Not the *Tamarindo Gazette* again. I've told them three times now, I'm not paying for that bloody ad."

"No, not them." Luis looked down at the slip of paper in his hand. "He said he was calling from En Bee See. He wants to speak to someone about the emeralds."

NBC? "Hold on, I'll be right there." Ben rose to his feet and dashed back inside. He had a sneaking suspicion they might not have to search long for new clients.

Ana slid off her sandals and walked along the beach, barefoot. A gust of wind ruffled her hair. She ignored the burning sky and the sparkling waves, staring instead at the rocks and twigs and the dirt in the sand. She should have been relieved; instead, she felt nothing at all.

Her phone beeped twice. A new text message. It read in Spanish, "Should have paid when you had the chance."

She pulled up her inbox. There it was: the email from Juan, the one with attachments that he'd sent to all of her family and friends. Ana's worst fear. She tapped on the message and held her breath. The screen flooded with photos.

Every last one was corrupted beyond recognition. All she could make out was the small message in the corner of each of them that read, *"Juan es un picha."*

She laughed, and then she started to cry.

Finally, Ana mourned her uncle.

Miguel found Ana sitting on the beach, a lone figure on the vast expanse of sand, dwarfed by towering palms that bobbed in the wind. Her cheeks were streaked with tears.

"Do you want some company?" he asked softly.

She nodded, and he sat down beside her. They sat together in silence for a time. Finally, he leaned closer and said, "Thank you."

Ana looked puzzled. "What for?"

"For starting the boat when you did." He lightly touched the bruise on his neck. "If you hadn't . . ."

"I am sure you would have been fine on your own." She brushed the tears from her eyes.

"I'm not so sure," Miguel said. He vividly remembered the

feel of Vasquez's hands around his neck, the way sound had faded out and his vision had turned to black as he'd started to lose consciousness. It had been a rough couple of days since then. Everyone thought they were doing him a favor by giving him time to rest and heal, but he couldn't sleep. The dreams were back again. But at least his heart no longer felt as though it would burst from his chest. Until now.

"Ana, I . . ." he stammered. "There's something you need to know—"

"I know, Miguel." She leaned her head on his shoulder. "And there is a lot that you need to know, too. But for now, let's just spend some time together. *Ta bien?*"

He wrapped his arms around her and gave her a gentle kiss on the forehead.

Miguel and Victoria wandered back down to the beach later that evening, drinks in hand. Ben had already built a bonfire that popped and cracked as the flames spread through the pile of driftwood. He gazed into the embers, a perfect pint of cold beer in his hand.

"How'd the calls go?" Victoria asked.

Rather than relay Tara's message, Ben finally told his friends about the many attempts to unlock his bank account.

"Ben." Miguel slowly nodded. "That's deep, brother. Really deep."

"That's the stupidest thing I've ever heard," Victoria said. "You should have asked us for help."

"You would have figured it out sooner?" Ben asked.

"Of course not. But it would have been hilarious. Like watching a Labrador try its paw at calculus." Victoria shook her head. "Seriously? A grizzly bear?"

Ben checked his new watch. One minute to go. "Did you bring them?"

Miguel tapped his pocket.

"Me too," Victoria said, "Though if we were doing this properly, we would have done mine ages ago."

"Stop being a spoilsport." Ben reached into his pocket, pulled out a slip of paper, and held it above the fire. Miguel and Victoria did the same.

Ben said, "At six—"

"Wait." Victoria cut him off. "Are you *sure* you didn't grab Enrico's check by accident?"

"Yes, Victoria. I'm sure." Ben surreptitiously double-checked the slip in his hand, then continued, "At six forty eight p.m., Air Canada flight 4354 departed San José, Costa Rica for Toronto, Canada. Two passengers never boarded." He looked at Victoria. "Flight 4410 left Liberia one week earlier. One passenger was absent." He glanced again at his watch. "It is now seven p.m., which means these airline tickets are now worthless."

"A toast." Victoria raised her glass. "To pursuing a dream."

Miguel clinked his against hers. "To leaving the past behind."

Ben raised his glass to theirs in turn. "To starting over."

They dropped their tickets into the bonfire, where they were consumed by the crackling flames and cast into the sky in a cloud of smoke and ash.

ABOUT THE AUTHOR

Ryan Aldred finished his first novel while still in high school, a work that was never published and since exiled to the recycle bin of history. Fifteen years went by before Ben, Miguel, and Victoria burst forth from some forgotten corner of his mind and refused to leave until he told their story. Four months later, *Rum Luck* was on its way to an intrepid band of beta readers.

When not writing, Ryan runs a small Canadian charity that supports education in Afghanistan, Tanzania, Uganda, and other at-risk regions. He previously worked as a defense analyst and continues to serve as a sergeant in the Canadian Forces Reserve. He's never met a beach he doesn't like.

Ryan and his family live in beautiful Prince Edward County, Canada.

S0-BZW-477

SUNSET PARK

Paul Auster is the bestselling author of *Invisible*, *The Brooklyn Follies*, *The Book of Illusions*, *The New York Trilogy*, among many other works. In 2006 he was awarded the Prince of Asturias Prize for Literature and inducted into the American Academy of Arts and Letters. Among his other honours are the Independent Spirit Award for the screenplay of *Smoke* and the Prix Médicis étranger for *Leviathan*. He has also been shortlisted for both the International IMPAC Dublin Literary Award (*The Book of Illusions*) and the PEN/Faulkner Award for Fiction (*The Music of Chance*). His work has been translated into more than thirty languages. He lives in Brooklyn, New York.

SUNSET PARK

PAUL AUSTER

faber and faber

First published in the USA in 2010
by Henry Holt and Company, LLC
175 Fifth Avenue
New York, New York 10010

First published in the UK in 2010
by Faber and Faber Ltd
Bloomsbury House
74–77 Great Russell Street
London WC1B 3DA
This export paperback edition published in 2010

Printed in England by CPI Mackays, Chatham

All rights reserved
© Paul Auster, 2010

The right of Paul Auster to be identified as author of this work
has been asserted in accordance with Section 77 of the
Copyright, Designs and Patents Act 1988

A CIP record for this book
is available from the British Library

ISBN 978-0-571-25879-6

2 4 6 8 10 9 7 5 3 1

SUNSET PARK

MILES HELLER

1

For almost a year now, he has been taking photographs of abandoned things. There are at least two jobs every day, sometimes as many as six or seven, and each time he and his cohorts enter another house, they are confronted by the things, the innumerable cast-off things left behind by the departed families. The absent people have all fled in haste, in shame, in confusion, and it is certain that wherever they are living now (if they have found a place to live and are not camped out in the streets) their new dwellings are smaller than the houses they have lost. Each house is a story of failure—of bankruptcy and default, of debt and foreclosure—and he has taken it upon himself to document the last, lingering traces of those scattered lives in order to prove that the vanished families were once here, that the ghosts of people he will never see and never know are still present in the discarded things strewn about their empty houses.

The work is called trashing out, and he belongs to a four-man crew employed by the Dunbar Realty Corporation, which subcontracts its "home preservation" services to the local banks that now own the properties in question. The sprawling flatlands of south Florida are filled with these orphaned structures, and because it is in the interest of the banks to resell them as quickly as possible, the vacated houses must be cleaned, repaired, and made ready to be shown to prospective buyers. In a collapsing world of economic ruin and relentless, ever-expanding hardship, trashing out is one of the few thriving businesses in the area. No doubt he is lucky to have found this job. He doesn't know how much longer he can bear it, but the pay is decent, and in a land of fewer and fewer jobs, it is nothing if not a good job.

In the beginning, he was stunned by the disarray and the filth, the neglect. Rare is the house he enters that has been left in pristine condition by its former owners. More often there will have been an eruption of violence and anger, a parting rampage of capricious vandalism—from the open taps of sinks and bathtubs overflowing with water to sledge-hammered, smashed-in walls or walls covered with obscene graffiti or walls pocked with bullet holes, not to mention the ripped-out copper pipes, the bleach-stained carpets, the piles of shit deposited on the living room floor. Those are extreme examples, perhaps, impulsive acts triggered by the rage of the dispossessed, disgusting but understandable statements of despair, but even if he is not always gripped by revulsion when he enters a house, he never opens a door without a feeling of dread. Inevitably, the first thing to contend with is the smell, the onslaught of sour air rushing into his nostrils, the ubiquitous, commingled aromas of mildew, rancid milk, cat litter, crud-caked toilet bowls, and food rotting on the kitchen counter. Not even fresh air pouring in through open windows can wipe out the smells; not even the tidiest, most circumspect removal can erase the stench of defeat.

Then, always, there are the objects, the forgotten possessions, *the abandoned things.* By now, his photographs number in the thousands, and among his burgeoning archive can be found pictures of books, shoes, and oil paintings, pianos and toasters, dolls, tea sets, and dirty socks, televisions and board games, party dresses and tennis racquets, sofas, silk lingerie, caulking guns, thumbtacks, plastic action figures, tubes of lipstick, rifles, discolored mattresses, knives and forks, poker chips, a stamp collection, and a dead canary lying at the bottom of its cage. He has no idea why he feels compelled to take these pictures. He understands that it is an empty pursuit, of no possible benefit to anyone, and yet each time he walks into a house, he senses that the things are calling out to him, speaking to him in the voices of the people who are no longer there, asking him to be looked at one last time before they are carted away. The other members of the crew make fun of him for this obsessive picture taking, but he pays them no heed. They are of little account in his opinion, and he despises them all. Brain-dead Victor, the crew boss; stuttering, chatterbox Paco; and fat, wheezing Freddy—the three musketeers of doom. The law says that all salvageable objects above a certain value must be handed over to the bank, which is obliged to return them to their owners, but his co-workers grab whatever they please and never give it a second thought. They consider him a fool for turning his back on these spoils—the bottles of whiskey, the radios, the CD players, the archery equipment, the dirty magazines—but all he wants are his pictures—not things, but the pictures of things. For some time now, he has made it his business to say as little as possible when he is on the job. Paco and Freddy have taken to calling him El Mudo.

He is twenty-eight years old, and to the best of his knowledge he has no ambitions. No burning ambitions, in any case, no clear idea of what building a plausible future might entail for him. He knows that he will not stay in Florida much longer, that the moment is coming when he will feel the need to move on again, but until that need ripens into a necessity to act, he is content to remain in the present and not look ahead. If he has accomplished anything in the seven and a half years since he quit college and struck out on his own, it is this ability to live in the present, to confine himself to the here and now, and although it might not be the most laudable accomplishment one can think of, it has required considerable discipline and self-control for him to achieve it. To have no plans, which is to say, to have no longings or hopes, to be satisfied with your lot, to accept what the world doles out to you from one sunrise to the next—in order to live like that you must want very little, as little as humanly possible.

Bit by bit, he has pared down his desires to what is now approaching a bare minimum. He has cut out smoking and drinking, he no longer eats in restaurants, he does not own a television, a radio, or a computer. He would like to trade in his car for a bicycle, but he can't get rid of the car, since the distances he must travel for work are too great. The same applies to the cell phone he carries around in his pocket, which he would dearly love to toss in the garbage, but he needs it for work as well and therefore can't do without it. The digital camera was an indulgence, perhaps, but given the drear and slog of the endless trash-out rut, he feels it is saving his life. His rent is low, since he lives in a small apartment in a poor neighborhood, and beyond spending money on bedrock necessities, the only luxury he allows himself is buying books, paperback books, mostly novels, American novels, British novels, foreign novels in translation, but in the end books are not luxuries so much as necessities, and reading is an addiction he has no wish to be cured of.

If not for the girl, he would probably leave before the month was out. He has saved up enough money to go anywhere he wants, and there is no question that he has had his fill of the Florida sun—which, after much study, he now believes does the soul more harm than good. It is a Machiavellian sun in his opinion, a hypocritical sun, and the light it generates does not illuminate things but obscures them—blinding you with its constant, overbright effulgences, pounding on you with its blasts of vaporous humidity, destabilizing you with its miragelike reflections and shimmering waves of nothingness. It is all glitter and dazzle, but it offers no substance, no tranquillity, no respite.

Still, it was under this sun that he first saw the girl, and because he can't talk himself into giving her up, he continues to live with the sun and try to make his peace with it.

Her name is Pilar Sanchez, and he met her six months ago in a public park, a purely accidental meeting late one Saturday afternoon in the middle of May, the unlikeliest of unlikely encounters. She was sitting on the grass reading a book, and not ten feet away from her he too was sitting on the grass reading a book, which happened to be the same book as hers, the same book in an identical soft-cover edition, *The Great Gatsby*, which he was reading for the third time since his father gave it to him as a present on his sixteenth birthday. He had been sitting there for twenty or thirty minutes, inside the book and therefore walled off from his surroundings, when he heard someone laugh. He turned, and in that first, fatal glimpse of her, as she sat there smiling at him and pointing to the title of her book, he guessed that she was even younger than sixteen, just a girl, really, and a little girl at that, a small adolescent girl wearing tight, cut-off shorts, sandals, and a skimpy halter top, the same clothes worn by every half-attractive girl throughout the lower regions of hot, sun-spangled Florida. No more than a baby, he said to himself, and yet there she was with her smooth, uncovered limbs and alert, smiling face, and he who rarely smiles at anyone or anything looked into her dark, animated eyes and smiled back at her.

Six months later, she is still underage. Her driver's license says she is seventeen, that she won't be turning eighteen until May, and therefore he must act cautiously with her in public, avoid at all costs doing anything that might arouse the suspicions of the prurient, for a single telephone call to the police from some riled-up busybody could easily land him in jail. Every morning that is not a weekend morning or a holiday morning, he drives her to John F. Kennedy High School, where she is in her senior year and doing well, with aspirations for college and a future life as a registered nurse, but he does not drop her off in front of the building. That would be too dangerous. Some teacher or school official could catch sight of them in the car together and raise the alarm, and so he glides to a halt some three or four blocks before they reach Kennedy and lets her off there. He does not kiss her good-bye. He does not touch her. She is saddened by his restraint, since in her own mind she is already a full-grown woman, but she accepts this sham indifference because he has told her she must accept it.

Pilar's parents were killed in a car wreck two years ago, and until she moved into his apartment after the school year ended last June, she lived with her three older sisters in the family house. Twenty-year-old Maria, twenty-three-year-old Teresa, and twenty-five-year-old Angela. Maria is enrolled in a community college, studying to become a beautician. Teresa works as a teller at a local bank. Angela, the prettiest of the bunch, is a hostess in a cocktail lounge. According to Pilar, she sometimes sleeps with the customers for money. Pilar hastens to add that she loves Angela, that she loves all her sisters, but she's glad to have left the house now, which is filled with too many memories of her mother and father, and besides, she can't stop herself, but she's angry at Angela for doing what she does, she considers it a sin for a woman to sell her body, and it's a relief not to be arguing with her about it anymore. Yes, she says to him, his apartment is a shabby little nothing of a place, the house is much bigger and more comfortable, but the apartment doesn't have eighteen-month-old Carlos Junior in it, and that too is an immense relief. Teresa's son isn't a bad child as far as children go, of course, and what can Teresa do with her husband stationed in Iraq and her long hours at the bank, but that doesn't give her the right to pawn off babysitting duties on her kid sister every other day of the week. Pilar wanted to be a good sport, but she couldn't help resenting it. She needs time to be alone and to study, she wants to make something of herself, and how can she do that if she's busy changing dirty diapers? Babies are fine for other people, but she wants no part of them. Thanks, she says, but no thanks.

He marvels at her spirit and intelligence. Even on the first day, when they sat in the park talking about *The Great Gatsby*, he was impressed that she was reading the book for herself and not because a teacher had assigned it at school, and then, as the conversation continued, doubly impressed when she began to argue that the most important character in the book was not Daisy or Tom or even Gatsby himself but Nick Carraway. He asked her to explain. Because he's the one who tells the story, she said. He's the only character with his feet on the ground, the only one who can look outside of himself. The others are all lost and shallow people, and without Nick's compassion and understanding, we wouldn't be able to feel anything for them. The book depends on Nick. If the story had been told by an omniscient narrator, it wouldn't work half as well as it does.

Omniscient narrator. She knows what the term means, just as she understands what it is to talk about *suspension of disbelief, biogenesis, antilogarithms,* and *Brown v. Board of Education.* How is it possible, he wonders, for a young girl like Pilar Sanchez, whose Cuban-born father worked as a letter carrier all his life, whose three older sisters dwell contentedly in a bog of humdrum daily routines, to have turned out so differently from the rest of her family? Pilar wants to know things, she has plans, she works hard, and he is more than happy to encourage her, to do whatever he can to help advance her education. From the day she left home and moved in with him, he has been drilling her on the finer points of how to score well on the SATs, has vetted every one of her homework assignments, has taught her the rudiments of calculus (which is not offered by her high school), and has read dozens of novels, short stories, and poems out loud to her. He, the young man without ambitions, the college dropout who spurned the trappings of his once privileged life, has taken it upon himself to become ambitious for her, to push her as far as she is willing to go. The first priority is college, a good college with a full scholarship, and once she is in, he feels the rest will take care of itself. At the moment, she is dreaming of becoming a registered nurse, but things will eventually change, he is certain of that, and he is fully confident that she has it in her to go on to medical school one day and become a doctor.

She was the one who proposed moving in with him. It never would have occurred to him to suggest such an audacious plan himself, but Pilar was determined, at once driven by a desire to escape and enthralled by the prospect of sleeping with him every night, and after she begged him to go to Angela, the major breadwinner of the clan and therefore the one with the final word on all family decisions, he met with the oldest Sanchez girl and managed to talk her into it. She was reluctant at first, claiming that Pilar was too young and inexperienced to consider such a momentous step. Yes, she knew her sister was in love with him, but she didn't approve of that love because of the difference in their ages, which meant that sooner or later he would grow bored with his adolescent plaything and leave her with a broken heart. He answered that it would probably end up being the reverse, that he would be the one left with a broken heart. Then, brushing aside all further talk of hearts and feelings, he presented his case in purely practical terms. Pilar didn't have a job, he said, she was a drag on the family finances, and he was in a position to support her and take that burden off their hands. It wasn't as if he would be abducting her to China, after all. Their house was only a fifteen-minute walk from his apartment, and they could see her as often as they liked. To clinch the bargain, he offered them presents, any number of things they craved but were too strapped to buy for themselves. Much to the shock and jeering amusement of the three clowns at work, he temporarily reversed his stance on the do's and don'ts of trash-out etiquette, and over the next week he calmly filched an all-but-brand-new flat-screen TV, a top-of-the-line electric coffeemaker, a red tricycle, thirty-six films (including a boxed collector's set of the *Godfather* movies), a professional-quality makeup mirror, and a set of crystal wineglasses, which he duly presented to Angela and her sisters as an expression of his gratitude. In other words, Pilar now lives with him because he bribed the family. He bought her.

Yes, she is in love with him, and yes, in spite of his qualms and inner hesitations, he loves her back, however improbable that might seem to him. Note here for the record that he is not someone with a special fixation on young girls. Until now, all the women in his life have been more or less his own age. Pilar therefore does not represent an embodiment of some ideal female type for him—she is merely herself, a small piece of luck he stumbled across one afternoon in a public park, an exception to every rule. Nor can he explain to himself why he is attracted to her. He admires her intelligence, yes, but that is finally of scant importance, since he has admired the intelligence of other women before her without feeling the least bit attracted to them. He finds her pretty, but not exceptionally pretty, not beautiful in any objective way (although it could also be argued that every seventeen-year-old girl is beautiful, for the simple reason that all youth is beautiful). But no matter.

He has not fallen for her because of her body or because of her mind. What is it, then? What holds him here when everything tells him he should leave? Because of the way she looks at him, perhaps, the ferocity of her gaze, the rapt intensity in her eyes when she listens to him talk, a feeling that she is entirely present when they are together, that he is the only person who exists for her on the face of the earth.

Sometimes, when he takes out his camera and shows her his pictures of the abandoned things, her eyes fill up with tears. There is a soft, sentimental side to her that is almost comic, he feels, and yet he is moved by that softness in her, that vulnerability to the aches of others, and because she can also be so tough, so talkative and full of laughter, he can never predict what part of her will surge forth at any given moment. It can be trying in the short run, but in the long run he feels it is all to the good. He who has denied himself so much for so many years, who has been so stolid in his abnegations, who has taught himself to rein in his temper and drift through the world with cool, stubborn detachment has slowly come back to life in the face of her emotional excesses, her combustibility, her mawkish tears when confronted by the image of an abandoned teddy bear, a broken bicycle, or a vase of wilted flowers.

The first time they went to bed together, she assured him she was no longer a virgin. He took her at her word, but when the moment came for him to enter her, she pushed him away and told him he mustn't do that. The *mommy hole* was off-limits, she said, absolutely forbidden to male members. Tongues and fingers were acceptable, but not members, under no condition at any time, not ever. He had no idea what she was talking about. He was wearing a condom, wasn't he? They were protected, and there was no need to worry about anything. Ah, she said, but that's where he was wrong. Teresa and her husband always believed in condoms too, and look what happened to them. Nothing was more frightening to Pilar than the thought of becoming pregnant, and she would never risk her fate by trusting in one of those iffy rubbers. She would rather slit her wrists or jump off a bridge than get herself knocked up. Did he understand? Yes, he understood, but what was the alternative? The *funny hole*, she said. Angela had told her about it, and he had to admit that from a strictly biological and medical standpoint it was the one truly safe form of birth control in the world.

For six months now, he has abided by her wishes, restricting all member penetration to her funny hole and putting nothing more than tongue and fingers in her mommy hole. Such are the anomalies and idiosyncrasies of their love life, which is nevertheless a rich love life, a splendid erotic partnership that shows no signs of abating anytime soon. In the end, it is this sexual complicity that binds him fast to her and holds him in the hot nowhereland of ruined and empty houses. He is bewitched by her skin. He is a prisoner of her ardent young mouth. He is at home in her body, and if he ever finds the courage to leave, he knows he will regret it to the end of his days.

2

He has told her next to nothing about himself. Even on the first day in the park, when she heard him speak and understood that he came from somewhere else, he didn't tell her that the somewhere else was New York City, the West Village in Manhattan to be precise, but vaguely answered that his life had begun *up north*. A bit later, when he started the SAT drills and introduced her to calculus, Pilar quickly learned that he was more than just an itinerant trash-out worker, that he was in fact a highly educated person with a nimble mind and a love of literature so vast and so informed that it made her English teachers at John F. Kennedy High look like impostors. Where had he gone to school? she asked him one day. He shrugged, not wanting to mention Stuyvesant and the three years he had spent at Brown. When she continued to press him, he looked down at the floor and muttered something about a small state college in New England. The following week, when he gave her a novel written by Renzo Michaelson, who happened to be his godfather, she noticed that it had been published by a company called Heller Books and asked him if there was any connection. No, he said, it's just a coincidence, Heller turns out to be a fairly common name. This prompted her to ask the simple, altogether logical next question about which Heller family he happened to belong to. Who were his parents, and where did they live? They're both gone, he replied. Gone as in dead and gone? I'm afraid so. Just like me, she said, her eyes suddenly filling with tears. Yes, he answered, just like you. Any brothers and sisters? No. I'm an only child.

Lying to her in this way has spared him the discomfort of having to talk about things he has been struggling to avoid for years. He doesn't want her to know that six months after he was born his mother walked out on his father and divorced him to marry another man. He doesn't want her to know that he has not seen or spoken to his father, Morris Heller, founder and publisher of Heller Books, since the summer after his third year at Brown. Least of all does he want her to know anything about his stepmother, Willa Parks, who married his father twenty months after the divorce, and nothing, nothing, nothing about his dead stepbrother, Bobby. These matters do not concern Pilar. They are his own private business, and until he finds an exit from the limbo that has encircled him for the past seven years, he will not share them with anyone.

Even now, he can't be sure if he did it on purpose or not. There is no question that he pushed Bobby, that the two of them were arguing and he pushed him in anger, but he doesn't know if the push came before or after he heard the oncoming car, which is to say, he doesn't know if Bobby's death was an accident or if he was secretly trying to kill him. The entire story of his life hinges on what happened that day in the Berkshires, and he still has no grasp of the truth, he still can't be certain if he is guilty of a crime or not.

It was the summer of 1996, roughly one month after his father had given him *The Great Gatsby* and five other books for his sixteenth birthday. Bobby was eighteen and a half and had just graduated from high school, having squeaked through by the skin of his teeth in no small part thanks to the efforts of his stepbrother, who had written three final term papers for him at the cut-rate price of two dollars per page, seventy-six dollars in all. Their parents had rented a house outside Great Barrington for the month of August, and the two boys were on their way to spend the weekend with them. He was too young to drive, Bobby was the one with the license, and therefore it was Bobby's responsibility to check the oil and fill the tank before they left—which, needless to say, he failed to do. About fifteen miles from the house, traveling along a twisty, hilly, back-country road, the car ran out of gas. He might not have become so angry if Bobby had shown some remorse, if the dim-witted slacker had taken the trouble to apologize for his mistake, but true to form, Bobby found the situation hilarious, and his first response was to burst out laughing.

Cell phones existed back then, but they didn't have one, which meant they had to get out of the car and walk.

It was a hot, oppressively humid day, with squadrons of gnats and mosquitoes swarming around their heads, and he was in a foul temper, irritated by Bobby's moronic nonchalance, by the heat and the bugs, by having to walk down that crummy, narrow little road, and before long he was lashing out at his stepbrother, calling him names, trying to provoke a fight. Bobby kept shrugging him off, however, refusing to respond to his insults. Don't get worked up over nothing, he said, life is full of unexpected turns, maybe something interesting would happen to them because they were on this road, maybe, just maybe, they would discover two beautiful girls around the next bend, two completely naked beautiful girls who would take them into the woods and make love to them for sixteen straight hours. Under normal circumstances, he would laugh whenever Bobby started talking like that, fall willingly under the spell of his stepbrother's inane prattle, but nothing was normal about what was happening just then, and he was in no mood to laugh. It was all so idiotic, he wanted to punch Bobby in the face.

Whenever he thinks about that day now, he imagines how differently things would have turned out if he had been walking on Bobby's right instead of his left. The shove would have pushed him off the road rather than into the middle of it, and that would have been the end of the story, since there wouldn't have been a story, the whole business would have amounted to less than nothing, a brief outburst that would have been forgotten in no time at all. But there they were, for no special reason arrayed in that particular left-right tandem, he on the inside, Bobby on the outside, walking along the shoulder of the road in the direction of the oncoming traffic, of which there was none, not a single car, truck, or motorcycle for ten minutes, and after he'd been haranguing Bobby nonstop for those ten minutes, his stepbrother's jocular indifference to their plight slowly turned into peevishness, then belligerence, and a couple of miles after they started out, the two of them were shouting at each other at the top of their lungs.

How often had they fought in the past? Countless times, more times than he is able to remember, but there was nothing unusual about that, he feels, since brothers always fight, and if Bobby wasn't his flesh-and-blood brother, he nevertheless had been there for the full span of his conscious life. He was two years old when his father married Bobby's mother and the four of them started living together under the same roof, which necessarily makes it a time beyond recall, a period now wholly expunged from his mind, and therefore it would be legitimate to say that Bobby had always been his brother, even if that wasn't strictly the case. There had been the customary squabbles and conflicts, then, and because he was the younger by two and a half years, his body had received the bulk of the punishment. A dim recollection of his father stepping in to pull a screaming Bobby off him one rainy day somewhere in the country, of his stepmother scolding Bobby for *playing too rough*, of kicking Bobby in the shins when he yanked a toy out of his hands. But it hadn't been all war and combat, there had been lulls and truces and good times as well, and beginning when he was seven or eight, meaning when Bobby was nine or ten or eleven, he can remember actively liking his brother, perhaps even loving him, and that he was liked and perhaps even loved in return. But they were never close, not close in the way some brothers are, even fighting, antagonistic brothers, and no doubt that had something to do with the fact that they belonged to an artificial family, a constructed family, and each boy's deepest loyalty was reserved for his own parent. It wasn't that Willa had been a bad mother to him or that his father had been a bad father to Bobby. Quite the reverse. The two adults were steadfast allies, their marriage was solid and remarkably free of trouble, and each one bent over backward to give the other's kid every benefit of the doubt. But still, there were invisible fault lines, microscopic fissures to remind them that they were a patched-together entity, something not completely whole. The matter of Bobby's name, for example. Willa was Willa Parks, but her first husband, who had died of cancer at thirty-six, was Nordstrom, and Bobby was Nordstrom as well, and because he had been Nordstrom for the first four and a half years of his life, Willa had been reluctant to change it to Heller. She felt Bobby might be confused, but more to the point, she couldn't bring herself to wipe out the last traces of her first husband, who had loved her and was dead through no fault of his own, and to deprive his son of his name would have made her feel that he was being killed for a second time. The past, then, was part of the present, and the ghost of Karl Nordstrom was the fifth member of the household, an absent spirit who had left his mark on Bobby—who was both a brother and not a brother, both a son and not a son, both a friend and a foe.

They lived under the same roof, but apart from the fact that their parents were husband and wife, they had little in common. By temperament and outlook, by inclination and behavior, by all the measures used to gauge who and what a person is, they were different, deeply and unalterably different. As the years went by, each drifted off into his own separate sphere, and by the time they were bumping along through early adolescence, they rarely intersected anymore except at the dinner table and on family outings. Bobby was bright, quick, and funny, but he was an atrocious student who detested school, and because he was a reckless and defiant mischief maker on top of that, he was labeled *a problem*. By contrast, his younger stepbrother consistently earned the highest grades in his class. Heller was quiet and withdrawn, Nordstrom was extroverted and rambunctious, and each thought the other was going about the business of life in the wrong way. To make matters worse, Bobby's mother was a professor of English at NYU, a woman with a passion for books and ideas, and how difficult it must have been for her son to listen to her praise Heller for his academic achievements, exult at his acceptance by Stuyvesant, and talk to him over dinner about goddamned bloody *existentialism*. By fifteen, Bobby had turned into a serious pothead, one of those glassy-eyed high school stoners who puke their stomachs out at weekend parties and make small drug deals to keep themselves in extra cash. Stick-in-the-mud Heller, bad-boy Nordstrom, and never the twain could meet. Verbal attacks were occasionally delivered from each side, but the physical fighting had stopped—largely due to the mysteries of genetics. When they found themselves on that road in the Berkshires twelve years ago, the sixteen-year-old Heller stood a couple of centimeters below six feet and weighed one hundred and seventy pounds. Nordstrom, derived from scrawnier stock, was five-eight and weighed one forty-five. The mismatch had canceled all potential bouts. For some time now, they had belonged in different divisions.

What were they arguing about that day? What word or sentence, what series of words or sentences had so enraged him that he lost control of himself and pushed Bobby to the ground? He can't remember clearly. So many things were said during that argument, so many accusations flew back and forth between them, so many buried animosities came roiling to the surface in so many gusts of vehemence and vindictiveness that he has trouble pinpointing the one particular phrase that set him off. At first, it was all quite childish. Irritation on his part over Bobby's negligence, yet one more botch in a long line of botches, how could he be so stupid and careless, look at the mess you've gotten us into now. On Bobby's part, irritation over his brother's tight-assed response to a minor inconvenience, his sancti-monious rectitude, the know-it-all superiority he'd been busting his balls with for years. Boys' stuff, hotheaded adolescent boys' stuff, nothing terribly alarming. But then, as they continued going at each other and Bobby warmed up to the battle, the dispute reached a deeper, more reso-nant level of bitterness, the nether lode of bad blood. It became the family then and not just the two of them. It was about how Bobby resented being the outcast of the holy four, how he couldn't stand his mother's attachment to Miles, how he'd had it up to here with the punishments and groundings that had been meted out to him by heart-less, vengeful adults, how he couldn't bear to listen to another word about academic conferences and publishing deals and why this book was better than that book—he was sick of it all, sick of Miles, sick of his mother and step-father, sick of everyone in that stinking household, and he couldn't wait to be gone from there and off at college next month, and even if he flunked out of college, he was through with them and wouldn't be coming back. Adios, assholes. Fuck Morris Heller and his goddamned son. Fuck the whole fucking world.

He can't remember which word or words pushed him over the edge. Perhaps it isn't important to know that, per-haps it will never be possible to remember which insult from that rancorous spew of invective was responsible for the shove, but what is important, what counts above all else, is to know if he heard the car coming toward them or not, the car that was suddenly visible after rounding a sharp curve at fifty miles an hour, visible only when it was already too late to prevent his brother from being hit. What is certain is that Bobby was shouting at him and he was shouting back, telling him to stop, telling him to shut up, and all through that insane shouting match they were continuing to walk down the road, oblivious to everything around them, the woods to their left, the meadow to their right, the hazy sky above them, the birds singing in every pocket of the air, finches, thrushes, warblers, all those things had disappeared by then, and the only thing left was the fury of their voices. It seems certain that Bobby didn't hear the approaching car—or else he wasn't concerned by it, since he was walking on the shoulder of the road and didn't feel he was in danger. But what about you? Miles asks himself. Did you know or didn't you know?

It was a hard, decisive shove. It knocked Bobby off balance and sent him staggering onto the road, where he fell down and cracked his head against the asphalt. He sat up almost immediately, rubbing his head and cursing, and before he could climb to his feet, the car was mowing him down, crushing the life out of him, changing all their lives forever.

That is the first thing he refuses to share with Pilar. The second thing is the letter he wrote to his parents five years after Bobby's death. He had just finished his junior year at Brown and was planning to spend the summer in Providence, working as a part-time researcher for one of his history professors (nights and weekends in the library) and a full-time deliveryman for a local appliance store (installing air conditioners, lugging TVs and refrigerators up narrow flights of stairs). A girl had recently entered the picture, and since she lived in Brooklyn, he played hooky from his research job one weekend in June and drove down to New York to see her. He still had the keys to his parents' apartment on Downing Street, his old bedroom was still intact, and ever since he'd left for college the arrangement was that he could come and go as he pleased, with no obligation to announce his visits. He started out late on Friday after finishing work at the appliance store and didn't enter the apartment until well past midnight. Both of his parents were asleep. Early the next morning, he was awakened by the sound of their voices coming from the kitchen. He climbed out of bed, opened the door of his room, and then hesitated. They were speaking more loudly and more urgently than usual, there was an anguished undertow in Willa's voice, and if they weren't exactly quarreling (they rarely quarreled), something important was taking place, some crucial business was being settled or hashed about or reexamined, and he didn't want to interrupt them.

The proper response would have been to go back into his room and shut the door. Even as he stood in the hallway listening to them, he knew he had no right to be there, that he must and should withdraw, but he couldn't

He couldn't bear to listen anymore. They were chopping him into pieces, dismembering him with the calm and efficient strokes of pathologists conducting a postmortem, talking about him as if they thought he was already dead. He slipped back into the bedroom and quietly shut the door. They had no idea how much he loved them. For five years he had been walking around with the memory of what he had done to his brother on that road in Massachusetts, and because he had never told his parents about the shove and how deeply he was tormented by it, they misread the guilt that had spread through his system as a form of sickness. Maybe he was sick, maybe he did come across as a shut-down, thoroughly unlikable person, but that didn't mean he had turned against them. Complex, high-strung, infinitely generous Willa; his open-hearted, genial father—he hated himself for having caused them so much sorrow, so much unnecessary grief. They looked on him now as a walking dead man, as someone without a future, and as he sat down on the bed and considered that futureless future hovering dimly before him, he realized that he didn't have the courage to face them again. Perhaps the best thing for all concerned would be to remove himself from their lives, to disappear.

Dear Parents, he wrote the next day, Forgive the abruptness of my decision, but after finishing yet another year of college, I find myself feeling a little burned out on school and think a pause might do me some good. I've already told the dean that I want to take a leave of absence

for the fall semester, and if that turns out to be insuffi-
cient, for the spring semester as well. I'm sorry if this dis-
appoints you. The one bright spot is that you won't have to
worry about paying my tuition for a while. Needless to say,
I don't expect any money from you. I have work and will
be able to support myself. Tomorrow, I'm taking off for
L.A. to visit my mother for a couple of weeks. After that,
as soon as I settle in wherever I happen to wind up living,
I will be in touch. Hugs and kisses to you both, Miles.

It's true that he left Providence the following morning, but he didn't go to California to see his mother. He
settled in somewhere. Over the past seven-plus years he
has settled in at any number of new addresses, but he still
hasn't been in touch.

3

It is 2008, the second Sunday in November, and he is lying in bed with Pilar, flipping through the *Baseball Encyclopedia* in search of odd and amusing names. They have done this once or twice in the past, and it counts heavily for him that she is able to see the humor in this absurd enterprise, to grasp the Dickensian spirit locked inside the two thousand seven hundred pages of the revised, updated, and expanded 1985 edition, which he bought for two dollars at a used bookstore last month. He is roaming among the pitchers this morning, since he always gravitates toward the pitchers first, and before long he stumbles upon his first promising find of the day. Boots Poffenberger. Pili scrunches up her face in an effort not to laugh, then shuts her eyes, then holds her breath, but she can't resist for more than a few seconds. The air comes bursting out of her in a tornado of yelps, screeches, and firecracker guffaws. When the fit subsides, she tears the book from his hands, accusing him of having made it up. He says: I would never do that. Games like this aren't fun unless you take them seriously.

And there it is, sitting in the middle of page 1977: Cletus Elwood "Boots" Poffenberger, born July 1, 1915, in

Williamsport, Maryland, a five-foot-ten-inch right-hander who played two years with the Tigers (1937 and 1938) and one year with the Dodgers (1939), compiling a career record of sixteen wins and twelve losses.

He continues on through Whammy Douglas, Cy Slapnicka, Noodles Hahn, Wickey McAvoy, Windy McCall, and Billy McCool. On hearing this last name, Pili groans with pleasure. She is smitten. For the rest of the morning, he is no longer Miles. He is Billy McCool, her sweet and beloved Billy McCool, ace of the staff, ace in the hole, her ace of hearts.

On the eleventh, he reads in the paper that Herb Score has died. He is too young to have seen him pitch, but he remembers the story his father told about the night of May 7, 1957, when a line drive off the bat of Yankee infielder Gil McDougald hit Score in the face and put an end to one of the most promising careers in baseball history. According to his father, who was ten years old at the time, Score was the best left-hander anyone had ever seen, possibly even better than Koufax, who was also pitching then but didn't come into his own until several years later. The accident occurred exactly one month before Score's twenty-fourth birthday. It was his third season with the Cleveland Indians, following his rookie-of-the-year performance in 1955 (16–10, 2.85 earned run average, 245 strikeouts) and an even more impressive performance the next year (20–9, 2.53 earned run average, 263 strikeouts). Then came the pitch to McDougald on that chilly spring night at Municipal

Stadium. The ball knocked Score down *as if he'd been shot by a rifle* (his father's words), and as his motionless body lay crumpled on the field, blood was pouring from his nose, mouth, and right eye. The nose was broken, but more devastating was the injury to the eye, which was hemorrhaging so badly that most people feared he would lose it or be blinded for life. In the locker room after the game, McDougald, utterly distraught, promised to quit baseball *if Herb loses the sight in his eye.* Score spent three weeks in a hospital and missed the rest of the season with blurred vision and depth-perception difficulties, but the eye eventually healed. When he attempted a comeback the next season, however, he was no longer the same pitcher. The sting in his fastball was gone, he was wild, he couldn't strike anyone out. He struggled for five years, won only seventeen games in fifty-seven starts, and then packed it in and went home.

Reading the obituary in the *New York Times*, he is astonished to learn that Score was a cursed man from the beginning, that the 1957 accident was only one of many mishaps that plagued him throughout his life. In the words of obit writer Richard Goldstein: *When he was three, he was struck by a bakery truck, which severely injured his legs. He missed a year of school with rheumatic fever, broke an ankle slipping on a wet locker-room floor and separated his left shoulder slipping on wet outfield grass while in the low minor leagues.* Not to speak of hurting his left arm during the comeback year of 1958, being gravely injured in a car crash in 1998, and suffering a stroke in 2002, from which he never fully recovered. It doesn't seem possible for a man to have encountered so much bad luck in the course of a single lifetime. For once, Miles is tempted to call his father, to chat with him about Herbert Jude Score and the imponderables of fate, the strangeness of life, the what-ifs and might-have-beens, all the things they used to talk about so long ago, but now isn't the time, if there ever is a time it mustn't begin with a long-distance phone call, and consequently he fights off the impulse, holding on to the story until he is with Pilar again that evening.

As he reads the obituary to her, he is alarmed by the sadness that washes over her face, the depth of misery emanating from her eyes, her downturned mouth, the dejected droop of her shoulders. He can't be certain, but he wonders if she isn't thinking about her parents and their abrupt and terrible deaths, the bad luck that took them from her when she was still so young, still so much in need of them, and he regrets having brought up the subject, feels ashamed of himself for having caused her this hurt. To lift her spirits, he tosses the paper aside and launches into another story, another one of the many stories his father used to tell him, but this one is special, it was folklore around the house for years, and he hopes it will erase the gloom from her eyes. Lucky Lohrke, he says. Has she ever heard of him? No, of course not, she answers, smiling ever so slightly at the sound of the name. Another

baseball player? Yes, he replies, but not a very distin-
guished one. A utility infielder for the Giants and Phillies
in the late forties and early fifties, a career .240 hitter, of
no particular interest except for the fact that this fellow,
Jack Lohrke, a.k.a. Lucky, is the mythic embodiment of a
theory of life that contends that not all luck is bad luck.
Consider this, he says. While serving in the army during
World War II, not only did he survive the D-day invasion
and the Battle of the Bulge, but one afternoon, in the thick
of combat, he was marching along with four other soldiers, two on either side of him, when a bomb exploded.
The four other soldiers were killed instantly, but Lohrke
walked through without a scratch. Or this, he continues.
The war ends, and Lucky is about to get on a plane that
will fly him back home to California. At the last moment,
a major or a colonel shows up, pulls rank on him, takes
his seat, and Lucky is bumped from the flight. The plane
takes off, the plane crashes, and everyone on board is killed.

This is a true story? Pilar asks.

One hundred percent true. If you don't believe me,
look it up.

You know the weirdest things, Miles.

Wait. There's still one more to go. It's nineteen forty-
six, and Lucky is back on the West Coast, playing baseball
in the minor leagues. His team is on the road, traveling by
bus. They stop somewhere for lunch, and a call comes for
the manager, telling him that Lucky has been promoted to
a higher league. Lucky has to report to his new team right

away, on the double, and so rather than get back on the bus with his old team, he gathers up his belongings and hitchhikes home. The bus continues, it's a long trip, hours and hours of driving, and in the middle of the night it starts to rain. They're high up in the mountains some-where, surrounded by darkness, wetness, and the driver loses control of the wheel, the bus goes tumbling into a ravine, and nine players are killed. Awful. But our little man has been spared again. Think of the odds, Pili. Death comes looking for him three times, and three times he manages to escape.

Lucky Lohrke, she whispers. Is he still alive?

I think so. He'd be well into his eighties by now, but yes, I think he's still with us.

Some days after that, Pilar finds out the scores of her SATs. The news is good, as good or better than he hoped it would be. With her unbroken run of A's in high school and these results from the test, he is convinced she will be accepted by any college she applies to, any college in the country. Ignoring his oath about not eating in restaurants, he takes her to a celebratory dinner the next night and struggles throughout the meal not to touch her in public. He is so proud of her, he says, he wants to kiss every inch of her body, to gobble her up. They discuss the various possibilities in front of her, and he urges her to think about leaving Florida, to take a stab at some of the Ivy League schools up north, but Pilar is reluctant to consider such a step, she can't imagine being so far away from her sisters. You never know, he tells her, things could change between now and then, and it won't do any harm to try—just to see if you can get in. Yes, she answers, but the applications are expensive, and it doesn't make sense to throw away money for no reason. Don't worry about the money, he says to her. He will pay. She mustn't worry about anything.

By the end of the following week, she is up to her neck in forms. Not just from the state universities in Florida, but from Barnard, Vassar, Duke, Princeton, and Brown as well. She fills them out, composes all the required essays (which he reads over but does not alter or correct, since no alterations or corrections are necessary), and then they return to life as they once knew it, before the college madness began. Later that month, he receives a letter from an old friend in New York, one of the boys from the gang of *crazy kids* he used to run around with in high school. Bing Nathan is the only person from the past he still writes to, the only person who has known each one of his many addresses over the years. At first, he was mystified by his willingness to make this exception for Bing, but after he had been gone for six or eight months, he understood that he couldn't cut himself off completely, that he needed at least one link to his old life. It isn't that he and Bing have ever been particularly close. The truth is that he finds Bing somewhat off-putting, at times even obnoxious, but Bing looks up to him, for unknown reasons he has attained the

status of exalted figure in Bing's eyes, and that means
Bing can be trusted, relied upon to keep him informed
about any changes on the New York front. That is the nub
of it. Bing was the one who told him about his grandmother's death, the one who told him about his father's
broken leg, the one who told him about Willa's eye operation. His father is sixty-two years old now, Willa is sixty,
and they aren't going to live forever. Bing has his ear to
the ground. If anything happens to either one of them, he
will be on the phone the next minute.

Bing reports that he is now living in an area of Brooklyn called Sunset Park. In mid-August, he and a group of
people took over a small abandoned house on a street
across from Green-Wood Cemetery and have been camped
out there as squatters ever since. For reasons unknown,
the electricity and the heat are still functioning. That
could change at any second, of course, but for now it
appears there is a glitch in the system, and neither Con
Ed nor National Grid has come to shut off the service.
Life is precarious, yes, and each morning they wake up to
the threat of immediate and forcible eviction, but with the
city buckling under the pressure of economic hard times,
so many government jobs have been lost that the little
band from Sunset Park seems to be flying under the
municipal radar, and no marshals or bailiffs have shown
up to kick them out. Bing doesn't know if Miles is looking for a change, but one of the original members of the
group has recently left town, and a room is available for

him if he wants it. The previous occupant was named Millie, and to replace Millie with Miles seems alphabetically coherent, he says. *Alphabetically coherent.* Another example of Bing's wit, which has never been his strong point, but the offer seems genuine, and as Bing goes on to describe the other people who are living there (a man and two women, a writer, an artist, and a graduate student, all in their late twenties, all poor and struggling, all with talent and intelligence), it is clear that he is trying to make a move to Sunset Park sound as attractive as possible. Bing concludes that at last word all was well with Miles's father and that Willa left for England in September, where she will be spending the academic year as a visiting professor at Exeter University. In a brief postscript he adds: Think it over.

Does he want to return to New York? Has the moment finally come for the wayward son to crawl home and put his life together again? Six months ago, he probably wouldn't have hesitated. Even one month ago, he might have been tempted to consider it, but now it is out of the question. Pilar has claimed dominion over his heart, and the mere thought of going off without her is unbearable to him. As he folds up Bing's letter and puts it back in the envelope, he silently thanks his friend for having clarified the issue in such stark terms. Nothing matters anymore except Pilar, and when the time is right, meaning when a little more time has passed and she has reached her next birthday, he will ask her to marry him. It is far from clear that she will accept, but he has every intention of asking her. That is his answer to Bing's letter. Pilar.

The problem is that Pilar is more than just Pilar. She is a member of the Sanchez family, and even if her relations with Angela are somewhat strained at the moment, Maria and Teresa are as close to her as ever. All four girls are still grieving over the loss of their parents, and strong as Pilar's attachment to him might be, her family still comes first. After living with him since June, she has forgotten how determined she was to fly out of the nest. She has become nostalgic for the old days, and not a week goes by now when she doesn't stop by the house to visit with her sisters at least twice. He stays out of it and accompanies her only rarely, as little as possible. Maria and Teresa are polite and innocuous motormouths, unobjectionable but boring company for more than an hour at a stretch, and Angela, who is anything but boring, rubs him the wrong way. He doesn't like how she keeps looking at him, scrutinizing him with that odd combination of contempt and seductiveness in her eyes, as if she can't quite believe her baby sister has snagged him—not that she has any interest in him herself (how could anyone be interested in a grubby trash-out worker?), but it's the principle of the thing, since reason dictates that he should be attracted to her, the beautiful woman, whose job in life is to be a beautiful woman and make men fall for her. That is bad enough, but he still carries around the memory of the bribes he paid her last summer, the countless stolen presents he showered on her every day for a week, and even if it was all to a good purpose, he couldn't help feeling revolted by her avidity, her inexhaustible craving for those ugly, stupid things.

On the twenty-seventh, he allows Pilar to talk him into going to the Sanchez house for Thanksgiving dinner. He does it against his better judgment, but he wants to make her happy, and he knows that if he stays behind he will do nothing but sulk in the apartment until she returns. For the first hour, all goes reasonably well, and he is startled to discover that he is actually enjoying himself. As the four girls prepare the meal in the kitchen, he and Maria's boyfriend, a twenty-three-year-old auto mechanic named Eddie, go into the backyard to keep an eye on little Carlos. Eddie turns out to be a baseball fan, a well-read and knowledgeable student of the game, and in the aftermath of Herb Score's recent death, they fall into a conversation about the tragic destinies of various pitchers from decades past.

It begins with Denny McLain of the Detroit Tigers, the last man to win thirty games and no doubt the last one who ever will, the top pitcher in America from 1965 to 1969, whose career was destroyed by compulsive gambling binges and a penchant for choosing mobsters as his closest friends. Gone from the scene by the time he was twenty-eight, he later went to prison for drug trafficking, embezzlement, and racketeering, gorged himself up to a titanic three hundred and thirty pounds, and returned to prison for six years in the nineties for stealing two and a half million dollars from the pension fund of the company he worked for.

He did it to himself, Eddie says, so I can't feel no pity for him. But think of a guy like Blass. What the hell happened to him?

He is referring to Steve Blass, who played for the Pittsburgh Pirates from the mid-sixties to the mid-seventies, a consistent double-digit winner, pitching star of the 1971 World Series, who went on to have his best season in 1972 (19–8, 2.49 earned run average), and then, following the end of that season, on the last day of the year, Roberto Clemente, his future Hall of Fame teammate, was killed in a plane crash on his way to deliver emergency relief packages to the survivors of an earthquake in Nicaragua. The next season, Blass could no longer throw strikes. His once excellent control was gone, he walked batter after batter—eighty-four in eighty-eight innings—and his record dropped to 3–9 with a 9.85 earned run average. He tried again the next year, but after one game (five innings pitched, seven batters walked), he quit the game for good. Was Clemente's death responsible for Blass's sudden downfall? No one knows for certain, but according to Eddie, most people in baseball circles tend to believe that Blass was suffering from something called survivor's guilt, that his love for Clemente was so great he simply couldn't go on after his friend was killed.

At least Blass had seven or eight good years, Miles says. Think about poor Mark Fidrych.

Ah, Eddie replies, Mark "the Bird" Fidrych, and then the two of them launch into a eulogy for the brief and flamboyant career of the out-of-nowhere sensation who dazzled the country for the space of a few miraculous months, the twenty-one-year-old boy who was perhaps the most lovable person ever to play the game. No one had seen his like before—a pitcher who talked to the ball, who got down on his knees and smoothed out the dirt on the mound, whose entire fidgety being seemed to be electrified by constant jolts of hectic, nervous energy—not a man so much as a perpetual motion machine in the shape of a man. For one season he was dominant: 19–9, a 2.34 earned run average, starting pitcher for the American League in the All-Star game, rookie of the year. A few months later, he damaged the cartilage in his knee while horsing around in the outfield during spring training, and then, even worse, tore up his shoulder just after the start of the regular season. His arm went dead, and just like that, the Bird was gone— from pitcher to ex-pitcher in the blink of an eye.

Yes, Eddie says, a sad case, but nothing to compare with what happened to Donnie Moore.

No, nothing to compare, says Miles, nodding in agreement.

He is old enough to have lived through the story himself, and he can still remember the stunned expression in his father's eyes when he looked up from his newspaper at breakfast twenty years ago and announced that Moore was dead. Donnie Moore, a relief pitcher with the California

Angels, was brought in to shut down a ninth-inning rally by the Boston Red Sox in the fifth game of the 1986 American League Championship Series. The Angels were ahead by a run, on the verge of winning their first pennant, but with two outs and a runner on first base, Moore delivered one of the most unfortunate pitches ever thrown in the annals of the sport—the one that Boston outfielder Dave Henderson knocked out of the park for a home run, the one that turned the course of the game and led to the Angels' defeat. Moore never recovered from the humiliation. Three years after throwing that life-altering pitch, by then out of baseball, dogged by financial and marital difficulties, perhaps certifiably insane, Moore got into an argument with his wife in the presence of their three children. He pulled out a gun, fired three nonfatal shots into his wife's body, and then turned the gun on himself and blew his brains out.

Eddie looks at Miles and shakes his head in disbelief. I don't get it, he says. What he did wasn't no worse than what Branca did when he threw that pitch to Thomson in fifty-one. But Branca didn't kill himself, did he? He and Thomson are buddies now, they go around the country signing goddamned baseballs together, and whenever you see a picture of them they're smiling at each other, two old coots without a care in the world. Why isn't Donnie Moore out there signing balls with Henderson instead of lying in his grave?

Miles shrugs. It's a question of character, he says.

Every man is different from every other man, and when rough things happen, each man reacts in his own way. Moore cracked. Branca didn't.

He finds it soothing to talk about these things with Eduardo Martinez in the late afternoon light of this Thanksgiving Thursday, and even if the subject matter could be considered somewhat grim—stories about failure, disappointment, and death—baseball is a universe as large as life itself, and therefore all things in life, whether good or bad, whether tragic or comic, fall within its domain. Today they are examining instances of despair and blighted hope, but the next time they meet (assuming they meet again), they could fill an afternoon with scores of funny anecdotes that would make their stomachs hurt from laughing so hard. Eddie strikes him as an earnest, well-meaning kid, and he is touched that Maria's new boyfriend has donned a jacket and tie for this holiday visit to the Sanchez household, that he is sporting a fresh haircut, and that the air is filled with the smell of the cologne he has put on for the occasion. The boy is pleasant company, but just as useful as *pleasant* is the simple fact that Eddie is there, that he has been given a male ally in this country of women. When they are called in for dinner, Eddie's presence at the table seems to neutralize Angela's hostility toward him, or at least deflect her attention from him and reduce the number of challenging looks he normally receives from her. There is another person to look at now, another stranger to be sized up and judged, to be deemed worthy or unworthy of yet another

[45]

younger sister of hers. Eddie seems to be passing the test, but it puzzles Miles that Angela hasn't bothered to arrange a date of her own for the evening, that she is apparently without a boyfriend. Teresa's husband is far away, of course, and he fully expected her to be without a male companion, but why hasn't Angela invited a man to join them? Maybe Miss Beautiful doesn't like men, he thinks. Maybe her work at the Blue Devil cocktail lounge has soured her on the whole business.

Sergeant Lopez has not been home for ten months, and the meal begins with a silent prayer for his continued safety. A few seconds after they begin, everyone looks up as Teresa sniffs back a sudden onrush of tears. Pilar, who is sitting next to her, puts her arm around Teresa's shoulder and kisses her on the cheek. He looks down at the tablecloth again and resists addressing his thoughts to God. God has nothing to do with what is happening in Iraq, he says to himself. God has nothing to do with anything. He imagines George Bush and Dick Cheney being lined up against a wall and shot, and then, for Pilar's sake, for the sake of everyone there, he hopes that Teresa's husband will be lucky enough to make it back in one piece.

He is beginning to think he will get through this trial without any unpleasantness from Angela. They have polished off several courses by now, everyone is attacking the dessert, and afterward, as a gesture of goodwill, he will offer to do the dishes, do them by himself with no help from anyone, and once he has washed and dried the innumerable plates and glasses and utensils, once he has scrubbed the pots and pans and put everything back in the cupboards, he will go out to the living room and fetch Pilar, telling them that it's late, that he has to work tomorrow, and off they'll go, just the two of them, slipping out of the house and climbing into his car before another word can be spoken. An excellent plan, perhaps, but the moment Angela finishes the last forkful of her pumpkin pie (no Cuban food today, everything strictly American, from the big bird with the stuffing in it to the cranberry sauce and the gravy and the sweet potatoes and the traditional dessert), she puts down her fork, removes the napkin from her lap, and stands up. I need to talk to you, Miles, she says. Let's go out back where we can be alone, okay? It's very important.

It isn't important. It isn't the least bit important. Angela is feeling deprived, that's all it is. Christmas is coming soon, and she wants him to help her out again. What does she mean by that? he asks. Stuff, she says. Like what he did for her this summer. Impossible, he tells her, it's against the law to steal, and he doesn't want to lose his job.

You did it for me once, she says. There's no reason why you can't do it again.

I can't, he repeats. I can't risk getting into trouble.

You're full of shit, Miles. Everybody does it. I hear stories, I know what's been going on. Those trash-out jobs are like walking into a department store. Grand pianos, sailboats, motorcycles, jewelry, all kinds of expensive stuff. The workers pinch everything they can lay their hands on.

Not me.

I'm not asking for a sailboat. And what do I need a piano for when I can't even play? But nice stuff, you know what I mean? Good stuff. Stuff that will make me happy.

You're knocking on the wrong door, Angela.

You're really a stupid guy, aren't you, Miles?

Come to the point. I assume you're trying to tell me something, but all I hear is static.

Have you forgotten how old Pilar is?

You're not serious . . .

No?

You wouldn't dare. She's your own sister, remember?

One call to the cops, and you're toast, my friend.

Cut it out. Pilar would spit in your face. She'd never talk to you again.

Think about the stuff, Miles. Pretty stuff. Big mounds of pretty stuff. It's a lot better than thinking about jail, isn't it?

In the car on the way home, Pilar asks what Angela wanted to talk to him about, but he avoids telling her the truth, not wanting her to know how much contempt he feels for her sister, how profoundly he despises her. He mutters something about Christmas, a secret plan the two of them have been cooking up together that involves the whole family, but he can't breathe a word because Angela has made him promise to keep quiet about it until further notice.

This seems to satisfy Pilar, who grins at the prospect of whatever good thing is in store for them, and by the time they are halfway back to their apartment, they are no longer talking about Angela, they are discussing their impressions of Eddie. Pilar finds him *sweet* and not at all bad-looking, but she wonders if he is smart enough for Maria—to which he offers no comment. In his mind, the question is whether Maria is smart enough for Eddie, but he isn't about to offend Pilar by insulting her sister's intelligence. Instead, he reaches out his right hand and begins stroking her hair, asking her what she thinks of the book he gave her this morning, *Dubliners*.

He goes back to work the next day, convinced that Angela's threat is nothing more than a bluff, a nasty little piece of theater designed to break down his resistance and get him to start stealing for her again. He isn't going to fall for such a mindless, transparent trick, and over his dead body will he give her a single thing—not even a toothpick, not even a used paper napkin, not even one of Paco's farts.

On Sunday afternoon, Pilar goes to the Sanchez house to spend a couple of hours with her sisters. Again, he has no wish to join her and remains in the apartment to prepare their dinner while she is gone (he is the one who shops and cooks for them), and when Pilar returns at six o'clock, she tells him that Angela asked her to remind him not to forget about their deal. She says she can't wait forever, Pilar adds, repeating her sister's words with a confused, questioning look in her eyes. What in the world does she mean by that? she asks. Nothing, he says, dismissing this new threat with a curt shake of the head. Absolutely nothing.

Two more days of work, three more days of work, four more days of work, and then, late on Friday, just after wrapping up the final trash-out operation of the week, as he walks away from yet another empty house and heads for his car across the street, he spots two men leaning against the front and back doors of the red Toyota, two large men, one Anglo and the other Latino, two very large men who look like defensive tackles or professional bodybuilders or nightclub bouncers, and if they are bouncers, he thinks, perhaps they are employed by an establishment called the Blue Devil. The wisest course of action would be to turn and run, but it is already too late, the men have already seen him approaching, and if he runs now, he will only make things worse for himself, since it is altogether certain that they will catch up to him in the end. It's not that he is a small person or that he shies away from fights. He stands at six-two now, he weighs one hundred and eighty-seven pounds, and after years of working at jobs that have asked more from his body than his mind, he is in better than passable condition—well built, muscular, strong. But not as strong as either one of the two men waiting for him, and because they are two and he is one, he can only hope the men are here to talk and not to demonstrate their fighting skills.

Miles Heller? the Anglo asks.

What can I do for you? he replies.

We have a message from Angela.

Why doesn't she give it to me herself?

Because you don't listen to her when she talks to you. She thought you might pay more attention if we delivered the message for her.

All right, I'm listening.

Angela is pissed off, and she's beginning to lose her patience. She says you have one more week, and if you don't come through for her by then, she's going to pick up the phone and make that call. You got it?

Yes, I've got it.

Are you sure?

Yes, yes, I'm sure.

Are you sure you're sure?

Yes.

Good. But just to make sure you don't forget you're sure, I'm going to give you a little present. Like one of those strings you tie around your finger when you want to remember something. You know what I'm talking about?

I think so.

Without warning, the man hauls off and punches him in the gut. It is a cannonball of a punch, a punch so colossal in its force and so devastating in its effect that it knocks him to the ground, and as he is knocked to the ground the air is knocked out of his lungs, and along with the air that comes bursting through his windpipe there also comes the entire contents of his stomach, his lunch and his breakfast, remnant particles from last night's dinner, and everything

[51]

that was inside him a moment ago is now outside him, and as he lies there puking and gasping for breath and clutching his belly in pain, the two large men walk off to their čar, leaving him alone in the street, a wounded animal felled by that single blow, a man wishing he were dead.

An hour later, Pilar knows everything. The bluff was not a bluff, and therefore he can no longer hold out on her. They are suddenly in a dangerous spot, and it is essential for her to know the truth. She cries at first, finding it impossible to believe that her sister could act like this, threatening to put him in jail, willing to ruin her happiness for the sake of a few measly things, none of it makes any sense to her. It's not the things, he says. The things are only an excuse. Angela doesn't like him, she's been against him from the start, and Pilar's happiness means nothing to her if that happiness is connected to him. He doesn't understand why she should feel such animosity, but there it is, it's a fact, and they have no choice but to accept it. Pilar wants to jump into the car, drive over to the house, and slap Angela across the face. That's what she deserves, he says, but you can't do it now. You have to wait until after I'm gone.

It is a horrible solution, an unthinkable solution, but the only one left to them under the circumstances. He must leave the state. There is no alternative. He must get out of Florida before Angela picks up the phone and calls the police, and he mustn't come back until the morning of May twenty-third, when Pilar turns eighteen. He is tempted to ask her to marry him right then and there, but too many things are happening at once, they are both miserable and overwrought, and he doesn't want to pressure her or confuse her, to complicate an already complicated business when so little time is left.

He tells her that a friend has a room for him somewhere in Brooklyn. He gives her the address and promises to call every day. Since going back to the family house is out of the question now, she will remain in the apartment. He writes out a check to cover six months' rent in advance, signs over the title of his car to her, and then takes her to the bank, where he shows her how to use the automated teller machine. There are twelve thousand dollars in his account. He withdraws three thousand for himself and leaves the remaining nine thousand for her. After slipping the bank card into her hand, he puts his arm around her as they walk out into the blaze of the midafternoon sun. It is the first time he has touched her in public, and he does it consciously, as an act of defiance.

He packs a small bag with two changes of clothes, his camera, and three or four books. He leaves everything else where it is—to convince her that he will be coming back.

Early the next morning, he is sitting on a bus headed for New York.

4

It is a long, tedious trip, more than thirty hours from start to finish, with close to a dozen stopovers ranging from ten minutes to two hours, and from one leg of the journey to the next the seat adjacent to his is variously occupied by a round, wheezing black woman, a sniffing Indian or Pakistani man, a bony, throat-clearing white woman of eighty, and a coughing German tourist of such indeterminate aspect that he can't tell whether the person sitting next to him is a woman or a man. He says nothing to any of them, keeping his nose in his book or pretending to sleep, and every time there is a break in the journey he scampers out of the bus and calls Pilar.

In Jacksonville, the longest stopover of the trip, he works his way through two fast-food hamburgers and a large bottle of water, chewing and swallowing with care, since his stomach muscles are still exceedingly tender from the punch that knocked him down on Friday. Yes, the pain is just as effective as a string you tie around your finger, and the large man with the stone fist was right to assume he wouldn't forget it. After finishing his snack, he wanders over to the terminal kiosk, where everything from licorice sticks to condoms are for sale. He buys several newspapers and magazines, stocking up on additional reading material in case he wants a pause between books during the hundreds of miles still ahead. Two and a half hours later, as the bus is approaching Savannah, Georgia, he opens the *New York Times*, and on the second page of the arts section, in a column of squibs about upcoming events and the doings of well-known personalities, he sees a small picture of his mother. It is not unusual for him to come across pictures of his mother. It has been happening to him for as long as he can remember, and given that she is a well-known actress, it is only natural that her face should turn up frequently in the press. The short article in the *Times* is of special interest to him, however. Having spent most of her life working in movies and television, his mother is returning to the New York stage after an absence of ten years to appear in a production that will be opening in January. In other words, there is a better than even chance that she is already in New York rehearsing her role, which means that for the first time in how many years, in how many long, excruciating centuries, both his mother and father will be living in New York at the same moment, which is the selfsame moment when their son will find himself there as well. How odd. How terribly odd and incomprehensible. No doubt it means nothing, nothing whatsoever, and yet why now, he asks himself, why did he choose to go back now? Because he didn't choose. Because the choice was made for him by a large fist that knocked him down and commanded him to run from Florida to a place called Sunset Park. Just another roll of the dice, then, another lottery pick scooped out of the black metal urn, another fluke in a world of flukes and endless mayhem.

Half his life ago, when he was fourteen years old, he was out walking with his father, just the two of them, without Willa or Bobby, who were off somewhere else that day. It was a Sunday afternoon in late spring, and he and his father were walking side by side through the West Village, on no particular errand, he remembers, just walking for the sake of walking, out in the air because the weather was especially fine that day, and after they had been strolling for an hour or an hour and a half, they sat down on a bench in Abingdon Square. For reasons that escape him now, he started asking his father questions about his mother. How and where they met, for example, when they were married, why they hadn't stayed married, and so on. He saw his mother only twice a year, and on his last visit to California he had asked her similar questions about his father, but she hadn't wanted to talk about it, she had brushed him off with a brief sentence or two. The marriage was a mistake from the start. His father was a decent man, but they were wrong for each other, and why bother to go into it now? Perhaps that was what prompted him to interrogate his father that Sunday afternoon in Abingdon Square fourteen years ago. Because his mother's answers had been so unsatisfactory, and he was hoping his father would be more receptive, more willing to talk.

He first saw her onstage, his father said, undaunted by the question, speaking without bitterness, in a neutral tone from the first sentence to the last, no doubt thinking that his son was old enough to know the facts, and now that the boy had asked the question, he deserved a straight and honest answer. Curiously enough, the theater wasn't far from where they were sitting now, his father said, the old Circle Rep on Seventh Avenue. It was October 1978, and she was playing Cordelia in a production of *King Lear,* a twenty-four-year-old actress named Mary-Lee Swann, a glorious name for an actress in his opinion, and she gave a moving performance, he was stirred by the strength and groundedness of her interpretation, which bore no resemblance to the saintly, simpering Cordelias he had seen in the past. *What shall Cordelia speak? Love, and be silent.* She delivered those words with a self-questioning hesitation that seemed to open up her very insides to the audience. An extraordinary thing to behold, his father said. Utterly heartbreaking.

Yes, his father seemed willing to talk, but the story he told that afternoon was vague, ever so vague and difficult to follow. There were details, of course, the recounting of various incidents, starting with that first night when his father went out for drinks after the play with the director, who was an old friend of his, along with a few members of the cast, Mary-Lee among them. His father was thirty-two at the time, unmarried and unattached, already the publisher of Heller Books, which had been in operation for five years and was just beginning to gain momentum, largely because of the success of Renzo Michaelson's second novel, *House of Words.* He told his son that the attraction was immediate on both sides. An unexpected congruency, perhaps, in that she was a country girl from a backwater in central Maine and he was a lifelong New Yorker, born into a modicum of wealth whereas she came from little or nothing, the daughter of a man who worked as the manager of a hardware store, and yet there they were, making eyes at each other across the table in that little bar off Sheridan Square, he with his two university degrees and she with a high school diploma and a stint at the American Academy of Dramatic Arts, a waitress between roles, a person without interest in books whereas publishing books was his life's work, but who can penetrate the mysteries of desire, his father said, who can account for the unbidden thoughts that rush through a man's mind? He asked his son if he understood. The boy nodded, but in fact he understood nothing.

He was blinded by her talent, his father continued. Anyone who could perform as she had in that demanding, delicate role must have had a greater depth of heart and a wider range of feeling than any of the women he had known in the past. But pretending to be a person and actually being a person were two different things, weren't they? The wedding took place on March 12, 1979, less than five months after their first meeting. Five months after that, the marriage was already in trouble. His father didn't want to bore him by reciting a litany of their disputes and incompatibilities, but what it came down to was this: they loved each other, but they couldn't get along. Did that make any sense to him?

No, it made no sense to him at all. The boy was utterly confused by then, but he was too afraid to admit it to his father, who was making every effort to treat him as an adult, but he wasn't up to the job that day, the world of adults was unfathomable to him at that point in his life, and he couldn't grasp the paradox of love and discord coexisting in equal measure. It had to be one or the other, love or not-love, but not love and not-love at the same time. He paused for a moment to collect his thoughts, and then he asked the only question that seemed relevant to him, the only question that had any pertinent meaning. If they disliked each other so much, why did they have a baby?

It was going to rescue them, his father said. That was the plan, in any case: make a child together and then hope the love they would inevitably feel for their son or daughter would arrest the disenchantment that was growing between them. She was happy about it at first, his father said, they were both happy about it, but then—. His father abruptly cut himself off in midsentence, looked away for a moment as he shifted mental gears, and finally said: She wasn't prepared to be a mother. She was too young. I shouldn't have pushed her into it.

The boy understood that his father was trying to spare his feelings. He couldn't come out and bluntly declare that his mother hadn't wanted him, could he? That would have been too much, a blow that no person could ever fully absorb, and yet his father's silence and sympathetic evasion of the brute particulars amounted to an admission of that very fact: his mother had wanted no part of him, his birth was a mistake, there was no tenable reason for him to be alive.

When had it started? he wondered. At what point had her early happiness turned into doubt, antipathy, dread? Perhaps when her body began to change, he thought, when his presence inside her began to show itself to the world and it was too late to ignore the bulging extrusion that now defined her, not to speak of the alarm caused by the thickening of her ankles and the spreading of her bottom, all the extra weight that was distorting her once slender, ravishing self. Was that all it was—a fit of vanity? Or was it fear that she would lose ground by having to take time off from work just when she was being offered better, more interesting roles, that she was disrupting her progress at the worst possible moment and might never get back on track? Three months after she gave birth to him (July 2, 1980), she auditioned for the lead in a film to be directed by Douglas Flaherty, *Innocent Dreamer*. She got the part, and three months after that she headed for Vancouver, British Columbia, leaving her infant son in New York with his father and a live-in baby nurse, Edna Smythe, a two-hundred-pound Jamaican woman of forty-six who went on working as his nanny (and later Bobby's too) for the next seven years. As for his mother, that role launched her career in films. It also brought her a new husband (Flaherty, the director) and a new life in Los Angeles. No, his father said when the boy asked the question, she didn't fight for custody. She was *torn apart,* his father explained, quoting what she had said to him at the time, *giving up Miles was the toughest, most awful decision she had ever made,* but under the circumstances, *there didn't seem to be anything else she could do.* In other words, his father said to him that afternoon in Abingdon Square, she ditched us. You and me both, kid. She gave us the old heave-ho, and that was that.

But no regrets, he quickly added. No second thoughts or morbid exhumations of the past. His marriage to Mary-Lee hadn't worked out, but that didn't mean it could be called a failure. Time had proved that the real purpose of the two years he spent with her was not about building a sustainable marriage, it was about creating a son, and because that son was the single most important creature in the world for him, all the disappointments he'd endured with her had been worth it—no, more than worth it, absolutely necessary. Was that clear? Yes. On that point, the boy did not question what his father was saying to him. His father smiled, then put his arm around his shoulder, drew him in toward his chest, and kissed him on the top of his head. You're the apple of my eye, he said. Never forget that.

It was the only time they talked about his mother in this way. Both before and after that conversation fourteen years ago, it was largely a matter of practical arrangements, scheduling phone calls, buying plane tickets to California, reminding him to send birthday cards, figuring out how to coordinate his school holidays with his mother's acting jobs. She might have disappeared from his father's life, but lapses and inconsistencies notwithstanding, she remained a presence in his. From the very beginning, then, he was the boy with two mothers. His real mother, Willa, who had not given birth to him, and his blood mother, Mary-Lee, who played the role of exotic stranger. The early years do not exist anymore, but going back to when he was five or six years old, he can remember flying across the country to see her, the unaccompanied minor indulged by stewardesses and pilots, sitting in the cockpit before takeoff, drinking the sweet sodas he was rarely allowed to have at home, and the big house up in the hills above Los Angeles with the hummingbirds in the garden, the red and purple flowers, the junipers and mimosas, the cool nights after warm, light-flooded days. His mother was so terribly pretty back then, the elegant, lovely blonde who was sometimes referred to as the second coming of Carroll Baker or Tuesday Weld, but more gifted than they were, more intelligent in her choice of roles, and now that he was growing up, now that it was evident to her that she would not be having any more children, she called him her little prince, her precious angel, and the same boy who was the apple of his father's eye was anointed the peach of his mother's heart.

She never knew quite what to make of him, however.
There were considerable amounts of goodwill, he supposed,
but not much knowledge, not the kind of knowledge Willa
had, and consequently he seldom felt that he was standing
on solid ground with her. From one day to the next, from
one hour to the next, she could turn from ebullience to
distraction, from joking affability to withdrawn, irritable
silence. He learned to be on his guard with her, to prepare
himself for these unpredictable shifts, to savor the good
moments while they lasted but not to expect them to last
very long. She was usually between jobs when he visited,
and that might have added to the anxiety that seemed to
permeate the household. The telephone would start ringing early in the morning, and then she would be talking
to her agent, to a producer, to a director, to a fellow actor,
or else accepting or refusing to be interviewed or photo-
graphed, to appear on television, to present this or that
award, not to mention where to have dinner that night,
what party to go to next week, who said what about whom.
It was always calmer when Flaherty was around. Her husband helped smooth out the rough patches and keep her
nighttime drinking under control (she tended to get a bit
slurry when he was off on a job somewhere), and because
he had a child of his own from an earlier marriage, his
stepfather had a better feel for what he was thinking than
his own mother did. His daughter's name was Margie,
Maggie, he can't remember now, a girl with freckles and
chubby knees, and they sometimes played together in the

garden, squirting each other with the hose or staging pretend tea parties as they acted out various bits from the Mad Hatter scene in *Alice in Wonderland*. How old was he then? Six years old? Seven years old? When he was eight or nine, Flaherty, a transplanted Englishman with no interest in baseball, took it upon himself to drive them out to Chavez Ravine one night to watch the Dodgers play against the Mets, his hometown team, the club he pulled for through good years and bad. He was an amiable sort, old Flaherty, a man with much to recommend him, but when Miles returned to California six months later, Flaherty was gone, and his mother was going through her second divorce. Her new man was Simon Korngold, a producer of low-budget independent films, and against all odds, considering her record with his father and Douglas Flaherty, he is still her man today after seventeen years of marriage.

When he was twelve, she came into his room and asked him to take off his clothes. She wanted to see how he was *developing*, she said, and he reluctantly obliged her by stripping down to his bare skin, sensing that it wasn't within his power to turn down her request. She was his mother, after all, and no matter how frightened or embarrassed he felt to be standing naked in front of her, she had a right to see her son's body. She looked him over quickly, told him to turn around in a circle, and then, fixing her eyes on his genitals, she said: Promising, Miles, but still a long way to go.

When he was thirteen, after a year of tumultuous changes, to both his inner self and his physical self, she made the same request. He was sitting by the pool this time, wearing nothing but a bathing suit, and although he was even more nervous and hesitant than he had been the previous year, he stood up, peeled down the top of his trunks, and gave her a glimpse of what she wanted to see. His mother smiled and said: The little fellow isn't so little anymore, is he? Watch out, ladies. Miles Heller is in town.

When he was fourteen, he flatly said no. She looked somewhat disappointed, he felt, but she didn't insist. It's your call, kid, she said, and then she left the room.

When he was fifteen, she and Korngold threw a party at their house, a large, clamorous party with over a hundred guests, and even though many familiar faces were there, actors and actresses he had seen in films and on television, famous actors, all of them good actors, people who had either moved him or made him laugh many times over the years, he couldn't stand the noise, the sound of all those chattering voices was making him ill, and after doing his best for more than an hour, he stole upstairs to his room and lay down on the bed with a book, his book of the moment, whatever book it happened to be, and he remembers thinking that he much preferred to spend the rest of the evening with the writer of that book than with the thunderous mob downstairs. After fifteen or twenty minutes, his mother burst into the room with a drink in her hand, looking both angry and a little smashed. What did he think he was doing? Didn't he know there was a party going on, and how dare he walk out in the middle of it? So-and-so was here, and so-and-so was here, and so-and-so was here, and who gave him the right to insult them by going upstairs to read a goddamned *book*? He tried to explain that he wasn't feeling well, that he had a bad head-ache, and what difference did it make anyway if he wasn't in the mood to stand around yakking with a bunch of grown-ups? You're just like your father, she said, growing more and more exasperated. A bred-in-the-bone sourpuss. You used to be such a fun kid, Miles. Now you've turned into a pill. For some reason, he found the word *pill* deeply funny. Or perhaps it was the sight of his mother standing there with a vodka tonic in her hand that amused him, his flustered, irate mother insulting him with baby words like *sourpuss* and *pill*, and all of a sudden he started to laugh. What's so funny? she asked. I don't know, he answered, I just can't help myself. Yesterday I was your peach, and today I'm a pill. To tell you the truth, I don't think I'm either one. At that moment, which was no doubt his moth-er's finest moment, her expression changed from one of anger to mirth, changed from one to the other in a single instant, and suddenly she was laughing too. Fuck me, she said. I'm acting like a real bitch, aren't I?

When he was seventeen, she promised to come to New York for his high school graduation, but she never showed up. Curiously, he didn't hold it against her. After Bobby's death, things that had once mattered to him no longer mattered at all. He figured she had forgotten. Forgetting is not a sin—it is simple human error. The next time he saw her, she apologized, bringing up the subject before he had a chance to mention it, which he never would have done in any case.

His visits to California became less frequent. He was in college now, and during the three years he spent at Brown he went out there only twice. There were other meetings, however, lunches and dinners in New York restaurants, several long telephone conversations (always at her initiative), and a weekend together in Providence with Korngold, whose decade of steadfast loyalty to her had made it impossible for him to feel anything but admiration for the man. In some ways, Korngold reminded him of his father. Not in looks or affect or bearing, but in the work he did, which was scrambling to make small, worthwhile films in a world of mega-junk, just as his father was scrambling to publish worthwhile books in a world of fads and weightless ephemera. His mother was well into her forties by then, and she seemed more comfortable with herself than she'd been at the summit of her beauty, less involved in the intrigues of her own life, more open to others. During that weekend in Providence, she asked him if he'd thought about what he wanted to do after graduation. He wasn't sure, he said. One day he was convinced he would become a doctor, the next day he was tilting toward photography, and the day after that he was planning to go into teaching. Not writing or publishing? she asked. No, he didn't think so, he said. He loved to read books, but he had no interest in making them.

Then he vanished. His mother had nothing to do with the impetuous decision to turn on his heels and run, but once he left Willa and his father, he left her as well. For better or worse, it had to be that way, and it has to be that way now. If he goes to see his mother, she will immediately contact his father and tell him where he is, and then everything he has struggled to accomplish over the past seven and a half years will have been for naught. He has turned himself into a black sheep. That is the role he has willed himself to play, and he will go on playing it even in New York, even as he wanders back to the edge of the flock he left behind. Will he dare to go to the theater and knock on his mother's dressing room door? Will he dare to ring the bell of the apartment on Downing Street? Possibly, but he doesn't think so—or at least he can't think about it now. After all this time, he still doesn't feel quite ready.

Just north of Washington, as the bus enters the final leg of the trip, snow begins to fall. They are moving into winter now, he realizes, the cold days and long nights of his boyhood winters, and suddenly the past has turned into the future. He closes his eyes, thinking about Pilar's face, running his hands over her absent body, and then, in the darkness behind his lids, he sees himself as a black speck in a world made of snow.

BING NATHAN
AND COMPANY

Bing Nathan

He is the warrior of outrage, the champion of discontent, the militant debunker of contemporary life who dreams of forging a new reality from the ruins of a failed world. Unlike most contrarians of his ilk, he does not believe in political action. He belongs to no movement or party, has never once spoken out in public, and has no desire to lead angry hordes into the streets to burn down buildings and topple governments. It is a purely personal position, but if he lives his life according to the principles he has established for himself, he feels certain that others will follow his example.

When he talks about the world, then, he is referring to his world, to the small, circumscribed sphere of his own life, and not to the world-at-large, which is too large and too broken for him to have any effect on it. He therefore concentrates on the local, the particular, the nearly invisible details of quotidian affairs. The decisions he makes are necessarily small ones, but small does not always mean unimportant, and day after day he struggles to adhere to the fundamental rule of his discontent: to stand in opposition to things-as-they-are, to resist the status quo on all fronts. Since the war in Vietnam, which began nearly twenty years before he was born, he would argue that the concept known as *America* has played itself out, that the country is no longer a workable proposition, but if anything continues to unite the fractured masses of this defunct nation, if American opinion is still unanimous about any one idea, it is a belief in the notion of progress. He contends that they are wrong, that the technological developments of the past decades have in fact only diminished the possibilities of life. In a throwaway culture spawned by the greed of profit-driven corporations, the landscape has grown ever more shabby, ever more alienating, ever more empty of meaning and consolidating purpose. His acts of rebellion are petty ones, perhaps, peevish gestures that accomplish little or nothing even in the short run, but they help to enhance his dignity as a human being, to ennoble him in his own eyes. He takes it for granted that the future is a lost cause, and if the present is all that matters now, then it must be a present imbued with the spirit of the past. That is why he shuns cell phones, computers, and all things digital—because he refuses to participate in new technologies. That is why he spends his weekends playing drums and percussion in a six-man jazz group—because jazz is dead and only the happy few are interested in it anymore. That is why he started his business three years ago— because he wanted to fight back. The Hospital for Broken Things is located on Fifth Avenue in Park Slope. Flanked by a laundromat on one side and a vintage clothing shop on the other, it is a hole-in-the-wall storefront enterprise devoted to repairing objects from an era that has all but vanished from the face of the earth: manual typewriters, fountain pens, mechanical watches, vacuum-tube radios, record players, wind-up toys, gumball machines, and rotary telephones. Little matter that ninety percent of the money he earns comes from framing pictures. His shop provides a unique and inestimable service, and every time he works on another battered artifact from the antique industries of half a century ago, he goes about it with the willfulness and passion of a general fighting a war.

Tangibility. That is the word he uses most often when discussing his ideas with his friends. The world is tangible, he says. Human beings are tangible. They are endowed with bodies, and because those bodies feel pain and suffer from disease and undergo death, human life has not altered by a single jot since the beginning of mankind. Yes, the discovery of fire made man warmer and put an end to the raw-meat diet; the building of bridges enabled him to cross rivers and streams without getting his toes wet; the invention of the airplane allowed him to hop over continents and oceans while creating new phenomena such as jet lag and in-flight movies—but even if man has changed the world around him, man himself has not changed. The facts of life are constant. You live and then you die. You are born out of a woman's body, and if you manage to survive your birth, your mother must feed you and take care of you to ensure that you go on surviving,

and everything that happens to you from the moment of
your birth to the moment of your death, every emotion
that wells up in you, every flash of anger, every surge
of lust, every bout of tears, every gust of laughter, everything you will ever feel in the course of your life has also
been felt by everyone who came before you, whether you
are a caveman or an astronaut, whether you live in the
Gobi Desert or the Arctic Circle. It all came to him in a
sudden, epiphanic burst when he was sixteen years old.
Paging through an illustrated book about the Dead Sea
scrolls one afternoon, he stumbled across some photographs of the things that had been unearthed along with
the parchment texts: plates and eating utensils, straw baskets, pots, jugs, all of them perfectly intact. He studied
them carefully for several moments, not quite understanding why he found these objects so compelling, and then,
after several more moments, it finally came to him. The
decorative patterns on the dishes were identical to the patterns on the dishes in the window of the store across the
street from his apartment. The straw baskets were identical to the baskets millions of Europeans use to shop with
today. The things in the pictures were two thousand years
old, and yet they looked utterly new, utterly contemporary. That was the revelation that changed his thinking
about human time: if a person from two thousand years
ago, living in a far-flung outpost of the Roman Empire,
could fashion a household item that looked exactly like a
household item from today, how was that person's mind or

heart or inner being any different from his own? That is the story he never tires of repeating to his friends, his counterargument to the prevailing belief that new technologies alter human consciousness. Microscopes and telescopes have permitted us to see more things than ever before, he says, but our days are still spent in the realm of normal sight. E-mails are faster than posted letters, he says, but in the end they're just another form of letter writing. He reels off example after example. He knows he drives them crazy with his conjectures and opinions, that he bores them with his long, nattering harangues, but these are important issues to him, and once he gets started, he finds it difficult to stop.

He is a large, hulking presence, a sloppy bear of a man with a full brown beard and a gold stud in his left earlobe, an inch under six feet tall but a wide and waddling two hundred and twenty pounds. His daily uniform consists of a pair of sagging black jeans, yellow work boots, and a plaid lumberjack shirt. He changes his underwear infrequently. He chews his food too loudly. He has been unlucky in love. Of all the things he does in life, playing the drums gives him the most pleasure. He was a boisterous child, a noisemaker of undisciplined exuberance and clumsy, scattershot aggression, and when his parents presented him with a drum set on his twelfth birthday, hoping his destructive urges might take a new form, their hunch proved correct. Seventeen years later, his collection has grown from the standard kit (snare drums, tom-toms, side drum, bass drum, suspended cymbals, hi-hat cymbals) to include more than two dozen drums of various shapes and sizes from around the world, among them a murumba, a batá, a dar-buka, an okedo, a kalangu, a rommelpot, a bodhrán, a dhola, an ingungu, a koboro, a ntenga, and a tabor. Depend-ing on the instrument, he plays with sticks, mallets, or hands. His percussion closet is stocked with standbys such as bells, gongs, bull-roarers, castanets, clappers, chimes, washboards, and kalimbas, but he has also performed with chains, spoons, pebbles, sandpaper, and rattles. The band he belongs to is called Mob Rule, and they average two or three gigs a month, mostly in small bars and clubs in Brooklyn and lower Manhattan. If they earned more money, he would gladly drop everything and spend the rest of his life touring the world with them, but they barely earn enough to cover the costs of their rehearsal space. He loves the harsh, dissonant, improvised sound they create—shit-kicking funk, as he sometimes calls it—and they are not without their loyal followers. But there aren't enough of them, not nearly enough, and so he spends his morn-ings and afternoons in the Hospital for Broken Things, putting frames around movie posters and mending relics that were built when his grandparents were children.

When Ellen Brice told him about the abandoned house in Sunset Park this past summer, he saw it as an opportu-nity to put his ideas to the test, to move beyond his invis-ible, solitary attacks on the system and participate in a communal action. It is the boldest step he has yet taken, and he has no trouble reconciling the illegality of what they are doing with their right to do it. These are desperate times for everyone, and a crumbling wooden house standing empty in a neighborhood as ragged as this one is nothing if not an open invitation to vandals and arsonists, an eyesore begging to be broken into and pillaged, a menace to the well-being of the community. By occupying that house, he and his friends are protecting the safety of the street, making life more livable for everyone around them. It is early December now, and they have been squatting there for close to four months. Because it was his idea to move there in the first place, and because he was the one who picked the soldiers of their little army, and because he is the only one who knows anything about carpentry, plumbing, and electric wiring, he is the unofficial leader of the group. Not a beloved leader, perhaps, but a tolerated leader, for they all know the experiment would fall apart without him.

Ellen was the first person he asked. Without her, he never would have set foot in Sunset Park and discovered the house, and therefore it seemed only fitting to give her the right of first refusal. He has known her since they were small children, when they went to elementary school together on the Upper West Side, but then they lost contact for many years, only to find out seven months ago that they were both living in Brooklyn and were in fact not terribly distant Park Slope neighbors. She walked into the Hospital one afternoon to have something framed, and

although he didn't recognize her at first (could anyone recognize a twenty-nine-year-old woman last seen as a girl of
twelve?), when he wrote down her name on the order form
he instantly understood that this was the Ellen Brice he
had known as a boy. Strange little Ellen Brice, all grown
up now and working as a real estate agent for a firm on
Seventh Avenue and Ninth Street, an artist in her spare
time in the same way he is a musician in his spare time,
although he has the semblance of a career and she does
not. That first afternoon in the shop, he blundered in with
his usual friendly, tactless questions and soon learned that
she was still unmarried, that her parents had retired to a
coastal town in North Carolina, and that her sister was
pregnant with twin boys. His first meeting with Millie
Grant was still six weeks in the future (the same Millie who
is about to be replaced by Miles Heller), and because he
and Ellen were both officially available, he asked her out
for a drink.

Nothing came of that drink, nor of the dinner he
invited her to three nights later, but there had been nothing between them as children and that continued to be the
case in adulthood as well. They were both at loose ends,
however, and even if romance was not in the picture, they
went on seeing each other from time to time and began to
build a modest friendship. It didn't matter to him that she
hadn't liked the Mob Rule concert she attended (the clang-
ing chaos of their work was not for everyone), nor was he

unduly concerned that he found her drawings and paintings
dull (meticulous, well-executed still lifes and cityscapes
that lacked all flair and originality, he felt). What counted
was that she seemed to enjoy listening to him talk and that
she never turned him down when he called. Something in
him responded to the sense of loneliness that enveloped
her, he was touched by her quiet goodness and the vulnerability he saw in her eyes, and yet the more their friendship advanced, the less he knew what to make of her. Ellen
was not an unattractive woman. Her body was trim, her face
was pleasant to look at, but she projected an aura of anxiety and defeat, and with her too pale skin and flat, luster-
less hair, he wondered if she wasn't mired in some sort of
depression, living out her days in an underground room at
the Hotel Melancholia. Whenever he saw her, he did everything in his power to make her laugh—with mixed results.

Early in the summer, on the same scorching day that
Pilar Sanchez moved in with Miles Heller down in southern Florida, a crisis broke out up north. The lease on the
storefront that housed the Hospital for Broken Things was
about to expire, and his landlord was demanding a twenty
percent rent increase. He explained that he couldn't afford
it, that the extra monthly charges would drive him out of
business, but the prick refused to budge. The only solution was to leave his apartment and find a cheaper place
somewhere else. Ellen, who worked in the rental division
of her real estate company on Seventh Avenue, told him

about Sunset Park. It was a rougher neighborhood, she said, but it wasn't far from where he was living now, and rents were a half or a third of the rents in Park Slope. That Sunday, the two of them went out to explore the territory between Fifteenth and Sixty-fifth streets in western Brooklyn, an extensive hodgepodge of an area that runs from Upper New York Bay to Ninth Avenue, home to more than a hundred thousand people, including Mexicans, Dominicans, Poles, Chinese, Jordanians, Vietnamese, American whites, American blacks, and a settlement of Christians from Gujarat, India. Warehouses, factories, abandoned waterfront facilities, a view of the Statue of Liberty, the shut-down Army Terminal where ten thousand people once worked, a basilica named Our Lady of Perpetual Help, biker bars, check-cashing places, Hispanic restaurants, the third-largest Chinatown in New York, and the four hundred and seventy-eight acres of Green-Wood Cemetery, where six hundred thousand bodies are buried, including those of Boss Tweed, Lola Montez, Currier and Ives, Henry Ward Beecher, F.A.O. Schwarz, Lorenzo Da Ponte, Horace Greeley, Louis Comfort Tiffany, Samuel F. B. Morse, Albert Anastasia, Joey Gallo, and Frank Morgan—the wizard in *The Wizard of Oz*.

Ellen showed him six or seven listings that day, none of which appealed to him, and then, as they were walking along the edge of the cemetery, they turned at random down a deserted block between Fourth and Fifth avenues and saw the house, a dopey little two-story wooden house with a roofed-over front porch, looking for all the world like something that had been stolen from a farm on the Minnesota prairie and plunked down by accident in the middle of New York. It stood between a trash-filled vacant lot with a stripped-down car in it and the metal bones of a half-built mini–apartment building on which construction had stopped more than a year ago. The cemetery was directly across the way, which meant there were no houses lining the other side of the street, which further meant that the abandoned house was all but invisible, since it was a house on a block where almost no one lived. He asked Ellen if she knew anything about it. The owners had died, she said, and because their children had been delinquent in paying the property taxes for several years running, the house now belonged to the city.

A month later, when he made up his mind to do the impossible, to risk everything on the chance to live in a rent-free house for as long as it took the city to notice him and give him the boot, he was stunned when Ellen accepted his offer. He tried to talk her out of it, explaining how difficult it would be and how much trouble they might be getting themselves into, but she held her ground, saying yes meant yes, and why bother to ask if he wanted her to say no?

They broke in one night and discovered that there were four bedrooms, three small ones on the top floor and a larger one below, which was part of an extension built onto the back of the house. The place was in lamentable condition, every surface coated with dust and soot, water stains streaking the wall behind the kitchen sink, cracked linoleum, splintered floorboards, a team of mice or squirrels running relay races under the roof, a collapsed table, legless chairs, spiderwebs dangling from ceiling corners, but remarkably enough not one broken window, and even if the water from the taps spurted out brown, looking more like English Breakfast tea than water, the plumbing was intact. Elbow grease, Ellen said. That's all it was going to take. A week or two of scrubbing and painting, and they would be in business.

He spent the next several days looking for people to fill the last two bedrooms, but no one from the band was interested, and as he went down the list of his other friends and acquaintances, he discovered that the idea of living as a squatter in an abandoned house did not have the broad appeal he had supposed it would. Then Ellen happened to talk to Alice Bergstrom, her old college roommate, and learned that she was about to be kicked out of her rent-controlled sublet in Morningside Heights. Alice was a graduate student at Columbia, already well into her dissertation, which she hoped to finish within a year, and moving in with her boyfriend was out of the question. Even if they had wanted to live together, it wouldn't have been possible. His apartment was the smallest of small, postage-stamp studios, and there simply wasn't enough space for two people to work in there at the same time. And they both needed to work at home. Jake Baum was a fiction writer, until now exclusively a writer of short stories (some of them published, most of them not), and he barely managed to scrape by on the salary he earned from his part-time teaching job at a community college in Queens. He had no money to lend Alice, could offer no help in her search for a new apartment, and since Alice herself was nearly broke, she didn't know where to turn. Her fellowship came with a small stipend, but it wasn't enough to live on, and even with her part-time job at the PEN American Center, where she worked for the Freedom to Write Program, she was subsisting on a diet of buttered noodles, rice and beans, and an occasional egg sandwich. After hearing out the story of her friend's predicament, Ellen suggested that she have a talk with Bing.

The three of them met at a bar in Brooklyn the following night, and after ten minutes of conversation he was convinced that Alice would make a worthy addition to the group. She was a tall, big-boned Scandinavian girl from Wisconsin with a round face and meaty arms, a person of heft and seriousness who also happened to have a quick mouth and a sharp sense of humor—a rare combination, he felt, which made her a shoo-in from the word go. Just as important, he liked the fact that she was Ellen's friend. Ellen had proven herself to be an admirable sidekick, for reasons he would never understand she had taken on his mad, quixotic venture as her own, but he still worried about her, was still troubled by the closed-in, unabated sadness that seemed to accompany her wherever she went, and he was heartened to see how she loosened up in Alice's presence, how much happier and more animated she looked as the three of them sat there talking in the bar, and he hoped that sharing the house with her old friend would be good medicine for her.

Before he met Alice Bergstrom, he had already met Millie Grant, but it took him several weeks after that night in the bar to screw up his courage and ask her if she had any interest in taking over the fourth and last bedroom. He was in love with her by then, in love with her in a way he had never loved anyone in his life, and he was too frightened to ask her because the thought that she might turn him down was more than he could bear. He was twenty-nine years old, and until he ran into Millie after a Mob Rule gig at Barbès on the last day of spring, his history with women had been one of absolute, unending failure. He was the fat boy who never had a girlfriend in school, the bumbling naïf who didn't lose his virginity until he was twenty, the jazz drummer who had never picked up a stranger in a club, the dumbbell who bought blow jobs from hookers when he was feeling desperate, the sex-starved moron who jerked off to pornography in the darkness of his bedroom. He knew nothing about women. He had less experience with women than most adolescent boys. He had dreamed of women, he had chased after women, he had declared his love to women, but again and again he had been rebuffed. Now, as he was about to take the biggest gamble of his life, as he stood on the brink of illegally occupying a house in Sunset Park and perhaps landing in jail, he was going into it with a team composed entirely of women. His hour of triumph had come at last.

Why did Millie fall for him? He doesn't quite know, cannot be sure of anything when it comes to the murky realms of attraction and desire, but he suspects it might be connected to the house in Sunset Park. Not the house itself, but the plan to move in there, which was already turning around in his head by the time he met her, already mutating from whim and vague speculation into a concrete decision to act, and he must have been burning with his idea that night, emitting a shower of mental sparks that surrounded him like a magnetic field and charged the atmosphere with a new and vital energy, an irresistible force, as it were, making him more attractive and desirable than usual perhaps, which could have been the reason why she was drawn to him. Not a pretty girl, no, not by the conventional standards that define prettiness (nose too sharp, left eye veering off slightly, too thin lips), but she had a terrific head of wiry red hair and a lithe, fetching body. They wound up in bed together that night, and when he understood that she wasn't put off by his shaggy, overly round *corpus horrendous*, he asked her out to dinner the following night, and they wound up in bed again. Millie Grant, a twenty-seven-year-old part-time dancer, part-time restaurant hostess, born and raised in Wheaton, Illinois, a girl with four small tattoos and a navel ring, an advocate of numerous conspiracy theories (from the Kennedy assassination to the 9/11 attacks to the dangers of the public drinking-water system), a lover of loud music, a nonstop talker, a vegetarian, an animal rights activist, a vivacious, tightly sprung piece of work with a quick temper and a machine-gun laugh—someone to hold on to for the long haul. But he couldn't hold on to her. He doesn't understand what went wrong, but after two and a half months of communal living in the house, she woke up one morning and declared that she was going to San Francisco to join a new dance company. She had auditioned for them in the spring, she said, had been the last person cut, and now that one of the dancers was pregnant and had been forced to drop out, she had been hired. Sorry, Bing. It was nice while it lasted and all that, but this was the chance she'd been waiting for, and she'd be a fool not to jump at it. He didn't know whether to believe her or not, whether *San Francisco* was simply a term that meant *good-bye* or if she was really going there. Now that she is gone, he wonders if he performed well enough in bed with her, if he was able to satisfy her sexually. Or, just the opposite, if she felt he was too interested in sex, if all his dirty talk about the bizarre couplings he had witnessed in porno films had finally driven her away. He will never know. She has not been in touch since the morning she left the house, and he is not expecting to hear from her again.

Two days after Millie's departure, he wrote to Miles Heller. He got a little carried away, perhaps, claiming there were four people in the house rather than three, but four was a better number than three somehow, and he

didn't want Miles to think that his great anarchist insur-
rection had been whittled down to his own paltry self
and a pair of women. In his mind, the fourth person was
Jake Baum, the writer, and while it's true that Jake comes
around to visit Alice once or twice a week, he is not a permanent member of the household. He doubts that Miles
will care one way or the other, but if he does care, it will
be easy enough to invent some fib to account for the dis-
crepancy.

He loves Miles Heller, but he also thinks that Miles is
insane, and he is glad his friend's lonesome cowboy act is
finally coming to an end. Seven years ago, when he received
the first of the fifty-two letters Miles has written to him, he
didn't hesitate to call Morris Heller and tell him that his
son wasn't dead as everyone had feared but working as a
short-order cook in a diner on the South Side of Chicago.
Miles had been missing for over six months by then. Just
after his disappearance, Morris and Willa had asked Bing
over to their apartment to question him about Miles and
what he thought could have happened to him. He will never
forget how Willa broke down in tears, never forget the
anguished look on Morris's face. He had no suggestions to
offer that afternoon, but he promised that if he ever heard
from Miles or heard anything about him, he would contact
them at once. He has been calling them for seven years
now—fifty-two times, once after every letter. It grieves
him that Morris and Willa have not jumped on a plane and
flown off to any of the several spots where Miles has parked

his bones—not to drag him back, necessarily, but just to see him and force him to explain himself. But Morris says there is nothing to be done. As long as the boy refuses to come home, they have no option but to wait it out and hope he will eventually change his mind. Bing is glad that Morris Heller and Willa Parks are not his parents. No doubt they are both good people, but they are just as stubborn and crazy as Miles.

Alice Bergstrom

No one is watching them. No one cares that the empty house is now occupied. They have settled in.

When she took the plunge and decided to join forces with Bing and Ellen last summer, she imagined they would be forced to live in the shadows, slinking in and out the back door whenever the coast was clear, hiding behind blackout shades to prevent any light from seeping through the windows, always afraid, always looking over their shoulders, always expecting the boom to fall on them at any moment. She was willing to accept those conditions because she was desperate and felt she had no choice. She had lost her apartment, and how can a person rent a new apartment when the person in question doesn't have the money to pay for it? Things would be easier if her parents were in a position to help, but they are barely getting by themselves, living on their Social Security checks and clipping coupons out of the newspaper in a perpetual hunt for bargains, sales, gimmicks, any chance to shave a few pennies from their monthly costs. She was anticipating a grim go of it, a scared and mean little life in a broken-down shithole of a house, but she was wrong about that, wrong about many things, and even if Bing can be intolerable at times, pounding his fist on the table as he subjects them to another one of his dreary exhortations, slurping his soup and smacking his lips and letting crumbs fall into his beard, she misjudged his intelligence, failed to realize that he had worked out a thoroughly sensible plan. No skulking around, he said. Acting as if they didn't belong there would only alert the neighborhood to the fact that they were trespassers. They had to operate in broad daylight, hold their heads high, and pretend they were the legitimate owners of the house, which they had bought from the city for next to nothing, yes, yes, at a shockingly low price, because they had spared them the expense of having to demolish the place. Bing was right. It was a plausible story, and people accepted it. After they moved in last August, there was a brief fluster of curiosity about their comings and goings, but that passed soon enough, and by now the short, sparsely populated block has adjusted to their presence. No one is watching them, and no one cares. The old Donohue place has finally been sold, the sun continues to rise and set, and life goes on as if nothing ever happened.

For the first few weeks, they did what they could to make the rooms habitable, diligently attacking all manner of blight and decay, treating each small task as if it were a momentous human endeavor, and bit by bit they turned their wretchedly inadequate pigsty into something that might, with some generosity, be classified as a hovel. It is far from comfortable there, countless inconveniences impinge on them every day, and now that the weather has turned cold, bitter air rushes in on them through a thousand cracks in the walls and embrasures, forcing them to bundle up in heavy sweaters and put on three pairs of socks in the morning. But she doesn't complain. Not having to pay rent or utility bills for the past four months has saved her close to thirty-five hundred dollars, and for the first time in a long while she can breathe without feeling her chest tighten up on her, without feeling that her lungs are about to explode. Her work is moving forward, she can see the end looming on the far horizon, and she knows that she has the stamina to finish. The window in her room faces the cemetery, and as she writes her dissertation at the small desk positioned directly below that window, she often stares into the quiet of Green-Wood's vast, rolling ground, where more than half a million bodies are buried, which is roughly the same number as the population of Milwaukee, the city where she was born, the city where most of her family still lives, and she finds it strange, strange and even haunting, that there are as many dead lying under that ground across from her window as the number of people living in the place where her life began.

She isn't sorry that Millie is gone. Bing is in shock, of course, still staggered by his girlfriend's abrupt exit from the house, but she feels the group will be better off without that fractious, redheaded storm of gripes and thoughtless digs, she of the unwashed dinner plates and the blaring radio, who nearly pulverized poor, fragile Ellen with her comments about her drawings and paintings. A man named Miles Heller will be joining them tomorrow or the day after. Bing says he is hands down the smartest, most interesting person he has ever known. They met when they were teenagers apparently, all the way back in the early years of high school, so their friendship has gone on long enough for Bing to have some perspective on what he is saying—which is rather extreme in her opinion, but Bing is often given to hyperbole, and only time will tell if Señor Heller measures up to this powerful endorsement.

It is a Saturday, a gray Saturday in early December, and she is the only person in the house. Bing left an hour ago to rehearse with his band, Ellen is spending the day with her sister and the little twins on the Upper West Side, and Jake is in Montclair, New Jersey, visiting his brother and sister-in-law, who have just had a child as well. Babies are popping out all over, in every part of the globe women are huffing and heaving and disgorging fresh battalions of newborns, doing their bit to prolong the human race, and at some point in the not-too-distant future she hopes to put her womb to the test and see if she can't contribute as well. All that remains is choosing the right father. For close to two years, she felt that person was Jake Baum, but now she is beginning to have doubts about Jake, something seems to be crumbling between them, small daily erosions have slowly begun to mar their patch of ground, and if things continue to deteriorate, it won't be long before entire shorelines are washed away, before whole villages are submerged under water. Six months ago, she never would have asked the question, but now she wonders if she has it in her to carry on with him. Jake was never an expansive person, but there was a gentleness in him that she admired, a charming, ironical approach to the world that comforted her and made her feel they were well matched, comrades under the skin. Now he is pulling away from her. He seems angry and dejected, his once lighthearted quips have taken on a new edge of cynicism, and he never seems to tire of denigrating his students and fellow teachers. LaGuardia Community College has turned into Pifflebum Tech, Asswipe U, and the Institute for Advanced Retardation. She doesn't like to hear him talk that way. His students are mostly poor, working-class immigrants, attending school while holding down jobs, never an easy proposition as she damned well knows, and who is he to make fun of them for wanting an education? With his writing, it's more or less the same story. A flood of caustic remarks every time another piece is rejected, an acid contempt for the literary world, an abiding grudge against every editor who has failed to recognize his gifts. She is convinced that he has talent, that his work has been progressing, but it is a small talent in her eyes, and her expectations for his future are equally small. Perhaps that is part of the problem. Perhaps he senses that she doesn't believe in him enough, and in spite of all the pep talks she has given him, all the long conversations in which she has cited the early struggles of one important writer after another, he never seems to take her words to heart. She doesn't blame him for feeling frustrated—but does she want to spend the rest of her life with a frustrated man, a man who is rapidly becoming a failure in his own eyes?

She mustn't exaggerate, however. More often than not, he is kind to her, and he has never once hinted that he is weary of their affair, has never once suggested that they break it off. He is still young, after all, not yet thirty-one, which is extremely young for a fiction writer, and if his stories keep improving, chances are that something good will happen, a success of one kind or another, and with that turn his spirits would undoubtedly improve as well. No, she can weather his disappointments if she has to, that isn't the problem, she can put up with anything as long as she feels he is solidly with her, but that is precisely what she doesn't feel anymore, and even if he seems content to glide along with her out of old habits, the reflex of old affections, she is becoming ever more certain, no, *certain* is probably too strong a word for it, she is becoming ever more willing to entertain the idea that he has stopped loving her. It isn't anything he ever says. It's the way he looks at her now, the way he has been looking at her for the past few months, without any noticeable interest, his eyes blank, unfocused, as if looking at her were no different from looking at a spoon or a washcloth, a speck of dust. He rarely touches her anymore when they are alone, and even before she moved to the house in Sunset Park, their sex life was in precipitous decline. That is the crux of it, without question the problem begins and ends there, and she blames herself for what has happened, she can't help believing that the fault rests entirely on her shoulders. She was always a big person, always bigger than the other girls at school—taller, broader, more robust, more athletic, never chubby, never overweight for her size, just big. When she met Jake two and a half years ago, she was five feet ten inches tall and weighed one hundred and fifty-seven pounds. She is still five-ten, but now she weighs one-seventy. Those thirteen pounds are the difference between a strong, imposing woman and a mountain of a woman. She has been dieting ever since she landed in Sunset Park, but no matter how severely she limits her intake of calories, she has not managed to lose more than three or four pounds, which she always seems to gain back within a day or two. Her body repulses her now, and she no longer has the courage to look at herself in the mirror. I'm fat, she says to Jake. Again and again she says it, I'm fat, I'm fat, unable to stop herself from repeating the words, and if she is repulsed by the sight of her own body, imagine what he must feel when she takes off her clothes and climbs into bed with him.

The light is fading now, and as she stands up from her bed to switch on a lamp, she tells herself that she must not cry, that only weaklings and imbeciles feel sorry for themselves, and therefore she must not feel sorry for herself, for she is neither a weakling nor an imbecile, and she knows better than to think that love is simply a question of bodies, the size and shape and heft of bodies, and if Jake can't cope with his somewhat overweight, furiously dieting girl-friend, then Jake can go to hell. A moment later, she is sitting at her desk. She turns on the laptop, and for the next half hour she vanishes into her work, reading over and correcting the newest passages from her dissertation, which were written this morning.

Her subject is America in the years just after World War II, an examination of the relations and conflicts between men and women as shown in books and films from 1945 to 1947, mostly popular crime novels and commercial Hollywood movies. It is a broad terrain for an academic study, perhaps, but she couldn't picture herself spending years of her life comparing rhyme schemes in Pope and Byron (one of her friends is doing that) or analyzing the metaphors in Melville's Civil War poetry (another friend is doing that). She wanted to take on something larger, something of human importance that would engage her personally, and she knows she is working on this subject because of her grandparents and her great-uncles and great-aunts, all of whom participated in the war, lived through the war, were changed forever by the war. Her argument is that the traditional rules of conduct between men and women were destroyed on the battlefields and the home front, and once the war was over, American life had to be reinvented. She has limited herself to several texts and films, the ones that feel most emblematic to her, that expose the spirit of the time in the clearest, most forceful terms, and she has already written chapters on *The Air-Conditioned*

Nightmare by Henry Miller, the brutal misogynism of Mickey Spillane's *I, the Jury,* the virgin-whore female split presented in Jacques Tourneur's film noir *Out of the Past,* and has carefully dissected a bestselling anti-feminist tract called *Modern Woman: The Lost Sex.* Now she is about to begin writing on William Wyler's 1946 film, *The Best Years of Our Lives,* a work that is central to her thesis and which she considers to be the national epic of that particular moment in American history—the story of three men broken by war and the difficulties they confront when they return to their families, which is the same story that was being lived out by millions of others at the time.

The entire country saw the film, which won the Academy Award for best picture, best director, best leading actor, best supporting actor, best editor, best original score, and best adapted screenplay, but while most critics responded with enthusiasm (*some of the most beautiful and inspiriting demonstrations of human fortitude that we have had in films,* wrote Bosley Crowther of the *New York Times*), others were less impressed. Manny Farber trashed it as *a horse-drawn truckload of liberal schmaltz,* and in his long, two-part review published in the *Nation,* James Agee both condemned and praised *The Best Years of Our Lives,* calling it *very annoying in its patness, its timidity,* and then concluded by saying: *Yet I feel a hundred times more liking and admiration for the film than distaste or disappointment.* She agrees that the movie has its faults, that it is often too tame and sentimental, but in the end she feels its virtues outweigh its deficits. The acting is strong throughout, the script is filled with memorable lines (*Last year it was kill Japs, this year it's make money; I think they ought to put you in mass production; I'm in the junk business, an occupation for which many people feel I'm well qualified by training and temperament*), and the cinematography by Gregg Toland is exceptional. She pulls out her copy of Ephraim Katz's *Film Encyclopedia* and reads this sentence from the William Wyler entry: *The revolutionary deep-focus shot perfected by Toland enabled Wyler to develop his favorite technique of filming long takes in which characters appear in the same frame for the duration of entire scenes, rather than cutting from one to another and thus disrupting intercharacter relationships.* Two paragraphs down, at the end of a brief description of *The Best Years of Our Lives*, the author remarks that the film contains *some of the most intricate compositions ever seen on celluloid*. Even more important, at least for the purposes of the dissertation she is writing, the story concentrates on precisely those elements of male-female conflict that most interest her. The men no longer know how to act with their wives and girlfriends. They have lost their appetite for domesticity, their feel for home. After years of living apart from women, years of combat and slaughter, years of grappling to survive the horrors and dangers of war, they have been cut off from their civilian pasts, crippled, trapped in nightmare repetitions of their experiences, and the women they left behind have become strangers to them.

So the film begins. Peace has broken out, but what in God's name happens now?

She owns a small television set and a DVD player. Because there is no cable hookup in the house, the television doesn't receive normal broadcasts, but she can watch films on it, and now that she is about to begin her chapter on *The Best Years of Our Lives,* she feels she should take another look at it, have one last run-through before getting down to work. Night has fallen now, but as she settles onto her bed to begin watching, she turns off the lamp in order to study the film in total darkness.

It is deeply familiar to her, of course. After four or five viewings, she practically knows the film by heart, but she is determined to look for small things that might have escaped her notice earlier, the quickly passing details that ultimately give a film its texture. Already in the first scene, when Dana Andrews is at the airport, unsuccessfully trying to book a ticket back to Boone City, she is struck by the businessman with the golf clubs, Mr. Gibbons, who calmly pays his excess-baggage charge while ignoring air force captain Andrews, who has just helped win the war for Mr. Gibbons and his fellow countrymen, and from now on, she decides, she will take note of each act of civilian indifference toward the returning soldiers. She is gratified to see how rapidly they mount up as the film progresses: the desk clerk at the apartment building where Fredric March lives, for example, who is reluctant to let the uniformed sergeant into his own house, or the manager of Midway

Drugs, Mr. Thorpe, who snidely dismisses Andrews's war record as he offers him a low-paying job, or even Andrews's wife, Virginia Mayo, who tells him to *snap out of it*, that he won't get anywhere until he stops thinking about the war, as if going to war ranked as a minor inconvenience, equivalent to a painful session at the dentist.

More details, more small things: Virginia Mayo removing her false eyelashes; the rheumy Mr. Thorpe squirting nasal spray into his left nostril; Myrna Loy trying to kiss the sleeping Fredric March, who nearly slugs her in response; the choked sob from Harold Russell's mother when she sees her son's prosthetic hooks for the first time; Dana Andrews reaching into his pocket to look for his bank roll after Teresa Wright wakes him up, suggesting in one quick, instinctive move how many nights he must have spent with low-life women overseas; Myrna Loy putting flowers on her husband's breakfast tray, then deciding to take them off; Dana Andrews picking up the photo from the country club dinner, tearing it in half to preserve the shot of Teresa Wright sitting next to him, and then, after a brief hesitation, tearing up that half as well; Harold Russell stumbling over his marriage vows in the wedding scene at the end; Dana Andrews's father awkwardly trying to conceal his gin bottle on his son's first day home from the war; a sign seen through the window of a passing cab: *Settle for a Hot Dog?*

She is especially interested in Teresa Wright's performance in the role of Peggy, the young woman who falls in love with unhappily married Dana Andrews. She wants to know why she is drawn to this character when everything tells her that Peggy is too perfect to be credible as a human being—too poised, too good, too pretty, too smart, one of the purest incarnations of the ideal American girl she can think of—and yet each time she watches the film, she finds herself more involved with this character than any of the others. The moment Wright makes her first appearance on-screen, then—early in the film, when her father, Fredric March, returns home to Myrna Loy and his two children—she makes up her mind to track every nuance of Wright's behavior, to scrutinize the finest points of her performance in order to understand why this character, who is potentially the weakest link in the film, ends up holding the story together. She is not alone in thinking this. Even Agee, so harsh in his judgment of other aspects of the movie, is effusive in his admiration of Wright's accomplishment. *This new performance of hers, entirely lacking in big scenes, tricks or obstreperousness—one can hardly think of it as acting—seems to be one of the wisest and most beautiful pieces of work I have seen in years.*

Just after the long two-shot of March and Loy embracing at the end of the hall (one of the signature moments in the film), the camera cuts to a close-up of Wright—and just then, during those few seconds when Peggy occupies the screen alone, Alice knows what she has to look for. Wright's performance is concentrated entirely in her eyes and face. Follow the eyes and face, and the riddle of her mastery is solved, for the eyes are unusually expressive eyes, subtly but vividly expressive, and the face registers her emotions with such a highly sensitive, understated authenticity that you can't help but believe in her as a fully embodied character. Because of her eyes and face, Wright as Peggy is able to bring the inside to the outside, and even when she is silent, we know what she is thinking and feeling. Yes, she is without question the healthiest, most earnest character in the film, but how not to respond to her angry declaration to her parents about Andrews and his wife, *I'm going to break that marriage up*, or the irritated brush-off she gives her rich, handsome dinner date when he tries to kiss her, saying *Don't be a bore, Woody,* or the short, complicitous laugh she shares with her mother when they say good night to each other after the two drunken men have been put to bed? That explains why Andrews thinks she should be put in mass production. Because there is only one of her, and how much better off the world would be (how much better off men would be!) if there were more Peggys to go around.

She is doing her best to concentrate, to keep her eyes fixed on the screen, but midway into the film her thoughts begin to wander. Watching Harold Russell, the third male protagonist along with March and Andrews, the nonprofessional actor who lost his hands during the war, she begins to think about her great-uncle Stan, the husband of her grandmother's sister Caroline, the one-armed D-day veteran with the bushy eyebrows, Stan Fitzpatrick, belting back drinks at family parties, telling dirty jokes to her brothers on their

grandparents' back porch, one of the many who never managed to pull themselves together after the war, the man with
thirty-seven different jobs, old Uncle Stan, dead for a good
ten years now, and the stories her grandmother has told her
lately about how he used to *knock Caroline around a bit,*
the now departed Caroline, knocked around so much she
lost a couple of teeth one day, and then there are her two
grandfathers, both of them still alive, one fading and the
other lucid, who fought in the Pacific and Europe as young
men, such young men they were scarcely older than boys,
and even though she has tried to get the lucid grandfather to
talk to her, Bill Bergstrom, the husband of her one surviving grandmother, he never says much, speaks only in the
foggiest generalities, it simply isn't possible for him to talk
about those years, they all came home insane, damaged for
life, and even the years after the war were still part of the
war, the years of bad dreams and night sweats, the years of
wanting to punch your fist through walls, so her grandfather humors her by talking about going to college on the
G.I. Bill, about meeting her grandmother on a bus one day
and falling in love with her at first sight, bullshit, bullshit
from start to finish, but he is one of those men who can't
talk, a card-carrying member from the generation of men
who can't talk, and therefore she has to rely on her grandmother for the stories, but she wasn't a soldier during the
war, she doesn't know what happened over there, and all
she can talk about are her three sisters and their husbands,
the dead Caroline and Stan Fitzpatrick and Annabelle, the

one whose husband was killed at Anzio and who later married again, to a man named Jim Farnsworth, another vet from the Pacific, but that marriage didn't last long either, he was unfaithful to her, he forged checks or was involved in a stock swindle, the details are unclear, but Farnsworth vanished long before she was born, and the only husband she ever knew was Mike Meggert, the traveling salesman, who never talked about the war either, and finally there is Gloria, Gloria and Frank Krushniak, the couple with the six children, but Frank's war was different from the others' war, he faked a disability and never had to serve, which means that he has nothing to say either, and when she thinks of that generation of silent men, the boys who lived through the Depression and grew up to become soldiers or not-soldiers in the war, she doesn't blame them for refusing to talk, for not wanting to go back into the past, but how curious it is, she thinks, how sublimely incoherent that her generation, which doesn't have much of anything to talk about yet, has produced men who never stop talking, men like Bing, for example, or men like Jake, who talks about himself at the slightest prompting, who has an opinion on every subject, who spews forth words from morning to night, but just because he talks, that doesn't mean she wants to listen to him, whereas with the silent men, the old men, the ones who are nearly gone now, she would give anything to hear what they have to say.

Ellen Brice

She is standing on the front porch of the house, looking into the fog. It is Sunday morning, and the air outside is almost warm, too warm for the beginning of December, making it feel like a day from another season or another latitude, a damp, balmy sort of weather that reminds her of the tropics. When she looks across the street, the fog is so dense that the cemetery is invisible. A strange morning, she says to herself. The clouds have descended all the way to the ground, and the world has become invisible—which is neither a good thing nor a bad thing, she decides, merely strange.

It is early, early for a Sunday in any case, a few minutes past seven o'clock, and Alice and Bing are still asleep in their beds on the second floor, but she is up at first light again as usual, even if there is little light to speak of on this dull, fog-saturated morning. She can't remember the last time she managed to sleep for six full hours, six uninterrupted hours without waking from a rough dream or discovering her eyes had opened at dawn, and she knows these sleep difficulties are a bad sign, an unmistakable warning of trouble ahead, but in spite of what her mother keeps telling her, she doesn't want to go back on the medication. Taking one of those pills is like swallowing a small dose of death. Once you start with those things, your days are turned into a numbing regimen of forgetfulness and confusion, and there isn't a moment when you don't feel your head is stuffed with cotton balls and wadded-up shreds of paper. She doesn't want to shut down her life in order to survive her life. She wants her senses to be awake, to think thoughts that don't vanish the moment they occur to her, to feel alive in all the ways she once felt alive. Crack-ups are off the agenda now. She can't allow herself to surrender anymore, but in spite of her efforts to hold her ground in the here and now, the pressure has been building up inside her again, and she is beginning to feel twinges of the old panic, the knot in her throat, the blood rushing too quickly through her veins, the clenched heart and frantic rhythms of her pulse. Fear without an object, as Dr. Burnham once described it to her. No, she says to herself now: fear of dying without having lived.

There is no question that coming here was the right move, and she has never regretted leaving behind that small apartment on President Street in Park Slope. She feels emboldened by the risk they have taken together, and Bing and Alice have been so good to her, so generous and protective, so constant in their friendship, but in spite of the fact that she is less lonely now, there have been times, many times in fact, when being with them has only made things worse. When she lived on her own, she never had to compare herself with anyone. Her struggles were her struggles, her failures were her failures, and she could suffer through them within the confines of her small, solitary space. Now she is surrounded by impassioned, energetic people, and next to them she feels like a dim sluggard, a hopeless nonentity. Alice will soon have her Ph.D. and an academic post somewhere, Jake is publishing story after story in little magazines, Bing has his band and his goofy underground business, and even Millie, the sharp-tongued, never-to-be-missed Millie, is thriving as a dancer. As for her, she is getting nowhere fast, faster than it takes for a young dog to become an old dog, faster than it takes for a flower to bloom and wilt. Her work as an artist has crashed into a wall, and the bulk of her time is spent showing empty apartments to prospective tenants—a job for which she is thoroughly ill-suited and which she fears she could be fired from any day. All that has been hard enough, but then there is the business of sex, the fucking she has had to listen to through the thin walls upstairs, the fact of being the only single person in a house of two couples. It has been a long time since anyone made love to her, eighteen months by her latest reckoning, and she is so starved for physical contact that she can barely think about anything else now. She masturbates in her bed every night, but masturbation isn't a solution, it offers only temporary relief, it's like an aspirin you take to kill the pain of a throbbing tooth, and she doesn't know how much longer she can go on without being kissed, without being loved.

Bing is available now, it's true, and she can feel that he is interested in her, but somehow she can't imagine herself with Bing, can't see herself putting her arms around his broad, hairy back or trying to find his lips through the bramble of that thick beard. Again and again since Millie's departure, she has thought about making an advance on him, but then she sees Bing at breakfast in the morning and knows it isn't possible.

Her thoughts have begun to disturb her, the little games she plays in her mind without wanting to, the sudden, uncontrollable fugues into the dark. Sometimes they come to her in brief flashes—an impulse to burn down the house, to seduce Alice, to steal money from the safe at her real estate firm—and then, just as quickly as they arrive, they dwindle off into nothing. Others are more constant, more enduring in their impact. Even going out is fraught with hazards now, for there are days when she can no longer look at the people she passes on the street without undressing them in her imagination, stripping off their clothes with a quick, violent tug and then examining their naked bodies as they walk by. These strangers aren't people to her anymore, they are simply the bodies that belong to them, structures of flesh wrapped around bones and tissue and inner organs, and with the heavy pedestrian traffic that moves along Seventh Avenue, the street where her office is located, hundreds if not thousands of specimens are thrust before her eyes every day. She sees the enormous, unwieldy breasts of fat women, the tiny penises of young boys, the budding pubic hair of thirteen-year-old children, the pink vaginas of mothers pushing their babies in strollers, the assholes of old men, the hairless pudenda of little girls, luxuriant thighs, skinny thighs, vast, quivering buttocks, chest hair, recessed navels, inverted nipples, bellies scarred by appendix operations and cesarean births, turds sliding out of open anuses, piss flowing from long, partly erect penises. She is revolted by these images, appalled that her mind is capable of manufacturing such filth, but once they start coming to her, she is powerless to make them go away. Sometimes she even goes so far as to imagine herself pausing to slip her tongue into the mouth of each passerby, each and every person who falls within her sight, whether old or young, whether beautiful or deformed, pausing to lick the entire length of each naked body, pushing her tongue into moistened vaginas, putting her mouth around thick, hardened penises, giving herself with equal fervor to every man, woman, and child in an orgy of indiscriminate, democratic love. She doesn't know how to stop these visions. They leave her feeling wretched and exhausted, but the wild thoughts enter her head as if they were planted there by someone else, and even though she battles to suppress them, it is a battle she never wins.

Transient detours, mental conniptions, ordure rising from the inner depths, but out in the external world of solid things she has allowed her desires to run away from her only once, only once with any lasting consequences.

The ballad of Benjamin Samuels dates back to the summer of 2000, eight years ago, eight and a half years ago to be exact, which means that close to one-third of her life has been lived since then, and still it remains with her, she has never stopped listening to the song in her mind, and as she stands on the porch this foggy Sunday morning, she wonders if anything as momentous will ever happen to her again. She was twenty years old and had just finished her sophomore year at Smith. Alice was going back to Wisconsin to work as head counselor at a summer camp near Lake Oconomowoc, and she asked her if she wanted a job there as well, which was something she could easily arrange. No, she wasn't interested in summer camps, she said, she'd had an unhappy experience at camp when she was eleven, and so she wound up taking another job closer to home, for Professor Samuels and his wife, who had rented a place in southern Vermont for two and a half months and needed someone to look after their kids—Bea, Cora, and Ben, girls of five and seven and a boy of sixteen. The boy was too old to require looking after, but he had messed up in school that year, barely passing several of his courses, and she was supposed to tutor him in English, American history, and algebra. He was in a foul temper when the summer began—barred from attending his beloved soccer camp in Northampton and faced with the prospect of eleven weeks of excruciating exile with his parents and sisters in the middle of nowhere. But she was beautiful then, never more beautiful than she was that summer, so much rounder and softer than the scrawny creature she has turned into now, and why would a sixteen-year-old boy complain about having to take lessons from an enticing young woman in sleeveless tank tops and black spandex shorts? By the beginning of the second week they were friends, and by the beginning of the third week they were spending most of their evenings together in the pavilion, a small outbuilding about fifty yards from the main house, where they watched the films she would pick up from Al's Video Store on her shopping excursions to Brattleboro. The girls and their parents were always asleep by then. Professor Samuels and his wife were both writing books that summer, and they kept to a rigid schedule, up at five-thirty every morning and lights out by nine-thirty or ten. They weren't the least bit concerned that she and their son were spending so much time together in the pavilion. She was Ellen Brice, after all, the soft-spoken, dependable girl who had done so well in Professor Samuels's art history class, and they could count on her to behave responsibly in all situations.

Having sex with Ben wasn't her idea—at least not at first. She loved looking at him, the strength and leanness of his soccer player's body often aroused her, but he was still just a boy, less than six months ago he had been fifteen, and however attractive she might have found him, she had no intention of doing anything about it. But one month into the two and a half months she stayed there, on a warm July night filled with the sounds of tree frogs and a million cicadas, the boy made the first move. They were

[111]

sitting in their usual positions at opposite ends of the small sofa, the moths were banging against the screen windows as usual, the night air smelled of pines and damp earth as usual, a dumb comedy or western was playing as usual (the selection at Al's was limited), and she was beginning to feel drowsy, drowsy enough to lean back her head and close her eyes for a few seconds, perhaps ten seconds, perhaps twenty seconds, and before she was able to open them again, young Mr. Samuels had moved over to her side of the sofa and was kissing her on the mouth. She should have pushed him away, or turned her head away, or stood up and walked away, but she couldn't think fast enough to do any of those things, and so she remained where she was, sitting on the sofa with her eyes closed, and allowed him to go on kissing her.

They were never caught. For a month and a half they carried on with their little sex affair (she could never bring herself to think of it as a love affair), and then the summer came to an end. She might not have fallen in love with Ben, but she was in love with his body, and even now, eight and a half years later, she still thinks about the uncanny smoothness of his skin, the feel of his long arms wrapped around her, the sweetness of his mouth, the taste of him. She would have continued seeing Ben in Northampton after the summer, but his miserable academic performance the previous year had alarmed his parents so much that they shipped him off to a boarding school in New Hampshire, and suddenly he was gone from her life. She missed him a good deal more than she was expecting to, but before she understood how long it would take to get over him, how many weeks or months or years, she found herself in a new kind of fix. Her period was late. She told Alice about it, and her friend promptly dragged her off to the nearest pharmacy to buy a home-pregnancy-test kit. The results were positive, which is to say, negative, disastrously and irrevocably negative. She thought they had been so prudent, so careful to avoid just this thing from happening, but clearly they had slipped up somewhere along the way, and now what was she going to do? She couldn't tell anyone who the father was. Not even Alice, who pressed her about it again and again, and not even the father himself, who was just a sixteen-year-old boy, and why punish him with this news when there was nothing he could do to help her, when she was the one to blame for the whole sordid business? She couldn't talk to Alice, she couldn't talk to Ben, and she couldn't talk to her parents—not just about who the father was, but about who she was as well. A pregnant girl, an idiot college girl with a baby growing inside her. Her mother and father could never know what had happened. The mere thought of trying to tell them about it was enough to make her want to die.

If she had been a braver person, she would have had the child. In spite of the upheavals a full-term pregnancy would have caused, she wanted to go ahead with it and let the baby be born, but she was too scared of the questions she would be asked, too ashamed to confront her family, too weak to assert herself and drop out of school to join the ranks of *unwed mothers*. Alice drove her to the clinic. It was supposed to be a quick, uncomplicated procedure, and in medical terms everything came off as advertised, but she found it gruesome and humiliating, and she hated herself for having gone against her deepest impulses, her deepest convictions. Four days later, she downed half a bottle of vodka and twenty sleeping pills. Alice was supposed to be gone for the weekend, and if she hadn't changed her plans at the last minute and returned to their dormitory suite at four o'clock that afternoon, her sleeping roommate would still be sleeping now. They took her to Cooley Dickinson Hospital and pumped her stomach, and that was the end of Smith, the end of Ellen Brice as a so-called normal person. She was transferred to the psych ward of the hospital and kept there for twenty days, and then she returned to New York, where she spent a long, infinitely depressing period living with her parents, sleeping in her old childhood bedroom, seeing Dr. Burnham three times a week, attending group therapy sessions, and ingesting her daily quantum of the pills that were supposed to make her feel better but didn't. Eventually, she took it upon herself to enroll in some drawing classes at the School of Visual Arts, which turned into painting classes the following year, and little by little she began to feel that she was almost living in the world again, that there might be something that resembled a future for her, after all. When her sister's husband's brother-in-law offered her a job with his real estate firm in

Brooklyn, she finally moved out of her parents' apartment and started living on her own. She knew that it was the wrong job for her, that having to talk to so many people every day could become an unrelenting trial on her nerves, but she accepted the job anyway. She needed to get out, needed to be free of the ever-worried eyes of her mother and father, and this was her only chance.

That was five years ago. Now, as she stands on the front porch of the house wrapped in her overcoat and drinking her morning coffee, she realizes that she must begin again. Painful as it was to listen to Millie's words two months ago, the brutal and dismissive condemnation of her drawings and canvases was fully deserved. Her work doesn't speak to anyone. She knows she is not without skill, not without talent even, but she has boxed herself into a corner by pursuing a single idea, and that idea isn't strong enough to bear the weight of what she has been trying to accomplish. She thought the delicacy of her touch could lead her to the sublime and austere realm that Morandi had once inhabited. She wanted to make pictures that would evoke the mute wonder of pure thingness, the holy ether breathing in the spaces between things, a translation of human existence into a minute rendering of all that is *out there* beyond us, around us, in the same way she knows the invisible graveyard is standing there in front of her, even if she cannot see it. But she was wrong to put her trust in things, to trust in things only, to have squandered her time on the innumerable buildings she has drawn and painted, the empty streets devoid of people, the garages and gas stations and factories, the bridges and elevated highways, the red bricks of old warehouses glinting in the dusky New York light. It comes across as timid evasion, an empty exercise in style, whereas all she has ever wanted is to draw and paint representations of her own feelings. There will be no hope for her unless she starts again from the beginning. No more inanimate objects, she tells herself, no more still lifes. She will return to the human figure and force her strokes to become bolder and more expressive, more gestural, more wild if need be, as wild as the wildest thought within her.

She will ask Alice to pose for her. It is Sunday, a quiet Sunday without much of anything going on, and even if Alice will be working on her dissertation today, she might be able to spare her a couple of hours between now and bed. She goes back into the house and walks up the stairs to her room. Bing and Alice are still asleep, and she moves cautiously so as not to wake them, pulling off her overcoat and the flannel nightgown under it and then climbing into a pair of old jeans and a thick cotton sweater, not bothering with panties or a bra, just her bare skin under the soft fabrics, wanting to feel as loose and mobile as she can this morning, unencumbered for the day ahead. She takes her drawing pad and a Faber-Castell pencil off the top of the bureau, then sits down on the bed and opens the pad to the first empty page. Holding the pencil in her right hand, she raises her left hand in the air, tilts it at a forty-five-degree angle, and keeps it suspended about twelve inches from her face, studying it until it no longer seems attached to her body. It is an alien hand now, a hand that belongs to someone else, to no one, a woman's hand with its slender fingers and rounded nails, the half-moons above the cuticles, the narrow wrist with its small bump of bone sticking out on the left side, the ivory-shaded knuckles and joints, the nearly translucent white skin sheathed over rivulets of veins, blue veins bearing the red blood that meanders through her system as her heart beats and the air moves in and out of her lungs. Digits, carpus, metacarpus, phalanges, dermis. She presses the point of the pencil against the blank page and begins to draw the hand.

At nine-thirty, she knocks on Alice's door. Diligent Bergstrom is already at work, a swarm of fingers darting across the keyboard of her laptop, eyes fixed on the screen in front of her, and Ellen apologizes for interrupting her. No, no, Alice says, it's perfectly all right, and then she stops typing and turns to her friend with one of those warm Alice smiles on her face, no, more than just a warm smile, a maternal smile somehow, not the way Ellen's mother smiles at her, perhaps, but the kind of smile all mothers should give their children, a smile that is not a greeting so much as an offering, a benediction. She thinks: Alice will make a terrific mother when the time comes . . . a superior mother, she says to herself, and then, because of

the juxtaposition of those two words, she transforms Alice
into a Mother Superior, suddenly seeing her in a nun's
habit, and because of this momentary digression she loses
her train of thought and doesn't have time to ask Alice if
she would be willing to pose for her before Alice is asking
a question of her own:

Have you ever seen *The Best Years of Our Lives*?

Of course, Ellen says. Everyone knows that film.

Do you like it?

Very much. It's one of my favorite Hollywood movies.

Why do you like it?

I don't know. It touches me. I always cry when I see it.

You don't find it a little too pat?

Of course it's pat. It's a Hollywood movie, isn't it? All
Hollywood movies are a bit contrived, don't you think?

Good point. But this one is a little less contrived than
most—is that what you're saying?

Think of the scene when the father helps prepare his
son for bed.

Harold Russell, the soldier who lost his hands in the
war.

The boy can't take off the hooks by himself, he can't
button up his own pajamas, he can't put out his cigarette.
His father has to do everything for him. As I remember it,
there's no music in that scene, hardly a word of dialogue,
but it's a great moment in the film. Completely honest.
Incredibly moving.

Does everyone live happily ever after?

Maybe yes, maybe no. Dana Andrews tells the girl—
Teresa Wright—

He tells Teresa Wright that they're going to get kicked around a lot. Maybe they will, maybe they won't. And the Fredric March character is a drunk, a serious, nonstop, raving alcoholic, so his life isn't going to be much fun a few years down the road.

What about Harold Russell?

He marries his sweetheart at the end, but what kind of marriage is it going to be? He's a simple, good-hearted boy, but so damned inarticulate, so bottled up emotionally, I don't see how he's going to make his wife very happy.

I hadn't realized you knew the film so well.

My grandmother was crazy about it. She was about sixteen when the war broke out, and she always said *The Best Years of Our Lives* was *her* movie. We must have watched it together five or six times.

They go on talking about the film for a few more minutes, and then she finally remembers to ask Alice the question that prompted her to knock on the door in the first place. Alice is busy now, but she will be glad to break for an hour after lunch and pose for her then. What Alice doesn't understand is that Ellen isn't interested in doing a portrait of her face, she wants to make a drawing of her whole body, and not that body hidden by clothes but a full nude sketch, perhaps several sketches, similar to the ones she did in her life classes at art school. It is therefore an awkward moment for both of them when they go upstairs to Ellen's room after lunch and Ellen asks Alice to take off her clothes. Alice has never worked as a model, she is not accustomed to having her naked body scrutinized by anyone, and although she and Ellen occasionally catch glimpses of each other going in and out of the bathroom, that has nothing to do with the torture of having to sit stock-still for an hour as your closest friend looks you over from top to bottom, especially now, when she is feeling so miserable about her weight, and even though Ellen tells Alice that she is beautiful, that she has nothing to worry about, it is merely an art exercise, artists are used to looking at other people's bodies, Alice is too embarrassed to give in to her friend's request, she is sorry, terribly sorry, but she can't go through with it and must say no. Ellen is stung by Alice's refusal to do this simple thing for her, which is in fact the first step in reinventing herself as an artist, which is no less than reinventing herself as a woman, a human being, and while she understands that Alice has no intention of hurting her, she can't help feeling hurt, and when she asks Alice to leave the room, she closes the door, sits down on the bed, and starts to cry.

Miles Heller

He thinks of it as a six-month prison sentence with no time off for good behavior. The Christmas and Easter holidays will give Pilar temporary visiting rights, but he will be confined to his cell for the full six months. He mustn't dream of escape. No digging of tunnels in the middle of the night, no confrontations with the guards, no hacking through barbed wire, no mad dashes into the woods pursued by dogs. If he can last through his term without running into trouble or going to pieces, he will be on a bus heading back to Florida on May twenty-second, and on the twenty-third he will be with Pilar to celebrate her birthday. Until then, he will go on holding his breath.

Going to pieces. That was the phrase he kept using during the course of his trip, during the seven conversations he had with her over the thirty-four hours he spent on the road. *You mustn't go to pieces.* When she wasn't sobbing into the phone or ranting against her maniac bitch of a sister, she seemed to understand what he was trying to tell her. He heard himself uttering platitudes that just two days earlier he couldn't have imagined would ever cross his lips, and yet a part of him believed in what he was saying.

They had to be strong. This was a test, and their love would only deepen because of it. And then there was the practical advice, the injunctions to go on doing well at school, to remember to eat enough, to go to bed early every night, to change the oil in the car at regular intervals, to read the books he left for her. Was it a man talking to his future wife or a father talking to his child? A little of both, perhaps. It was Miles talking to Pilar. Miles doing his best to hold the girl together, to hold himself together.

He walks into the Hospital for Broken Things at three o'clock on Monday afternoon. That was the arrangement. If he came in after six o'clock, he was to head straight for the house in Sunset Park. If he arrived during the day, he was to meet Bing at his store on Fifth Avenue in Brooklyn. A bell tinkles as he opens and shuts the door, and when he steps inside he is struck by how small the place is, surely it is the smallest hospital in the world, he thinks, a dingy, cluttered shrine with ancient typewriters on display, a cigar-store Indian standing in the far corner to his left, model biplanes and Piper Cubs hanging from the ceiling, and the walls covered with signs and posters advertising products that left the American scene decades ago: Black Jack gum, O'Dell's Hair Trainer, Geritol, Carter's Little Liver Pills, Old Gold cigarettes. At the sound of the bell, Bing emerges from a back room behind the counter, looking larger and bushier than he remembers, a great big grinning oaf rushing toward him with open arms. Bing is all smiles and laughs, all bear hugs and kisses on the

cheek, and Miles, caught off guard by this slobbering welcome, bursts out laughing himself as he wriggles free of
his friend's crushing embrace.

Bing closes up the Hospital early, and because he suspects Miles is hungry after the long trip, he leads him a
few blocks down Fifth Avenue to what he calls his favorite
lunch place, a scruffy beanery that serves fish and chips,
shepherd's pies, bangers and mash, a full menu of authentic
Limey grub. No wonder Bing has broadened so much,
Miles thinks, lunching on this greasy slop several times a
week, but the truth is that he is famished just now, and
what could be better than a hot shepherd's pie to fill you
up on a cold day? Meanwhile, Bing is talking to him about
the house, about his band, about his failed love affair with
Millie, punctuating his remarks every so often with a brief
word about how well he thinks Miles is looking and how
glad he is to see him again. Miles doesn't say much in
response, he is busy with his food, but he is impressed by
Bing's high spirits and lunging goodwill, and the more
Bing talks, the more he feels that his pen pal of the past
seven years is the same person he was when they last saw
each other, a little older, of course, a little more in posses-
sion of himself, perhaps, but essentially the same person, whereas he, Miles, is altogether different now, a black
sheep who bears no resemblance to the lamb he was seven
years ago.

Toward the end of the meal, a look of discomfort comes
over Bing's face. He pauses for a few moments, fidgeting

with his fork, casting his eyes down at the table, apparently at a loss for words, and when he finally speaks again, his voice is far more subdued than it was earlier, almost hushed.

I don't mean to pry, he says, but I was wondering if you have any plans.

Plans to do what? Miles asks.

To see your parents, for one thing.

Is that any of your business?

Yes, unfortunately it is. I've been your source for a long time now, and I think I want to retire.

You already have. The moment I stepped off the bus today, you were given your gold watch. For years of devoted service. You know how grateful I am to you, don't you?

I don't want your gratitude, Miles. I just don't want to see you fuck up your life anymore. It hasn't been easy on them, you know.

I know. Don't think I don't know.

Well? Are you going to see them or not?

I want to, I'm hoping to . . .

That's no kind of answer. Yes or no?

Yes. Of course I will, he says, not knowing if he will or not, not knowing that Bing has talked to his parents fifty-two times in the past seven years, not knowing that his father and mother and Willa have all been told he will be landing in New York today. Of course I will, he says again. Just give me a chance to settle in first.

The house is like no house he has ever seen in New York.

He is aware that the city is filled with anomalous structures that have no apparent connection to urban life—the brick houses and garden apartments in certain sections of Queens, for example, with their timid, suburban aspirations, or the few remaining wooden houses in the northernmost parts of Brooklyn Heights, historical remnants from the 1840s— but this house in Sunset Park is neither suburban nor historic, it is merely a shack, a forlorn piece of architectural stupidity that would not fit in anywhere, neither in New York nor out of it. Bing didn't send any photographs with his letter, didn't describe what it looked like in any detail, and therefore he had no idea what to expect, but if he did expect anything, it certainly wasn't this.

Cracked gray shingles, red trim around the three sash windows on the second floor, a flimsy balustrade on the porch with diamond-shaped openings painted white, the four posts propping up the roof on the porch painted red, the same brick red as the trim around the windows, but no paint on the front steps or handrails, which are too splintered for a paint job and have been left as bare, weathered wood. Alice and Ellen are both still at work when he and Bing walk up the six steps to the front porch and go inside. Bing gives him the grand tour, clearly proud of all they have accomplished, and while the house seems cramped to him (not just because of the size of the rooms or the number of rooms but because of the many things that have been jammed into them—Bing's drums, Ellen's canvases, Alice's books), the interior is remarkably clean, with a

patched-up, freshly painted brightness, and therefore perhaps even livable. The kitchen, the bathroom, and the back
bedroom downstairs; the three bedrooms upstairs. But no
living room or parlor, which means that the kitchen is the
only communal space—along with the porch in times of
good weather. He will be inheriting Millie's old bedroom
on the ground floor, which is something of a relief, since
that room affords the most privacy, if living in a room off
the kitchen can be considered privacy. He puts his bag
down on the bed, and as he looks out the windows on
either side of him, the one with a view of the vacant lot
with the junked car in it, the other with a view of the abandoned construction site, Bing is telling him about the
various routines and protocols that have been established
since they moved in. Each person has a job to perform,
but beyond the responsibilities of that job, everyone is free
to come and go at will. He is the handyman-janitor, Ellen
is the cleaning woman, and Alice does the shopping and
most of the cooking. Perhaps Miles would like to share
Alice's job with her, taking turns with the shopping and
cooking. Miles has no objection. He enjoys cooking, he
says, he's developed a knack for it over the years, and that
won't be a problem. Bing goes on to say they generally eat
breakfast and dinner together because they are all low on
money and are trying to spend as little as they can. Pool-
ing their resources has helped them get by, and now that
Miles has joined the household, everyone's expenses will
go down accordingly. They will all benefit because he is

here, and by that he isn't talking only about money, it's about everything Miles will add to the spirit of the house, and Bing wants him to understand how happy it makes him to know that he is finally back where he belongs. Miles shrugs, saying he hopes he can manage to fit in, but secretly he is wondering if he is cut out for this sort of group living, if he wouldn't be better off looking for a place of his own. The only problem is cash, the same problem all the others are facing. He no longer has a job, and the three thousand dollars he brought with him amount to little more than pennies. Like it or not, then, for the time being he is stuck, and unless something comes along that dramatically alters his circumstances, he will just have to make the best of it. So his prison sentence begins. Pilar's sister has turned him into the newest member of the Sunset Park Four.

That night, they throw a dinner in his honor. It is a gesture of welcome, and although he would prefer not to have been made the center of attention, he tries to get through it without showing how uncomfortable he feels. What are his first impressions of them? He finds Alice to be the most likable, the most grounded, and he is rather taken by her blunt, boyish, midwestern approach to things. A well-read person with a good mind, he discovers, but unaffected, self-deprecating, with a talent for tossing off subtle wisecracks at unexpected moments. Ellen is more of a puzzle to him. She is both attractive and not attractive, both open and closed off, and from one minute to the next her personality seems to change. Long, awkward silences, and then, when she finally speaks, she rarely fails to deliver some astute remark. He senses inner turbulence, disarray, and yet deep kindness as well. If only she wouldn't stare at him so much, he might be able to warm up to her a little, but her eyes have been on him ever since they sat down at the table, and he feels discomfited by her blatant, overly intrusive interest in him. Then there is Jake, the sometime visitor to Sunset Park, a thin, balding person with a sharp nose and big ears, Jake Baum the writer, Alice's boyfriend. For the first few minutes he seems pleasant enough, but then Miles begins to change his opinion of him, noticing that he barely takes the trouble to listen to anyone but himself, especially Alice, whom he interrupts again and again, often cutting her off in mid-sentence to pursue some thought of his own, and before long Miles concludes that Jake Baum is a bore, even if he can recite Pound from memory and reel off the opponents from every World Series since 1932. Thankfully, Bing seems to be in top fettle, exuberantly playing his role as master of ceremonies, and in spite of the invisible tensions in the air, he has deftly maintained the frivolous tone of the evening. Each time another bottle of wine is opened, he stands up to pronounce a toast, celebrating Miles's homecoming, celebrating the imminent four-month anniversary of their little revolution, celebrating the rights of squatters all over the world. The only negative in all this conviviality is the fact that Miles doesn't drink, and he knows that when people meet someone who abstains from alcohol, they automatically assume he is a recovering drunk. Miles was never an alcoholic, but there was a time when he felt he was drinking too much, and when he cut himself off three years ago, it was as much about saving money as it was about his health. They can think whatever they like, he tells himself, it's of no importance to him, but each time Bing lifts his glass for another toast, Jake turns to Miles and urges him to join in. An honest mistake the first time, perhaps, but there have been two more toasts since then, and Jake has kept on doing it. If he knew what Miles was capable of when he is angry, the needling would stop at once, but Jake doesn't know, and if he does it again the next time, he could end up with a bloody nose or a broken jaw. All the years of battling to keep his temper under control, and now, on his first day back in New York, Miles is seething again, ready to tear someone apart.

It gets worse. Before the dinner, he asked Bing not to let anyone know who his parents were, to keep the names Morris Heller and Mary-Lee Swann out of the discussion, and Bing said of course, that went without saying, but now, just when the dinner is finally coming to an end, Jake starts talking about Renzo Michaelson's most recent novel, *The Mountain Dialogues*, which was published by his father's company in September. Perhaps there is nothing unusual about that, the book is doing extremely well, no doubt many people are talking about it, and Baum is a writer himself, which means that he is bound to be acquainted with Renzo's work, but Miles doesn't want to listen to him blather on about it, not about this book in any case, which he read down in Florida when it was first published, read only when Pilar wasn't around the apartment because it was too much for him, he understood on the first page that the two sixty-year-old men sitting and talking on that mountaintop in the Berkshires were in fact based on Renzo and his father, and it was impossible for him to read that book without breaking down in tears, knowing that he himself was implicated in the sorrows of that story, the two men talking back and forth about the things they had lived through, old friends, the best of old friends, his father and his godfather, and here is pompous Jake Baum making his declarations about that book, and with all his heart Miles wishes he would stop. Baum says he would love to interview Michaelson. He knows he rarely talks to journalists, but there are so many questions he would like to ask him, and wouldn't it be *a feather in his cap* if he could persuade Michaelson to give him a couple of hours? Baum is thinking only about his own petty ambitions, trying to aggrandize himself by feeding off someone who is ten thousand times greater than he will ever be, and then stupid Bing pipes in with the news that he is the person who cleans and repairs Renzo's typewriter, good old Michaelson, one of the last of a dying breed, a novelist who still hasn't switched over to a computer, and yes, he knows him a little bit, and maybe he could put in a word for Jake the next time Renzo comes into the shop. By now, Miles is ready to jump on

Bing and strangle him, but just then, fortunately, the conversation is deflected onto another subject when Alice lets out a loud, booming sneeze, and suddenly Bing is talking about flus and winter colds, and no more mention is made of interviewing Renzo Michaelson.

After that dinner, he resolves to make himself scarce whenever Jake is around, to avoid having any more meals with him. He doesn't want to do anything he will later regret, and Jake is the kind of man who inevitably brings out the worst in him. As it happens, the problem is not as grave as he supposes it will be. Baum comes by only once in the next two weeks, and although Alice spends a couple of nights with him in Manhattan, Miles senses there is trouble between them, that they are facing a rugged patch or perhaps even the end. It shouldn't concern him, but now that he has come to know Alice, he hopes it is the end, for Baum doesn't deserve a woman like Alice, and she herself deserves far better.

Three days after his arrival, he calls his father's office. The receptionist tells him that Mr. Heller is out of the country and won't be returning to work until January fifth. Would he like to leave a message? No, he says, he'll call back next month, thank you.

He reads in the paper that previews of his mother's play will begin on January thirteenth.

He doesn't know what to do with himself. Besides his daily conversations with Pilar, which tend to last between one and two hours, there is no structure to his life anymore.

He wanders around the streets, trying to familiarize himself with the neighborhood, but he quickly loses interest in Sunset Park. There is something dead about the place, he finds, the mournful emptiness of poverty and immigrant struggle, an area without banks or bookstores, only check-cashing operations and a decrepit public library, a small world apart from the world where time moves so slowly that few people bother to wear a watch.

He spends an afternoon taking photographs of some of the factories near the waterfront, the old buildings that house the last surviving companies in the neighborhood, manufacturers of windows and doors, swimming pools, ladies' clothes and nurses' uniforms, but the pictures are nondescript somehow, lacking in urgency, uninspired. The next day, he ventures up to the Chinatown on Eighth Avenue, with its dense grouping of shops and businesses, its crowded sidewalks, the ducks hanging in the butchers' windows, a hundred potential scenes to capture, vivid colors all around him, but still he feels flattened out, unengaged, and he leaves without taking a single picture. He will need time to adjust, he tells himself. His body might be here now, but his mind is still with Pilar in Florida, and even if he is home again, this New York is not his New York, not the New York of his memory. For all the distance he has traveled, he might just as well have come to a foreign city, a city anywhere else in America.

Little by little, he has been acclimating himself to Ellen's eyes. He no longer feels threatened by her curiosity in him, and if she talks less than anyone else at their shared breakfasts and dinners around the kitchen table, she can be quite voluble when he is alone with her. She communicates largely by asking questions, not personal questions about his life or past history, but questions about his opinions on topics ranging from the weather to the state of the world. Does he like winter? Who does he think is a better artist, Picasso or Matisse? Is he worried about global warming? Was he happy when Obama was elected last month? Why do men like sports so much? Who is his favorite photographer? No doubt there is something infantile about her directness, but at the same time her questions often provoke spirited exchanges, and following the path of Alice and Bing before him, he feels an ever-growing responsibility to protect her. He understands that Ellen is lonely and would like nothing better than to spend every night in his bed, but he has already told her enough about Pilar for her to know that this won't be possible. On one of her days off, she invites him to go walking with her in Green-Wood Cemetery, a visit to the City of the Dead, as she calls it, and for the first time since coming to Sunset Park, he feels something stir inside him. There were the abandoned things down in Florida, and now he has stumbled upon the abandoned people of Brooklyn. He suspects it is a terrain well worth exploring.

With Alice, he has been given the chance to talk to someone about books, a thing that has happened to him only rarely in the years between college and Pilar. Early on, he discovers that she is mostly ignorant of European and South American literature, which comes as a small disappointment, but she is one of those specialized academics steeped in her narrow Anglo-American world, far more familiar with *Beowulf* and Dreiser than with Dante and Borges, but that hardly qualifies as a problem, there is still much they can talk about, and before many days have passed they have already developed a private shorthand to express their likes and dislikes, a language consisting of grunts, frowns, raised eyebrows, nods of the head, and sudden slaps to the knee. She doesn't talk to him about Jake, and therefore he doesn't ask her any questions. He has told her about Pilar, however, but not much, not much of anything beyond her name and the fact that she will be coming up from Florida to visit over Christmas break. He uses the word *break* instead of *vacation*, since *break* suggests college and *vacation* always means school, and he doesn't want anyone in the house to know how young Pilar is until she is already here—at which point, he hopes, no one will bother to ask her age. But even if it happens, he isn't worried. The only person to worry about is Angela, and Angela won't know that Pilar is gone. He has discussed this detail with Pilar again and again. She mustn't let any of her sisters know that she is leaving, not just Angela, but Teresa and Maria as well, for the minute one of them knows, they will all know, and even if the odds are against it, Angela might just be crazy enough to follow Pilar to New York.

He has bought a small illustrated book about Green-Wood Cemetery, and he goes in there every day with his camera now, roaming among the graves and monuments and mausoleums, nearly always alone in the frigid December air, carefully studying the lavish, often bombastic architecture of certain plots, the marble pillars and obelisks, the Greek temples and Egyptian pyramids, the enormous statues of supine, weeping women. The cemetery is more than half the size of Central Park, ample enough space for a person to get lost in there, to forget that he is a prisoner serving out his time in a dreary part of Brooklyn, and to walk among the thousands of trees and plantings, to climb the hillocks and traverse the sweeping paths of this vast necropolis is to leave the city behind you and enclose yourself in the absolute quiet of the dead. He takes pictures of the tombs of gangsters and poets, generals and industrialists, murder victims and newspaper publishers, children dead before their time, a woman who lived seventeen years beyond her hundredth birthday, and Theodore Roosevelt's wife and mother, who were buried next to each other on the same day. There is Elias Howe, inventor of the sewing machine, the Kampfe brothers, inventors of the safety razor, Henry Steinway, founder of the Steinway Piano Company, John Underwood, founder of the Underwood Typewriter Company, Henry Chadwick, inventor of the baseball scoring system, Elmer Sperry, inventor of the gyroscope. The crematory built in the mid-twentieth century has incinerated the bodies of John Steinbeck, Woody

Guthrie, Edward R. Murrow, Eubie Blake, and how many more, both known and unknown, how many more souls have been transformed into smoke in this eerie, beautiful place? He has embarked on another useless project, employing his camera as an instrument to record his stray, useless thoughts, but at least it is something to do, a way to pass the time until his life starts again, and where else but in Green-Wood Cemetery could he have learned that the real name of Frank Morgan, the actor who played the Wizard of Oz, was Wuppermann?

MORRIS HELLER

1

It is the last day of the year, and he has come home from
England a week early to attend the funeral of Martin Rothstein's twenty-three-year-old daughter, who committed suicide in Venice the night before Christmas Eve. He has
been publishing Rothstein's work since the founding of
Heller Books. Marty and Renzo were the only Americans
on the first list, two Americans along with Per Carlsen
from Denmark and Annette Louverain from France, and
thirty-five years later he is still publishing them all, they
are the core writers of the house, and he knows he would
be nothing without them. The news came on the evening
of the twenty-fourth, a mass e-mail sent to hundreds of
friends and acquaintances, which he read on Willa's computer in their room at the Charlotte Street Hotel in London, the grim, naked message from Marty and Nina that
Suki had taken her own life, with further information to
follow about the date of the funeral. Willa didn't want him
to go. She thought the funeral would be too hard on him,
there had been too many funerals in the past year, too
many of their friends were dying now, and she knew how
ravaged he was by the losses, that was the word she used,

ravaged, but he said he had to be there for them, it wouldn't be possible not to go, the duties of friendship demanded it, and four days later he was on a plane back to New York.

Now it is December thirty-first, late morning on the final day of 2008, and as he steps off the No. 1 train and climbs the stairs to Broadway and Seventy-ninth Street, the air is clogged with snow, a wet, heavy snow is falling from the white-gray sky, thick flakes tumbling through the blustery dimness, muting the colors of the traffic lights, whitening the hoods of passing cars, and by the time he reaches the community center on Amsterdam Avenue, he looks as if he is wearing a hat of snow. Suki Rothstein, birth name Susanna, the baby girl he first glimpsed sleeping in the crook of her father's right arm twenty-three years ago, the young woman who graduated summa cum laude from the University of Chicago, the budding artist, the precociously gifted thinker, writer, photographer who went to Venice this past fall to work as an intern at the Peggy Guggenheim Collection, and it was there, in the women's room of that museum, just days after conducting a seminar about her own work, that she hanged herself. Willa was right, he knows that, but how not to feel ravaged by Suki's death, how not to put himself inside her father's skin and suffer the ravages of this pointless death?

He remembers running into her some years back on Houston Street in the brightness of a late afternoon at the end of spring, the beginning of summer. She was on her way to her high school prom, decked out in a flamboyant red dress, as red as the reddest Jersey tomato, and Suki was all lit up with smiles when he chanced upon her that afternoon, surrounded by her friends, happy, affectionately kissing him hello and good-bye, and from that day forward he held that picture of her in his mind as the quintessential embodiment of youthful exuberance and promise, a singular example of *youth on fire*. Now he thinks about the dank chill of Venice in the dead of winter, the canals overflowing onto streets knee-deep in water, the shivering loneliness of unheated rooms, a head splitting open from the sheer force of the darkness within it, a life broken apart by the too-much and too-little of this world.

He shuffles into the building with the other people, a slowly gathering crowd that builds to two or three hundred, and he sees any number of familiar faces in the throng, Renzo's among them, but also Sally Fuchs, Don Willingham, Gordon Field, any number of old friends, writers, poets, artists, editors, and many young people as well, dozens and dozens of young men and women, Suki's friends from childhood, from high school, from college, and everyone is speaking in low voices, as if speaking above a whisper would be an offense, an insult against the silence of the dead, and as he looks at the faces around him, everyone seems numb and depleted, not quite fully there, *ravaged*. He makes his way to a small room at the end of the corridor where Marty and Nina are welcoming the visitors, the guests, the mourners, whatever word is used to describe people who come to a funeral, and as he steps forward to put his arms around his old friend, tears are pouring down Marty's face, and then Marty throws his arms around him and presses his head against his shoulder, saying Morris, Morris, Morris as his body convulses against him in a spasm of breathless sobs.

Martin Rothstein is not a man built for tragedies of this magnitude. He is a person of wit and effervescent charm, a comic writer of baroque, hilariously constructed sentences and spot-on satirical flair, an intellectual agitator with grand appetites and countless friends and a sense of humor equal to the best of the Borscht Belt wise guys. Now he is weeping his heart out, overcome by grief, by the cruelest, most lacerating form of grief, and Morris wonders how anyone can expect a man in this condition to stand up and talk in front of all these people when the service begins. And yet, sometime later, when the mourners have taken their seats in the auditorium and Marty climbs onto the stage to deliver his eulogy, he is calm, dry-eyed, completely recovered from his breakdown in the reception room. He reads from a text he has written, a text no doubt made possible by the length of time it took for Suki's body to be shipped from Venice to New York, making the gap between death and burial longer than usual, and in those empty, unsettled days of waiting for his daughter's corpse to arrive, Marty sat down and wrote this text. With Bobby, there had been no words. Willa hadn't been capable of writing or saying anything, he hadn't been capable of writing or saying anything, the accident had crushed them into a state of mute incomprehension, a dumb, bleeding sorrow that had lasted for months, but Marty is a writer, his whole life has been spent putting words and sentences together, paragraphs together, books together, and the only way he could respond to Suki's death was to write about her.

The coffin is on the stage, a white coffin surrounded by red flowers, but it is not a religious service. No rabbi has come to officiate, no prayers are recited, and no one who appears onstage tries to draw any meaning or consolation from Suki's death—there is nothing more than the fact of it, the horror of it. Someone plays a solo piece for saxophone, someone else plays a Bach chorale on the piano, and at one point Suki's younger brother, Anton, wearing red nail polish in honor of his sister, performs an unaccompanied, dirgelike rendition of a Cole Porter song (Ev'ry time we say good-bye / I die a little) that is so drastically slowed down, so drenched in melancholy, so painful to listen to that most of the gathering is in tears by the time he comes to the end. Writers walk up to the lectern and read poems by Shakespeare and Yeats. Friends and classmates tell stories about Suki, reminisce, evoke the *burning intensity of her spirit*. The director of the gallery where she had her one and only exhibition talks about her work. Morris follows every word spoken, listens to every note played and sung, on the verge of disintegration throughout the entire one-and-a-half-hour service, but it is Marty's speech that comes closest to destroying him, a brave and stunning piece of eloquence that shocks him with its candor, the brutal precision of its thinking, the rage and sorrow and guilt and love that permeate each of its articulations. All during Marty's twenty-minute talk, Morris imagines himself trying to talk about Bobby, about Miles, about the long-dead Bobby and the absent Miles, but he knows he would never have the courage to stand up in public and express his feelings with such naked honesty.

Afterward, there is a pause. Only the Rothsteins and their closest relatives will be going to the cemetery in Queens. Everyone is invited to Marty and Nina's apartment at four o'clock, but for now the mourners must disperse. He is glad to have been spared the ordeal of watching the coffin being lowered into the ground, the bulldozer pushing the dirt back into the hole, the sight of Marty and Nina collapsing into tears again. Renzo tracks him down in the entrance hall, and the two of them go back out into the snow together to look for a place to have lunch. Renzo is intelligent enough to have brought along an umbrella, and as Morris squeezes in beside him, Renzo puts his arm around his shoulder. Neither one of them says a word. They have been friends for fifty years, and each knows what the other is thinking.

They wind up in a Jewish delicatessen on Broadway in the low Eighties, a throwback to their New York childhoods, the all but vanished cuisine of chopped liver, matzo-ball soup, corned beef and pastrami sandwiches, pot roasts, cheese blintzes, sour pickles. Renzo has been traveling, they haven't seen each other since the publication of *The Mountain Dialogues* in September, and Morris feels that Renzo is looking tired, more haggard than usual. How did they get to be so old? he wonders. They are both sixty-two now, and while neither of them is in bad health, neither one of them fat or bald or ready for the glue factory, their heads have turned gray, their hairlines are receding, and they have reached that point in their lives when women under thirty, perhaps even forty, look right through them. He remembers Renzo as a young, young writer just out of college, living in a forty-nine-dollar-a-month apartment on the Lower East Side, one of those tenement railroad flats with a tub in the kitchen and six thousand cockroaches holding political conventions in every cupboard, so poor that he had to limit himself to one meal a day, working for three years on his first novel, which he destroyed because he felt it wasn't good enough, destroyed in the face of Morris's protests, his girlfriend's protests, who both felt it was very good indeed, and now look at him, Morris thinks, after how many books since that burned manuscript (seventeen? twenty?), published in every country of the world, even Iran, for God's sake, with how many literary prizes, how many medals, keys to cities, honorary doctorates, how many books and dissertations written about his work, and none of it matters to him, he is

glad to have some money now, glad to be free of the suffocating hardships of the early years, but his fame leaves
him cold, he has lost all interest in himself as a so-called
public figure. I just want to disappear, he once told Morris, muttering in the lowest of low voices, staring off with
a pained look in his eyes, as if he were talking to himself.
I just want to disappear.

They order their soups and sandwiches, and when the
Latino waiter walks off with their menus (a Latino waiter
in a Jewish restaurant, they both like that), Morris and
Renzo start talking about the funeral, sharing their impressions of what they have just witnessed in the community
center auditorium. Renzo didn't know Suki, he met her
only once when she was a small child, but he agrees with
Morris that Rothstein's talk was a powerful piece of work,
almost unimaginable when you consider that it was written under the most appalling duress, at a time when few
people would have the strength to pull themselves together
and write a single word, let alone the passionate, complex,
and clear-sighted eulogy they heard this morning. Renzo
has no children, two ex-wives but no children, and given
what Marty and Nina are going through now, given what
he and Willa have already gone through, first with Bobby
and then with Miles, Morris feels something close to envy,
thinking that Renzo made the right decision all those
years ago to steer clear of the kid business, to avoid the
unavoidable mess and potential devastation of fatherhood.
He is half-expecting Renzo to start talking about Bobby

now, the parallel is so evident, and surely he understands how difficult this funeral has been for him, but precisely because Renzo does understand, he does not talk about it. He is too discreet for that, too aware of what Morris is thinking to barge in on his pain, and just seconds afterward Morris himself understands his friend's reluctance to intrude on him when Renzo changes the subject, skirting past Bobby and the gloomy realm of dead children, and asks him how he is weathering the crisis, meaning the economic crisis, and whither Heller Books in this storm of trouble?

Morris tells him that the ship is still afloat, but listing somewhat to the starboard side now, and for the past few months they have been throwing excess equipment overboard. His primary concern is to keep the staff intact, and so far he hasn't had to let anyone go, but the list has been reduced, cut down by twenty or twenty-five percent. Last year, they published forty-seven books, this year thirty-eight, but their profits have gone down by only eleven percent, in large part thanks to *The Mountain Dialogues*, which is in its third printing, with forty-five thousand hardcovers sold. The Christmas sales figures won't be in for a while, but even if they turn out to be lower than expected, he isn't predicting out-and-out disaster. Louverain, Wyatt, and Tomesetti all published strong books this fall, and the paperback crime series seems to be off to a good start, but it's a rough time for first novels, very rough, and he's been forced to reject some good young writers, books he would have taken a chance on a year or two ago, and he finds that troubling, since the whole point of Heller Books is to encourage new talent. They're planning only thirty-three books for 2009, but Carlsen is on the list, Davenport is on the list, and then, needless to say, there is Renzo's novella, the little book he wrote just after *The Mountain Dialogues*, the unanticipated bonus book he has such high hopes for, and who knows, if every independent bookstore in America doesn't go bankrupt in the next twelve months, they might be in for a decent year. Listening to himself talk, he almost begins to feel optimistic, but he is telling Renzo only part of the story, leaving out the fact that when the returns start coming in on *The Mountain Dialogues* sales will fall by seven to ten thousand, leaving out the fact that 2008 will be the worst year for the house in three decades, leaving out the fact that he needs a new investor to put additional capital into the company or the ship will go down within two years. But there is no need for Renzo to know any of this. Renzo writes books, and he publishes them, and Renzo will go on writing and publishing books even if he is no longer in business.

After the soup comes, Renzo asks: What's the latest on the boy?

He's here, Morris says. As of two or three weeks ago.

Here in New York?

In Brooklyn. Living in an abandoned house in Sunset Park with some other people.

Our drummer friend told you this?

Our drummer friend is one of the people living there. He invited Miles to come up from Florida, and the boy accepted. Don't ask me why.

It sounds like good news to me.

Maybe. Time will tell. Bing says he's planning to call me, but no messages yet.

And what if he doesn't call?

Then nothing changes.

Think about it, Morris. All you have to do is jump in a cab, drive out to Brooklyn, and knock on the door. Aren't you tempted?

Of course I'm tempted. But I can't do it. He's the one who left, and he's the one who has to come back.

Renzo doesn't insist, and Morris is thankful to him for letting the matter drop there. As godfather to the boy and longtime friend of the father, Renzo has been participating in this grim saga for seven years, and by now there is little of anything left to say. Morris asks him about his recent travels, the trips to Prague, Copenhagen, and Paris, his reading at the Max Reinhardt Theater in Berlin, the prize he was given in Spain, and Renzo says it was a welcome diversion, he has been in a slump lately, and it felt good to be somewhere else for a few weeks, someplace other than inside his own head. Morris has been listening to this kind of talk from Renzo for as long as he can remember. Renzo is always in a slump, each book he finishes is always the last book he will ever write, and then, somehow, the slump mysteriously ends, and he is back in his room writing another book. Yes, Renzo says, he knows he's talked this way in the past, but this time it feels different, he doesn't know why, this time the paralysis is beginning to feel permanent. *Night Walk* was finished at the end of June, he says, more than six months ago, and since then he's done nothing of any account. It was such a short book, just a hundred and fifty-something pages, but it seemed to take everything out of him, he wrote it in a kind of frenzy, less than three months from beginning to end, working harder and with more concentration than at any time in all the years he has been writing, pushing, pushing, like a runner sprinting at full tilt for seven miles, and exhilarating as it was to work at that pace, something in him collapsed when he crossed the finish line. For six months he has had no plans, no ideas, no project to occupy his days. When he hasn't been traveling, he has felt listless and without motivation, with no desire to return to his desk and start writing again. He has experienced similar lulls in the past, yes, but never anything as stubborn and protracted as this one, and although he hasn't reached a state of alarm yet, he is beginning to wonder if this isn't the end, if the old fire hasn't been extinguished at last. Meanwhile, he spends his days doing next to nothing—reading books, thinking, going out for walks, watching films, following the news of the world. In other words, he is resting, but for all that it is a strange kind of rest, he says, *an anxious repose.*

The waiter brings them their sandwiches, and before Morris can say anything about this half-serious, half-mocking account of mental exhaustion, Renzo, in an abrupt about-face, contradicting everything he has just said, tells Morris that a small notion occurred to him while he was flying home from Europe the other day, the tiniest germ of an idea—for an essay, a piece of nonfiction, something. Morris smiles. I thought you had run out of ideas, he says. Well, Renzo answers, shrugging defensively, but with a glint of humor in his eye, one does have an occasional *flicker.*

He was on the plane, he says, a first-class ticket paid for by the people who gave him the prize, the dread of flying dulled somewhat by soft leather seats, caviar and champagne, imbecilic luxe among the clouds, with an abundant choice of films at his disposal, not just new films from Europe and America but old ones as well, venerated classics, ancient fluff from the dream factories on both sides of the Atlantic. He wound up watching *The Best Years of Our Lives,* something he had seen once a long time ago and therefore had utterly forgotten, a nice movie, he felt, well played by the actors, a charming piece of propaganda designed to persuade Americans that the soldiers returning from World War II will eventually adjust to civilian life, not without a few bumps along the way, of course, but in the end everything will work out, because this is America, and in America everything always works out. Be that as it may, he enjoyed the film, it helped pass

the time, but what interested him most about the film was
not the film itself but a minor role played by one of the
actors in it, Steve Cochran. He has only one bit of any
importance, a short, smirking confrontation with the hero,
whose wife has been running around with Cochran on
the sly, but that finally isn't what interested him either,
Cochran's performance is a matter of complete indifference to him, what counts is the story his mother once told
him about having known Cochran during the war, yes, his
mother, Anita Michaelson, née Cannobio, who died four
years ago at the age of eighty. His mother was an elusive
woman, not given to opening up about the past, but when
Cochran died at forty-eight in 1965, just after Renzo had
turned nineteen, she must have been thrown sufficiently
off guard to feel a need to unburden herself, and so she
told him about her brief infatuation with the theater in
the early forties, a girl of fifteen, sixteen, seventeen, and
how she crossed paths with Cochran in some New York
theater group and *fell for him*. He was such a handsome
man, she said, one of those rugged black-Irish heart-
throbs, but what *falling* meant was never quite clear to
Renzo. Did his mother lose her virginity to Steve Cochran
in 1942 when she was seventeen years old? Did they have
an actual fling—or was it only a thing, an adolescent crush
on an up-and-coming twenty-five-year-old actor? Impossible to say, but what his mother did report was that Cochran
wanted her to go to California with him, and she was prepared to go, but when her parents got wind of what was

brewing, they put an immediate stop to it. No daughter of theirs, no scandals in this family, forget it, Anita. So Cochran left, his mother stayed and married his father, and that was how he came to be born—because his mother hadn't run off with Steve Cochran. That is the idea he is toying with, Renzo says, to write an essay about the things that don't happen, the lives not lived, the wars not fought, the shadow worlds that run parallel to the world we take to be the real world, the not-said and the not-done, the not-remembered. Chancy territory, perhaps, but it could be worth exploring.

After he came home, Renzo says, he felt curious enough to do a little digging into Cochran's life and career. Gangster roles for the most part, a couple of plays on Broadway with Mae West, of all people, *White Heat* with James Cagney, the lead in Antonioni's *Il Grido,* and appearances on various television shows in the fifties: *Bonanza, The Untouchables, Route 66, The Twilight Zone.* He formed his own production company, which produced little or nothing (information is scant, and although Renzo is curious, he is not curious enough to explore this point further), but Cochran seems to have acquired a reputation as one of the most active skirt chasers of his time. This probably explains why his mother fell for him, Renzo continues, sadly contemplating how easy it must have been for a practiced seducer to soften the heart of an inexperienced seventeen-year-old girl. How could she have resisted the man who later went on to have affairs with Joan Crawford,

Merle Oberon, Kay Kendall, Ida Lupino, and Jayne Mansfield? There was also Mamie Van Doren, who apparently wrote at great length about her sex life with Cochran in an autobiography published twenty years ago, but Renzo has no plans to read the book. In the end, what fascinates him most is how thoroughly he suppressed the facts about Cochran's death, which he must have heard about when he was nineteen, but even after the conversation with his mother (which theoretically should have made the story impossible to forget), he forgot everything. In 1965, hoping to rejuvenate his moribund production company, Cochran developed a project for a film to be set in Central or South America. With three young women between the ages of fourteen and twenty-five, supposedly hired as assistants, he set out for Costa Rica on his forty-foot yacht to begin scouting locations. Some weeks later, the boat washed ashore along the coast of Guatemala. Cochran had died on board from a severe lung infection, and the three panic-stricken young women, who knew nothing about sailing, nothing about navigating forty-foot yachts, had been drifting through the ocean for the past ten days, alone with Cochran's putrefying corpse. Renzo says he cannot efface the image from his mind. The three frightened women lost at sea with the decomposing body of the dead movie star below deck, convinced they will never touch land again.

So much, he says, for the best years of our lives.

2

He has been invited to four New Year's Eve parties in four different parts of Manhattan, East Side and West Side, uptown and downtown, but after the funeral, after the lunch with Renzo, after the two hours spent at Marty and Nina's place, he has no desire to see anyone. He goes home to the apartment on Downing Street, unable to stop thinking about Suki, unable to free himself of the story Renzo told about the dead actor on the drifting boat. How many corpses has he seen in his life? he wonders. Not the embalmed dead lying in their open coffins, the wax-museum figures drained of blood who no longer appear to have been human, but actual dead bodies, the vivid dead, as it were, before they could be touched by the mortician's scalpel? His father, thirty years ago. Bobby, twelve years ago. His mother, five years ago. Three. Just three in more than sixty years.

He goes into the kitchen and pours himself a scotch. He already knocked off two of them at Marty and Nina's place, but he doesn't feel the least bit wobbly or disabled, his head is clear, and after the enormous lunch he consumed at the delicatessen, which is still sitting in his stomach like a stone, he has no appetite for dinner. He tells himself that he will end the year by catching up on the manuscripts he should have read in England, but he understands that this is merely a ruse, a trick to propel him into the comfortable armchair in the living room, and once he sits down in that chair, he will not return to Samantha Jewett's novel, which he has already decided not to publish.

It is seven-thirty, four and a half hours before another year begins, the tired ritual of noisemakers and fireworks, the blast of drunken voices that will echo across the neighborhood at midnight, always the same eruption on this particular midnight, but he is far from that now, alone with his scotch and his thoughts, and if he can go deeply enough into those thoughts, he won't even hear the voices and the clamor when the time comes. Five years ago this past May, the call from his mother's cleaning woman, who had just let herself into the apartment with her duplicate key. He was at the office, he remembers, a Tuesday morning around ten o'clock, talking with Jill Hertzberg about Renzo's latest manuscript and whether to use an illustration on the cover or go with pure graphics. Why remember a detail like that? No reason, no reason that he can think of, except that reason and memory are nearly always at odds, and then he was in a cab heading up Broadway to West Eighty-fourth Street, trying to get his mind around the fact that his mother, who had been wisecracking with him over the phone on Saturday, was now dead.

The body. That is what he is thinking about now, the

corpse of his mother lying on the bed five years ago, and the terror he felt when he looked down at her face, the blue-gray skin, the half-open-half-closed eyes, the terrifying *immobility* of what had once been a living person. She had been lying there for roughly forty-eight hours before she was discovered by the cleaning woman. Still dressed in her nightgown, his mother had been reading the Sunday edition of the *New York Times* when she died—no doubt of a sudden, cataclysmic heart attack. One bare leg was hanging over the edge of the bed, and he wondered if she had tried to get up when the attack began (to search for a pill? to call for help?), and if so, given that she had moved only a few inches, it struck him that she must have died within seconds.

He looked at her for a brief moment, for several moments, and then he turned away and walked into the living room. It was too much for him; to see her in that state of frozen vulnerability was more than he could bear. He can't remember if he looked at her again when the police arrived, if it was necessary for him to make a formal identification of the body or not, but he is certain that when the paramedics came to pack up the corpse in a black rubber body bag, he couldn't look. He remained in the living room staring down at the rug, studying the clouds through the window, listening to himself breathe. It was simply too much for him, and he couldn't bring himself to look anymore.

The revelation of that morning, the blunt, incontestable

minim of knowledge he finally grasped when the paramedics were wheeling her out of the apartment, the idea
that has continued to haunt him ever since: there can be
no memories of the womb, not for him or anyone else, but
he accepts it as an article of faith, or else wills himself to
understand it through a leap of the imagination, that his
own life as a sentient being began as part of the now dead
body they were pushing through the opened door, that his
life began *within her.*

She was a child of the war, just as Renzo's mother was,
just as all their parents were, whether their fathers had
fought in the war or not, whether their mothers had been
fifteen or seventeen or twenty-two when the war began.
A strangely optimistic generation, he thinks now, tough,
dependable, hardworking, and a little stupid as well, perhaps, but they all bought into the myth of American greatness, and they lived with fewer doubts than their children
did, the boys and girls of Vietnam, the angry postwar children who saw their country turn into a sick, destructive
monster. Spunky. That is the word that comes to him whenever he thinks about his mother. Spunky and outspoken,
strong-willed and loving, impossible. She remarried twice
after his father's death in seventy-eight, lost both of the
new husbands to cancer, one in ninety-two, the other in
oh-three, and even then, in the last year of her life, at age
seventy-nine, eighty, she was still hoping to catch another
man. I was born married, she said to him once. She had
turned into the Wife of Bath, and fitting as that role might

have been for her, playing the son of the Wife of Bath had not been entirely pleasant. His sisters had shared the burden with him, of course, but Cathy lives in Millburn, New Jersey, and Ann is in Scarsdale, just out of reach, on the fringes of the combat zone, and because he was the oldest, and because his mother trusted men more than women, he was the one she came to with her troubles, which were never classified as troubles (all negative words had been expunged from her vocabulary) but as *little somethings*, as in, I have a little something to discuss with you. Willful blindness is what he called it, an obdurate insistence on looking for silver linings, moral victories, a darkest-before-the-dawn attitude in the face of the most wrenching facts—burying three husbands, the disappearance of her grandson, the accidental death of her stepgrandson—but that was the world she came from, an ethical universe patched together from the righteous platitudes of Hollywood films—pluck, spunk, and never say die. Admirable in its way, yes, but also maddening, and as the years moved forward he understood that much of it was a sham, that inside her supposedly indomitable spirit there was also fear and panic and crushing sadness. Who could blame her? Having lived through the various maladies of her three husbands, how could she not have turned into a world-class hypochondriac? If your experience has taught you that all bodies must and will betray the person they belong to, why wouldn't you think that a small pain in the stomach is a prelude to stomach cancer, that a headache signifies brain tumor, that a forgotten word or name is an augury of dementia? Her last years were spent visiting doctors, dozens of specialists for this condition or that syndrome, and it's true that she was having problems with her heart (two angioplasties), but no one thought she was in any real danger. He figured she would go on complaining about her imaginary illnesses until she was ninety, that she would outlive him, that she would outlive them all, and then, without warning, less than twenty-four hours after cracking jokes to him on the phone, she was dead. And once he had come to terms with it, the frightening thing about her death was that he felt relieved, or at least some part of him felt relieved, and he hates himself for being callous enough to admit it, but he knows he is lucky to have been spared the rigors of seeing her through a long old age. She left the world at the right time. No prolonged suffering, no descent into decrepitude or senility, no broken hips or adult diapers, no blank stares into empty space. A light goes on, a light goes off. He misses her, but he can live with the fact that she is gone.

He misses his father more. He is callous enough to admit that, too, but his father has been dead for thirty years now, and he has spent half his life walking beside that ghost. Sixty-three, just one year older than he is now, in good condition, still playing tennis four times a week, still strong enough to trounce his thirty-two-year-old son in three sets of singles, probably still strong enough to beat him at arm wrestling, a strict nonsmoker, alcohol consumption close to zero, never ill with anything, not even colds or flus, a broad-shouldered six-one, without flab or gut or stoop, a man who looked ten years younger than his age, and then a minor problem, an attack of bursitis in his left elbow, the proverbial tennis elbow, extremely painful, yes, but hardly life-threatening, and so he went to a doctor for the first time in how many years, a quack who prescribed cortisone pills instead of some mild painkiller, and his father, unaccustomed to taking pills, carried around the cortisone in his pocket as if it were a bottle of aspirin, tossing another pill down his throat every time the elbow acted up, thus tampering with the functioning of his heart, putting undue strain on his cardiovascular system without even knowing it, and one night, as he was making love to his wife (a consoling thought: to know that his parents were still active in the sex department at that point in their marriage), the night of November 26, 1978, as Alvin Heller was approaching an orgasm in the arms of his wife, Constance, better known as Connie, his heart gave out on him, rupturing inside his chest, exploding inside his chest, and that was the end.

There were never any of the conflicts he witnessed so often with his friends and their fathers, the boys with the slapping fathers, the shouting fathers, the aggressive fathers who pushed their frightened six-year-old sons into swimming pools, the contemptuous fathers who sneered at their adolescent sons for liking the wrong music, wearing the wrong clothes, looking at them in the wrong way, the war-veteran fathers who punched out their twenty-year-old sons for resisting the draft, the weak fathers who were afraid of their grown-up sons, the shut-down fathers who couldn't remember the names of their sons' children. From beginning to end, there had been none of those antagonisms or dramas between them, no more than some sharp differences of opinion, small punishments doled out mechanically for small infractions of the rules, a harsh word or two when he was unkind to his sisters or forgot his mother's birthday, but nothing of any significance, no slaps or shouts or angry insults, and unlike most of his friends, he never felt embarrassed by his father or turned against him. At the same time, it would be wrong to presume that they were especially close. His father wasn't one of those warmhearted buddy fathers who thought his son should be his best pal, he was simply a man who felt responsible for his wife and children, a quiet, even-tempered man with a talent for making money, a skill his son failed to appreciate until the last years of his father's life, when his father became the principal backer and founding partner of Heller Books, but even if they weren't close in the way some fathers and sons are, even if the one thing they ever talked about with any passion together was sports, he knew that his father respected him, and to have that unflagging respect from beginning to end was more important than any open declaration of love.

When he was very young, five years old, six years old, he felt disappointed that his father had not fought in the war, unlike the fathers of most of his friends, and that while they had been off in far-flung parts of the world killing Japs and Nazis and turning themselves into heroes, his father had been in New York, immersed in the petty details of his real estate business, buying buildings, managing buildings, endlessly repairing buildings, and it puzzled him that his father, who seemed so strong and fit, had been rejected by the army when he tried to join up. But he was still too young at that point to understand how badly his father's eye was injured, to have been told that his father had been legally blind in his left eye since the age of seventeen, and because his father had so thoroughly mastered the art of living with and compensating for his handicap, he failed to understand that his powerhouse of a father was impaired. Later on, when he was eight or nine and his mother finally told him the story of the injury (his father never talked about it), he realized that his father's wound was no different from a war wound, that a part of his life had been shot down on that Bronx ball field in 1932 in the same way a soldier's arm can be shot off on a battlefield in Europe. He was the top pitcher for his high school baseball team, a hard-throwing left-hander who was already beginning to attract attention from major league scouts, and when he took the mound for Monroe that day in early June, he had an undefeated record and what appeared to be an unhittable arm. On the first pitch of the game, just as the fielders were settling into their positions behind him, he threw a low fastball to the Clinton shortstop, Tommy DeLucca, and the line drive that came flying back at him was struck so hard, with such ferocious power and speed, that he had no time to lift his glove and protect his face. It was the same injury that destroyed Herb Score's career in 1957, the same bone-breaking shot that changes the course of a life. And if that ball hadn't slammed his father in the eye, who is to say he wouldn't have been killed in the war—before his marriage, before the birth of his children? Now Herb Score is dead, too, Morris thinks, dead as of six or seven weeks ago, Herb Score, with the prophetic middle name of Jude, and he remembers how badly shaken his father was when he read about Score's injury in the morning paper, and how, for years after, right up to the end of his life, he would periodically refer to Score, saying that injury was one of the saddest things that ever happened in the history of the game. Never a word about himself, never the slightest hint of any personal connection. Only Score, poor Herb Score.

Without his father's help, the publishing house never would have been born. He knew he didn't have the stuff to become a writer, not when he had the example of young Renzo to compare himself to, his dormitory roommate for four years at Amherst, the immense, grinding struggle of it, the long solitary hours, the everlasting uncertainty and compulsive need, and so he opted for the next best thing, teaching literature instead of making it, but after one year of graduate school at Columbia, he withdrew from the Ph.D. program, understanding that he wasn't cut out for

an academic life either. He wandered into publishing
instead, spent four years rising through the ranks of two
different companies, at last finding a place for himself, a
mission, a calling, whatever word best applies to a sense of
commitment and purpose, but there were too many frustrations and compromises at the top levels of commercial
publishing, and when, in the space of two short months,
his senior editor quashed his recommendation that they
publish Renzo's first novel (the one following the burned
manuscript) and similarly rejected his proposal to publish
Marty's first novel, he went to his father and told him he
wanted to quit the august company he was working for
and start a little house of his own. His father knew nothing
about books or publishing, but he must have seen something in his son's eyes that persuaded him to throw a los-
able fraction of his money into a venture that was all but
certain to fail. Or perhaps he felt this certain failure would
teach the boy a lesson, help him work the bug out of his
system, and before long he would return to the security of
a normal job. But they didn't fail, or at least the losses
were not egregious enough to make them want to stop, and
after that inaugural list of just four books, his father opened
his pockets again, staking him to a new investment worth
ten times the amount of his initial outlay, and suddenly
Heller Books was off the ground, a small but viable entity,
a real publishing house with an office on lower West Broadway (dirt-cheap rents back then in a Tribeca that was not
yet Tribeca), a staff of four, a distributor, well-designed

catalogues, and a growing stable of authors. His father never interfered. He called himself *the silent partner*, and for the last four years of his life he used those words to announce himself whenever they talked on the phone. No more *This is your father* or *This is your old man* but, without fail, one hundred percent of the time, *Hello there, Morris, this is your silent partner.* How not to miss him? How not to feel that every book he has published in the past thirty-five years is a product of his father's invisible hand?

It is nine-thirty. He meant to call Willa to say happy new year, but it is two-thirty in England now, and no doubt she has been asleep for hours. He returns to the kitchen to pour himself another scotch, his third since coming back to the apartment, and it is only now, for the first time all evening, that he remembers to check the answering machine, suddenly thinking that Willa might have called while he was at Marty and Nina's or on his way home from the Upper West Side. There are twelve new messages. One by one, he listens to them all—but no word from Willa.

He is being punished. That is why she accepted the job at Exeter for the year, and that is why she never calls— because she is punishing him for the meaningless indiscretion he committed eighteen months ago, a stupid act of sexual weakness that he regretted even as he was crawling into bed with his partner in crime. Under normal circumstances (but when is anything ever normal?) Willa never would have found out, but not long after he did what he did, she went to her gynecologist for her semi-annual checkup and was told she had something called chlamydia, a mild but unpleasant condition that can be contracted only through sexual intercourse. The doctor asked her if she had slept with anyone besides her husband lately, and because the answer was no, the culprit could have been none other than said husband, and when Willa confronted him with the news that evening, he had no choice but to confess. He didn't provide any names or details, but he admitted that when she was in Chicago delivering her paper on George Eliot, he had gone to bed with someone. No, he wasn't having an affair, it had happened only that one time, and he had no intention of ever doing it again. He was sorry, he said, deeply and truly sorry, he had been drinking too much, it was a terrible mistake, but even though she believed him, how could he blame her for feeling angry, not just because he had been unfaithful to her for the first time in their marriage, no, that was bad enough, but because he had infected her as well. A venereal disease! she shouted. It's disgusting! You stick your dumb-ass penis into another woman's vagina, and you wind up infecting me! Aren't you ashamed of yourself, Morris? Yes, he said, he was horribly ashamed, more ashamed than he had ever been in his life.

It torments him to think about that evening now, the idiocy of it all, the frantic little coupling that led to such enduring havoc. A dinner invitation from Nancy Greenwald, a literary agent in her early forties, someone he had been doing business with for six or seven years, divorced, not unattractive, but until that night he had never given her much thought. A dinner for six at Nancy's apartment in Chelsea, and the only reason he accepted was because Willa was out of town, a fairly tedious dinner as it turned out, and when the four other guests gathered up their things and left, he agreed to stay on for a last drink before walking home to the Village. That was when it happened, about twenty minutes after the others disappeared, a quick crazy fuck of no earthly importance to anyone. After Willa's announcement about chlamydia, he wondered how many other dumb-ass penises had found comfort in Nancy's vagina, although the truth was that there hadn't been much comfort for him, and even as they went at it together, he had felt too wretched about betraying Willa to lose himself in the supposed pleasure of the moment.

After his confession, after the round of antibiotics that purged the venereal microbes from Willa's system, he thought that would be the end of it. He knew she believed him when he told her it had happened only once, but this tiny lapse of attention, this breach of solidarity after close to twenty-four years of marriage, had shaken Willa's confidence in him. She doesn't trust him anymore. She believes he is on the prowl, searching for younger and more beautiful women, and even if he isn't up to anything at this particular moment, she has convinced herself that sooner or later it is bound to happen again. He has done everything he can to reassure her, but his arguments seem to have no effect. He is too old for adventures now, he says, he wants to live out the rest of his days with her and die in her arms. And she says: A sixty-two-year-old man is still young, a sixty-year-old woman is old. He says: After all they've been through together, all the nightmares and sorrows, all the poundings they've taken, all the miseries they've survived, how can a little thing like this make any difference? And she answers: Maybe it's been too much for you, Morris. Maybe you want a fresh start with someone else.

The trip to England didn't help. They had been apart for three and a half months when he finally went over there for the Christmas break, and he understood that she was using this enforced separation as a test, to see whether it would be possible for her to live without him over the long haul. So far, the experiment seems to be working rather well. Her anger toward him has changed into a kind of willed detachment, an aloofness that made him feel awkward around her for much of the visit, never quite sure what he should say or how he should act. The first night, she was reluctant to have sex with him, but then, just as he was drifting off, she reached out for him in bed and started kissing him in the old way, giving herself up to the old intimacies as if there were no trouble between them. That was the thing that so confounded him—their silent companionship in bed at night followed by moody, disjointed days, tenderness and irritability alternating in wholly unpredictable patterns, a feeling that she was both pushing him away from her and trying to hold on to him at the same time.

There was only one vicious outburst, one full-blown argument. It occurred on the third or fourth day, when they were still in her Exeter flat, taking out their bags to prepare for their trip to London, and the quarrel began as many others had in the past few years, with Willa attacking him for not wanting to have children of their own, for being content with her son and his son as their only family, but no family of their own, just the two of them and their own boy or girl, without the specters of Karl and Mary-Lee hovering in the background, and now that Bobby was dead and Miles had gone missing, just look at them, she said, they were nothing, they had nothing, and it was his fault for talking her out of another child all those years ago, and she was a goddamned fool for listening to him. In principle, he didn't disagree with her, had never disagreed with her, but how could they have known what would happen, and by the time Miles took off, they were too old to think about having babies. He didn't resent her for bringing up the subject again, it was altogether natural for her to feel this grief, this loss, the history of the past twelve years could have produced no other outcome, but then she said something that shocked him, that hurt him so badly he still hasn't recovered from it. But Miles is back in New York, he said. He'll be contacting them any day now, any week, and before long the whole miserable chapter will come to an end. Instead of answering him, Willa picked up her suitcase and threw it angrily on the floor—a furious gesture, more violent than any response he had ever seen from her. It's too late, she shouted. Miles is sick. Miles is no good. Miles has wrecked them, and from this day forward she cuts him out of her heart. She doesn't want to see him. Even if he calls, she doesn't want to see him. Never again. It's finished, she said, it's finished, and every night she will get down on her knees and pray he doesn't call.

It was somewhat better in London. The hotel was neutral ground, a no-man's-land devoid of any associations with the past, and there were some good days of walking through museums and sitting in pubs, seeing old friends for dinner, browsing in bookstores, not to mention the sublime indulgence of doing nothing at all, which seemed to have a restorative effect on Willa. One afternoon, she read aloud to him from the most recent chapter of the book she is writing on the late novels of Dickens. The next morning, over breakfast, she asked him about his search for a new investor, and he told her about his meeting with the German at the Frankfurt Book Fair in October, his conversation with the Israeli in New York last month, the steps he has taken to find the needed cash. Several good days, or at least not bad days, and then came the e-mail from Marty and the news of Suki's death. Willa didn't want him to go back to New York, she argued fiercely and persuasively why she thought the funeral would be too much for him, but when he asked her to make the trip with him, her face tensed up, she seemed thrown by the suggestion, which was an entirely reasonable suggestion to his mind, and then she said no, she couldn't. He asked her why. Because she couldn't, she said, repeating her answer as she searched for the right words, clearly at war with herself, unprepared to make any crucial decisions at that moment, because she wasn't ready to go back, she said, because she needed more time. Again, she asked him to stay, to remain in London until January third as originally planned, and he understood that she was testing him, forcing him to make a choice between her and his friends, and if he didn't choose her, she would feel betrayed. But he had to go back, he said, it was out of the question not to go back.

One week later, as he sits in his New York apartment on New Year's Eve, sipping scotch in the darkened living room and thinking about his wife, he tells himself that a marriage can't stand or fall on a simple matter of leaving London a few days early to attend a funeral. And if it does stand or fall on that matter, perhaps it was destined to fall in the first place.

He is in danger of losing his wife. He is in danger of losing his business. As long as there is breath in him, he says to himself, remembering that homely, worn-out phrase, which he has always been fond of, as long as there is breath in him he will not allow either one of those things to happen.

Where is he now? Straddling the border between inevitable extinction and the possibility of continued life. Overall, the situation is bleak, but there are some encouraging signs that have given him cause for hope—or, if not quite hope, a sense that it is still too early to succumb to resignation and despair. How much he reminds himself of his mother whenever he starts thinking like this, how obstinately she goes on living inside him. Let the house come crashing down around him, let his marriage burst into flames, and Connie Heller's son will find a way to rebuild the house and put out the fire. Lucky Lohrke walking calmly through a barrage of bullets. Or else the ghost dance of the Oglala Sioux—and the conviction that the white man's bullets would evaporate into thin air before they ever touched them.

He drinks another scotch and then staggers off to bed. Exhausted, so exhausted that he is already asleep before the shouting and the fireworks begin.

3

He knows why Miles left. Even before the letter came, he was all but certain the boy had spent the night in the apartment, the night preceding the morning when he and Willa had talked so brutally about him in the kitchen. After breakfast, he had cracked open the door of Miles's room to find out if the boy had come home for the weekend, and when he saw that the bed was empty, he went in to discover an ashtray filled with cigarette butts, a forgotten paperback anthology of Jacobean drama lying on the floor, and a flattened, unplumped pillow on the hastily made bed—sure signs that the boy had spent the night there, and if he had stolen off early that morning without bothering to greet them, without a hello or a good-bye, it could only mean that he had overheard the cruel things that had been said about him and was too upset to face his parents. Morris didn't mention his discovery to Willa, but at that point there was no reason to suspect the conversation would lead to such a drastic response from Miles. He felt terrible about having said those things, angry with himself for not having defended the boy more vociferously against Willa's harsh attacks, but he figured he would have a chance to apologize the next time they saw each other, to clear the air somehow and put the matter behind them. Then came the letter, the mad, falsely cheerful letter with the disturbing news that Miles had quit college. *Burned out on school*. The boy wasn't burned out. He loved being in school, he was sailing through with top honors, and just two weeks before, when they met for Sunday breakfast at Joe Junior's, Miles had been talking about the courses he was planning to take in his senior year. No, quitting had been a hostile act of revenge and self-sabotage, a symbolic suicide, and there was no doubt in Morris's mind that it was a direct result of that conversation overheard in the apartment a few days earlier.

Still, there was no reason to panic. Miles was going to L.A. to spend a couple of weeks with his mother, and all Morris had to do was pick up the telephone and call him. He would do what he could to talk some sense into the boy, and if that didn't work, he would fly to California and have it out with him face to face. But not only was Miles not at Mary-Lee's, Mary-Lee was not at home either. She was in San Francisco, filming the pilot of a new television series, and the person he spoke to was Korngold, who told him that Miles hadn't been heard from in more than a month and that as far as he knew there were no plans for him to visit California anytime that summer.

From that moment on, they were in it together, all four of them, the two parents and the two stepparents, and when they hired a private detective to look for the missing boy, each couple bore half the cost, living through eight dismal months of progress reports that reported no progress, no leads, no signs of hope, not a single microdot of information. Morris held fast to the theory that Miles had vanished on purpose, but after three or four months both Willa and Korngold began to waver, gradually coming to the conclusion that Miles was dead. An accident of some kind, they thought, perhaps murdered, perhaps killed by his own hand, it was impossible to say. Mary-Lee took an agnostic position on the matter—she simply didn't know. He could have been dead, yes, but on the other hand, the kid had *issues,* the thing with Bobby had been an absolute devastation, Miles had closed in on himself since then, and it was clear that he had *a lot of stuff to work out.* Running away was a stupid thing to do, of course, but maybe some good would come of it in the end, maybe being on his own for a while would give him a chance to straighten himself out. Morris didn't disagree with this analysis. In fact, he found Mary-Lee's attitude rather impressive—calm, compassionate, and thoughtful, not judging Miles so much as trying to understand him—and now that they were locked in this crisis together, he realized that the indifferent, irresponsible mother was far more attached to her son than he had imagined. If anything positive emerged from Miles's disappearance, it was this shift in his perception of Mary-Lee. They were no longer enemies. They had become allies now, perhaps even friends.

Then Bing Nathan called, and everything turned

upside down again. Miles was working as a short-order cook in Chicago, and Morris's first impulse was to go out there and talk to him—not to make any demands, merely to find out what was going on—but Willa was against it, and after he called California to share the good news with Mary-Lee and Korngold, they took Willa's side. Their argument was this: the boy was twenty-one now and capable of making his own decisions; as long as his health was sound, as long as he wasn't in trouble with the law, as long as he wasn't in a mental hospital, as long as he wasn't asking them for money, they had no right to force him to do anything against his will—not even to make him talk to them, which he obviously had no wish to do. Give him time, they said. He'll figure it out.

But Morris didn't listen to them. He took a plane to Chicago the next morning, and by three o'clock he had parked his rented car across the street from Duke's, a shabby, heavily frequented diner in a rough neighborhood on the South Side. Two hours later, Miles walked out of the restaurant wearing his leather jacket (the one Morris had bought for him on his nineteenth birthday) and looking well, very well in fact, a bit taller and more filled out than he'd been at that Sunday breakfast eight and a half months ago, and at his side there was a tall, attractive black woman who appeared to be in her mid-twenties, and the moment the two of them walked out the door, Miles put his arm around the woman's shoulder, drew her toward him, and planted a kiss on her mouth. It was a joyful kiss, somehow, the kiss of a man who has just put in eight hours of work and is back with the woman he loves, and the woman laughed at this sudden outburst of affection, threw her arms around him, and returned his kiss with one of her own. A moment after that, they were walking down the street together, holding hands and talking in that intense, intimate way that is possible only in the closest friend-ships, the closest loves, and Morris just sat there, frozen in the seat of his rented car, not daring to roll down the window and call out to Miles, not daring to jump out and run after him, and ten seconds later Miles and the woman turned left at the first corner they came to and vanished from sight.

He has done it three more times since then, once in Arizona, once in New Hampshire, and once in Florida, always watching from a place where he couldn't be seen, the warehouse parking lot where Miles was loading crates onto the back of a truck, the hotel lobby where the boy rushed past him in a bellhop's uniform, the little park he sat in one day as his son read *The Great Gatsby* and then talked to the cute high school girl who happened to be reading the same book, always tempted to step forward and say something, always tempted to pick a fight with him, to punch him, to take him in his arms, to take the boy in his arms and kiss him, but never doing anything, never saying anything, keeping himself hidden, watching Miles grow older, watching his son turn into a man as his own life dwindles into something small, too small to care

about anymore, listening to Willa's tirade in Exeter, all
the damage that has been done to her, his brave, battered
Willa, Bobby on the road, Miles gone, and yet he grimly
perseveres, never quite able to let go of it, still thinking
the story hasn't come to an end, and when thinking about
the story becomes unbearable, he sometimes diverts himself with childish reveries about dressing up in costumes,
disguising himself so thoroughly that not even his own
son would recognize him, a demon of disguise in the spirit
of Sherlock Holmes, not just the clothes and the shoes but
an entirely different face, entirely different hair, an entirely
different voice, an utter transformation from one being
into another, and how many different old men has he
invented since the idea occurred to him, wrinkled pen-
sioners hobbling along with their canes and aluminum
walkers, old men with flowing white hair, flowing white
beards, Walt Whitman in his dotage, a friendly old fellow
who has lost his way and stops the young man to ask for
directions, and then they would begin to talk, the old man
would invite the young man for a drink, and little by little
the two of them would become friends, and now that Miles
is living in Brooklyn, out there in Sunset Park next to
Green-Wood Cemetery, he has come up with another character, a New York character he calls the Can Man, one of
those old, broken-down men who forage among dumpsters
and recycling bins for bottles and cans, five cents a bottle,
five cents a can, a tough way to make a living, but times
are tough and one mustn't complain, and in his mind the

Can Man is a Mohawk Indian, a descendent of the Mohawks who settled in Brooklyn in the early part of the last century, the community of Mohawks who came here to become construction workers on the tall buildings going up in Manhattan, Mohawks because for some reason Mohawks have no fear of heights, they feel at home in the air and were able to dance along the beams and girders without the slightest dread or vertiginous wobble, and the Can Man is a descendent of those fearless people who built the towers of Manhattan, a crazy customer, alas, not quite right in the head, a daft old loon who spends his days pushing his shopping cart through the neighborhood, collecting the bottles and cans that will fetch him five cents apiece, and when the Can Man speaks, more often than not he will punctuate his remarks with absurd, outlandishly inappropriate advertising slogans, such as, *I'd walk a mile for a Camel*, or: *Don't leave home without it*, or: *Reach out and touch someone*, and perhaps Miles will be amused by a man who would walk a mile for a Camel, and when the Can Man wearies of his advertising slogans, he will start quoting from the Bible, saying things like: *The wind goeth toward the south, and turneth about unto the north, it whirleth about continually* or *And that which is done is that which shall be done*, and just when Miles is about to turn around and walk away, the Can Man will push his face up against his and shout: *Remember, boy! Bankruptcy is not the end! It's just a new beginning!*

It is ten o'clock in the morning, the first morning of

the new year, and he is sitting in a booth at Joe Junior's, the diner on the corner of Sixth Avenue and Twelfth Street where he last spoke to Miles more than two thousand seven hundred days ago, sitting, as it happens, in the same booth the two of them sat in that morning, eating his scrambled eggs and buttered toast as he toys with the notion of turning himself into the Can Man. Joe Junior's is a small place, a simple, down-at-the-heels neighborhood joint featuring a curved Formica counter with chrome trim, eight swivel stools, three tables by the window in front, and four booths along the northern wall. The food is ordinary at best, the standard greasy-spoon fare of two dozen breakfast combinations, grilled ham-and-cheese sandwiches, tuna fish salads, hamburgers, hot open turkey sandwiches, and fried onion rings. He has never sampled the onion rings, but legend has it that one of the old regulars, Carlton Rabb, now deceased, was so enamored of them that he added a clause to his will stipulating that an order of Joe Junior's fried onion rings be smuggled into his coffin before his body was laid to rest. Morris is fully aware of Joe Junior's shortcomings as a dining establishment, but among its advantages are the total absence of music, the chance to eavesdrop on stimulating, often hilarious conversations, the broad spectrum of its clientele (from homeless beggars to wealthy home owners), and, most important, the role it plays in his memory. Joe Junior's was the site of the ritual Saturday breakfast, the place where he brought the boys every week throughout their childhoods, the quiet Saturday mornings when the three of them would tiptoe out of the apartment as Willa caught an extra hour or two of sleep, and to sit in this place now, this drab little restaurant on the corner of Sixth Avenue and Twelfth Street, is to return to those countless Saturdays of long ago and remember the Eden he once lived in.

Bobby lost interest in coming here when he was thirteen (the boy liked his sleep), but Miles carried on the tradition all the way to the end of high school. Not every Saturday morning, of course, at least not after he turned seven and started playing in the local kids' baseball league, but often enough to feel that the room is still saturated with his presence. Such a bright young thing, such an earnest young thing, so little laughter in that somber face of his, but just below the surface a frolicking sort of inner mirth, and the pleasure he took in the various teams they made up together with the names of real players, the all-body-parts team, for example, with a lineup of Bill Hands, Barry Foote, Rollie Fingers, Elroy Face, Ed Head, and Walt "No-Neck" Williams, along with substitutes such as Tony Armas (Arm) and Jerry Hairston (Hair), or the all-finance team, consisting of Dave Cash, Don Money, Bobby Bonds, Barry Bonds, Ernie Banks, Elmer Pence, Bill Pounds, and Wes Stock. Yes, Miles loved that nonsense when he was a boy, and when laughter did come out of him, it was propulsive and unstoppable, red-faced, breathless, as if an unseen phantom were tickling him all over his body. But most often the breakfasts were subdued affairs, quiet conversations about his classmates, his aversion to his piano lessons (he eventually quit), his disagreements with Bobby, his homework, the books he was reading, the fortunes of the Mets and football Giants, the finer points of pitching. Of all the regrets Morris has accumulated over the course of his life, there is the lingering sadness that his father did not live long enough to know his grandson, but if he had, and if by some miracle he had lasted into the boy's teens, there would have been the happiness of seeing Miles pitch, the right-handed version of his young self, living proof that all the hours he had spent teaching his son how to throw properly had not been wasted, that even if Morris never developed much of an arm himself, he had passed on his father's lessons to his own son, and until Miles quit in his junior year, the results had been promising—no, more than promising—excellent. Pitching was the ideal position for him. Solitude and strength, concentration and will, the lone wolf standing in the middle of the infield, carrying the entire game on his back. It was all fastballs and changeups back then, two pitches and endless work on his delivery, the fluid motion, the arm whipping forward at the same angle every time, the coiled right leg pushing off the rubber until the moment of release, but no curveballs or sliders, at sixteen he was still growing, and young arms can be ruined by the unnatural torque required to snap off a good breaking ball. He was disappointed, yes, but he never blamed Miles for quitting when he did. The self-flagellating grief of surviving Bobby had demanded a sacrifice of some kind, and so he gave up the thing he loved doing most at that point in his life. But willing yourself out of something is not the same as renouncing it in your heart. Four years ago, when Bing called to report the arrival of another letter—from Albany, California, just outside Berkeley—he mentioned that Miles was pitching for a team in a Bay Area amateur league, competing against ex–college players who hadn't been good enough or interested enough to turn pro, but serious competition for all that, and he was holding his own, Miles said, winning twice as many games as he lost, and he had finally taught himself how to throw a curveball. He went on to say that the San Francisco Giants were sponsoring an open tryout later that month, and his teammates were urging him to go, recommending that he lie about his age and tell them he was nineteen, not twenty-four, but he wasn't going to do it. Imagine him signing a contract to play in the low minor leagues, he said. Preposterous.

The Can Man is thinking, remembering, sifting through the countless Saturday mornings he ate breakfast here with the boy, and now, as he lifts his arm and asks for the check, just a minute or two before he will be stepping out into the cold air again, he stumbles across something that hasn't occurred to him in years, an unearthed shard, a shining piece of glass to put in his pocket and take home with him. Miles was ten or eleven. It was one of the first times they came here without Bobby, just the two of them sitting across from each other in one of the booths, perhaps this booth, perhaps another, he can't recall which one now, and the boy had brought along a book report he had written for his fifth- or sixth-grade class, no, not a report exactly, a short paper of six or seven hundred words, an analysis of the book the teacher had assigned to the pupils, the book they had been reading and discussing for the past several weeks, and now each child had to produce a paper, an interpretation of the novel they had all finished, *To Kill a Mockingbird*, a sweet book, Morris felt, a good book for children of that age, and the boy wanted his father to read over what he had done. The Can Man remembers how tense the boy looked as he removed the three sheets of paper, the four sheets of paper from his backpack, awaiting his father's judgment on what he had written, his first attempt at literary criticism, his first grown-up assignment, and from the look in the boy's eyes, his father understood how much work and thought had gone into this little piece of writing. The paper was about wounds. The father of the two children, the lawyer, is blind in one eye, the boy wrote, and the black man he defends against the false charge of rape has a withered arm, and late in the book, when the lawyer's son falls out of the tree, he breaks his arm, the same arm as the withered arm of the innocent black man, left or right, the Can Man no longer remembers, and the point of all this, the young Miles wrote, is that wounds are an essential part of life, and until you are wounded in some way, you cannot become a man. His father wondered how it was possible for a ten- or eleven-year-old child to read a book so carefully, to pull together such disparate, unemphasized elements of a story and see a pattern develop over the course of hundreds of pages, to hear the repeated notes, notes so easily lost in the whirl of fugues and cadenzas that form the totality of a book, and not only was he impressed by the mind that had paid such close attention to the smallest details of the novel, he was impressed by the heart that had come up with such a profound conclusion. Until you are wounded, you cannot become a man. He told the boy he had done a superior job, that most readers twice or three times his age could never have written anything half as good as this, and only a person with a great soul could have thought about the book in this way. He was very moved, he said to his son that morning seventeen or eighteen years ago, and the fact is that he is still moved by the thoughts expressed in that short paper, and as he collects his change from the cashier and walks out into the cold, he goes on thinking about these thoughts, and just before he reaches his house, the Can Man stops and says to himself: When?

4

She has come to New York to act in Samuel Beckett's *Happy Days*. She will be Winnie, the woman buried up to her waist in Act I and then buried up to her neck in Act II, and the challenge in front of her, the formidable challenge will be to hold forth within these constricted emplacements for an hour and a half, delivering what amounts to a sixty-page monologue, with occasional interruptions from the hapless, mostly invisible Willie, and she can think of no theatrical role she has played in the past, neither Nora nor Miss Julie, neither Blanche nor Desdemona, that is more demanding than this one. But she loves Winnie, she responds deeply to the combination of pathos, comedy, and terror in the play, and even if Beckett is inordinately difficult, cerebral, at times obscure, the language is so clean and precise, so gorgeous in its simplicity, that it gives her physical pleasure to feel the words coming out of her mouth. Tongue, palate, lips, and throat are all in harmony as she pronounces Winnie's long, halting rambles, and now that she has finally mastered and memorized the text, the rehearsals have been steadily improving, and when the previews begin ten days from now, she hopes she will be ready to give the performance she hopes to give. Tony Gilbert has been hard on her, and every time the young director cuts her off for making the wrong gesture or not pausing long enough between phrases, she consoles herself with the thought that he begged her to come to New York to play Winnie, that again and again he has told her that no actress alive could do a better job in this role. He has been hard on her, yes, but the play is hard, and she has worked hard because of it, even letting her body go to hell in order to put on the twenty extra pounds she felt she needed to become Winnie, to inhabit Winnie (*About fifty, well preserved, blond for preference, plump, arms and shoulders bare, low bodice, big bosom* . . .), and she has done much homework in preparation, reading up on Beckett, studying his correspondence with Alan Schneider, the original director of the play, and she now knows that a *bumper* is a brimming glass, that *bast* is a fibrous twine used by gardeners, that the words Winnie speaks at the beginning of Act II, *Hail, holy light,* are a quotation from Book III of *Paradise Lost,* that *beechen green* comes from *Ode to a Nightingale,* and that *bird of dawning* comes from *Hamlet.* What world the play is set in has never been clear to her, a world without darkness, a world of hot, unending light, a sort of purgatory, perhaps, a post-human wilderness of ever-diminishing possibilities, ever-diminishing movement, but she also suspects that this world might be none other than the stage she will be performing on, and even if Winnie is essentially alone, talking to herself and Willie, she is also aware that she is in the presence of others, that the audience is out there in the dark. *Someone is looking at me still. Caring for me still. That is what I find so wonderful. Eyes on my eyes.* She can understand this. Her entire life has been about this, only this.

It is the third day of the year, the evening of Saturday, January third, and Morris is having dinner with Mary-Lee and Korngold at the Odeon, not far from the Tribeca loft they have rented for their four-month stay in New York. They arrived in the city just as he was preparing to leave for England, and although they have talked on the telephone several times in the past few months, they have not seen each other in a long while, not since 2007, he thinks, perhaps even 2006. Mary-Lee has just turned fifty-four, and their brief, disputatious marriage is no more than a dim memory now. He bears her no grudge or ill will, is in fact quite fond of her, but she is still a conundrum to him, a puzzling mixture of warmth and distance, keen intelligence hidden behind brash, rough-and-tumble manners, by turns good-hearted and selfish, droll and boring (she tends to go on at times), vain and utterly indifferent to herself. Witness the increased poundage for her new role. She has always taken pride in her slim, well-maintained figure, has fretted over the fat content of every morsel of food that enters her mouth, has made a religion of eating *properly*, but now, for the sake of her work, she has calmly tossed her diet to the four winds. Morris is intrigued by this fuller, more ample version of his ex-wife, and he tells her that she is looking beautiful, to which she responds, laughing and then puffing out her cheeks: A big, beautiful hippo. But she *is* beautiful, he thinks, still beautiful even now, and unlike most actresses of her generation, she has not marred her face with cosmetic surgery or wrinkle-removing injections, for the simple reason that she intends to go on working as long as she can, deep into her old age if possible, and, as she once jokingly put it to him, If all the sixty-year-old broads come across as bizarre-looking thirty-year-olds, who's going to be left to play the mothers and grandmothers?

She has been acting steadily for a long time now, ever since she was in her early twenties, and there is not a person in the crowded restaurant who does not know who she is, glance after glance is directed toward their table, *eyes are on her eyes*, but she pretends to pay no attention, she is used to this kind of thing, but Morris senses that she is secretly enjoying it, that silent adulation of this sort is a boon that never grows old. Not many actors manage to keep it going for thirty years, especially women, especially women who act in films, but Mary-Lee has been smart and flexible, willing to reinvent herself at each step along the way. Even during the early run of successful films that got her started, she would take time off to work in plays, always good plays, the best plays, the Bard and his modern heirs, Ibsen, Chekhov, Williams, Albee, and then, when she was in her mid-thirties and the big studios stopped making films for grown-ups, she didn't hesitate to accept parts in small, low-budget independent films (many of them produced by Korngold), and then, more years down the road, when she reached the point at which she was beginning to play mothers, she jumped into television, starring in a weekly series called *Martha Kane, Attorney-at-Law*, something Morris and Willa actually watched from time to time, and during the five-year span of that show she attracted an audience in the millions and grew ever more popular, which is very popular indeed. Drama and comedy, good girls and bad girls, feisty secretaries and drug-addicted hookers, wives, lovers, and mistresses, a singer and a painter, an undercover cop and the mayor of a large city, she has played all kinds of roles in all kinds of films, many of them quite decent, a few clumsy stinkers, but no mediocre performances that Morris can recall, with a number of memorable turns that have touched him in the same way he was touched when he first saw her as Cordelia in 1978. He is glad she is doing the Beckett, he thinks she is wise to have accepted such a daunting role, and as he looks at her across the table now, he wonders how this attractive but wholly ordinary woman, this woman with her fluctuating moods and vulgar passion for dirty jokes, has it in her to transform herself into so many distinct and totally different characters, to make one feel she carries all humanity inside her. Does it require an act of courage to stand up and turn your guts inside out before an audience of strangers, or is it a compulsion, a need to be looked at, a reckless lack of inhibition that drives a person to do what she does? He has never been able to put his finger on the line that separates life from art. Renzo is the same as Mary-Lee, they are both prisoners of what they do, for years both have been plunging forward from one project to the next, both have produced lasting works of art, and yet their lives have been a bollix, both divorced twice, both with a tremendous talent for self-pity, both ultimately inaccessible to others—not failed human beings, exactly, but not successful ones either. Damaged souls. The walking wounded, opening their veins and bleeding in public.

He finds it odd to be with her now, sitting across from his ex-wife and her husband, sitting in yet another booth in yet another New York restaurant, odd because the love he once felt for her is entirely gone, and he knows that Korngold is a far better husband for her than he ever could have been, and she is lucky to have a man like this to take care of her, to prop her up whenever she begins to stagger, to give her the advice she has been listening to and following for years, to love her in a way that has tamped down her anxieties and frantic distempers, whereas he, Morris, was never up to the task of loving her in the way she needed to be loved, could never give her advice about her career, could never prop her up or understand what was whirling about in that beautiful head of hers. She is so much better than she was thirty years ago, and he gives Korngold all the credit, he admires him for having rescued her after two bad marriages, for throwing out the vodka bottles and the pill bottles she began collecting after the second divorce, for sticking by her through what must have been some harrowing moments, and beyond what Korngold has done for Mary-Lee, Morris admires him pure and simple, in and of himself, not just because he was good to his son during the years when the boy was still visible, not just because he has anguished over Miles's disappearance as a true member of the family, but because he discovered many years ago that Simon Korngold is a thoroughly likable person, and what Morris likes most about him is the fact that he never complains. Everyone is suffering because of the crash, the slump, whatever word people are using to talk about the new depression, book publishers not excepted, of course, but Simon is in much worse shape than he is, the independent film business has been destroyed, production companies and distributors are folding up like collapsible chairs every day of the week, and it has been two years now since he last put a movie together, which means that he unofficially retired this fall, accepting a job to teach film courses at UCLA instead of making films, but he isn't bitter about it, or at least he shows no bitterness, and the only thing he says to account for what has happened to him is to mention that he is fifty-eight years old and that independent film producing is a young person's job. The grinding search for money can crush the spirit out of you unless you're made of steel, he says, and the tall and short of it is that he isn't made of steel anymore.

But that comes later. The talk about Winnie and *Hail, holy light* and men of steel does not begin until after they have talked about why Mary-Lee called Morris three hours ago and asked him to dinner on such short notice. There is news. That is the first article on the agenda, and moments after they enter the restaurant and take their seats at the table, Mary-Lee tells him about the message she found on her answering machine at four o'clock this afternoon.

It was Miles, she says. I recognized his voice.

His voice, Morris says. You mean he didn't give his name?

No. Only the message—a short, confusing message. As follows, in its entirety. *Um.* Long pause. *Sorry.* Long pause. *I'll call back.*

Are you sure it was Miles?

Positive.

Korngold says: I'm still trying to figure out what *sorry* means. Sorry for calling? Sorry because he was too flustered to leave a proper message? Sorry for everything he's done?

Impossible to say, Morris replies, but I would tend to go with flustered.

Something's going to happen, Mary-Lee says. Very soon. Any day now.

I talked to Bing this morning, Morris says, just to check in and see if everything is all right. He told me Miles has a girlfriend, a young Cuban girl from Florida, and that she's been in New York for the past week or so visiting him. I think she went back today. According to Bing, Miles was planning to get in touch with us as soon as she left. That would explain the message.

But why call me and not you? Mary-Lee asks.

Because Miles thinks I'm still in England and won't be reachable until Monday.

And how does he know that? Korngold says.

Apparently, he called my office two or three weeks ago and was told I'd be back at work on the fifth. That's what Bing reported, in any case, and I don't see why the boy would lie to him.

We owe Bing Nathan a lot, Korngold says.

We owe him everything, Morris says. Try to imagine these past seven years without him.

We should do something for him, Mary-Lee says. Write him a check, send him on a world cruise, something.

I've tried, Morris says, but he won't take any money from me. He was very insulted the first time I offered, and even more insulted the second time. He says: You don't accept money for acting like a human being. A young man with principles. I can respect that.

What else? Mary-Lee asks. Any word on how Miles is doing?

Not much, Morris answers. Bing says he mostly keeps to himself, but the other people in the house like him and he gets on well with them. Quiet, as usual. A bit low, as usual, but then he perked up when the girl came.

And now she's gone, Mary-Lee says, and he's left a

message on my machine saying he'll call me back. I don't know what I'm going to do when I see him. Slap him across the face—or throw my arms around him and kiss him?

Do both, Morris says. The slap first, and then the kiss.

They stop talking about Miles after that and move on to *Happy Days,* the future of independent films, the strange death of Steve Cochran, the advantages and disadvantages of living in New York, Mary-Lee's new rotundity (which inspires the puffed-out cheeks and the beautiful-hippo comment), the forthcoming novels from Heller Books, and Willa, needless to say Willa, it is the polite question that must be asked, but Morris has no desire to tell them the truth, no desire to unburden himself and talk about his fear that he might be losing her, that he has already lost her, and so he says that Willa is flourishing, in top form, that his trip to England was like a second honeymoon, and he is hard-pressed to recall a time when he ever felt happier. His answer comes and goes in just a few seconds, and then they move on to other things, other digressions, other chatter about any number of relevant and irrelevant subjects, but Willa is on his mind now, he can't shake free of her, and watching Korngold and his ex-wife across the table, the comfort and amiability of their interactions, the furtive, unspoken complicity that exists between them, he understands how lonely he is, how lonely he has become, and now that the dinner is nearing its conclusion, he dreads returning to the empty apartment on Downing Street. Mary-Lee has drunk enough wine to be in one of those expansive, bountiful moods of hers, and when the three of them go outside to part company, she opens her arms and says to him, Give us a hug, Morris. A nice long squeeze for the fat old woman. He embraces the bulky winter overcoat hard enough to feel the flesh inside it, the body of the mother of his son, and as he does so, she holds on to him just as tightly, and then, with her left hand, she begins patting the back of his head, as if to tell him not to worry anymore, the dark time will soon be over, and all will be forgiven.

He walks back to Downing Street in the cold, his red scarf wrapped around his neck, hands thrust deep into the pockets of his coat, and the wind shooting off the Hudson is especially strong tonight as he heads up Varick toward the West Village, but he doesn't stop to flag down a taxi, he wants to walk this evening, the rhythm of his steps calms him in the way that music sometimes calms him, in the way children can be calmed when their parents rock them to sleep. It is ten o'clock, not late, several hours to go before he will be ready for sleep himself, and as he unlocks the door of the apartment, he imagines he will settle into the comfortable chair in the living room and spend the last hours of the day reading a book, but which book, he asks himself, which book from all the thousands crammed onto the shelves of the two floors of the duplex, perhaps the Beckett play if he can find it, he thinks, the one Mary-Lee is doing now, the one they talked about tonight, or if not that play perhaps another play by Shakespeare, the little project he has taken on in Willa's absence, rereading all of

Shakespeare, the words that have filled the hours between work and sleep these past months, and he is up to *The Tempest* now, he believes, or perhaps *The Winter's Tale*, and if reading is too much for him tonight, if his thoughts are too jumbled with Miles and Mary-Lee and Willa for him to concentrate on the words, he will watch a film on television, the one sedative that can always be counted on, the tranquilizing flicker of images, voices, music, the pull of the stories, always the stories, the thousands of stories, the millions of stories, and yet one never tires of them, there is always room in the brain for another story, another book, another film, and after pouring himself a scotch in the kitchen, he walks into the living room thinking film, he will opt for a film if anything watchable is playing tonight.

Before he can sit down in the comfortable chair and switch on the TV, however, the telephone starts ringing in the kitchen, and so he turns around and walks back into the kitchen to answer it, puzzled by the lateness of the call, wondering who could possibly want to talk to him at ten-thirty on a Saturday night. His first thought is Miles, Miles following up his call to his mother with a call to his father, but no, that couldn't be it, Miles won't be calling him until Monday at the earliest, unless he supposes, perhaps, that his father has already returned from England and is spending the weekend at home, or, if not that, perhaps he simply wants to leave a message on the machine, in the same way he left a message on his mother's machine this afternoon.

It is Willa, calling from Exeter at three-thirty in the morning, Willa sobbing and in distress, saying that she is cracking apart, that her world is in ruins, that she no longer wants to be alive. Her tears are relentless, and the voice talking through those tears is barely audible, high-pitched, the voice of a child, and it is a true collapse, he tells himself, a person beyond anger, beyond hope, a person entirely spent, miserable, miserable, pulverized by the weight of the world, a sadness as heavy as the weight of the world. He doesn't know what to do except talk to her in the most comforting voice he can manage, to tell her he loves her, that he will be on the early plane to London tomorrow morning, that she must hold on until he gets there, less than twenty-four hours, just one more day, and he reminds her of the breakdown about a year after Bobby's death, the same tears, the same weakened voice, the same words, and she pulled through that crisis then and will pull through this crisis now, trust him, he knows what he is talking about, he will take care of her, he will always take care of her, and she mustn't blame herself for things that aren't her fault. They talk for an hour, for two hours, and eventually the tears subside, eventually she begins to calm down, but just when he is beginning to feel it will be safe to hang up the phone, the tears begin again. She needs him so much, she says, she can't survive without him, she has been so horrible to him, so mean and vindictive and cruel, she has become a horrible person, a monster, and she hates herself now, she can never forgive herself, and again he tries to soothe her, telling her that she must go to sleep now, that she is exhausted and must go to sleep, that he will be there with her tomorrow, and finally, finally, she promises that she will go to bed, and even if she can't sleep, she promises not to do anything stupid, she will behave herself, she promises. They hang up at last, and before another night falls in New York City, Morris Heller is back in England, traveling between London and Exeter to see his wife.

ALL

Miles Heller

It was the best thing that could have happened to him, it was the worst thing that could have happened to him. Eleven days with Pilar in New York, and then the agony of putting her on the bus and sending her back to Florida.

One thing is certain, however. He loves her more than any other person on this earth, and he will go on loving her until the day he stops breathing.

The joy of looking at her face again, the joy of holding her again, the joy of listening to her laugh again, the joy of hearing her voice again, the joy of watching her eat again, the joy of looking at her hands again, the joy of looking at her naked body again, the joy of touching her naked body again, the joy of kissing her naked body again, the joy of watching her frown again, the joy of watching her brush her hair again, the joy of watching her paint her nails again, the joy of standing in the shower with her again, the joy of talking to her about books again, the joy of watching her eyes fill up with tears again, the joy of watching her walk again, the joy of listening to her insult Angela again, the joy of reading out loud to her again, the joy of listening to her burp again, the joy of watching her brush her teeth again, the joy of undressing her again, the joy of putting his mouth against her mouth again, the joy of looking at her neck again, the joy of walking down the street with her again, the joy of putting his arm around her shoulders again, the joy of licking her breasts again, the joy of entering her body again, the joy of waking up beside her again, the joy of discussing math with her again, the joy of buying clothes for her again, the joy of giving and receiving back rubs again, the joy of talking about the future again, the joy of living in the present with her again, the joy of being told she loves him again, the joy of telling her he loves her again, the joy of living under the gaze of her fierce dark eyes again, and then the agony of watching her board the bus at the Port Authority terminal on the afternoon of January third with the certain knowledge that it will not be until April, more than three months from now, that he will have a chance to be with her again.

It was her first trip to New York, the only time she has ever set foot outside the state of Florida, her maiden voyage to the land of winter. Miami is the one large city she is familiar with, but Miami is not large when compared to New York, and he hoped she wouldn't feel intimidated by the jangle and immensity of the place, that she wouldn't be put off by the noise and the dirt, the crowded subway cars, the bad weather. He imagined he would have to lead her into it cautiously, like someone walking into a cold lake with a young swimmer, giving her time to adjust to the frigid water, letting her tell him when she was ready to go in up to her waist, up to her neck, and if and when she wanted to put her head under. Now that she is gone, he cannot fathom why he felt so timid on her behalf, why or how he could have underestimated her resolve. Pilar ran into the lake with flapping arms, whooping excitedly as the cold water hit her bare skin, and seconds after that she was taking the plunge, dunking her head below the surface and gliding along as smoothly as a practiced veteran. The little one had done her homework. During the long trek up the Atlantic coast, she digested the contents of three guidebooks and a history of New York, and by the time the bus pulled into the terminal, she had already drawn up a list of the places she wanted to see, the things she wanted to do. Nor had she neglected his advice to prepare herself for the low temperatures and possible storms. She had gone out and bought a pair of snow boots, a couple of warm sweaters, a scarf, woolen gloves, and a snappy green down parka with a fur-fringed hood. She was Nanook of the North, he said, his intrepid Eskimo girl armed to beat back the assaults of the harshest climes, and yes, she looked adorable in that thing, and again and again he told her the Cuban-American-Eskimo look was destined to stay in fashion for years to come.

They went to the top of the Empire State Building, they walked through the marble halls of the Public Library at Fifth Avenue and Forty-second Street, they visited Ground Zero, they spent one day going from the Metropolitan Museum to the Frick Collection to MoMA, he bought her

a dress and a pair of shoes at Macy's, they walked across
the Brooklyn Bridge, they ate oysters at the Oyster Bar in
Grand Central Station, they watched the ice skaters at
Rockefeller Center, and then, on the seventh day of her
visit, they rode the subway uptown to 116th Street and
Broadway and checked out the Barnard College campus,
the Columbia campus across the street, the various semi-
naries and music academies spread across Morningside
Heights, and he said to her, Look, all this is possible for
you now, you're as good as any of the people studying here,
and when they send you your letter of acceptance this
spring, which I'm sure they will, there's a better than eighty
percent chance they're going to want you, think long and
hard before you decide to stay in Florida, all right? He
wasn't telling her what to do, he was merely asking her to
consider the matter carefully, to weigh the consequences of
accepting or turning down what in all likelihood would be
offered to her, and for once Pilar was silent, not willing to
share her thoughts with him, and he didn't press her to say
anything, for it was clear from the look in her eyes that she
was already pondering this very question, trying to project
herself into the future, trying to imagine what going to
college in New York would mean to her or not mean to her,
and as they walked among the deserted grounds and studied the façades of the buildings, he felt as if she were changing in front of him, growing older in front of him, and he
suddenly understood what she would be like ten years from
now, twenty years from now, Pilar in the full vigor of her

evolving womanhood, Pilar all grown into herself and yet still walking with the shadow of the pensive girl walking beside him now, the young woman walking beside him now.

He wishes they could have been alone for the full eleven days, living and sleeping in a room or an apartment not shared with anyone else, but the only option available to them was the house in Sunset Park. A hotel would have been perfect, but he didn't have the money for a hotel, and besides, there was the question of Pilar's age, and even if he could have afforded to put them up in style, there was the same risk in New York as there was in Florida, and he wasn't willing to take it. About a week before Christmas, he and Ellen discussed the possibility of borrowing the keys to one of the empty apartments on her firm's rental list, but little by little they talked themselves out of that absurd idea. Not only could Ellen have found herself in serious trouble, with instant dismissal from her job just one of the many gruesome things that could happen to her, but when they pictured what it would be like to hole up in a place without furniture, without blinds or curtains, without electricity, without a bed to sleep in, they both realized that staying in the shabby little house across from Green-Wood Cemetery would be far better.

Pilar knows they are squatting there illegally, and she doesn't approve. Not only is it wrong to break the law, she says, but she is frightened that something will happen to him, something bad, something irreversible, and how ironic it would be, she says (they have had this conversation on the phone more than once), if he left Florida to avoid going to jail only to land in another jail up north. But he won't go to jail for squatting, he tells her, the worst that can happen is an untimely eviction, and she mustn't forget that living there is only a stopgap arrangement for him, and once he heads back to Florida on May twenty-second, his little adventure in trespassing will be over. At this point in the conversation, Pilar invariably starts talking about Angela, cursing her greedy, no-good sister for having done this to them, the injustice of it all, the sickness of it all, and now she lives in constant fear that something will happen to him, and Angela is entirely to blame for it.

Because the house frightened her, she wanted to spend as little time there as possible. For very different reasons, he felt the same way, which meant they were out and about for the better part of her visit, mostly in Manhattan, mostly eating dinner in restaurants, cheap restaurants so as not to waste their money, diners and pizzerias and Chinese dumpling houses, and ninety percent of the time they spent in the house they were in his room, either making love or sleeping. Still, there were the unavoidable encounters with the others, the breakfasts in the morning, the accidental meetings in front of the bathroom door, the night when they returned to the house around ten o'clock and Alice asked them up to her room to watch a movie, which she described as her *obsession of the moment,* a film called *The Best Years of Our Lives,* since she wanted to know what they thought of it (he gave it a B-plus overall and an A for photography, Pilar gave it an A for everything), but his objective was to keep her contacts with the rest of the household to a minimum. It wasn't that they weren't friendly to her, but he had watched their faces when he introduced her to them on the first evening, and one by one he had noted the brief instant of shock when they understood how young she was, and he felt reluctant to expose her to situations in which she could be patronized by them, talked down to, hurt. It might have been different if she were taller than five feet four, if her breasts were larger, if her hips were wider, but Pilar must have struck them as a tiny, childlike thing, just as she had struck him the first time he saw her, and there was no point in trying to undo their initial impressions of her. The visit was going to be too short for that, and he wanted her to himself anyway. To be fair to them, however, nothing unpleasant happened. Alice had agreed to cook all the dinners while Pilar was in town, and therefore it was up to him to do the grocery shopping, which he took care of first thing every morning, and while he was out at the store, Alice and Pilar had a number of one-on-one talks at the kitchen table. It didn't take Alice long to figure out how intelligent Pilar was, and later on, after they had left the house, Pilar would tell him how impressed she was by Alice, how she admired the work she was doing, how much she liked her. But Alice was the only one who actively reached out to Pilar. Bing seemed nonplussed, a bit bowled over, befuddled by her presence, and by the second day he had adopted a jocular persona to communicate with her (Bing trying to be funny), talking in the voice of a movie cowboy, addressing her as Miss Pilar and coming out with such original remarks as Howdy there, Miss Pilar, and how's the purdy lady this mornin'? Ellen was polite but distant, and the one time Jake was there, he ignored her.

She is coping with her altered circumstances in Florida, but this is the first time she has lived alone, and there have been some difficult days, dark days when she has had to struggle against the urge to let go and cry for hours on end. She is still on good terms with Teresa and Maria, but the rift with Angela is absolute and forever, and she avoids going to the house when her oldest sister will be there. Maria continues to date Eddie Martinez, and Teresa's husband, Carlos, is coming to the end of his tour of duty and is scheduled to be rotated out of Iraq in March. She is bored with school, she hates going there every morning, and it requires an enormous effort of will not to cut classes, not to skip whole days, but she forges on because she doesn't want to disappoint him. She finds the other students to be idiots, especially the boys, and she has only two or three friends, just two or three girls in her A.P. English class who seem worth talking to. She has been careful with the money, spending as little as she can, and the only unforeseen expense came just before her trip to New York, when she had to replace the carburetor and spark plugs in the Toyota.

She is still a pathetic cook, but a little less pathetic than before, and she hasn't lost or gained any weight, which must mean she is on top of things in spite of her shortcomings. Lots of fruits and vegetables, rice and beans, an occasional chicken cutlet or hamburger (both are easy to cook), and a real breakfast every morning—melon, plain yogurt and berries, Special K. It's been a strange time, she said to him on her last morning in New York, the strangest time she has ever known, and she wishes the days would pass more quickly down there, that they wouldn't drag so much, but each turn of the clock creeps along like a tired fat man walking up a hundred flights of stairs, and now that she has to go back, it's bound to be even worse, because at least there was New York to look forward to after he left, for three weeks that was the thing that kept her going, but now they are looking at three months, she can barely wrap her mind around that thought, three months before she gets to see him again, and it will be like living in limbo, like going on a vacation in hell, and all because of a stupid date on her birth certificate, an arbitrary number, an irrational number that means nothing to anyone.

All during her visit, he was tempted to tell her the truth about himself, to open up to her and give the full story about everything—his parents and Bobby, his childhood in New York, the three years at Brown, the seven and a half years of crazed, self-inflicted exile, everything. On the morning they walked around the Village, they went past Saint Vincent's, the hospital where he was born, went past P.S. 41, the school he attended as a boy, went past the house on Downing Street, the place where his father and stepmother still live, and then they ate lunch at Joe Junior's, the family canteen for the first twenty years of his life, a whole morning and part of an afternoon in the very heart of his old stomping grounds, and that was the day when he came closest to doing it, but desperate as he was to tell her these things about himself, he held back and told her nothing. It wasn't a question of fear. He could have told her then, but he didn't want to spoil the good time they were having together. Pilar was struggling down in Florida, the trip to New York had reanimated her and brought her back to her hopeful, spirited self, and it simply wasn't the moment to confess his lies to her, to pull her down into the bleakness of the Heller family chronicle. He will do it when the time is right, and that time will come only after he has talked to his father and mother, only after he has seen his father and mother, only after he has asked them to take him back into their lives. He is ready to face them now, ready to confront the terrible thing he did to them, and Pilar is solely responsible for giving him the courage to do this—because in order to be worthy of Pilar, he must have this courage.

She left for Florida on the third, two days ago. Wretched farewells, the agony of looking at her face through the window, and then the bus drove down the ramp and disappeared. He took the subway back to Sunset Park, and the moment he walked into his room, he sat down on the bed, took out his cell phone, and called his mother. He wouldn't be able to talk to his father until Monday, but he had to do something now, watching the bus drive down the ramp had made it impossible not to do something, and if his father wasn't available, then he would begin with his mother. He was about to call the theater first, thinking that would be the best way to get hold of her, but then it occurred to him that perhaps her cell phone number was the same one she had seven years ago. He called to find out, and there was her voice telling the world that she would be in New York for the next four months, and if you wanted to get in touch with her there, this was the number. It was a Saturday afternoon, a cold Saturday afternoon in early January, and he assumed she would be at home on a crummy day like this, keeping her toes warm and doing crossword puzzles on the sofa, and when he called the New York number, he was fully confident she would pick up on the second or third ring. But she didn't. The telephone rang four times, and then a message came on, another message with her voice, telling the caller that she was out and please wait for the beep. He was so flummoxed by this unexpected turn that he suddenly went blank, and all he could think to say was: *Um*. Long pause. *Sorry*. Long pause. *I'll call back*.

He decided to reverse course, return to his original plan, and talk to his father first.

It is Monday morning now, January fifth, and he has just called his father's office, only to be told that his father flew back to England yesterday on urgent business. He asks when Mr. Heller will be coming back to New York. It isn't clear, the voice tells him. Call at the end of the week. There might be some news then.

Nine hours later, he calls his mother's New York number again. This time she is in. This time she picks up the phone and answers it.

Ellen Brice

Two trumps one. One is better than four. Three can be too many or just enough. Five is taking it too far. Six is delirium.

She is advancing now, traveling deeper and deeper into the netherworld of her own nothingness, the place in her that coincides with everything she is not. The sky above her is gray or blue or white, sometimes yellow or red, at times purple. The earth below her is green or brown. Her body stands at the juncture of earth and sky, and it belongs to her and no one else. Her thoughts belong to her. Her desires belong to her. Stranded in the realm of the one, she conjures up the two and three and four and five. Sometimes the six. Sometimes even the sixty.

After the unfortunate scene with Alice last month, she understood that she would have to carry on alone. Because of her job, she is too busy to enroll in a class, to waste precious hours riding on subways to and from Pratt or Cooper Union or SVA. The work is what counts, and if she intends to make any progress, she must work continually, with or without a teacher, with or without live models, for the essence of the work resides in her hand, and whenever she manages to lift herself out of herself and put her mind in abeyance, she can will that hand to see. Experiment has taught her that wine helps. A couple of glasses of wine to make her forget who she is, and then she can keep on going for hours, often far into the night.

The human body is strange and flawed and unpredictable. The human body has many secrets, and it does not divulge them to anyone, except those who have learned to wait. The human body has ears. The human body has hands. The human body is created inside another human body, and the human being who emerges from that other human body is necessarily small and weak and helpless. The human body is created in the image of God. The human body has feet. The human body has eyes. The human body is multitudinous in its forms, its manifestations, its degrees of size and shape and color, and to look at one human body is to apprehend only that human body and no other. The human body can be apprehended, but it cannot be comprehended. The human body has shoulders. The human body has knees. The human body is an object and a subject, the outside of an inside that cannot be seen. The human body grows from the small of infancy to the large of adulthood, and then it begins to die. The human body has hips. The human body has elbows. The human body lives in the mind of one who possesses a human body, and to live inside the human body possessed of the mind that perceives another human body is to live in a world of others. The human body has hair. The human body has a mouth.

The human body has genitals. The human body is created out of dust, and when that human body is no more, it returns to the dust from whence it came.

She works from several different sources now: reproductions of paintings and drawings by other artists, black-and-white photographs of male and female nudes, medical photographs of babies, children, and old people, the body-length mirror she attached to the wall opposite her bed in order to have a full view of herself, porn magazines aimed at various appetites and proclivities (from cheesecake shots of women to two-sex copulations to male-male copulations to female-female copulations to threesome, foursome, and fivesome copulations in all their mathematical permutations), and the small hand mirror she uses to study her own vagina. A door has opened inside her, and she has crossed the threshold into a new way of thinking. The human body is an instrument of knowledge.

There is no time for painting now. Drawing is faster and more tactile, better suited to the urgency of her project, and she has filled sketchbook after sketchbook this past month with her attempts to break free of her old methods. For the first hour after setting to work, she warms up by concentrating on details, isolated areas of a body culled from her collection of images or found in one of the two mirrors. A page of hands. A page of eyes. A page of buttocks. A page of arms. Then she moves on to whole bodies, portraits of single figures in various poses: a naked woman standing with her back to the viewer, a naked man sitting on the floor, a naked man stretched out on a bed, a naked girl squatting on the ground and urinating, a naked woman sitting in a chair with her head thrown back as she cups her right breast in her right hand and squeezes the nipple of her left breast with her left hand. These are intimate portraits, she tells herself, not erotic drawings, human bodies doing what human bodies do when no one is watching them, and if many of the men in these single portraits have erections, that is because the average man has fifty erections and semi-erections per day—or so she has been told. Then, in the last part of the exercise, she brings these figures together. A naked woman holding a naked infant in her arms. A naked man kissing the neck of a naked woman. An old naked man and an old naked woman sitting on a bed with their arms around each other. A naked woman kissing a naked man's penis. Two trumps one, followed by the mystery of three: three naked women; two naked women and one naked man; one naked woman and two naked men; three naked men. The porn magazines are quite explicit about what goes on in these situations, and their frankness inspires her to work without fear or inhibition. Fingers have entered vaginas. Mouths have encircled erect penises. Penises have entered vaginas. Anuses have been breached. It is important to note the difference between photography and drawing, however. If one leaves nothing to the imagination, the other dwells exclusively in the realm of the imagination, and therefore her entire being is ablaze when she works on these drawings, since she never simply copies the photograph she is looking at but uses it to imagine a new scene of her own invention. She is sometimes aroused by what her pencil does to the page in front of her, aroused because of the pictures bubbling in her head as she draws, which are similar to the pictures that bubble in her head when she masturbates at night, but arousal is only a minor by-product of the effort, and mostly what she feels are the demands of the work itself, the constant, ever-pressing desire to get it right. The drawings are rough and usually left unfinished. She wants her human bodies to convey the miraculous strangeness of being alive—no more than that, as much as all that. She doesn't concern herself with the idea of beauty. Beauty can take care of itself.

Two weeks ago, there was a heartening development, something unexpected that is still in the process of playing itself out. Several days before the girl from Florida came to Brooklyn and destroyed her hopes of ever conquering Miles, Bing asked to see her new work. She took him upstairs to her bedroom after dinner, trepidation mounting in her with each step they climbed, certain he would laugh at her as he casually flipped through the sketchbooks and then dismiss her with a polite smile and a pat on the shoulder, but she felt she had to risk this potential humiliation, she was burning up inside, the drawings were consuming her now, and someone had to look at them besides herself. Normally, she would have asked Alice, but Alice had let her down that day in December when the fog had blanked out the cemetery, and even though they had long since forgiven each other for that ludicrous misunderstanding, she was afraid to ask Alice because she thought Alice would be embarrassed by the pictures, shocked by them, repulsed by them even, because good and loyal a friend as Alice has been to her, she has always been something of a stodge. Bing is more open-minded, more direct (if often crude) in discussing sexual matters, and as she walked up the stairs with him and opened the door, she realized there was a lot of sexy stuff in those drawings, pretty dirty stuff if you wanted to look at it that way, and maybe this obsession with human bodies was getting a little out of hand, maybe it showed that she was beginning to fall apart again—the first sign of another crack-up. But Bing loved the pictures, he thought they were *stupendous*, a bold, extraordinary breakthrough, and because he spontaneously jumped off the bed and kissed her after he had looked at the last drawing, she knew he wasn't lying to her.

Bing's opinion means nothing, of course. He has no understanding of visual art, no knowledge of the history of art, no ability to judge what he is seeing. When she showed him a reproduction of Courbet's *The Origin of the World*, his eyes opened wide, but when she showed him a similar image of a woman's private parts in one of her skin magazines, his eyes opened wide then too, and she felt saddened to be with someone who was so handi-capped aesthetically, a man unable to tell the difference between a brave and revolutionary work of art and a piece of impoverished, run-of-the-mill smut. Nevertheless, she was encouraged by his enthusiasm, stunned by how happy she felt as she listened to him praise her. Untutored or not, Bing's response to the drawings was visceral and genuine, he was moved by what she had done, he couldn't stop talking about how honest and powerful the work was, and in all the years she had been painting and drawing, no one had ever spoken like that to her, not once.

The goodwill emanating from Bing that night made her feel confident enough to ask a question, *the* question, the one question she had not dared ask anyone since Alice turned her down last month. Would he be willing to pose for her? Working from mirrors and two-dimensional images could take her only so far, she said, but if she meant to accomplish anything with this investigation of the human figure, she would have to begin working with live models at some point, three-dimensional people, living and breathing people. Bing seemed flattered by her request, but also a little pained. We're not talking about the body beautiful here, he said. Nonsense, she replied. You embody you, and because you don't want to be anyone but you, you mustn't be afraid.

They each drank two glasses of wine, which is to say, they finished off a bottle between them, and then Bing removed his clothes and sat down in the chair by the desk as she settled onto the bed, sitting Indian-style with the sketchbook in her lap. Remarkably enough, he didn't seem afraid. Lumpy body and all, with his bulging stomach and thick thighs and hirsute chest and broad, flaccid buttocks, he sat there calmly as she drew him, showing no signs of discomfort or timidity, and ten minutes into the first sketch, when she asked him how he was doing, he said fine, he trusted her, he hadn't known how much he would enjoy being looked at in this way. The room was small, they were no more than four feet apart, and when she began drawing his penis for the first time, it occurred to her that she wasn't looking at a penis anymore but a cock, that penis was the word for the thing in the drawing, but cock was the word for the thing just four feet in front of her, and, objectively speaking, she had to admit that Bing had a handsome cock, no longer or shorter than the majority of those she had seen in her life, but thicker than most, well formed and without peculiarities or blemishes, a first-rate example of male equipment, not what they call a pencil dick (where had she heard that phrase?) but a bulky fountain pen, a substantial plug for any orifice. By the third drawing, she asked him if he would mind playing with himself for a little while so she could see what happened to him when he was hard, and he said no problem, posing for her was actually making him rather hot, and he wouldn't mind at all. By the fourth drawing, she asked him to masturbate for her, and again he willingly obliged, but just to make sure, he asked her if she wouldn't prefer taking her clothes off and letting him join her on the bed, but she said no, she would rather keep her clothes on and continue drawing, but if, at the last moment, he would like to get out of the chair, walk over to the bed, and finish off what he was doing in her mouth, she would have no objection.

There have been five more sessions since then. The same thing has happened all five times, but they are no more than brief interruptions, small gifts they bestow on each other for the space of a few minutes, and then the work goes on as before. It is a perfectly fair arrangement, she feels. Her drawings have already improved because of Bing, and she is certain that the prospect of coming in her mouth will keep him interested in posing for her, at least for now, at least for the foreseeable future, and even if she has no desire to shed her clothes for him, the contact is comforting to her, and she takes pleasure in it as well. She would rather be drawing Miles, of course, and if Miles were the one who posed for her and not Bing, she wouldn't hesitate to shed her clothes for him and let him do whatever he wanted to her, but that will never happen, she knows that now, and she mustn't let her disappointment throw her off course. Miles scares her. The power he has over her scares her as much as anything has scared her in years, and yet she can't stop herself from wanting him. But Miles wants the girl from Florida, he adores the girl from Florida, and when the girl came to Brooklyn and she saw how Miles looked at her, she knew that was the end of it. Poor Ellen, she mutters, speaking to no one in the empty room, poor Ellen Brice who always loses out to someone else, don't feel sorry for yourself, go on with your drawings, go on letting Bing come in your mouth, and sooner or later all of you will be gone from Sunset Park, this ratty little house will be torn down and forgotten, and the life you are living now will fade into oblivion, not one person will remember you were ever here, not even you, Ellen Brice, and Miles Heller will vanish from your heart, in the same way you have already vanished from his heart, have never been in his heart, have never been in anyone's heart, not even your own.

Two is the only number that counts. One defines the real, perhaps, but all the others are pure fantasy, pencil lines on a blank white page.

On Sunday, January fourth, she goes to visit her sister on the Upper West Side, and one by one she holds the naked bodies of her twin nephews, Nicholas and Bruno. Such masculine names for such tiny fellows, she thinks, just two months old and everything still before them in a world coming apart at the seams, and as she holds first the one and then the other in her arms, she is awed by the softness of their skin, the smoothness of their bodies as she presses them against her neck and cheeks, feels the young flesh in the palms of her hands and along her bare forearms, and again she remembers the phrase that has been repeating itself to her ever since it came into her head last month: the strangeness of being alive. Just think, she says to her sister, Larry puts his cock in you one night, and nine months later out come these two little men. It doesn't make any sense, does it? Her sister laughs. That's the deal, honey, she says. A few minutes of pleasure, followed by a lifetime of hard work. Then, after a short pause, she looks at Ellen and says: But no, it doesn't make any sense—no sense at all.

Riding home on the subway that evening, she thinks about her own child, the child who was never born, and wonders if that was her only chance or if a time will come when a child starts growing inside her again. She takes out her notebook and writes:

The human body cannot exist without other human bodies.

The human body needs to be touched—not just small human bodies, but large human bodies as well.

The human body has skin.

Alice Bergstrom

Every Monday, Wednesday, and Thursday she takes the subway into Manhattan and goes to her part-time job at the PEN American Center at 588 Broadway, just south of Houston Street. She started working there last summer, abandoning her post as an adjunct at Queens College because that job ate up too many hours and left her with no time for her dissertation. Remedial English and freshman English, just two classes, but fifty students writing one paper a week, and then the obligatory three private conferences with each student every semester, one hundred and fifty conferences in all, seven hundred papers to read and correct and grade, preparation for class, drawing up reading lists, inventing good assignments, the challenge of holding the students' attention, the need to dress well, the long commute out to Flushing and back, and all for an insultingly low salary with no benefits, a salary that came out to less than the minimum wage (she did the math once and calculated how much she earned by the hour), which meant that the pay she received for doing work that prevented her from doing her own work was less than she would have made as a car-wash attendant or a flipper of

hamburgers. PEN doesn't pay much either, but she gives
them only fifteen hours a week, her dissertation is advancing again, and she believes in the purpose of the organiza-
tion, the only human rights group in the world devoted
exclusively to defending writers—writers imprisoned by
unjust governments, writers living under the threat of
death, writers banned from publishing their work, writers
in exile. P-E-N. Poets and publishers, essayists and editors,
novelists. They can pay her only twelve thousand seven
hundred dollars for her part-time position, but whenever
she walks into the building at 588 Broadway and takes the
elevator to the third floor, at least she knows she isn't wast-
ing her time.

She was ten years old when the fatwa was declared
against Salman Rushdie. She was already a committed
reader then, a girl who lived in the land of books, at that
point immersed in the eight novels of the Anne of Green
Gables series, dreaming of becoming a writer herself one
day, and then came the news about a man living in England
who had published a book that angered so many people in
distant parts of the world that the bearded leader of one
country actually stood up and declared that the man in
England should be killed for what he had written. This
was incomprehensible to her. Books weren't dangerous, she
said to herself, they brought only pleasure and happiness
to the people who read them, they made people feel more
alive and more connected to one another, and if the bearded
leader of that country on the other side of the world was

against the Englishman's book, all he had to do was stop reading it, put it away somewhere, and forget about it. Threatening to kill someone for writing a novel, a make-believe story set in a make-believe world, was the stupidest thing she had ever heard of. Words were harmless, with no power to hurt anyone, and even if some words were offensive to some people, words weren't knives or bullets, they were simply black marks on pieces of paper, and they couldn't kill or wound or cause any real damage. That was her response to the fatwa at ten, her naïve but earnest reaction to the absurd injustice that had been committed, and her outrage was all the more intense because it was tinged with fear, for this was the first time she had been exposed to the ugliness of brute, irrational hatred, the first time her young eyes had looked into the darkness of the world. The affair continued, of course, it went on for many years after that denunciation on Valentine's Day 1989, and she grew up with the story of Salman Rushdie—the bookstore bombings, the knife in the heart of his Japanese translator, the bullets in the back of his Norwegian publisher—the story was embedded inside her as she moved from childhood into adolescence, and the older she grew the more she understood about the danger of words, the threat to power words can represent, and in states ruled by tyrants and policemen, every writer who dares to express himself freely is at risk.

PEN's Freedom to Write Program is run by a man named Paul Fowler, a poet in his spare time, a human rights activist by profession, and when he gave Alice her job last summer, he told her that the underlying philosophy of their work was quite simple: to make a lot of noise, as much noise as possible. Paul has a full-time deputy, Linda Nicholson, a woman born on the same day as Alice, and the three of them make up the staff of the small department dedicated to the production of noise. About half of what they do is focused on international issues, the campaign to reform Article 301 of the Turkish penal code, for example, the insult law that has threatened the lives and safety of scores of writers and journalists for making critical remarks about their country, as well as the attempts to win the release of writers imprisoned in various places around the world, the Burmese writers, the Chinese writers, the Cuban writers, many of them suffering from grave medical problems because of harsh treatment and/or neglect, and by putting pressure on the various governments responsible for these violations of international law, exposing these stories to the world press, circulating petitions signed by hundreds of celebrated writers, PEN has often succeeded in embarrassing these governments into letting prisoners go, not as often as they would like, but often enough to know that these methods can work, often enough to keep on trying, and in many cases to keep on trying for years. The other half of what they do is concerned with domestic issues: the banning of books by schools and libraries, for example, or the ongoing Campaign for Core Freedoms, initiated by PEN in 2004 in response to the Patriot Act passed by the Bush administration, which has given the U.S. government unprecedented authority to monitor the activities of American citizens and collect information about their personal associations, reading habits, and opinions. In the report Alice helped Paul compose not long after starting her job, PEN is now calling for the following actions: expanding safeguards for bookstore and library records weakened by the Patriot Act; reining in the use of the National Security Letters; limiting the scope of secret surveillance programs; closing Guantánamo and all remaining secret prisons; ending torture, arbitrary detentions, and extraordinary rendition; expanding refugee resettlement programs for endangered Iraqi writers. On the day she was hired, Paul and Linda told her not to be alarmed by the clicking sounds she would hear when she used the phone. The lines at PEN were tapped, and both the U.S. and Chinese governments had hacked into their computers.

It is the first Monday of the new year, January fifth, and she has just traveled into Manhattan to begin another five-hour stint at PEN headquarters. She will be working from nine in the morning until two o'clock today, at which point she will return to Sunset Park and put in another few hours on her dissertation, forcing herself to sit at her desk until six-thirty, trying to eke out another paragraph or two on *The Best Years of Our Lives*. Six-thirty is when she and Miles arranged to meet in the kitchen to start preparing dinner. They will be cooking together for the first time since Pilar went back to Florida, and she is looking forward to it, looking forward to being alone with Señor Heller again for a little while, for Señor Heller has proved to be every bit as interesting as Bing advertised, and she takes pleasure in being near him, in talking to him, in watching him move. She has not fallen for him in the way poor Ellen has, has not lost her head or cursed the innocent Pilar Sanchez for robbing his heart, but the soft-spoken, brooding, impenetrable Miles Heller has touched a nerve in her, and she finds it difficult to remember what things were like in the house before he moved in. For the fourth night in a row, Jake will not be coming, and it pains her to realize that she is glad.

She is still thinking about Jake as she steps out of the elevator on the third floor, wondering if the moment has finally come for a showdown with him or if she should put it off a little longer, wait until the four pounds she lost in December have become eight pounds, twelve pounds, however many pounds it will take before she stops counting. Paul is already sitting at his desk, talking to someone on the telephone, and he waves to her from the other side of the glass window that separates his office from the outer room, where her desk is located, her small, cluttered desk, where she now sits down and switches on her computer. Linda comes in a couple of minutes later, cheeks flushed from the cold morning air, and before she removes her coat and gets to work, she walks over to Alice, plants a big kiss on her left cheek, and wishes her a happy new year.

Paul makes a grunting sound from within his office, a sound that could signify surprise or disappointment or dismay, nothing is clear, Paul often emits confusing sounds after he hangs up the phone, and as Alice and Linda turn to look through the glass window, Paul is already on his feet and walking toward them. There has been a new development. On December thirty-first, the Chinese authorities allowed Liu Xiaobo to be visited by his wife.

This is their new case, the most pressing case on the current agenda, and ever since Liu Xiaobo was detained in early December, they have worked on little else. Paul and Linda are both pessimistic about the immediate future, both are certain that the Beijing Public Security Bureau will hold Liu until enough evidence has been gathered against him to make a formal arrest on the charge of *inciting subversion of state power,* which could land him in prison for fifteen years. His offense: cowriting a document called Charter 08, a declaration calling for political reform, greater human rights, and an end to one-party rule in China.

Liu Xiaobo began as a literary critic and professor at Beijing Normal University, an important enough figure to have worked as a visiting scholar at a number of foreign institutions, notably the University of Oslo and Columbia University in New York, Alice's Columbia University, the place where she is pushing toward her doctorate, and Liu's activism dates all the way back to 1989, the year of years, the year the Berlin Wall came down, the year of the fatwa, the year of Tiananmen Square, and it was precisely then, in the spring of 1989, that Liu quit his post at Columbia and went back to Beijing, where he staged a hunger strike in Tiananmen Square in support of the students and advocated nonviolent methods of protest in order to prevent further bloodshed. He spent two years in prison for this, and then, in 1996, was sentenced to three years of *reeducation through labor* for suggesting that the Chinese government open discussions with the Dalai Lama of Tibet. More harassments have followed, and he has been living under police surveillance ever since. His latest arrest occurred on December 8, 2008, coincidentally or not coincidentally just one day before the sixtieth anniversary of the Universal Declaration of Human Rights. He is being held in an undisclosed location, with no access to a lawyer, no writing materials, no way to communicate with anyone. Does his wife's visit on New Year's Eve signify an important turn, or was it simply a small act of mercy that will have no bearing on the outcome of the case?

Alice spends the morning and early afternoon writing e-mails to PEN centers all around the world, enlisting support for the massive protest Paul wants to mount in Liu's defense. She works with a kind of righteous fervor, knowing that men like Liu Xiaobo are the bedrock of humanity, that few men or women are brave enough to stand up and risk their lives for others, and beside him the rest of us are nothing, walking around in the chains of our weakness and indifference and dull conformity, and when a man like this is about to be sacrificed for his belief in others, the others must do everything they can to save him, and yet even if Alice is filled with anger as she works, she works in a kind of despair as well, feeling the hopelessness of the effort they are about to launch, sensing that no amount of indignation will alter the plans of the Chinese authorities, and even if PEN can roust a million people to pound on drums across the entire globe, there is little chance those drums will be heard.

She skips lunch and works straight through until it is time for her to leave, and when she walks out of the building and heads for the subway, she is still under the spell of the Liu Xiaobo case, still trying to figure out how to interpret the visit from his wife on New Year's Eve, the same New Year's Eve she spent with Jake and a group of their friends on the Upper West Side, everyone kissing everyone else at midnight, a silly custom, but she enjoyed it anyway, she liked being kissed by everyone, and she wonders now, as she descends the stairs into the subway, if the Chinese police allowed Liu's wife to stay with him until midnight, and if they did, whether she and her husband kissed at the stroke of twelve, assuming they were allowed to kiss at all, and if they were, what it would be like to kiss your husband under those circumstances, with policemen watching you and no guarantee that you will ever see your husband again.

Normally, she carries along a book to read on the subway, but she overslept by half an hour this morning, and in

the scramble to get out of the house in time for work, she
forgot to take one with her, and because the train is nearly
empty at two-fifteen in the afternoon, there aren't enough
people on board for her to use the forty-minute ride to
study her fellow passengers, a cherished New York pas-
time, especially for a New York transplant who grew up in
the Midwest, and with nothing to read and not enough
faces to look at, she digs into her purse, pulls out a small
notebook, and jots down some remarks about the passage
she is planning to write when she gets home. Not only are
the returning soldiers estranged from their wives, she will
argue, but they no longer know how to talk to their sons.
There is a scene early in the movie that sets the tone for
this generational split, and that is what she will be tackling
today, that one scene, in which Fredric March presents his
high-school-age boy with his war trophies, a samurai sword
and a Japanese flag, and she finds it unexpected but entirely
appropriate that the boy shows no interest in these things,
that he would rather talk about Hiroshima and the prospect of nuclear annihilation than the presents his father
has given him. His mind is already fixed on the future, the
next war, as if the war that has just been fought is already
in the distant past, and consequently he asks his father no
questions, is not curious enough to learn how these souve-
nirs were obtained, and a scene in which one would have
imagined the boy wanting to hear his father talk about his
adventures on the battlefield ends with the boy forgetting
to take the sword and the flag with him when he walks out

of the room. The father is not a hero in the eyes of his son—he is a superannuated figure from a bygone age. A bit later, when March and Myrna Loy are alone in the room, he turns to her and says: It's terrifying. Loy: What is? March: Youth! Loy: Didn't you run across any young people in the army? March: No. They were all old men—like me.

Miles Heller is old. The thought comes to her out of nowhere, but once it settles in her mind, she knows that she has discovered an essential truth, the thing that sets him apart from Jake Baum and Bing Nathan and all the other young men she knows, the generation of talking boys, the logorrhea class of 2009, whereas Señor Heller says next to nothing, is incapable of making small talk, and refuses to share his secrets with anyone. Miles has been in a war, and all soldiers are old men by the time they come home, shut-down men who never talk about the battles they have fought. What war did Miles Heller march off to, she wonders, what action has he seen, how long has he been away? It is impossible to know, but there is no question that he has been wounded, that he walks around with an inner wound that will never heal, and perhaps that is why she respects him so much—because he is in pain, and he never says anything about it. Bing rants and Jake whines, but Miles holds his tongue. It is not even clear to her what he is doing in Sunset Park. One day early last month, just after he moved in, she asked him why he had left Florida, but his answer was so vague—*I have some unfinished business to take care of*—it could have meant anything. What unfinished business? And why move away from Pilar? He is so obviously in love with the girl, why on earth would he have come to Brooklyn?

If not for Pilar, she would actively worry about Miles. Yes, it was a little disconcerting to be introduced to someone so young, a *high school girl* in her funny green parka and red woolen gloves, but that sensation quickly wore off when one understood how bright and pulled together she was, and the best thing about this girl is the simple fact that Miles is devoted to her, and from Alice's observations during Pilar's visit, she believes she was looking at what is probably an exceptional love, and if Miles can love someone in the way he loves this girl, it must mean the damage inside him is not systemic, that his wounds are specific wounds in specific areas of his soul and are not bleeding into other parts of him, and therefore the darkness in Miles does not prey on her mind as it did before Pilar lived among them for those ten or eleven days. It was difficult not to feel some envy, of course, watching Miles as he looked at his beloved, talked to his beloved, touched his beloved, not because she wants him to look at her in that way but because Jake doesn't do it anymore, and foolish as it is to measure Jake against Señor Heller, there are times when she can't stop herself. Jake has brains, talent, and ambition, whereas Miles, for all his mental and physical virtues, is completely lacking in ambition, seems content to drift through his days without passion or purpose, and yet Miles is a man and Jake is still a boy, because Miles has been to war and has grown old. Perhaps that explains why the two of them seem to dislike each other so much. Even at the first dinner, when Jake began talking about interviewing Renzo Michaelson, she felt that Miles was ready to punch him or pour a drink over his head. Who knows why Michaelson provoked that response, but the animosity has continued—to such a degree that Miles is rarely at home when Jake comes for dinner. Jake is continuing to pester Bing about helping him set up a meeting with Michaelson, but Bing keeps putting him off, saying that Michaelson is an ornery, reclusive sort of person, and the best way to handle it is to wait until he comes into the store again to have his typewriter cleaned. Alice could probably arrange it herself if she wanted to. Michaelson is a longtime member of PEN, a past vice president with a special attachment to the Freedom to Write Program, and she talked to him on the phone only last week about the Liu Xiaobo case. She could easily call him tomorrow and ask if he has any time to talk to her boyfriend, but she doesn't want to do it. Jake has stuck a knife in her, and she isn't in the mood to do him any favors.

She returns to the empty house just after three o'clock. By three-thirty, she is sitting at her desk, typing up her notes about the father-son conversation in *The Best Years of Our Lives*. At three-fifty, someone starts knocking on the front door. Alice stands up and goes downstairs to see who it is. When she opens the door, a tall, blubbery man in a strange khaki uniform grins at her and tips his hat.

He has a splayed, multifaceted nose, pockmarked cheeks, and a large, full-lipped mouth, a curious assortment of facial characteristics that somehow reminds her of a platter of mashed potatoes. She also notes, with a certain sadness, that he is wearing a gun. When she asks him who he is, he says that he is Nestor Gonzalez, New York City marshal, and then he hands her a folded-up piece of paper, a document of some kind. What is this? Alice asks. A court order, Gonzalez says. For what? Alice asks, pretending that she doesn't know. You're breaking the law, ma'am, the marshal replies. You and your friends have to get out.

Bing Nathan

Miles is worried about money. He didn't have enough to begin with, and now that he has spent the better part of two weeks running around the city with Pilar, eating twice a day in restaurants, buying her clothes and perfume, springing for expensive theater tickets, his reserve has been melting even more quickly than he imagined it would. They talk about it on January third, a few hours after Pilar climbs onto the bus and heads back to Florida, a few minutes after Miles leaves the garbled message on his mother's answering machine, and Bing says there is a simple solution to the problem if Miles is willing to accept his offer. He needs help at the Hospital for Broken Things. Mob Rule has finally found a booking agent, and they will be out of town for two weeks at the end of January and two more weeks in February, playing at colleges in New York State and Pennsylvania, and he can't afford to shut down the business while he is away. He can teach Miles how to frame pictures, clean and repair typewriters, fix anything the customers want fixed, and if Miles agrees to work full-time for so many dollars an hour, they can catch up on the unfinished jobs that have been mounting over the past few

months, Bing can cut out early to practice with his band
whenever the mood strikes him, and whenever the band is
traveling, Miles will be in charge. Bing can cover an extra
salary now because of the money he has saved by living
rent-free in Sunset Park for the past five months—and
then, on top of that, it looks as if Mob Rule will be bringing
in more cash than at any time in its history. What does
Miles think? Miles looks down at his shoes, turns the proposition around for several moments, and then lifts his head
and says he is for it. He thinks it will be better to work at
the Hospital than to spend his days walking around the
cemetery taking photographs, and before he goes out to
shop for dinner, he thanks Bing for having rescued him
again.

What Miles doesn't understand is that Charles Bing-
ham Nathan would do anything for him, and even if Miles
had turned down the offer to work for so many dollars
an hour at the Hospital for Broken Things, his friend would
have been happy to advance him as much money as he
needed, with no obligation to pay back the loan anytime
before the end of the twenty-second century. He knows that
Miles is only half a person, that his life has been sundered
and will never be fully repaired, but the half of Miles that
remains is more compelling to him than two of anyone
else. It began when they met twelve years ago, in the fall
immediately after the death of Miles's brother, Miles just
sixteen and Bing a year older, the one following the smart-
kid road at Stuyvesant and the other in the music program

at LaGuardia, two angry boys who found common cause in their contempt for the hypocrisies of American life, and it was the younger one who taught the older one the value of resistance, how it was possible to refuse to participate in the meaningless games society was asking them to play, and Bing knows that much of what he has become in the years since then is a direct result of Miles's influence on him. It was more than what Miles said, however, more than any one of the hundreds of cutting observations he made about politics and economics, the clarity with which he broke down *the system*, it was what Miles said in combination with who Miles was, and how he seemed to embody the ideas he believed in, the gravity of his bearing, the grief-stricken boy with no illusions, no false hopes, and even if they never became intimate friends, he doubts there is anyone from his generation he admires more.

He was not the only one who felt that way. As far back as he can remember, Miles seemed different from everyone else, to possess some magnetic, animal force that changed the atmosphere whenever he walked into a room. Was it the power of his silences that made him attract so much attention, the mysterious, closed-in nature of his personality that turned him into a kind of mirror for others to project themselves onto, the eerie sense that he was both there and not there at the same time? He was intelligent and good-looking, yes, but not all intelligent and good-looking people exude that magic, and when you added in the fact that everyone knew he was the son of Mary-Lee

Swann, the only child of Mary-Lee Swann, perhaps the aura
of her fame helped to enhance the feeling that Miles was
one of the anointed. Some people resented him, of course,
boys in particular, boys but never girls, but why wouldn't
boys resent him for his luck with girls, for being the one
the girls wanted? Even now, so many years later, the Heller
touch seems to have survived the long odyssey to nowhere
and back. Look at Alice and Ellen. Alice finds him *wholly
admirable* (a direct quote), and Ellen, dear little Ellen, is
besotted with him.

Miles has been living in Sunset Park for a month now,
and Bing is glad he is here, glad the Paltry Three has been
turned back into the Solid Four, although he is still baffled
by Miles's sudden change of heart about coming to Brooklyn. First it was no, and the long letter explaining why he
wanted to stay in Florida, and then the urgent phone call
to the Hospital late one Friday, just as Bing was about to
close up and return to the house in Sunset Park, and Miles
telling him that *something had come up* and if a place was
still open for him, he would be on a bus to New York that
weekend. Miles will never explain himself, of course, and
it would be pointless to ask, but now that he is here, Bing
is heartened that old Mr. Sullen is finally prepared to
make peace with his parents and put a stop to the idiocy
that has been going on for so long, much too long, and that
his own role as double agent and liar will soon be coming
to an end. He feels no guilt about having deceived Miles.
If anything, he is proud of what he has done, and when

Morris Heller called the Hospital this morning to ask for the latest news, he felt a sense of victory when he was able to report that Miles had called his office while he was in England and would be calling back on Monday, and now that Miles has just told him he has called his mother as well, the victory is almost complete. Miles has come round at last, and it is probably a good thing that he is in love with Pilar, even if that love feels a bit strange, more than a little disturbing in fact, such a young girl, the last person one would expect Miles to get himself entangled with, but without question charming and pretty, old beyond her years perhaps, and therefore let Miles have his Pilar and think no more about it. Good news all around, positive things happening on so many fronts, and yet it has been a difficult month for him, one of the most anguishing months of his life, and when he hasn't been wallowing in mud baths of confusion and disarray, he has been close to despair. It started when Miles returned to New York, the moment when he saw Miles standing in the store and he threw his arms around him and kissed him, and ever since that day he has found it nearly impossible not to touch Miles, not to want to touch Miles. He knows that Miles doesn't like it, that he is put off by his spontaneous hugs, his pats on the back, his neck squeezes and shoulder squeezes, but Bing can't stop himself, he knows he should stop but he can't, and because he is afraid he has fallen in love with Miles, because he is afraid he has always been in love with Miles, he is living in a state of despair.

He remembers a summer outing eleven years ago, the summer after he graduated from high school, three boys and two girls packed into a little car driving north to the Catskills. Someone's parents owned a cottage up there, an isolated spot in the woods with a pond and a tennis court, and Miles was in the car with his love of the moment, a girl named Annie, and there was Geoff Taylor with his newest conquest, someone whose name has been forgotten, and last but not least himself, the one with no girlfriend, the odd man out as usual. They arrived late, sometime between midnight and one o'clock in the morning, and because they were hot and stiff after the long drive, someone suggested they cool off in the pond, and suddenly they were running toward the water, stripping off their clothes, and wading in. He remembers how pleasant it was, splashing around in that remote place with the moon and the stars overhead, the crickets singing in the woods, the warm breeze blowing against his back, along with the pleasure of seeing the bodies of the girls, the long-legged Annie with her flat stomach and delightfully curved rear end, and Geoff's girlfriend, short and round, with large breasts and frizzy strands of dark hair twining over her shoulders. But it wasn't sexual pleasure, there was nothing erotic about what they were doing, it was simple corporeal ease, the pleasure of feeling the water and the air against your skin, of lolling around in the open on a hot summer night, of being with your friends. He was the first one to come out, and as he stood at the edge of the pond, he saw that

the others had paired off, that the two couples were standing chest-deep in the water, and each couple was embracing, and as he watched Miles and Annie with their arms
around each other and their mouths locked in a prolonged
kiss, the strangest thought occurred to him, something
that took him completely by surprise. Annie was incon-
testably a beautiful girl, one of the loveliest girls he had
ever met, and the logic of the situation demanded that he
feel envious of Miles for having such a beautiful girl in his
arms, for being attractive enough to have won the affections of such a desirable creature, but as he watched the
two of them kissing in the water, he understood that
the envy he felt was directed toward Annie, not Miles, that
he wanted to be in Annie's place and to be kissing Miles
himself. A moment later, they began walking toward the
edge of the pond, walking straight toward him, and as
Miles's body emerged from the water, Bing saw that he
had an erection, a large, fully formed erection, and the
sight of that stiffened penis aroused him, excited him in a
way he never would have thought possible, and before
Miles had touched dry ground, Bing had an erection of his
own, a turn of events that so bewildered him that he ran
back into the pond and dove under the water to conceal his
embarrassment.

He suppressed the memory of that night for years,
never returned to it even in the darkest, most private
realms of his imagination, but then Miles came back, and
with Miles the memory came back, and for the past month

Bing has been replaying that scene in his head five times a day, ten times a day, and by now he no longer knows who or what he is. Does his response to that erect phallus glimpsed in the moonlight eleven years ago mean that he prefers men to women, that he is more attracted to male bodies than female bodies, and if that is the case, could that account for his singular run of failure with the women he has courted over the years? He doesn't know. The only thing he can say with any certainty is that he is drawn to Miles, that he thinks about Miles's body and that erect phallus whenever he is with him, which is often, and that he thinks about touching Miles's body and that erect phallus whenever he is not with him, which is more often, and yet to act on these desires would be a grave error, an error that would lead to the most horrendous consequences, for Miles has no interest in coupling with other men, and if Bing even suggested such a possibility, even whispered a single word about what is on his mind, he would lose Miles's friendship forever, which is something he devoutly does not wish to do.

Miles is off-limits, on permanent loan to the world of women. But the tormenting power of that erect phallus has driven Bing to consider other options, to think about looking elsewhere to satisfy his curiosity, for in spite of the fact that Miles is the only man he craves, he wonders if the time hasn't come to experiment with another man, which is the only way he will ever find out who and what he is—a man made for men, a man made for women, a man made for both men and women, or a man made for no one but himself. The problem is where to look. All the members of his band are married or living with their girlfriends, he has no gay friends he can think of, and the idea of cruising for some pickup in a gay bar leaves him cold. He has thought about Jake Baum a few times, plotting various strategies about how and when he could approach him without tipping his hand and humiliating himself in the event of a rebuff, but he suspects there is something ambiguous about Alice's boyfriend, and even if he is with a woman now, it is possible that he has been with men in the past and is not immune to the charms of phallic love. Bing regrets that he is not more attracted to Jake, but in the interests of scientific self-discovery he would be willing to bed down with him to see if he himself has any taste for phallic love. He has yet to do anything about it, however, for just when he was gearing up to cajole Baum into having sex with him by promising to arrange the interview with Renzo Michaelson (not the strongest idea, perhaps, but ideas have been hard to come by), Ellen asked him to pose for her, and his quest for knowledge was temporarily derailed.

He has no idea what they are up to. Something perverse, he feels, but at the same time altogether innocent and without danger. A silent pact of some sort, a mutual understanding that allows them to share their loneliness and frustrations, but even as they draw closer to each other in that silence, he is still lonely and frustrated, and he senses that Ellen is no better off than he is. She draws and he drums. Drumming has always been a way for him to scream, and Ellen's new drawings have turned into screams as well. He takes off his clothes for her and does everything she asks him to do. He doesn't know why he feels so comfortable with her, so unthreatened by her eyes, but donating his body to the cause of her art is a small thing, finally, and he intends to go on doing it until she asks him to stop.

On Sunday, January fourth, he spends eight hours with Miles at the Hospital for Broken Things, giving him his first lessons in the delicate, exacting work of picture framing, introducing him to the sturdy mechanisms of manual typewriters, familiarizing him with the tools and materials in the back room of the tiny shop. The next morning, Monday, January fifth, they go back for more of the same, but this time Miles seems worried, and when Bing asks him what is wrong, Miles explains that he has just called his father's office and was told his father returned to England yesterday *on urgent business*, and he is concerned that it might have something to do with his stepmother. Bing, too, is both worried and perplexed by this news, but he cannot reveal the full scope of his anxiety to Morris Heller's son, nor can he tell him that he spoke to Morris Heller just forty-eight hours ago and that nothing seemed amiss at the time. They work steadily until five-thirty, at which point Miles informs Bing that he wants to take another stab at calling his mother, and Bing deferentially withdraws to a

bar down the street, understanding that such a call
demands total privacy. Fifteen minutes later, Miles walks
into the bar and tells Bing that he and his mother have
arranged to meet for dinner tomorrow night. There are a
hundred questions Bing would like to ask, but he confines
himself to just one: How did she sound? Very well, Miles
says. She called him a no-good shithead, an imbecile, and a
rotten coward, but then she cried, then they both cried,
and afterward her voice became warm and affectionate, she
talked to him with far more kindness than he deserved,
and hearing her again after all these years was almost too
much for him. He regrets everything, he says. He thinks he
is the stupidest person who ever lived. If there were any
justice in the world, he should be taken outside and shot.

Bing has never seen Miles look more distressed than
he is now. For a few moments, he thinks Miles might actually break down in tears. Forgetting his vow not to touch
him anymore, he puts his arms around his friend and
holds on to him tightly. Cheer up, asshole, he says. At least
you know you're the stupidest person who ever lived. How
many people are smart enough to admit that?

They take a bus back to Sunset Park and walk into the
house a couple of minutes before six-thirty, a couple of
minutes before Miles's scheduled rendezvous with Alice
in the kitchen. As expected, Alice is already there, as is
Ellen, and both of them are sitting at the table, not preparing food, not doing anything but sitting at the table and
looking into each other's eyes. Alice is stroking the back

of Ellen's right hand, Ellen's left hand is stroking Alice's face, and both of them look miserable. What is it? Bing asks. This, Alice says, and then she picks up a piece of paper and hands it to him.

Bing has been expecting this piece of paper since the day they moved into the house last August. He knew it would come, and he knew what he was going to do when it came, which is precisely what he does now. Without even bothering to read the full text of the court order to vacate the premises, he tears the sheet once, twice, and then a third time, and then he tosses the eight scraps of paper onto the floor.

Don't worry, he says. This doesn't mean a thing. They've found out we're here, but getting us to move will take more than a dumb piece of paper. I know how this stuff works. They've given us notice, and now they'll forget about us for a while. In a month or so, they'll be back with another piece of paper, which we'll tear up and throw on the floor again. And another time, and another time after that, and maybe even another time after that. The city marshals won't do anything to us. They don't want trouble. Their job is to deliver pieces of paper, and that's it. We don't have to worry until they come with the cops. Then it gets serious, but we won't be seeing any cops around here for a long time—if ever. We're small potatoes, and the cops have better things to think about than four quiet people living in a quiet little house in a quiet little nothing neighborhood. Don't panic. We might have to leave someday, but that day isn't today, and until the cops show up, I'm not giving an inch. And even when they do come, they'll have to beat me over the head and drag me out in handcuffs. This is our house. It belongs to us now, and I'd rather go to jail than give up my right to live here.

That's the spirit, Miles says.

So you're with me? Bing asks.

Of course I am, Miles says, lifting his right hand into the air, as if taking an oath. Chief Miles no budge from tepee.

And what about you, Ellen? Do you want to leave or stay?

Stay, Ellen says.

And you, Alice?

Stay.

Mary-Lee Swann

Simon left last night, back to L.A. to teach his film history class, and so begins the grind of comings and goings, the poor man traveling back and forth across the country every week for the next three months, the diabolical red-eye, jet lag, sticky clothes and swollen feet, the awful air in the cabin, the pumped-in artificial air, three days in L.A., four days in New York, and all for the pittance they are paying him, but he says he enjoys the teaching, and surely it is better for him to stay busy, to be doing something rather than nothing, but the timing couldn't have been worse, how much she needs him to be with her now, how much she hates to sleep alone, and this part, Winnie, so grueling and difficult, she fears she will not be up to it, dreads she will fall on her face and become a laughing-stock, jitters, jitters, the old knot in the belly before the curtain rises, and how was she to know an emmet is an ant, an archaic word for ant, she had to look it up in the dictionary, and why would Winnie say emmet instead of ant, is it funnier to say emmet instead of ant, yes, no doubt it is funnier, or at least unexpected and therefore strange, *An emmet!*, which leads to Willie's one-word utterance,

Formication, very droll that, you think he is mispronouncing fornication, but she had to look that one up in the dictionary too before she got the joke, *a sensation of the body resembling that made by the creeping of ants on the skin*, and Fred delivers the word wonderfully well, he is a fine Willie, a good soul to work with, and how nicely he reads the paper early in the first act, *Opening for smart youth*, *Wanted bright boy*, she burst out laughing at the first read-through when he spoke those lines, Fred Derry, the same name as a character in that movie she watched with Simon the other night, the one he will be showing to his class today, *The Best Years of Our Lives*, an excellent old film, she choked up at the end and cried, and when she went to rehearsal the next day and asked Fred if his parents had named him after the character in that movie, her stage husband grinned at her and said, Alas, dear woman, no, I am an aged fart who crept into this world five years before that film was made.

Alas, dear woman. She doubts she has ever been dear. Many other things on the long journey from the first day to this day, but not dear, no, never that. Intermittently kind, intermittently lovable, intermittently loving, intermittently unselfish, but not often enough to qualify as dear.

She misses Simon, the place feels sickeningly empty without him, but perhaps it is just as well that he isn't here tonight, this one night, a Tuesday night in early January, the sixth night of the year, because in one hour Miles will

be ringing the bell downstairs, in one hour he will be
walking into this third-floor loft on Franklin Street, and
after seven and a half years of no contact with her son
(*seven and a half years*), it is probably best that she see
him alone, talk to him alone. She has no idea what will
happen, is entirely in the dark about what to expect from
the evening, and because she is too afraid to dwell on these
imponderables, she has concentrated her attention on the
dinner, the meal itself, what to serve and what not to serve,
and because rehearsal was going to run too late for her to
cook the meal herself, she has called two different restaurants to deliver food to the loft at eight-thirty sharp, two
restaurants because after ordering steak dinners from the
first, thinking steak was a good bet, everyone likes steak,
especially men with healthy appetites, she began to fret
that she had made the wrong choice, that maybe her son
has become a vegetarian or has an aversion to steak, and
she didn't want things to get off to an awkward start by
putting Miles in a position that would force him to eat
something he doesn't like or, even worse, to serve him a
meal that he couldn't or wouldn't eat, and therefore, just to
play it safe, she called a second restaurant and ordered
a second pair of dinners—meatless lasagna, salads, and
grilled winter vegetables. As with food, so with drink. She
remembers that he used to like scotch and red wine, but
his preferences might have changed since the last time she
saw him, and consequently she has bought one case each
of red wine and white wine and filled the liquor cabinet

[255]

with an abundant range of possibilities: scotch, bourbon, vodka, gin, tequila, rye, and three different brands of cognac.

She assumes that Miles has already seen his father, that he made the call to the office first thing yesterday morning as Bing Nathan said he would, and that the two of them had dinner together last night. She was expecting Morris to call her today and give a full account of what happened, but no word yet, no message on the machine or her cell phone, even though Miles must have told him he would be coming here tonight, since she and Miles spoke before dinner hour yesterday, in other words before Miles saw his father, and it is hard to imagine that the subject would not have come up somewhere in their conversation. Who knows why she hasn't heard from Morris? It could be that things went badly last night and he is still too upset to talk about it. Or else he was simply too busy today, his second day back at work after the trip to England, and maybe he got caught up in problems at the office, the publishing house is going through hard times just now, and it's even possible that he's still at the office at seven o'clock, eating Chinese takeout for dinner and settling in for a long night of work. Then, too, it could be that Miles lost his nerve and didn't make the call. Not likely, since he wasn't too afraid to call her, and if this is the week for burying hatchets, his father is the logical place to begin, the one he would go to first, since Morris had a hell of a lot more to do with raising him than she did, but still, it could be true, and while she mustn't let Miles know what Bing Nathan has been up to all these years, she can ask the question tonight and find out if he has been in touch with his father or not.

That was why she shouted at Miles on the phone yesterday—out of solidarity with Morris. He and Willa have borne the brunt of this long, wretched affair, and when she saw him at dinner on Saturday night, he looked so much older to her, the hair so gray now, the cheeks so thin, the eyes so dull with sadness, and she understood what a toll this story has taken on him, and now that she is older and presumably wiser (although that is a matter of some dispute, she believes), she was moved by the surge of affection she felt for him in the restaurant that night, the aging shadow of the man she married so long ago, the father of her only child, and it was for Morris's sake that she shouted at Miles, pretending to share Morris's anger at him for what he has done, trying to act like a proper parent, the hurt, scolding mother, but most of it was performance, nearly every word was a pretend word, the insults, the name-calling, for the fact is that she resents Miles far less than Morris does, and she has not walked around all these years feeling bitter about what happened—disappointed, yes, confused, yes, but not bitter.

She has no right to blame Miles for anything he has done, she has let him down by being such a fitful, incompetent mother, and she knows she has failed at this more dreadfully than anything else in her life, the two failed marriages included, every one of her lapses and bad deeds included, but she wasn't up to motherhood when Miles was born, twenty-six years old but still not ready, too distracted to concentrate, preoccupied by the jump from theater to film, indignant with Morris for having talked her into it, and struggle as she did to fulfill her duties for those first six months, she found herself bored with the baby, there was so little pleasure in taking care of him, and not even the pleasure of breast-feeding was enough, not even the pleasure of looking into his eyes and watching him smile back at her could compensate for the smothering tedium of it all, the incessant wailing, the wet, yellow shit in the diapers, the puked-up milk, the howls in the middle of the night, the lack of sleep, the mindless repetitions, and then *Innocent Dreamer* came along, and she bolted. Looking back on her actions now, she finds them unpardonable, and even if she did fall for the boy later, after the divorce, after he started growing up, she was no good at it, she kept letting him down, couldn't even remember to go to his bloody high school graduation for God's sake, but that was the turning point, the unpardonable sin of not being there when she should have been there, and from then on she became more conscientious, tried to make amends for all the sins she had committed over the years (the beautiful weekend in Providence with Simon, the three of them together as if they were a family, she was so happy there, so proud of the boy), and then, six months after that, he bolted. Mother bolts, boy bolts. Hence her tears on the phone yesterday. She shouted at him for Morris's sake, but the tears were for herself, and the tears spoke the truth. Miles is twenty-eight now, older than she was when she gave birth to him, but he is still her son, and she wants him back, she wants the story to begin again.

Pity the poor hippo, she thinks. Too fat, dear woman, too many extra pounds on the old bones. Why did it have to be Winnie now and not someone a little more graceful, a little more *svelte*? Svelte Salome, for instance. Because she is too old to play Salome, and Tony Gilbert has asked her to play Winnie. *That is what I find so wonderful. (Pause.) Eyes on my eyes.* She has changed three times since returning to the loft, but she still isn't satisfied with the results. The hour is fast approaching, however, and it is too late to consider a fourth option. Pale blue silk pants, white silk blouse, and a gauzy, loose-flowing, semi-transparent, knee-length jacket to mask the flab. Bracelets on each wrist, but no earrings. Chinese slippers. Winnie's short hair, nothing to be done about that. Too much makeup or too little makeup? The red lipstick a bit harsh, perhaps, remove some of it now. Perfume or no perfume? No perfume. And the hands, the telltale hands with their too plump fingers, nothing to be done about them either. A necklace would probably be too much, and besides, no one could see it under the gauzy wrap. What else? The nail polish. Winnie's nail polish, nothing to be done about that either. Jitters, jitters, the old lump in the gut before the emmet crawls out and formicates. *Your eyes on my eyes.*

She goes into the bathroom for a last look in the mirror. Old Mother Hubbard or Alice in Motherland? Somewhere in between, perhaps. *Wanted bright boy.* She goes into the kitchen and pours herself a glass of wine. Time for one sip, time for a second sip, and then the doorbell rings.

So much to absorb all at once, so many particulars bombarding her the instant the door opens, the tall young man with his father's dark hair and eyebrows, his mother's gray-blue eyes and mouth, so complete now, the work of growing finally finished, a sterner face than before, she thinks, but softer, more giving eyes, eyes looking into her eyes, and the fierce hug he gives her before either of them can say a word, feeling the great strength of his arms and shoulders through his leather jacket, and again she goes stupid on him without wanting to, breaking down and crying as she holds on to him for dear life, blubbering how sorry she is for all the misunderstandings and grievances that drove him away, but he says none of it has anything to do with her, she is entirely blameless, everything is his fault, and he is the one who is sorry.

He doesn't drink anymore. That is the first new fact she learns about him after she dries her eyes and leads him into the living room. He doesn't drink, but he isn't particular about food, he will be happy to have the steak or the meatless lasagna, whichever she prefers. Why does she feel so nervous around him, so apologetic? She has already apologized, he has already apologized, it is time to move on to more substantial matters, time to begin talking, but then she does the one thing she promised herself she wouldn't do, she mentions the play, she says that is why she is so large now, he is looking at Winnie, not Mary-Lee, an illusion, an imaginary character, and the boy who is no longer a boy smiles at her and says he thinks she is looking grand, *grand* she says to herself, what a curious word, such an old-fashioned way of putting it, no one says *grand* anymore, unless he is referring to her size, of course, her newly begotten rotundity, but no, he seems to be paying her a compliment, and yes, he adds, he has read about the play and is looking forward to seeing it. She notices that she is fidgeting with her bracelet, her lungs feel tight, she can't sit still. I'll go get the wine, she says, but what will it be for you, Miles? Water, juice, ginger ale? As she walks across the large open space of the loft, Miles stands up and follows her, saying he's changed his mind, he'll have some wine after all, he wants to celebrate, and who knows if he means it or is simply dying for a drink because he is just as nervous as she is?

They clink glasses, and as they do so she tells herself to be careful, to remember that Bing Nathan must be kept out of it, that Miles must not discover how closely they have kept track of him, the different jobs in all the different places for all these years, Chicago, New Hampshire, Arizona, California, Florida, the restaurants, the hotels, the warehouses, pitching for the baseball team, the women who have come and gone, the Cuban girl who was with him in New York just now, all the things they know about him must be suppressed, and she must feign ignorance whenever he divulges something, but she can do that, it is her business to do that, she can do that even when she has drunk too much, and from the way Miles has gulped down the first sip of his Pouilly-Fumé, it looks as if much wine will be consumed tonight.

And what about your father? she asks. Have you been in touch with him?

I've called twice, he says. He was in England the first time. They told me to call back on the fifth, but when I tried to reach him yesterday, they said he'd flown off to England again. Something urgent.

Strange, she says. I had dinner with Morris Saturday night, and he didn't say anything about going back. He must have left on Sunday. Very strange.

I hope everything is okay with Willa.

Willa. What makes you think she's in England?

I know she's in England. People tell me things, I have my sources.

I thought you turned your back on us. Not a peep in all this time, and now you tell me you know what we've been up to?

More or less.

If you still cared, why run away in the first place?

That's the big question, isn't it? (*Pause. Another sip of wine.*) Because I thought you'd be better off without me— all of you.

Or you'd be better off without us.

Maybe.

Then why come back now?

Because circumstances brought me up to New York, and once I was here, I understood that the game was over. I'd had enough.

But why so long? When you first went missing, I thought it would be for a few weeks, a few months. You know: confused young man lights out for the territories, grapples with his demons in the wilderness, and comes back a stronger, better person. But seven years, Miles, one-quarter of your life. You see how crazy that is, don't you?

I did want to become a better person. That was the whole point. Become better, become stronger—all very worthy, I suppose, but also a little vague. How do you know when you've become better? It's not like going to college for four years and being handed a diploma to prove you've passed all your courses. There's no way to measure your progress. So I kept at it, not knowing if I was better or not, not knowing if I was stronger or not, and after a while I stopped thinking about the goal and concentrated on the effort. (*Pause. Another sip of wine.*) Does any of this make sense to you? I became addicted to the struggle. I lost track of myself. I kept on doing it, but I didn't know why I was doing it anymore.

Your father thinks you ran away because of a conversation you overheard.

He figured that out? I'm impressed. But that conversation was only the start, the first push. I'm not going to deny how terrible it felt to hear them talking about me like that, but after I took off, I understood they were right, right to be so worried about me, right in their analysis of my fucked-up psyche, and that's why I stayed away—because I didn't want to be that person anymore, and I knew it would take me a long time to get well.

Are you well now?

(*Laughs.*) I doubt it. (*Pause.*) But not as bad off as I was then. Lots of things have changed, especially in the past six months.

Another glass, Miles?

Yes, please. (*Pause.*) I shouldn't be doing this. Out of practice, you know. But it's awfully good wine, and I'm awfully, awfully nervous.

(*Refilling both their glasses.*) Me too, baby.

It was never about you, I hope you understand that. But once I made the break with my father and Willa, I had to break with you and Simon as well.

It's all about Bobby, isn't it?

(*Nods.*)

You have to let it go.

I can't.

You have to.

(*Shakes his head.*) Too many bad memories.

You didn't run him over. It was an accident.

We were arguing. I pushed him into the road, and then the car came—going too fast, coming out of nowhere.

Let it go, Miles. It was an accident.

(*Eyes welling up with tears. Silence, four seconds. Then the downstairs buzzer rings.*)

It must be the food. (*Stands up, walks over to Miles, kisses him on the forehead, and then goes off to let in the deliveryman from the restaurant. Over her shoulder, addressing Miles.*) Which one do you think it is? The vegetarians or the carnivores?

(*Long pause. Forcing a smile.*) Both!

Morris Heller

The Can Man has been to England and back, and his experiences there have changed the color of the world. Since returning to New York on January twenty-fifth, he has given up his cans and bottles in order to devote himself to a life of pure contemplation. The Can Man nearly died in England. The Can Man contracted pneumonia and spent two weeks in a hospital, and the woman he went there to rescue from mental collapse and potential suicide wound up rescuing him from almost certain death and in so doing rescued herself from mental collapse and possibly saved a marriage as well. The Can Man is glad to be alive. The Can Man knows his days are numbered, and therefore he has put aside his quest for cans and bottles in order to study the days as they slip past him, one after the other, each one more quickly than the day before it. Among the numerous observations he has noted down in his book of observations are the following:

January 25. We do not grow stronger as the years advance. The accumulation of sufferings and sorrows weakens our capacity to endure more sufferings and sorrows, and since sufferings and sorrows are inevitable, even a small setback late in life can resound with the same force as a major tragedy when we are young. *The straw that broke the camel's back.* Your dumb-ass penis in another woman's vagina, for example. Willa was on the verge of collapse before that ignominious adventure ever occurred. She has been through too much in her life, has borne more than her fair share of pains, and tough as she has had to be, she is not half as tough as she thinks she is. A dead husband, a dead son, a runaway stepson, and an unfaithful second husband—a nearly dead second husband. What if you had taken the initiative years ago, when you first saw her in that seminar in Philosophy Hall at Columbia, the bright Barnard girl let into a class for graduate students, the one with the delicate, pretty face and slender hands? There was a strong attraction then, all those years ago, long before Karl and Mary-Lee, and young as you both were at the time, twenty-two and twenty, what if you had pursued her a bit harder, what if your little dalliance had led to marriage? Result: no dead husband, no dead son, no runaway stepson. Other sufferings and sorrows, of course, but not those. Now she has brought you back from the dead, averting the final eclipse of all hope, and your still-breathing body must be counted as her greatest triumph. Hope endures, then, but not certainty. There has been a truce, a declaration of a desire for peace, but whether this has been a genuine meeting of minds is not clear. The boy remains an obstacle. She cannot forgive and forget. Not even after he and his mother called from New York to find out how you were, not even after the boy went on calling every day for two weeks to ask for the latest news on your condition. She will remain in England for the Easter break, and you will not be going there again. Too much time has been lost already, and you are needed at the office, the captain of a sinking ship must not abandon his crew. Perhaps she will change her mind as the months roll on. Perhaps she will bend. But you cannot renounce the boy for her sake. Nor can you renounce her for the boy's sake. You want them both, you must have them both, and one way or another, you will, even if they do not have each other.

January 26. Now that you and the boy have spent an evening together, you find yourself curiously let down. Too many years of anticipation, perhaps, too many years of imagining how the reunion would unfold, and therefore a feeling of anticlimax when it finally happened, for the imagination is a powerful weapon, and the imagined reunions that played out in your head so many times over the years were bound to be richer, fuller, and more emotionally satisfying than the real thing. You are also disturbed by the fact that you can't help resenting him. If there is to be any hope for the future, then you too must learn to forgive and forget. But the boy is already standing between you and your wife, and unless your wife undergoes a change of heart and allows him into her world again, the boy will continue to represent the distance that has grown between you. Still and all, it was a miraculous occasion, and the boy is so earnestly repentant, one would have to be made of stone not to want a new chapter to begin. But it will take some time before the two of you feel comfortable together, before you can trust each other again. Physically, he looks well. Strong and fit, with an encouraging brightness in his eyes. Mary-Lee's eyes, the indelible imprint of his mother. He says he has been to two performances of *Happy Days* and thinks she is a splendid Winnie, and when you suggested that the two of you go to see her together—if he could stand to watch the play a third time—he eagerly accepted. He talked at length about the young woman he has fallen in love with, Pilar, Pilar Hernandez, Sanchez, Gomez, her last name escapes you now, and he is looking forward to introducing her to you when she comes back to New York in April. He has no definite plans for the future. For the time being, he is work-ing in Bing Nathan's store, but if he can put together enough money, he is toying with the idea of returning to college next year and getting his degree. Perhaps, maybe, it all depends. You didn't have the courage to confront him with difficult questions about the past. Why he ran away, for example, or why he kept himself hidden for so long. Not to speak of why he left his girlfriend in Florida and came to New York alone. There will be time for questions later. Last night was simply the first round, two boxers feeling each other out before getting down to business. You love him, of course, you love him with all your heart, but you no longer know what to think of him. Let him prove himself to be a worthy son.

January 27. If the company goes down, you will write a book called *Forty Years in the Desert: Publishing Literature in a Country Where People Hate Books*. The Christmas sales figures were even worse than you feared they would be, the worst showing ever. In the office, everyone looks worried—the old hands, the young kids, everyone from senior editors to baby-faced interns. Nor can the sight of your weakened, emaciated body inspire much confidence about the future. Nevertheless, you are glad to be back, glad to be in the place where you feel you belong, and even though the German and the Israeli have both turned you down, you feel less desperate about the situation than you did before you became ill. Nothing like a brief chat with Death to put things in perspective, and you figure that if you managed to avoid an untimely exit in that British hospital, you will find a way to steer the company through this nasty typhoon. No storm lasts forever, and now that you are back at the helm, you realize how much you savor your position as boss, how nourishing this little enterprise has been for you all these years. And you must be a good boss, or at least an appreciated boss, for when you returned to work yesterday, Jill Hertzberg threw her arms around you and said, Good God, Morris, don't ever do that again, please, I beg of you, and then, one by one, each member of the staff, all nine of them, men and women alike, came into your office and hugged you, welcoming you back after your long, tumultuous absence. Your own family might be in ruins, but this is your family as well, and your job is to protect them and make them understand that in spite of the idiot culture that surrounds them, books still count, and the work they are doing is important work. No doubt you are a senti-mental old fool, a man out of step with the times, but you enjoy swimming against the current, that was the found-ing principle of the company thirty-five years ago, and you have no intention of changing your ways now. They are all worried about losing their jobs. That is what you see in their faces when you watch them talking to one another, and so you called a general meeting this afternoon and told them to forget 2008, 2008 is history now, and even if 2009 is no better, there will be no layoffs at Heller Books. Consider the publishers' softball league, you said. Any reductions of staff and it will be impossible to field a team in the spring, and Heller Books' proud record of twenty-seven consecutive losing seasons would come to an end. No softball team this year? Unthinkable.

February 6. Writers should never talk to journalists. The interview is a debased literary form that serves no purpose except to simplify that which should never be simplified. Renzo knows this, and because he is a man who acts on what he knows, he has kept his mouth shut for years, but tonight at dinner, concluded just one hour ago, he informed you that he spent part of the afternoon talk-ing into a tape recorder, answering questions posed to him by a young writer of short stories, who intends to publish the results once the text has been edited and Renzo has given his approval. Special circumstances, he said, when you asked him why he had done it. The request came from Bing Nathan, who happens to be a friend of the young writer of short stories, and because Renzo is aware of the great debt you owe Bing Nathan, he felt it would have been rude to turn him down, unforgivable. In other words, Renzo has broken his silence out of friendship for you, and you told him how touched you were by this, grateful, glad he understood how much it meant to you that he could do something for Bing. An interview for Bing's sake, then, for your sake, but with certain restrictions the young writer had to accept before Renzo would agree to talk to him. No questions about his life or work, no questions about politics, no questions about anything except the work of other writers, dead writers, recently dead writers whom Renzo had known, some well, some casually, and whom he wanted to praise. No attacks, he said, only praise. He provided the interviewer with a list of names in advance and instructed him to choose some of them, just five or six, because the list was far too long to talk about them all. William Gaddis, Joseph Heller, George Plimpton, Leonard Michaels, John Gregory Dunne, Alain Robbe-Grillet, Susan Sontag, Arthur Miller, Robert Creeley, Kenneth Koch, William Styron, Ryszard Kapuściński, Kurt Vonnegut, Grace Paley, Norman Mailer, Harold Pinter, and John Updike, who died just last week, an entire generation gone in the space of a few years. You knew many of those writers as well, talked to them, rubbed shoulders with them, admired them, and as Renzo reeled off their names, you were astonished by how many there were, and a terrible sadness descended on both of you as you raised a glass to their memory. To brighten the mood, Renzo launched into a story about William Styron, an amusing little anecdote from many years ago concerning a French magazine, *Le Nouvel Observateur,* which was planning an entire issue on the subject of America, and among the features they were hoping to include was a long conversation between an older American novelist and a younger American novelist. The magazine had already contacted Styron, and he proposed Renzo as the younger writer he would like to talk to. An editor called Renzo, who was deep into a novel at the time (as usual), and when he told her he was too busy to accept—tremendously flattered by Styron's offer, but too busy—the woman was so shocked by his refusal that she threatened to kill herself, *Je me suicide!,* but Renzo merely laughed, telling her that no one commits suicide over such a trivial matter and she would feel better in the morning. He didn't know Styron well, had met him only once or twice, but he had his number, and after the conversation with the suicidal editor, he called Styron to thank him for suggesting his name, but he wanted him to know that he was hard at work on a novel and had turned down the invitation. He hoped Styron would understand. Completely, Styron said. In fact, that's why he'd suggested Renzo in the first place. He didn't want to do the conversation either, and he was fairly certain, more or less convinced, that Renzo would say no to them and get him off the hook. Thanks, Renzo, he said, you've done me a great favor. Laughter. You and Renzo both cracked up over Styron's remark, and then Renzo said: "Such a polite man, so well mannered. He simply didn't have the heart to turn the editor down, so he used me to do it for him. On the other hand, what would have happened if I had said yes? I suspect he would have pretended to be thrilled, delighted that the two of us would be given a chance to sit down together and shoot our mouths off about the state of the world. That's the way he was. A good person. The last thing he wanted was to hurt anyone's feelings." From Styron's goodness, the two of you went on to talk about the PEN campaign in support of Liu Xiaobo. A large petition signed by writers from all over the world was published on January 20, and PEN is planning to honor him in absentia at its annual fund-raising dinner in April. You will be there, of course, since you never fail to attend that dinner, but the situation looks bleak, and you have little hope that giving Liu Xiaobo a prize in New York will have any effect on his status in Beijing—detained man, no doubt soon-to-be arrested man. According to Renzo, a young woman who works at PEN lives in the same house where the boy is camped out in Brooklyn. A small world, no? Yes, Renzo, a small world indeed.

February 7. You have met with the boy twice more since your reunion on January twenty-sixth. The first time, you went to *Happy Days* together (courtesy of Mary-Lee, who had two tickets waiting for you at the box office), watched the play in a kind of stunned rapture (Mary-Lee was brilliant), and then went to her dressing room after the performance, where she assaulted you both with wild, ebullient kisses. The ecstasy of acting before a live audience, a superabundance of adrenaline coursing through her body, her eyes on fire. The boy looked inordinately pleased, especially at the moment when you and his mother embraced. Later on, you realized that this was probably the first time in his life he had seen this happen. He understands that the war is over now, that the combatants have long since put down their arms and beaten their swords into plowshares. Afterward, dinner with Korngold and Lady Swann in a small restaurant off Union Square. The boy said little but was extremely attentive. Some astute remarks about the play, parsing the opening line of the second act, *Hail, holy light,* and why Beckett chose to refer to Milton at that point, the irony of those words in the context of a world of everlasting day, since light cannot be holy except as an antidote to darkness. His mother's eyes looking at him while he spoke, glistening with adoration. Mary-Lee, the queen of excess, the Madonna of naked feelings, and yet you sat there watching her with a twinge of envy—somewhat amused, yes, but also asking yourself why you continue to hold back. You felt more at ease in the boy's presence that second time. Getting used to him again, perhaps, but still not ready to warm up to him. The next encounter was more intimate. Dinner at Joe Junior's tonight for old times' sake, just the two of you, chomping on greasy hamburgers and soggy fries, and mostly you talked about baseball, reminding you of numerous conversations you had with your own father, that passionate but wholly neutral subject, safe ground as it were, but then he brought up Herb Score's death and told you how badly he'd wanted to call you that day and talk about it, the pitcher whose career was ruined by the same kind of injury that knocked down your father, the grandfather he never met, but then he decided that a long-distance call was inappropriate, and how odd that his first contact with you ended up being by telephone anyway, the calls between Brooklyn and Exeter when you were in the hospital, and how afraid he was that he would never see you again. You took him back to Downing Street after dinner, and it was there, in the living room of the old apartment, that he suddenly broke down and wept. He and Bobby were fighting that day, he said, out on the hot road all those years ago, and just before the car came, he pushed Bobby, pushed the smaller Bobby hard enough to make him fall down, and that was why he was run over and killed. You listened in silence. No words were available to you anymore. All the years of not knowing, and now this, the sheer banality of it, an adolescent spat between stepbrothers, and all the damage that ensued from that push. So many things became clearer to you after the boy's confession. His savage withdrawal into himself, the escape from his own life, the punishing blue-collar jobs as a form of penance, more than a decade in hell because of one moment of anger. Can he be forgiven? You couldn't get the words out of your mouth tonight, but at least you had the sense to take him in your arms and hold him. More to the point: is there anything that needs to be forgiven? Probably not. But still, he must be forgiven.

February 8. The Sunday phone conversation with Willa. She is worried about your health, wonders how you are holding up, asks if it wouldn't be better if she quit her job and came home to take care of you. You laugh at the thought of your diligent, hardworking wife telling the university administrators: "So long, fellas, my man's got a tummy ache, gotta be going, and fuck the students I'm teaching, by the way, they can bloody well teach themselves." Willa giggles as you present that scene to her, and it is the first good laugh you have heard from her in some time, the best laugh in many months. You tell her about seeing the boy for dinner last night, but she is unresponsive, asks no questions, a small grunt to let you know she is listening but nothing more than that, and yet you forge on anyway, remarking that the boy finally seems to be coming into his own. Another grunt. Needless to say, you do not bring up the confession. A little pause, and then she tells you that at last she is feeling strong enough to return to her book, which is another good sign in your opinion, and then you tell her that Renzo sends his love, that you send your love, and you are covering her body with a thousand kisses. The conversation ends. Not a bad conversation, all in all, but after you hang up, you wander around the apartment feeling you have been stranded in the middle of nowhere. The boy has asked many questions about Willa, but you still haven't found the courage to tell him that she has *cut him out of her heart*. The Can Man dresses in a suit and tie now. The Can Man goes to work, pays his bills, and has become a model citizen. But the Can Man is still touched in the head, and on nights when the world closes in on him, he still gets down on his hands and knees and howls at the moon.

March 15. You have seen the boy six more times since the last entry about him on February seventh. A visit to the Hospital for Broken Things one Saturday afternoon, where you watched him framing pictures and asked yourself if this is all he aspires to, if he will be content to knock around from one odd job to another until he becomes an old man. You don't push him into making decisions, however. You leave him alone and wait to see what will happen next, although you are privately hoping he will return to college next fall and finish up his degree, which is something he still mentions from time to time. Another dinner foursome with Korngold and La Swann on a Monday night, when the theater was dark. A night out at the movies together to see Bresson's old masterpiece *A Man Escaped*. A midweek lunch, preceded by a visit to the office, where you showed him around and introduced him to your little band of stalwarts, and the mad thought that rushed through your head that afternoon, wondering if a boy with

his intelligence and interest in books might not find a place
for himself in publishing, as an employee of Heller Books,
for example, where he could be groomed as his father's suc-
cessor, but one mustn't dream too much, thoughts of that
kind can plant poisonous seeds in one's head, and it is best
to refrain from writing another person's future, especially
if that person is your son. A dinner with Renzo near his
house in Park Slope, the godfather in good spirits that
night, embarked on yet another novel, and no more talk of
slumps and doldrums and extinguished flames. And then
the visit out to the house where he is living, a chance to see
the Sunset Park Four in action. A sad little run-down place,
but you enjoyed seeing his friends, Bing most of all, of
course, who appears to be flourishing, as well as the two
girls, Alice, the one who works at PEN, who talked with
great intensity about the Liu Xiaobo case and then asked
you a number of probing questions about your parents'
generation, the young men and women of World War II,
and Ellen, so meek and pretty, who late in the evening
showed you a sketchbook filled with some of the raunchiest
erotic drawings you have ever seen, which made you stop
and wonder—just for an instant—if you couldn't rescue
your company by introducing a new line of pornographic
art books. They have already been served with two eviction
notices, and you expressed your concern that they were
pushing their luck and could wind up in a dangerous spot,
but Bing slammed his fist down on the table and said they
were holding out to the bitter end, and you didn't press

your argument any further, since it is not your business to tell them what to do, they are all grown people (more or less) and are perfectly capable of making their own decisions, even if they are the wrong ones. Six more times, and little by little you and the boy have grown closer. He has been opening up to you now, and on one of the nights when you were alone with him, after the Bresson film most likely, he told you the full story about the girl, Pilar Sanchez, and why he had to run away from Florida. To be perfectly honest, you were appalled when he told you how young she is, but after you had thought about it for a moment, you realized that it made sense for him to be in love with someone that age, for the boy's life has been stunted, cut off from its proper and natural development, and although he looks like a full-grown man, his inner self is stuck somewhere around eighteen or nineteen. There was a moment back in January when he was afraid he was going to lose her, he said, there was a terrible flare-up, their first serious argument, and he claimed it was largely his fault, entirely his fault, since when they first met and he still had no idea how important she would become to him, he had lied to her about his family, telling her that his parents were dead, that he had no brother, had never had a brother, and now that he had come back to his parents, he wanted her to know the truth, and when he did tell her the truth, she was so angry at him for having lied to her, she hung up the phone. A week of battles followed, and she was right to feel burned, he said, he had let her down, she had lost faith in him, and it was only when he asked her to marry him that she began to soften, to understand that he would never let her down again. Marriage! Engaged to a girl not yet out of high school! Wait until you meet her next month, the boy said. And you replied, as calmly as you could, that you were looking forward to it very much.

March 29. The Sunday phone conversation with Willa. You finally tell her about the boy's confession, not knowing if this will help matters or make them worse. It is too much for her to take in all at once, and therefore her reaction evolves through several distinct stages over the minutes that follow. First: total silence, a silence that lasts long enough for you to feel compelled to repeat what you have just told her. Second: a soft voice saying "This is horrible, this is too much to bear, how can it be true?" Third: sobbing, as her mind travels back to the road and she fills in the missing parts of the picture, imagines the fight between the boys, sees Bobby being crushed all over again. Fourth: growing anger. "He lied to us," she says, "he betrayed us with his lies," and you answer her by saying that he didn't lie, he simply didn't speak, he was too traumatized by his guilt to speak, and living with that guilt has nearly destroyed him. "He killed my son," she says, and you answer her by saying that he pushed her son into the road and that her son's death was an accident. The two of you go on talking for more than an hour, and again and again you tell her you love her, that no matter what she decides or how she chooses to deal with the boy, you will always love her. She breaks down again, finally putting herself in the boy's shoes, finally telling you that she understands how much he has suffered, but she doesn't know if understanding is enough, it isn't clear to her what she wants to do, she isn't certain if she will have the strength to face him again. She needs time, she says, more time to think it over, and you tell her there is no rush, you will never force her to do anything she doesn't want to do. The conversation ends, and once again you feel you have been stranded in the middle of nowhere. By late afternoon, you have begun to resign yourself to the fact that nowhere is your home now and that is where you will be spending the last years of your life.

April 12. She reminds you of someone you know, but you can't put your finger on who that person is, and then, five or six minutes after you are introduced to her, she laughs for the first time, and you know beyond a shadow of a doubt that the person is Suki Rothstein. Suki Rothstein in the incandescent sunlight of that late afternoon on Houston Street nearly seven years ago, laughing with her friends, decked out in her bright red dress, the promise of youth in its fullest, most glorious incarnation. Pilar Sanchez is the twin of Suki Rothstein, a small luminescent being who carries the flame of life within her, and may the gods be more gentle with her than they were with the doomed child of your friends. She arrived from Florida early Saturday evening, and the next day, Easter Sunday, she and the boy came to the apartment on Downing Street. The boy had trouble keeping his hands off her, and even as they sat side by side on the sofa talking to you in your comfortable chair, he was kissing her neck, stroking her bare knee, putting his arm around her shoulder. You had already seen her, of course, almost a year ago in that little park in southern Florida, you were a clandestine witness to their first encounter, their first conversation, but you were too far away from her to look into her eyes and see the power that is in them, the dark steady eyes that absorb everything around her, that emit the light that has made the boy fall in love with her. They came with good news, the boy said, the best news, and a moment later you were told that Pilar had been accepted at Barnard with a full scholarship and will be coming to live in New York immediately after her high school graduation in June. You told her that your wife went to Barnard as well, that you saw her for the first time when she was a Barnard student, and the torch has now been passed from the boy's stepmother to her. And then (you almost fell out of your chair when you heard this) the boy announced that he has enrolled in the School of General Studies at Columbia and will start the final leg toward his B.A. in the fall. You asked him how he was going to pay for it, and he said he has some money in the bank and will cover the rest by applying for a student loan. You were impressed that he didn't ask for your help, even though you would be willing to give it, but you know it is better for his morale to take on this burden himself. As the talk continued, you realized that you were becoming more and more happy, that you were happier today than you have been at any time in the past thirteen years, and you wanted to drink in this happiness, to become drunk on this happiness, and it occurred to you that no matter what Willa decides concerning the boy, you will be able to tolerate a split life with the two people you care about most in the world, that you will take your pleasures wherever and whenever you can find them. You booked a table for dinner at the Waverly Inn, that venerable establishment from the old New York, the New York that no longer exists, thinking Pilar would enjoy going to such a place, and she did enjoy it, she actually said she felt she was in heaven, and as the three of you packed away your Easter dinner, the girl was full of questions, she wanted to know everything about running a publishing house, how you met Renzo Michaelson, how you decide whether to accept a book or not, and as you answered her questions, you understood that she was listening to you with intense concentration, that she would not forget a word you had said. At one point, the talk drifted onto math and science, and you found yourself listening to a discussion about quantum physics, a subject that you freely admitted escapes you entirely, and then Pilar turned to you and said: "Think of it this way, Mr. Heller. In the old physics, three times two equals six and two times three equals six are reversible propositions. Not in quantum physics. Three times two and two times three are two different matters, distinct and separate propositions." There are many things in this world for you to worry about, but the boy's love for this girl is not one of them.

April 13. You wake up this morning to the news that Mark Fidrych is dead. Just fifty-four years old, killed on his farm in Northborough, Massachusetts, when the dump truck he was repairing collapsed on top of him. First Herb Score, and now Mark Fidrych, the two cursed geniuses who dazzled the country for a few days, a few months, and then vanished from sight. You remember your father's old refrain: Poor Herb Score. Now you add another casualty to the roster of the fallen: Mark Fidrych. May the Bird rest in peace.

Alice Bergstrom and Ellen Brice

It is Thursday, April thirtieth, and Alice has just completed another five-hour stint at the PEN American Center. Breaking from her established routine of the past several months, she will not be rushing home to Sunset Park to work on her dissertation. Instead, she is on her way to meet Ellen, who has Thursdays off, and the two of them will be splurging on a late lunch at Balthazar, the French brasserie on Spring Street in SoHo, less than a two-minute walk from the PEN offices at 588 Broadway. Yesterday, another court order was delivered to the house by yet another New York City marshal, bringing the total number of eviction notices they have received to four, and earlier in the month, when the third notice arrived, she and Ellen agreed that the next warning would be the last one, that they would turn in their squatters' badges at that point and move on, reluctantly move on. That is why they have arranged to meet in Manhattan this afternoon—to talk things over and figure out what to do next, calmly and thoughtfully, in an environment far from Bing and his aggressive, hotheaded pronouncements, and what better place for a calm and thoughtful discussion than this pricey,

[286]

elegant restaurant during the quiet interlude between lunch and dinner?

Jake is out of the picture now. The showdown she was preparing herself for when last seen on January fifth finally took place in mid-February, and the hurtful thing about that last conversation was how quickly he assented to her reading of their present circumstances, how little resistance he mounted to the idea of going their separate ways, calling it quits. Something was wrong with him, he said, but it was true that he no longer felt excited when he was with her, that he no longer looked forward to seeing her, and he blamed himself for this shift in his feelings and frankly could not understand what had happened to him. He told her that she was a remarkable person, with numerous outstanding qualities—intelligence, compassion, wisdom— and that he was a damaged soul incapable of loving her in the way she deserved to be loved. He did not explore the problem more deeply than that, did not, for example, delve into the reasons why he had lost interest in her sexually, but that would have been too much to hope for, she realized, since he openly admitted that these changes confused him just as much as they confused her. She asked him if he had ever thought about psychotherapy, and he said yes, he was considering it, his life was in a shambles and there was no question that he needed help. Alice sensed that he was telling her the truth, but she wasn't entirely certain of it, and whenever she replays that conversation in her mind now, she wonders if his passive, self-accusatory position was not simply the easiest way out for him, a lie to mask the fact that he had fallen for someone else. But which someone else? She doesn't know, and in the two and a half months since she last saw him, none of their mutual friends has talked to her about a new person in connection with Jake. It could be that there is no one—or else his love life has become a well-guarded secret. One way or the other, she misses him. Now that he is gone, she tends to recall the good moments they had together and ignore the difficult ones, and oddly enough, what she finds herself missing most about him are the occasional jags of humor that would pour out of him at unpredictable moments, the moments when the distinctly unhumorous Jake Baum would drop his defenses and begin impersonating various comical figures, mostly ones who spoke with heavy foreign accents, Russians, Indians, Kore-ans, and he was surprisingly good at this, he always got the voices just right, but that was the old Jake, of course, the Jake of a year ago, and the truth is that it had been a long time since he had made her laugh by turning himself into one of those funny characters. *Meese Aleece. Keese mee, Meese Aleece.* She doubts that another man will come along anytime soon, and this worries her, since she is thirty years old now, and the prospect of a childless future fills her with dread.

Her weight is down, however, more from lack of appe-tite than from scrupulous dieting, but one fifty-four is a decent number for her, and she has stopped thinking of herself as a repulsive cow—that is, whenever she thinks

about her body, which seems to happen less often now that
Jake is gone and there is no one to touch her anymore. Her
dissertation stalled for about two weeks after his departure, but then she pulled herself together and has been
working hard ever since, so hard, in fact, that she is well
into the concluding chapter now and feels she can finish
off the first draft in approximately ten days. For the past
three years, the dissertation has been an end in itself, the
mountain she set out to climb, but she has rarely thought
about what would happen to her after she reached the
top. If and when she did think about it, she complacently
assumed the next step would be to apply for a teaching
position somewhere. That's why you spend all those years
struggling to get your Ph.D., isn't it? They give you your
doctorate, and then you go out and teach. But now that the
end is in sight, she has been reexamining the question,
and it is by no means certain anymore that teaching is the
answer. She is still inclined to give it a shot, but after her
less than happy experience as an adjunct last year, she wonders if toiling in some English department for the next
four decades will be fulfilling enough to sustain her. Other
possibilities have occurred to her in the past month or so.
A bigger, more demanding job at PEN, for example. That
work has engaged her far more than she thought it would,
and she doesn't want to give it up, which she would be
forced to do if she landed a post in an English department—
which, by the by, would most likely be at a college eight
hundred miles to the south or west of New York. That's

the problem, she says to herself, as she pulls open the door of the restaurant and walks in, not the job but the place. She doesn't want to leave New York. She wants to go on living in this immense, unlivable city for as long as she can, and after all these years, the thought of living anywhere else strikes her as insane.

Ellen is already there, sitting at one of the tables along the eastern wall of the restaurant, nursing a glass of white wine as she waits for her friend to show up. Ellen knows more about what Alice's ex-lover has been up to for the past few months than Alice does, but Ellen hasn't said anything to Alice about these goings-on because she promised Bing to keep them a secret, and Ellen is not someone who breaks her word. Bing has continued posing for her once or twice a week throughout the first four months of the year, and many walls have come down between them in that time, all walls in fact, and they have shared confidences with each other that neither one of them would have been willing to share with anyone else. Ellen knows about Bing's infatuation with Miles, for example, and she knows about his anxieties concerning the man-woman problem, the man-man problem, and his doubts about who and what he is. She knows that sometime in late January Bing ventured up to Jake's small apartment in Manhattan and, with the aid of abundant quantities of alcohol and a guarantee to contact Renzo Michaelson about the interview Jake so earnestly wished to conduct with him, managed to seduce Alice's ex-amour into a sexual encounter.

That was Bing's first and last experiment in self-discovery, since he found little or no pleasure in Jake Baum's arms, mouth, or private parts, and grudgingly had to admit that while he was still deeply attracted to Miles, he had no interest in making love to men, not even to Miles. Jake, on the other hand, much as Bing had suspected, had been through a number of male-male experiences as an adolescent, and on the strength of his encounter with Bing, which brought him much pleasure, he realized that his interest in men had not waned with the years as he supposed it had. Two weeks later, when Alice forced him into the showdown, he quietly bowed out of their affair to pursue that other interest. Ellen knows about this because Jake and Bing are still in touch. Jake has told Bing about what he has been doing, Bing has passed along this information to Ellen, and Ellen has kept silent. Alice doesn't know it, but she is much better off without Jake, and if Ellen has any knowledge or understanding of the world, it won't be long before Alice finds herself another man.

This is the new Ellen, the Ellen Brice who last month overhauled the outward trappings of her person in order to express the new relation she has developed with her body, which is a product of the new relation she has developed with her heart, which in turn is a product of the new relation she has developed with her innermost self. In one bold, decisive week in the middle of March, she had her long, stringy hair cut into a short 1920s bob, threw out every article of clothing in her bureau and closet, and began adorning her face with lipstick, rouge, eyeliner, eye shadow, and mascara every time she left the house, so that the woman described in Morris Heller's journal as *meek*, the woman who for years inspired feelings of compassion and protectiveness in those who knew her, no longer projects an aura of victimhood and skittish uncertainty, and as she sits on the banquette along the eastern wall of Balthazar dressed in a black leather miniskirt and a tight cashmere sweater, sipping her white wine and watching Alice come through the door, heads turn when people walk past her, and she exults in the attention she receives, exults in the knowledge that she is the most desirable woman in the room. This revolution in her appearance was inspired by an unlikely event that occurred in February, just one week after Alice and Jake put an end to their tottering romance, when none other than Benjamin Samuels, the high school boy who impregnated Ellen nearly nine years ago in the pavilion of his parents' summer house in southern Vermont, walked into the real estate office where Ellen works, looking for an apartment to rent in Park Slope or one of its adjacent neighborhoods, a twenty-five-year-old Benjamin Samuels, fully grown now and employed as a cell phone salesman in a T-Mobile store on Seventh Avenue, a college dropout, a young man devoid of the intellectual skills required to pursue one of the professions, law or medicine, say, which his parents once hoped would be his destiny, but just as handsome as ever, more handsome than ever, the beautiful boy with the beautiful soccer player's body now

ripened into a large beautiful man. He didn't recognize
Ellen at first, and although she suspected that the broad-
shouldered fellow sitting across from her was the matured
incarnation of the boy she had given herself to so many
years earlier, she waited until he had filled in the blanks on
the rental application form before she announced who she
was. She spoke quietly and tentatively, not knowing if he
would be pleased or displeased, not knowing if he would
even remember her, but Ben Samuels did remember her,
and Ben Samuels was pleased to have found her again, so
pleased that he stood up from his chair, walked around to
the other side of Ellen's desk, and put his arms around her
in a great welcoming hug. They spent the afternoon walking in and out of empty apartments together, kissing in
the first apartment, making love in the second apartment,
and now that Ben Samuels has moved into the neighborhood, he and Ellen have continued making love nearly
every day. That is why Ellen cut her hair—because Ben is
aroused by the back of her neck—and once she cut her hair,
she understood that he would be even more aroused by her
if she started wearing different, more alluring clothes.
Until now, she has kept Ben a secret from Alice, Bing, and
Miles, but with so many changes suddenly afoot, the fourth
court order, the imminent dispersal of their little gang,
she has decided that this is the day she will tell Alice about
the extraordinary thing that has happened to her.

Alice is kissing her on the cheek now and smiling her
Alice smile, and as Ellen watches her friend sit down in

the chair facing the banquette, she wonders if she will ever be good enough to do a drawing that would fully capture that smile, which is the warmest, most luminous smile on earth, a smile that sets Alice apart from every other person she knows, has known, or will ever know until the end of her life.

Well, kid, Alice says, I guess the grand experiment is over.

For us, maybe, Ellen says, but not for Bing and Miles.

Miles is going back to Florida in three weeks.

I forgot. Bing alone, then. How sad.

I'm thinking ten more days. If I work hard, I should be able to finish the last chapter by then. Is that okay with you, or would you rather pull out now?

I don't ever want to pull out. It's just that I'm getting scared. If the cops show up, they'll toss our stuff out onto the street, things could get broken, Bing could go crazy, all sorts of unpleasant possibilities come to mind. Ten days is too long, Alice. I think you should start looking for a new place tomorrow.

How many rentals do you have?

Plenty in the Slope, not so many in Sunset Park.

But Sunset Park is cheaper, which means that Sunset Park is better.

How much can you afford to pay?

As little as the market will bear.

I'll check the listings after lunch and let you know what we have.

But maybe you've had enough of Sunset Park. If you want to go somewhere else, I have no problem with that. As long as I can pay my half of the rent, anywhere is fine.

Dear Alice . . .

What?

I hadn't realized you wanted to share.

Don't you?

In principle, yes, but something has come up, and I'm considering other options.

Options?

One option.

Oh?

He's called Benjamin Samuels, and he's asked me to move in with him.

You little devil. How long as this been going on?

A couple of months.

A couple of months? What's gotten into you? A couple of months, and you never even told me.

I wasn't sure enough to tell anyone. I thought it might be just a sex thing that would flame out before it was worth mentioning. But it seems to be getting bigger. Big enough for me to want to give it a try, I think.

Are you in love with him?

I don't know. But I'm crazy about him, that much I do know. And the sex is pretty sensational.

Who is he?

The one.

What one?

The one from the summer of two thousand.

The man who got you pregnant?

The boy who got me pregnant.

So, the story finally comes out . . .

He was sixteen, and I was twenty. Now he's twenty-five, and I'm twenty-nine. Those four years are a lot less important today than they were back then.

Christ. I thought it might have been the father, but never the son.

That's why I couldn't talk about it. He was too young, and I didn't want to get him into trouble.

Did he ever know what happened?

Not then, no, and not now either. There's no point in telling him, is there?

Twenty-five years old. And what does he do with himself?

Nothing much. He has a dreary little job, and he isn't terribly bright. But he adores me, Alice, and no one has ever treated me better. We fuck during our lunch break every afternoon in his apartment on Fifth Street. He turns me inside out. I swoon when he touches me. I can't get enough of his body. I feel I might be going mad, and then I wake up in the morning and realize that I'm happy, happier than I've been in a long, long time.

Good for you, El.

Yes, good for me. Who ever would have thought?

Miles Heller

On Saturday, May second, he reads in the morning paper that Jack Lohrke is dead at the age of eighty-five. The short obituary recounts the three miraculous escapes from certain death—the felled comrades in the Battle of the Bulge, the crashed airplane after the war, the bus that toppled into the ravine—but it is a skimpy article, a perfunctory article, which glides over Lucky's undistinguished major league career with the Giants and Phillies and mentions only one detail Miles was not aware of: in the most celebrated game of the twentieth century, the final round of the National League championship play-off between the Giants and the Dodgers in 1951, Don Mueller, the Giants' right fielder, broke his ankle sliding into third base in the last inning, and if the Giants had tied the score rather than win the game with a walk-off home run, Lohrke would have taken over for Mueller in the next inning, but Branca threw the pitch, Thomson hit the pitch, and the game ended before Lucky could get his name in the box score. The young Willie Mays on deck, Lucky Lohrke warming up to replace Mueller in right field, and then Thomson clobbered the final pitch of the season over the left-field wall, and the Giants

won the pennant, the Giants won the pennant. The obituary says nothing about Jack "Lucky" Lohrke's private life,
not a single word about marriage or children or grandchil-
dren, no information about the people he might have loved
or the people who might have loved him, simply the dull
and insignificant fact that the patron saint of good fortune
worked in security at Lockheed after he retired from baseball.

The instant he finishes reading the obituary, he calls
the apartment on Downing Street to commiserate with his
father over the death of the man they discussed so often
during the years of their own good fortune, the years before
anyone knew about roads in the Berkshires, the years
before anyone was buried or anyone else ran away, and his
father has of course read the paper over his morning coffee and knows about Lucky's departure from this world. A
bad stretch, his father says. First Herb Score in November, then Mark Fidrych in April, and now this. Miles says
he regrets they never wrote a letter to Jack Lohrke to tell
him what an important figure he was in their family, and
his father says, yes, that was a stupid oversight, why didn't
they think of that years ago? Miles answers that maybe it
was because they assumed their man would live forever,
and his father laughs, saying that Jack Lohrke wasn't
immortal, just lucky, and even if they considered him
their patron saint, he mustn't forget that saints die too.

The worst of it is behind him now. Just twenty days

before he is released from prison, then back to Florida until Pilar finishes school, and after that New York again, where they will spend the early part of the summer looking for a place to live uptown. In an astounding act of generosity, his father has offered to let them stay with him on Downing Street until they find their own apartment, which means that Pilar will never have to spend another night in the house in Sunset Park, which scared her even before the eviction notices started coming and now puts her in a full-blown panic. How much longer before the cops come to throw them out? Alice and Ellen have already made up their minds to decamp, and even though Bing went into a rage when they announced their decision at dinner two nights ago, they both held their ground, and Miles believes their position is the only sensible one to take anymore. They will be moving out the minute Ellen manages to find Alice an affordable replacement, which is likely to happen by the middle of next week, and if his circumstances were similar to theirs, he would be on his way out as well. Just twenty days, however, and in the meantime he must not abandon Bing, not when the venture is falling apart, not when Bing so desperately needs him to be here, and therefore he intends to stay put until the twenty-second and prays that no cops show up before then.

He wants those twenty days, but he does not get them. He gets the day and the night of the second, the day and the night of the third, and early in the morning on the fourth, there is a loud knock on the front door. Miles is fast asleep in his downstairs bedroom behind the kitchen, and by the time he wakes up and slips into his clothes, the house has already been invaded. He hears the tread of heavy footsteps clomping up the stairs, he hears Bing shouting angrily at the top of his voice (*Get your fucking hands off me!*), he hears Alice shrieking at someone to back off and leave her computer alone, and he hears the cops yelling (*Clear out! Clear out!*), how many cops he doesn't know, he thinks two, but there could be three, and by the time he opens the door of his room, walks across the kitchen, and reaches the entrance hall, the commotion upstairs has turned into a clamorous roar. He glances to his right, sees that the front door is open, and there is Ellen, standing on the porch with her hand over her mouth, her eyes wide with fear, with horror, and then he looks to his left, fixing his eyes on the staircase, at the top of which he sees Alice, large Alice trying to wrestle herself out of the arms of an enormous cop, and just then, as he continues looking up, he sees Bing on the top landing as well, his wrists shackled in handcuffs as a second enormous cop holds him by the hair with one hand and jabs a nightstick into his back with the other, and just when he is about to turn around and run out of the house, he sees the first enormous cop push Alice down the stairs, and as Alice tumbles toward him, cracking the side of her head against a wooden step, the enormous cop who pushed her races down the stairs, and before Miles can pause to think about what he is doing, he is punching that enormous cop in the jaw with his clenched fist, and as the cop falls down from the blow, Miles turns around, rushes out of the house, finds Ellen standing on the porch, takes hold of her right hand with his left hand, drags her down the front steps with him, and the two of them begin to run.

An entrance to Green-Wood Cemetery is just around the corner, and that is where they go, not certain if they are being chased or not, but Miles thinks that if there were two cops in the house and not three, then the uninjured cop would be tending to the cop he punched in the jaw, which would mean that no one is pursuing them. Still, they run for as long as they can, and when Ellen is out of breath and can go no farther, they flop down on the grass for a spell, leaning their backs against the headstone of a man named Charles Everett Brown, 1858–1927. Miles's hand is in terrific pain, and he fears it might be broken. Ellen wants to take him to the emergency room for X-rays, but Miles says no, that would be too dangerous, he must keep himself hidden. He has assaulted a police officer and that is a crime, a serious offense, and even if he hopes the bastard's jaw is broken, even if he feels no regret about smashing in the face of someone who threw a woman down a flight of stairs, Alice Bergstrom no less, the best woman in the world, there is no question that he is in bad trouble, the worst trouble he has ever known.

He doesn't have his cell phone, she doesn't have her cell phone. They are sitting on the grass in the cemetery with no way to reach anyone, no way to know if Bing has been arrested or not, no way to know if Alice has been hurt or not, and for the time being Miles is still too stunned to have formulated a plan about what to do next. Ellen tells him that she woke early as usual, six-fifteen or six-thirty, and that she was standing on the porch with her coffee when the cops arrived. She was the one who opened the door and let them in. What choice did she have but to open the door and let them in? They went upstairs, there were two of them, and she remained on the porch as the two cops went upstairs, and then all hell broke loose, she saw nothing, she was still standing on the porch, but Bing and Alice were both shouting, the two cops were shouting, everyone was shouting, Bing must have resisted, he must have started fighting, and no doubt Alice was afraid they would push her out before she could gather up her papers and books and films and computer, the computer in which her entire dissertation is stored, three years of work in one small machine, and no doubt that was why she snapped and started struggling with the cop, Alice's dissertation, Bing's drums, and all her drawings of the past five months, hundreds and hundreds of drawings, and all of it still in the house, in the house that is no doubt sealed up now, off-limits, and everything gone forever now. She wants to cry, she says, but she is unable to cry, she is too angry to cry, there was no need for all that pushing and shoving, why couldn't the cops have behaved like men instead of animals, and no, she can't cry even if she wants to, but please, Miles, she says, put your arms

around me, hold me, Miles, I need someone to hold me, and
Miles puts his arms around Ellen and strokes her head.

They have to do something about his hand. It is swelling now, the area around the knuckles looks bloated and
blue, and even if no bones are broken (he has discovered
that he can wiggle his fingers a bit without increasing the
pain), the hand must be iced to bring down the swelling.
Hematoma. He thinks that is the word he is looking for—
localized swelling filled with blood, a small lake of blood
sloshing around just under the skin. They must ice the
hand, and they also must eat something. They have been
sitting on the grass in the cemetery for close to two hours
now, and they are both hungry, although it is far from certain that either one of them would be able to eat if food
were set before them. They stand up and begin walking,
moving quickly past the tombs and mausoleums in the
direction of Windsor Terrace and Park Slope, the Twenty-
fifth Street entrance to the cemetery, the exit from the
cemetery, and once they reach Seventh Avenue, they go on
walking all the way to Sixth Street. Ellen tells Miles to
wait outside for her, and then she goes into a T-Mobile cell
phone store to talk to her new boyfriend, her old boyfriend, it's a complicated story, and a few moments later,
she is unlocking the door to Ben Samuels's apartment on
Fifth Street between Sixth and Seventh Avenues.

They can't stay here for long, she says, just a few hours,
she doesn't want Ben to get involved in this, but at least it's
something, a chance for a breather until they can figure out

what to do next. They wash up, Ellen makes them cheese sandwiches, and then she fills a plastic bag with ice cubes and hands it to Miles. He wants to call Pilar, but it is too early, she is at school now, and she doesn't switch on her phone until she returns to the apartment at four o'clock. Where do we go from here? Ellen asks. Miles thinks for a moment, and then he remembers that his godfather lives nearby, just a few blocks from where they are sitting, but when he calls Renzo's number, no one picks up, it is the answering machine that talks to him, and he knows that Renzo is either working or out of town and therefore does not bother to leave a message. There is no one left except his father, but just as Ellen is reluctant to involve her friend, he balks at the idea of dragging his father into this mess, his father is the last person in the world he wants to turn to for help now.

As if she is able to read his thoughts, Ellen says: You have to call your father, Miles.

He shakes his head. Impossible, he says. I've already put that man through enough.

If you won't do it, Ellen says, then I will.

Please, Ellen. Leave him alone.

But Ellen insists, and a moment later she is dialing the number of Heller Books in Manhattan. Miles is so upset by what she is doing that he walks out of the kitchen and locks himself in the bathroom. He can't bear to listen, he refuses to listen. He would rather stab himself in the heart than listen to Ellen talk to his father.

Time passes, how much time he doesn't know, three minutes, eight minutes, two hours, and then Ellen is knocking on the door, telling him to come out, telling him that his father knows everything about what happened in Sunset Park this morning, that his father is waiting for him on the other end of the line. He unlocks the door, sees that Ellen's eyes are rimmed with tears, gently touches her face with his left hand, and walks into the kitchen.

His father's voice says: Two detectives came to the office about an hour ago. They say you broke a policeman's jaw. Is that true?

He pushed Alice down the stairs, Miles says. I lost my temper.

Bing is in jail for resisting arrest. Alice is in the hospital with a concussion.

How bad is it?

She's awake, her head hurts, but no permanent damage. They'll probably let her out tomorrow morning.

To go where? She doesn't have a place to live anymore. She's homeless. We're all homeless now.

I want you to turn yourself in, Miles.

No chance. They'd lock me up for years.

Extenuating circumstances. Police brutality. First offense. I doubt you'd serve any time.

It's their word against ours. The cop will say Alice tripped and fell, and the jury will believe him. We're just a bunch of illegal trespassers, squatters, freeloading bums.

You don't want to spend the rest of your life running

from the police, do you? You've already done enough running. Time to stand up and face the music, Miles. And I'll stand up there with you.

You can't. You have a good heart, Dad, but I'm in this thing alone.

No, you're not. You'll have a lawyer. And I know some damned good ones. Everything is going to be all right, believe me.

I'm so sorry. So fucking, terribly sorry.

Listen to me, Miles. Talking on the phone is no good. We have to hash it out in person, face to face. The minute I hang up, I'll go straight home. Get yourself into a taxi and meet me there as soon as you can. All right?

All right.

You promise?

Yes, I promise.

Half an hour later, he is sitting in the backseat of a car-service Dodge, on his way to Downing Street in Manhattan. Ellen has gone to the bank for him with his ATM card and returned with a thousand dollars in cash, they have kissed and said good-bye, and as the car moves through the heavy traffic toward the Brooklyn Bridge, he wonders how long it will be before he sees Ellen Brice again. He wishes he could go to the hospital to see Alice, but he knows he can't. He wishes he could go to the jail where Bing is locked up, but he knows he can't. He presses the ice against his swollen hand, and as he looks at the hand, he thinks about the soldier with the missing hands in the movie he saw with Alice and Pilar last winter, the young soldier home from the war, unable to undress himself and go to bed without his father's help, and he feels he has become that boy now, who can do nothing without his father's help, a boy without hands, a boy who should be without hands, a boy whose hands have brought him nothing but trouble in his life, his angry punching hands, his angry pushing hands, and then the name of the soldier in the movie comes back to him, Homer, Homer Something, Homer as in the poet Homer, who wrote the scene about Odysseus and Telemachus, father and son reunited after so many years, in the same way he and his father have been reunited, and the name Homer makes him think of home, as in the word *homeless*, they are all homeless now, he said that to his father on the phone, Alice and Bing are homeless, he is homeless, the people in Florida who lived in the houses he trashed out are homeless, only Pilar is not homeless, he is her home now, and with one punch he has destroyed everything, they will never have their life together in New York, there is no future for them anymore, no hope for them anymore, and even if he runs away to Florida to be with her now, there will be no hope for them, and even if he stays in New York to fight it out in court, there will be no hope for them, he has let his father down, let Pilar down, let everyone down, and as the car travels across the Brooklyn Bridge and he looks at the immense buildings on the other side of the East River, he thinks about the missing buildings, the collapsed and

burning buildings that no longer exist, the missing buildings and the missing hands, and he wonders if it is worth
hoping for a future when there is no future, and from now
on, he tells himself, he will stop hoping for anything and
live only for now, this moment, this passing moment, the
now that is here and then not here, the now that is gone
forever.

Acknowledgments

Warm thanks to the following:

Charles Bernstein, Susan Bee, and their son, Felix.

Mark Costello.

Larry Siems and Sarah Hoffman of the PEN American Center.

My daughter, Sophie Auster, for her sixth-grade paper on *To Kill a Mockingbird* (1998).

Siri Hustvedt for *the strangeness of being alive*.